Mozart's Sister

Mozart's Sister

A NOVEL

Rita Charbonnier

Translated by
ANN GOLDSTEIN

THREE RIVERS PRESS
NEW YORK

Translation copyright © 2007 by Rita Charbonnier

Published in the United States by Three Rivers Press, an imprint of the
Crown Publishing Group, a division of Random House, Inc., New York.
www.crownpublishing.com

THREE RIVERS PRESS and the Tugboat design are registered trademarks of
Random House, Inc.

Originally published in Italy as La sorella di Mozart by Casa Editrice Corbaccio, s.r.l,
Milan, in 2006. Copyright © 2006 by Casa Editrice Corbaccio, s.r.l, Milano. Subsequently
published in the United States by Crown Publishers, an imprint of the Crown
Publishing Group, a division of Random House, Inc., New York, in 2007.

Library of Congress Cataloging-in-Publication Data
Charbonnier, Rita.
[Sorella di Mozart. English]
Mozart's sister: a novel / Rita Charbonnier; translated by Ann Goldstein.
1. Berchtold zu Sonnenburg, Maria Anna Mozart, Reichsfreiin von,
1751–1829—Fiction.   I. Goldstein, Ann, 1949–   II. Title.
PQ4903.H37S6713 2007
823'.6—dc22   2007020750

ISBN 978-0-307-34697-1

Printed in the United States of America

Design by Jennifer Ann Daddio

10 9 8 7 6 5 4 3 2 1

First English Paperback Edition

ACKNOWLEDGMENTS

Many people helped me directly in the production of the book you have in your hands. First of all, my heartfelt thanks to Crown and in particular to my editor, Allison McCabe, for her confidence, her perseverance, and her patience. I also wish to thank my Italian publisher, Corbaccio, in the person of Cecilia Perucci: she was the first to bet on my novel, and the result is deeply indebted to her. Last but not least, I would like to thank my literary agents, Dorie Simmonds and Roberta Oliva.

Many friends stood by me with encouragement and advice. My thanks to Doug McKinlay, who, as soon as I told him about my project, literally shouted in my face, "It's a great idea!" I would like to thank psychologist Giulia Corrao, for our long, intense conversations on the character of Nannerl, and for drawing attention to the most profound recesses of her soul.

Various people helped me indirectly: I refer to the teachers I have been fortunate to meet during my studies. I want to thank, above all, Lucia Lusvardi, my wonderful piano teacher. My thanks to Dara Marks, a teacher of screenwriting and storytelling, whose fascinating work is based on deep psychological research. I thank José Sanchis Sinisterra, a teacher of dramaturgy, a refined intellectual, and an exquisitely simple man.

Thanks to Genevieve Geffray, of the Mozarteum in Salzburg, who welcomed me within the precious walls of the Mozart Library and helped me with my research.

A special thank-you goes to my sister, Chiara, who, many years ago, first spoke to me of the mysterious sister of Wolfgang Amadeus Mozart.

Music is a moral law. It gives soul to the universe, wings to the mind, flight to the imagination, and charm and gaiety to life and to every thing.

—PLATO

A woman's education must therefore be planned in relation to man. To be pleasing in his sight, to win his respect and love, to train him in childhood, to tend him in manhood, to counsel and console, to make his life pleasant and happy, these are the duties of woman for all time, and this is what she should be taught while she is young.

—JEAN-JACQUES ROUSSEAU, *EMILE*

Mozart's Sister

Overture

Salzburg, February 21, 1777

Dearest Fräulein Mozart!

I am entrusting this letter to Victoria, on the eve of a mission that will keep me away from the city for some time, because I wish you, my charming young friend, to have in your hands something that, during this period, will remind you of me. It's a bold wish, I'm aware, but stronger than modesty is my fear that what happened may dissipate in our ordinary daily actions and remain confined to a single night.

The thought of you has been with me from the moment I saw you vanish into the darkness. I didn't want you to leave me, even if it was I who insisted; but it would not have been proper, I think, to stay longer, with the risk of being discovered by a passing watchman. I don't know what excuses you gave your family for your late return, and I do not intend to ask; I am sure that you did not involve me in the matter, and that is sufficient. Little Victoria, for her part, was fast asleep, and when I asked her to take this to you she didn't blink. I think, in fact, she was pleased.

Dear Fräulein Mozart, you must know how rare it is to meet a person who possesses such depth and clarity of thought, such a remarkable and keen sensibility. It was a pleasant surprise for me to discover these qualities in you, since in Salzburg (and I hope you are not upset by my frankness) you are known, rather, as a woman who is aloof, intimidating, and quick-tempered. You know that I don't frequent the salons of the beau monde and do not willingly indulge in gossip; besides, it would be unseemly, given my position. But whenever I have chanced to hear you named at the Palace by a colleague or an aide, it has been to contrast you with your brother, Wolfgang: he so lively, with his ability to entertain large audiences, not only through his music but, in particular, thanks to a ready tongue and a fluent and sometimes salacious wit; not to mention his generous spirit, which is legendary. Of you, however, people say the exact opposite!

In no uncertain terms I will tell you that I consider it a shame. Why do you conceal from the world your charm and sweetness, sides of you that I have had the great privilege to see?

But I care little for the world or its gossip. Truly, what is important to me is to give you a token of my friendship: a friendship that I hope may be affectionate, if you will allow me to offer it. I would be extremely happy to have the pleasure of your company again, as soon as I return to Salzburg, and, until then, to continue to write to you and to read with trepidation the longed-for replies that you might wish to send. When Victoria comes to her piano lesson, she will be able to bring you my letters, and in return take yours to send to me, thus enabling you to avoid embarrassing and premature explanations to your family.

If, however, your feelings are not the same as mine, I will withdraw

into the shadows without a word and not disturb you further; have no fear.
You don't even have to say no: confine yourself to not answering; and, I
pray you, in that case destroy this.

> With respectful admiration,
> Major Franz Armand d'Ippold

———

> Salzburg, February 28, 1777

Dearest Armand,

I have a suspicion that Victoria read your letter . . . and maybe you are
reading this, too, naughty girl! Fold it up immediately and don't you dare
interfere, do you understand? Otherwise you'll never have another lesson
with me, and your precious hands will be reduced to horrid dry twigs!

And now, my dear Armand, see how that image of intransigence and
scorn behind which I habitually hide, and behind which I have chosen not
to hide from you, suddenly lifts. Why conceal oneself from the world and
reveal oneself to few? Believe me, I don't do it on purpose; but I know that,
after all, in the little universe that I inhabit, my personal behavior matters
in a very relative way. What is most important is to be an outstanding
teacher of girls who aspire to play the piano; and if I have the reputation
of being severe, no one doubts that I am an equally capable teacher . . .
and this gratifies me, and satisfies me. And if at one time, in a child's too-
vivid fantasy, I had higher musical ambitions, today I am truly happy with
what I have, and of art I ask nothing more, truly nothing.

But now enough of these excuses . . . the letter inscribed by your hand
is here, beside me on the table, and the trembling light of the candle warms
your already affectionate words, which have roused so much emotion in me.
A drop of wax has fallen beside the words "little Victoria," as if to point
them out to me, as if to make me smile with greater tenderness toward the
one who bears that name, toward the one who gave it to her, and toward
that somewhat incongruous (forgive me . . .) adjective. Perhaps, dear

Armand, Victoria will forever be "little" to you; and yet she is the same age as Wolfgang, or only five years younger than me, so she is over twenty by now. My father, imagine, stopped considering me a child when I was barely twelve . . . but now that I'm speaking of it, I wonder if it was a good thing or not.

The truth is that I am writing to you without restraint, in the middle of the night, which is my friend, tossing out the thoughts as they come: for you are the first person to allow me this, the first who hasn't judged me. For that reason I am not afraid to open up to you . . . and for that reason, too, I long to see you and embrace you again. Yes, I wish for that moment, which I hope is not too distant, Major d'Ippold; I tell you that officially . . . and I respond to your declaration of friendship with an equally intense ardor; for indeed I, too, have been thinking of that night, from the moment we parted; and the thought of you is with me constantly, in every waking moment, and I am happy, yes, to begin this correspondence with you, as happy, perhaps, as I have ever been . . .

I will stop here, for now. With that fundamental mutual assurance, the rest can be tasted and enjoyed in every syllable, in every blink of an eye. Don't you think, my dearest?

With grateful affection,
Nannerl Mozart

Vienna, March 10, 1777

My dear, dearest Nannerl!

Your letter made me happier than I can ever remember being. You, sweetest girl, have wakened in me sensations I felt certain were closed off to me forever. In recent days I have performed every duty with a light heart, and even the other officers have noticed my state of mind. Thank you, Nannerl; thank you sincerely for responding to my feelings! Now, though we are distant, I can feel you near me, and it seems to me that I can caress your lovely face, and recall with intense emotion every moment spent at your side. Yet I don't think I know the right words to express what I feel; besides, I have never been good at expounding on certain subjects. The only thing I can tell you is that I, too, long for our next meeting and wish to do my utmost so that everything between us will be smooth, and a token of our growing affection.

I am writing to Victoria as well, separately, and among other things, I forbade her to read our correspondence. But you know my daughter well, and are aware that although she undoubtedly fears parental authority, she is nonetheless quite capable of happily violating the dictates it imposes on her. Therefore, when you reply to me, never forget that that young lady (because you are right, dear Nannerl, she is now of marriageable age!) could, as you say, "interfere" in our exchange of thoughts and emotions.

Thinking about Victoria and what she has told me about you as a teacher and a musician, and rereading your letter, I find something jarring, something that you experts would call a "dissonance." (I may allow myself these observations, may I not?) You say, dear Nannerl, that you once had higher musical ambitions but abandoned them graciously and without regret: it is that absence of regret that I find not entirely convincing. I know that you composed music from early childhood (because Victoria told me) and that, until some time ago (and everyone knows this), you often performed, as part of a duo with your brother and also as a soloist. But, of a sudden, you abruptly stopped both those activities, to devote yourself solely to teaching, in that way squandering (forgive my audacity, but by now I've made sure that my frankness doesn't wound you) your rare talent.

Was a choice of that kind truly made without regrets? And (what counts more) is it really an irreversible choice? Perhaps, if you were to go back on your decision, you would taste again joys that would gladden your heart. If I say all this to you, believe me, it is only because your happiness is as important to me as my own: rather, because mine is lovingly dependent on it.

With respect and esteem,
Major Franz Armand d'Ippold

Salzburg, March 24, 1777

Armand,

My first impulse was to answer you harshly, but then I made an effort and waited an entire week for my irritation to diminish. So only now—and I am still trying not to lose control—do I say to you: you don't want me to ask questions about poor Monika, right? Your beloved wife, who is unfortunately no longer among us, is a subject that I am not allowed even to touch on. In the same way, I would ask you not to make inferences of any sort regarding my decision to give up playing concerts and composing. Your words, Major, are salt in the wound. A wound that bleeds every day, because at every moment, even at this precise moment, exactly as when I was a child, the music presses inside me to come out; it's like an assault wave that rushes up from my guts to my throat and my brain and makes it whirl; it's an internal tempest that can't find an outlet, so the only possible choice is to ignore it and devote myself to something else. Is it clear to you now, Armand? Teaching, and in particular teaching Victoria, who, as you well know, is my best student, is the only narrow path into which I can channel this confusion, and silence it, at least temporarily. And you, like my brother, come to me now to say that I am wasting my talent? And with what right?

Forgive me; I haven't managed to moderate my tone. I don't even know if I will let you see this letter. Maybe I would do better to tear it up and wait until later, and then pretend to myself to have forgotten your words.

Nannerl Mozart

———

Vienna, April 5, 1777

My dear friend (I hope that you are still my friend),

You were very right to send me your letter, which I've finished reading just this instant; and you were even more right to reproach me for my unwarranted intrusion into matters that do not concern me and which I understand even less. I beg you sincerely to forgive me and I assure you that if you were here, or if I were where you are, I would ask your pardon on my knees and would not find peace until I had obtained it. The thought of having vexed you torments me, for it is the exact opposite of my deepest desires; it is the exact opposite (paradoxically) of what I wished to gain. But the truth is only this. You said you were happy that I, among the first in the world, did not judge you, and instead I have done so, like the greatest of fools, with regard to a decision for which you have taken every responsibility yourself; and I have also tried to make you go back on that decision, as if to transform you into someone who you, my dear perfect creature, are not.

While my pen runs on, my thoughts leap ahead, more rapidly, in a frantic search for something I can do to make up for it. What can I do? I beg you sincerely: tell me, Nannerl. And with my heart in my hand I implore you not to cut me out of your life. I swear to you that I will never again ask questions or make bold assumptions about your music—never. But I beg you, leave an opening for our friendship.

> With sorrow and regret,
> Armand

———

> Salzburg, April 15, 1777

Armand, my dear,

The idea of cutting you out of my life never occurred to me. If it had, not only would I not have sent you my previous letter but I wouldn't even have written it. In fact, what I wish for is precisely the opposite: I would like you to know as much as possible about me.

Because, as I pondered the little argument we've just had, and for which it is I who ought to ask forgiveness, I was surprised to find myself thinking that your intention of never again mentioning my music does not *augur well for our future: that there is something wrong with that (my fault, of course, and no one else's).*

So I've decided to tell you everything. I will do it myself: I won't leave you to ask me questions that at the moment you would certainly be afraid to ask. Naturally, my dearest confidant and loving friend, you remain free to interrupt the reading and respond to me, and write to me about other things, whenever you like . . .

Part One

The Kingdom of Back

I.

"Please, my love, let's go home . . . call a carriage, quickly," murmured the woman sitting wearily on a chair, pressing her stomach with her hands as if trying to hold it in. Her husband didn't answer; he was waiting for the harpsichordist, whose playing was execrable, to finish her ridiculous performance. As she caressed the keys, she moved her shoulders gently and smiled, opening and closing her lips. Every nobleman could be sure that he could approach those lips, and enjoy them, and enjoy her entire body: he had only to ask.

"My dear, I'm serious . . . we had better leave."

"Just a moment," he said in annoyance, as

feeble applause broke out. Then he turned and jumped up. "Where did she go?"

"There, look . . . but don't let it last too long, please."

With a leap, the man reached the child who was squatting in a corner, absorbed, as she repeatedly opened and closed a fan; he tore it from her hand, made her stand up, and adjusted her dress. "Be good, Nannerl . . . as you always are, my angel," he begged her, with a tremor of anxiety in his voice, while her blue eyes gazed into his and she uttered some strange monosyllables. She was odd, that girl. Anyone who didn't know her well might have thought she was slow-witted.

"Are you ready?"

She nodded, still muttering to herself.

"Then go. Now!"

The whisper was lost in the breeze of chatter that began to blow through the salon. The little girl trotted over to the stool in front of the harpsichord, and with some effort climbed up onto it.

"Excuse me . . . most noble ladies, honorable gentlemen, a moment of your attention, if you please!"

Suddenly the chattering stopped, and all eyes were directed toward the stranger. He was certainly not an aristocrat; who knew what recommendation had gained him entrance to that salon. He might even be a professional musician! Irritation crept in among the patricians of Salzburg. Another performance now, just as they were finally returning to gossiping, to flirting, to showing off? And what sort of music could be produced by that little blond dwarf, whose chubby hands could barely encompass a fifth?

"I have the honor to introduce to you this spectacular child prodigy . . . Maria Anna Walburga Ignatia Mozart! She is, truly, one of the best harpsichord players ever to touch an instrument, and, wonder of wonders, she is only five years old. I, Leopold Mozart, her father, was able to perceive her great talent thanks to my own activities as a musician, in service at the court of His Excellency the Prince Archbishop. It would be an outrage against God himself if that gift were to remain unknown and uncultivated."

The aristocratic irritation became palpable. One could only hope that the concert would quickly begin and end even more quickly, and that that pompous clown would stop strutting! Herr Mozart realized it, and hastily returned to his wife.

Impetuously the child began to play, and it was as if a lightning bolt had ripped through the frescoed ceiling, setting ablaze the curtains and the tapestries. There was nothing human about little Nannerl when she was making music; she seemed to be possessed by a primitive divinity, just waiting to get to an instrument to burst forth and leave listeners stunned. Her small hands produced clear and rapid sounds, obeying a supreme harmonic instinct, and the result was at the same time assured and undisciplined. The contradiction between her more-than-adult mastery and her child's body was disconcerting. Her notes were words of a language still unknown, a language both fascinating and disorienting. Where's the trick? No, there is no trick. And yet there must be! The lords and ladies approached, examined, were struck dumb; and, meanwhile, the child played melodies that she drew at random from her mind, inspired by the shapes of objects, by the crackle of the fire in the hearth, by the crash of a glass falling to the floor from the clumsy hands of one of the ladies.

Then, abruptly, she stopped, without even finishing the passage. She jumped down from the stool, ran to her father, took the fan, and began to open and close it again, swaying from one foot to the other and whispering strange words.

The ovation exploded, shaking the walls and the windows. How different from the applause for the voluptuous dilettante! It was the crash of an ancient tree trunk, the shouts and cries as a building falls. The women crowded around Leopold Mozart, who took his daughter in his arms and showed her off like a trophy, shaking jeweled hands,

offering her to rouged mouths. Nannerl, however, showed no interest in that adoration meant for her alone; the fan absorbed her attention completely.

No one could hear the hoarse appeals from the woman in the chair,
whose expression had become concentrated on a sudden internal
upheaval; she raised her voice, but they all continued to ignore her,
until a shrill cry burst from her.

"Leopold! Oh shit! Leopold!"

Those who heard her did not seem upset by the shocking words;
rather, they looked at her as a member of an alien species.

With a great effort she took a breath and spoke again, holding her
stomach: "Leopold . . . we're there . . . we're there; do you understand or not?"

II.

Through the bedroom door came utterly unfamiliar sounds. They
were cries and moans, and they were Mama's; she was in pain, and to
Nannerl it wasn't clear whether her father and the fat lady from
downstairs were helping her or were the torturers. Why had Papa forbidden her to enter? She had to intervene. The child stared at the
mother-of-pearl door handle, too high above her head, and wished
she were bigger. But a sudden sharp scream terrified her, and she
jumped back. Then she heard, too, the excited voice of her father, and
the fat lady's hysterical tones. Nannerl took refuge under the harpsichord and stuck her fingers in her ears as deeply as she could, until
she was practically digging out her eardrums: there, she no longer
heard the cries. But gradually they reemerged from her memory in an
amplified chorus, distorted and inhuman. Then she opened her mouth
to cry and burning tears flowed from her eyes.

Her father came in, but she didn't notice; she was crying too hard,
and the sorrowful symphony in her head was deafening. Leopold

drew her to him, put his arms around her, hugged her, while she struggled with her nightmare. For a long time the two remained sitting on the floor beside the harpsichord, holding each other, she out of terror, he out of love.

When Nannerl had calmed down, Leopold sat up on the stool and made her stand in front of him. He placed a finger on her nose: "Daughter, promise me that you won't cry anymore. Ever, in your life. Remember: tears are useless."

She nodded, drying her face with her sleeve.

"Now listen to me. Mama is fine, and you have a little brother."

She stood motionless, bewildered.

"Yes—a fine little boy, completely pink and completely bald. His name is Wolfgang Theophilus. Would you like to see him?"

Of course! And she sped across the threshold. Her mother's appearance alarmed her. She was in the bed, prostrate, and even though she was smiling, there was something abnormal about her. Everything in the room was abnormal; on the floor, at her feet, was a pile of blood-soaked rags, and, after wiping her hands, the fat lady threw another on top. Then, however, Nannerl saw the cradle; the sense of horror vanished miraculously, and she felt an intense desire to discover what sort of creature it held. She approached cautiously and slowly looked inside, enjoying every fraction of that memorable moment.

Wolfgang was pink, yes, and bald, yes, and he wasn't aware. His head was elongated, like a bean, and his small, toothless mouth was wailing. His eyes seemed not to grasp space; his gestures were without meaning. But the instant she saw him, Nannerl knew that she loved him with her whole self, and that she would never love anyone else in the world the way she loved him.

Do you have sisters, dear Armand? I sincerely hope so, for your sake. Everyone should be lucky enough to have a special relationship like the one between my brother and me! My mind and his have always been in unison, and we have never needed language in order to understand each other. As a child I liked to think we were a single body that had been divided by mistake. When I was eleven, in fact, an Italian painter made portraits of us, and it was disturbing to look at the paintings side by side. We had the same features: the same high forehead with prominent temples (which he naturally called "horns"), the same wide space between blond eyebrows and large light eyes, the same nose with the slightly downturned tip, the same full lips, with their mocking expression, the same strong-willed, pointed chin. Yet in character we were very different: he capricious, impertinent, and tirelessly in search of attention; I reserved, insecure, and fearful of imposing. I could express myself freely only in his company and in solitude—a condition not uncongenial to me even then.

In our games we were the king and queen of an imaginary land, the Kingdom of Back—a reality distinct from the tangible present and yet able to transform it and shatter its boundaries. How I yearn, dear Armand, for that enchanted land that I can no longer enter—a place inhabited only by children, where all make music the whole day long, and all are good and kind, and the bad are not admitted even for a visit. In the Kingdom of Back every pleasure was possible; you had only to utter the magic formula.

III.

"Here forever happy are we . . ."

"And nothing bad will ever be!"

The rhyme echoed between the narrow balconies of the inner courtyard, shooting upward until it reached the pentagonal patch of sky and disappeared among the clouds.

For Wolfgang and Nannerl, every action had a sound, and every sound had a meaning. The noise of the traffic on the Getreidegasse, the nasal chatter of two women at a window, the splashing of slops emptied out of a chamber pot; the scuff of feet on grass, the rustling of Nannerl's skirts and petticoats, the silent instant when she raised them to reveal long legs covered by scratches and bruises. And then the quick rhythm of running, he ahead and she behind, a tomboy, her hair loose and freely flying; and the crumbling mountain of garbage on whose summit rose the king's throne. Wolfgang climbed up, triumphant, a crown of leaves on his head and a sword of reeds in his hand.

"Your Majesty, I haven't done anything wrong!" Nannerl cried.

"When you speak to the king, you must kneel down!"

With a thud, she was on all fours. "Forgive me. I have no faults, my sovereign lord."

"It's not true! You don't love your brother!"

"No, I adore him, Your Majesty! I adore him—and even more," she said, seizing his feet and covering them with kisses.

"All right, I forgive you. You can be my queen again," the tyrant said with a magnanimous scowl, and then he got down from the throne to tap one of her shoulders with the sword. But at that moment, like a castle of cards, the mountain of trash came crashing down and a long metal rod tumbled to the ground, the noise echoing painfully in their ears. Closing their eyes tight and sticking out their tongues, the two children groaned and, as the last vibration faded, emitted, in chorus, a sigh of relief. "What a horrible B-flat!"

Their mother leaned out the window of their apartment, on the third floor, and her sharp cry was the final blow: "Nannerl! Wolfgang! In the house, this instant!"

IV.

"You must be quiet when Papa is working!" yelled Anna Maria Mozart, who was washing the floor, as soon as she saw her children at the door. "And you, you're older. You should be watching over your brother! Will you tie up that hair? You look like a witch!" She took a comb out of her own hair and started toward Nannerl, but the pail of dirty water was in the way and she bumped it with her clog so that the water sloshed out. "Holy shit!" she cried, raising her fists, as if to strike at random; she stood there like an enormous marble statue, the giantess Juno poised to transform the children into mice and the dirty water into a stormy sea, but instead she burst out laughing.

The children immediately followed, and how gaily! Wolfgang trotted around the puddle, and his laugh made the glasses on the shelf vibrate; Nannerl's laugh was deep, and though she covered her mouth with her hand, it escaped anyway. "Hush, children, hush," their mother begged. "Papa will be angry . . . Hush up, for heaven's sake." But she was giggling as she spoke, and could hardly be taken seriously. She pushed them along the hall with loving pats on the behind. "Go to the bedroom and be good. And please, be quiet." Then she went back to the kitchen, and as soon as she saw the mess on the floor the desire to laugh vanished.

Exhausted, the children threw themselves on their backs on the bed, in which both had been conceived and born. They lay there without moving, staring at the ceiling that their imagination opened up to the sky, while the sound of string playing wound its way through the door with the mother-of-pearl handle.

It was Wolfgang who spoke first. "I'm going to be a coachman when I grow up. I'll drive my carriage to the top of the mountains. I mean, to the top of the clouds."

"I'm going to be a musician when I grow up."

"What does that have to do with it! I'll do that, too. But you won't make it."

"Why not?"

"Because you'll be a mama. You'll have a bunch of children and you'll be lucky if you're even a music teacher."

"I don't want children. Not one! You're enough for me." She reached out a hand to cuddle him but encountered instead a large pear-shaped object hidden in the covers. "What's your new violin doing here?"

He shrugged, and hugged the instrument case as if it were a doll.

"Will you let me try it, Wolfgang?"

"No. It's mine."

"Let me at least pluck the strings. I just want to hear the sound."

"You're not even supposed to touch it!"

"Come on, Wolfgang, let me try it. You don't know how to play yet."

"I do so!"

She laughed in his face. "Who do you think you are? You haven't had a single lesson!"

A flash of defiance lighted the child's eyes, and in an instant he had climbed onto a stool and turned the door handle. She jumped up and tried to grab him, but he was already in the middle of the music room, standing behind the string players and brandishing his violin like the Archangel Gabriel with his flaming sword.

"Stop, stop! Don't you see there's a crescendo here?" Herr Mozart said to the second violin, a man with drink-reddened cheeks. "If the intensity diminishes at that point, the whole thing collapses! Concentration, please."

"Papa, I'll do it; I'll do the crescendo!"

Leopold made a grimace of irritation. "Anna Maria, come and get Wolfgang."

"My papa is right!" the child yelled. "That phrase has to be heard forte. You were playing like a pig. I can do it better!"

Faint smiles appeared among the players, and Leopold, brimming with parental indulgence, said, "Come, what do you know about these things? When you've learned to play, I'll let you rehearse with us. Now go and play with your sister."

"Why don't you let him try?" said the red-faced musician, launching into what he clearly imagined to be a good joke. "We're all eager to hear the interpretation of the illustrious Wolfgang Amadeus Mozart!"

There was a noisy burst of laughter.

"All right!" Leopold yielded. "Try the second-violin part, but

softly, so that no one will hear the mess you'll certainly make of it."
With a little shove he sent his son to his place.

Nannerl hid near the door and, under her incredulous gaze, as
the musicians began, her little brother joined in, following the score
attentively.

The second violinist watched him, smiling under his whiskers,
but his expression changed radically as he realized that Wolfgang
was playing . . . well. Yes, well! Imitating what he saw the adults
doing, he moved the bow and placed one note after the other; perhaps he made some mistakes in the fingering, but the notes were
right, and the sound was full—in a word, beautiful. Was it possible
that he had never had a violin in his hands? That he was only six
years old? The man laid down his instrument, amazed, and little
Mozart continued to play the part without the slightest hesitation.
The others, too, stopped playing, one at a time, staring in astonishment at this extraordinary child, who was now performing like a
soloist, as if it came naturally. Leopold, an expert teacher, and the
author of a method that was known throughout Europe, would have
sworn to God that such a thing wasn't possible; and now here was
his own son, the embodiment of this miracle before his very eyes!
What higher instinct had suggested the violinist's technique to this
prodigy? Maybe God himself!

Wolfgang ended the passage and bowed his head in a gesture of
thanks, as if he were already an accomplished performer. Mad with
joy, his father took him in his arms and held him up: "Gentlemen, my
son is a miracle! My son is a divine miracle!"

"Herr Mozart, the whole world must know him!" the second
violinist shouted. "Take him on tour! Have him play at the courts
of kings!"

Nannerl opened the door and entered the room. Her brother had
shown the way, and luckily he was there, and had had the courage;
from now on it would be possible to break into the rehearsals of adults
and play with them; and if you were good, you could even be

applauded! She grabbed her brother's violin and began playing a rapid, virtuosic passage.

No one looked at her, or seemed to be aware of her. The little group went off, Leopold in the lead, carrying the child in triumph, and Nannerl, in the deserted room, went on playing for herself.

V.

The young woman was on her knees talking and weeping at once, and behind the purple curtain the man of the church was hidden, but the grille did not drain her words of sorrow, or lighten their import. How much time does it take for a person's life to be ruined? For the attractive salon harpsichordist, the time taken for an intimacy consummated in a doorway had been enough, demanded by a count as a condition for engagement: an intimacy whose result was pregnancy, and not even the shadow of a ring. Her stomach was still flat; only the man directly responsible was aware of her condition, and he had denied his involvement.

The Reverend Joseph Bullinger had the girl leave the confessional and, taking her by the hand, led her toward the pews.

"I don't even know how I managed to get here," she sobbed. "I haven't eaten for days, and I don't have the strength to get up in the morning. If it were up to me, I would stay in bed until the end of my days."

"What did you tell your family?"

"A lot of lies." Awareness of that further sin made her cry even harder. "If I tell them, they'll throw me out of the house. And if the rumor spreads, there will be a scandal, and I can't even think of the consequences. I don't know what to do, Father. Help me."

There was only one solution, and he was silent as he searched for the words most suitable for proposing it; in the meantime, he observed her wrinkled clothes and tear-stained veil with a sad smile. He had been hearing ugly gossip about this tormented young woman for some time, and at first he had paid no attention to it. In his role as preceptor, Joseph Bullinger had regular contacts with the families of the aristocracy; he had never liked those vacuous circles, and was always hoping to improve them through education and culture.

"My child," he said, "don't cry. You have no reason to despair, believe me. Often the Lord indicates to us the just path in an unexpected way. When one reaches what seems a dead end, there may be a doorway to happiness: the doorway through which the Almighty offers you the chance to begin a new life, upright and pure, in His name."

The musician sniffed and looked at him, filled with hope.

"You will construct in your heart a system of new and just values, in the absence of which you have unfortunately committed this grave sin. You may repair the evil done through work and helping others, and learn to appreciate asceticism and contemplation."

"I understand," she said, but in fact she had understood nothing. "But what must I do, exactly?"

"Leave the city as soon as possible and, safe from the gossip, bring the pregnancy to term. I will take care of finding a good situation for the child when it is born; and for you, I already have in mind the convent where you will take your vows."

The harsh cry of dismay rattled the windows: "You mean, I am to become a nun?"

Protests followed, expressed in every form and every tone of voice, and a vain search for alternatives. As the reverend insisted, trying his best to convince her, she withdrew into a dangerous silence, accompanied by a new flood of tears, and so, disheveled and weeping, as she had arrived, she hurried to the door of the church and almost bumped into Leopold Mozart.

"Watch how you——" he grumbled, wiping his shoes on his calves, then he made the sign of the cross, approached the reverend, and uttered: *"Ave clare sacerdos! Magnum gaudium mihi affert in te incidere."*

Bullinger appeared to appreciate the learned phrases and answered in kind: *"Eadem laetitia afficior, carissime frater. Asside mihi."*

The priest was a man of influence, and Herr Mozart sat down beside him and started in on the speech that he had carefully prepared. "Reverend, I have formulated a particular plan for my life and that of my family; before putting it into action, however, I wish to confer with you, because your guidance is, for me, the one and only shining light."

Bullinger confined himself to a slight nod. The musician's ingratiating ways sometimes annoyed him.

"I intend to take Wolfgang on a tour. Not a short trip, like the one that took us to the court of Vienna, although that gave me great satisfaction. This time I intend to visit Munich, Frankfurt, and Brussels; then, God willing, I will go on to Paris and, finally, even to London."

It was an ambitious plan, and the Reverend Bullinger began to suspect that Leopold wanted something more than advice from him.

"You know how fond I am of our splendid city. And yet I feel that in this provincial environment my son's talent cannot receive the necessary stimulus to make it flourish and bear fruit as it deserves. Ours will not be a journey of mere promotion but one also of intense and thorough study: I want Wolfgang to have lessons from the finest masters."

"I take your point, Herr Mozart. But doesn't he seem too young for this?"

Leopold had foreseen this objection. "It is nature, not I, who rushes onward. My son, at his tender age, is already a composer: with his childish hands, he draws perfectly formed notes on the page. I can't let such a treasure be lost."

"I realize that. But aren't you worried about the risk of exposing him to diseases during the journey? You could undermine the health of your children irreparably."

"I trust in the protection of Our Lord. What He decides, I will accept with a heart full of faith. Naturally I will take every precaution so that my son—"

"Do I misremember, or don't you have a daughter as well?"

For this question, however, Leopold was not prepared. He looked at the priest, sincerely bewildered, and didn't know what to say.

"From the start of our conversation you have been speaking of your son," Bullinger continued. "And yet at the time I introduced you into the circles of the aristocracy, the girl was your pride and joy. Do you intend to leave her in Salzburg?"

"Of course not! Nannerl will perform duets with her brother! On the other hand, it's obvious that it wouldn't make any sense for a girl to learn composition."

"That is for you to decide—I cannot judge. I say only that all the creatures of the world are equal in the eyes of God, hence it is fitting that they should be also in the eyes of men."

"Yes, of course . . . Naturally, most reverend sir."

"Very well. Now explain to me how you propose to finance the journey."

Leopold gradually regained his confidence. "For one thing, I trust in gifts from the princes and so forth, and then, whenever possible, I will arrange for Wolfgang to give paid concerts, and, naturally, Nannerl, too! Also the girl, Reverend. In addition, my landlord has promised me a loan."

"I deduce, then, that that is not the reason you have come asking for my assistance. Shall we at last speak plainly, dear brother?"

"Yes, well . . . ," Leopold stammered, trying to hide his nervousness behind tight lips, "as you can certainly imagine, I will have to ask the archbishop for a long leave of absence, and, further, I would expect, once I have returned from the tour, to take up my post again, for without it, my family's subsistence would be in serious danger. Your intercession would be a great help."

"We have come to the point! I appreciate your frankness, Herr Mozart. On the other hand," he added, not entirely convinced, "you must realize that your request is rather exorbitant. What arguments do you imagine I should use with His Excellency?"

Leopold's face lighted up. This was the best part of his speech, the part that he had studded with solid rhetorical effects.

"One alone, beloved Father: that it was our Lord who gave a spark of musical genius to an ordinary child of Salzburg. Certainly it is not through any merit of mine, or of his mother, if this boy performs miracles with notes that have never been heard before. And if our Lord willed this, He did so in order that one day that child might sing His praises and celebrate His glory through music. We must all dedicate ourselves, each within the limits of his own role and using the humble means available to man, so that it may happen as soon as possible."

"That's enough! My stomach is beginning to complain about lunch." The priest rose stiffly. "All right, I will speak to the archbishop. *Cura ut valeas.*" And he went off.

And meanwhile I went on writing music, passionately. I always wrote at night. I waited until I heard the regular breathing of my brother, the quiet hum of my father exhaling, my mother's loud snoring. Then I got out of my bed, went barefoot along the hall, turned the mother-of-pearl handle, and let myself into the room with the instruments.

I have always liked the night. And now, when I'm writing to you, dearest Armand, it's the middle of the night, and between you and me there is only a lamp, a sheet of paper, and a pen. You and I are alone, and intimately, profoundly, close. You understand me, and you, too, have the same feelings, is that not true? And my family, from whom a mere wall separates me, are a million miles away.

They have never violated, and I don't think they have ever discovered, these lovely isolated moments of mine, when time expands, when no one has the power to tell me what I must or must not do. We live in a larger house now, and each of us has our own room, so I don't need to make complicated maneuvers to be alone, and there is no risk of being found out; but at that time, entering the music room meant the jealous, fearful crossing of the threshold between the world and myself.

In the silence I opened the window, listened to the rustling waters of the

Salzach, breathed in the cool air, stared into the darkness. Finally I lighted a candle and sat at the harpsichord, with the slow solemnity of one who is performing a rite. I couldn't play (I would have waked the entire building!), but to compose I had only to touch the keys, without pressing my fingers down; to listen to my internal ear. My knowledge of counterpoint was confined to what I managed to overhear of the lessons that my father gave Wolfgang, but I took this not as a limitation but as a stimulus. Arias, canons, lieder. Vocal music was what I loved, perhaps because I had some talent as a singer. My voice has been melodious since I was a child, and deep, even in speaking; I haven't trained it with any consistency, but if I had, I would be a mezzo-soprano or a contralto—the idea of being on the stage has never appealed to me. I've preferred the role of the one who, in the shadows, invents; and then, in the shadows, listens to the results.

I filled the pages with notes, I inscribed the titles in my best, most elegant handwriting, I blew on the ink, blotted it, and, finally, folded every page and put it in my secret pouch. I had sewn a kind of pouch that was fastened with long laces, and I tied it around my waist, hidden among my petticoats; thus my music never left me. During the day it sat at the table, worked, and played with me; at night, when I went to bed, it slept with me, warmed by the covers and by my skin. It was invisible to the world, but to me always present, like a limb, an organ, a lock of hair. I imagined giving it to my father, at the right moment, and then, I was sure, he would realize what I was capable of, and would encourage and support me. After all, the sister of the Prince Elector of Bavaria liked to write operas in the Italian style; I, who was Queen of the Kingdom of Back—couldn't I be like her?

VI.

"Put down the violin, Mama's little angel."

"No!"

"How can I sew the jacket if you've got both arms busy?"

"Papa said I can play the violin as much as I want. And now I want to play!"

Anna Maria resigned herself to working on the trousers. For her children's traveling clothes she had chosen fabrics that were durable but difficult to get the needle through; and if Wolfgang didn't stop playing with that damned instrument, sooner or later she would box his ears.

Nannerl was alone in the kitchen peeling potatoes. She was wearing a big apron, and amused herself by peeling in spirals, creating a single long strip for each potato; she also amused herself by listening to her brother's musical games, and singing along with him in an undertone. The larger the heap of peeled potatoes grew, the louder she sang, until Wolfgang heard her and answered with the violin.

"You little witch. Don't you start, too!" yelled her mother, but, far out of sight, Nannerl ignored the command, and sister and brother began tossing the music back and forth like a ball. Far, too, from the tedious lessons of their father! Who said that music has to be played in particular moments, in particular places, and in a particular way? Their notes ran, improvised and anarchic, wild and noisy, from one door to the other; they pursued, caught up, became entangled, and let go; they flew out the window, paused on the king's throne, blew over the hats of passersby, mixed with the rumble of a rushing carriage. Suddenly Nannerl left the kitchen and headed toward her brother; sight intensified their communication, and while their mother, pricking her finger, cursed, brother and sister sang and shouted more and more joyfully. Nannerl was still holding a potato, whose peel hung down to the floor; Wolfgang was bowing away like a gypsy. Then they exchanged objects and she found herself with the violin in hand and he the potato; and, meanwhile, the orgy of sound reached new heights. Their mother was yelling that in those conditions it was impossible for her to sew and she couldn't understand them in the least, but they paid no attention and went on with their wild music, until Anna Maria broke off a thread too energetically and Wolfgang's shorts split, leaving him with his bottom out.

At that moment, Leopold Mozart appeared in the doorway and the following sight presented itself to his horrified eyes: a wife desperate before a ripped garment, a daughter in an apron holding a violin, a son with his buttocks bared and a potato in his hand.

The sound of the door slamming interrupted the stream of sound like the blow of an ax and for a very long minute they all held their breath. Leopold stared at the three of them, flustered, as his eyes seemed to turn from blue to pitch black; then, with measured steps, he approached his daughter.

"Nannerl, this is the last time you touch a violin," he said. "Give it to me." And he held out his hand, palm up.

Her hands did not obey. They had turned rigid, becoming one with the sound box.

"The violin is not an instrument for girls. You are not to play it ever again. Do you understand me, Nannerl?"

The little girl's heart disappeared. In its place was a void, stillness, silence. Leopold seized the instrument and disappeared into the music room.

VII.

The great day has dawned! At the door of 9 Getreidegasse, impatient hooves pawed the ground, strong hooves that would consume the miles, and Joseph Bullinger pulled his coat tightly around him and looked up in annoyance at the third-floor window: How long could it take?

Hard to say. Anna Maria was pursuing Wolfgang, trying to dress him, and Nannerl was following Anna Maria and trying to dress herself. Open trunks and boxes of music were underfoot, and a servant was hurriedly packing a portable harpsichord. Leopold grabbed his

son by the collar, handed him to his mother, and descended the stairs
with the harpsichord on his back, shouting at her to hurry. She called
down that more than this she could not manage. She asked her son to
stand on an enormous trunk overflowing with clothes, to help her
close it, but it was still slightly open, so Wolfgang jumped on it. That
did the trick, though his mother almost lost an index finger. Panting,
Leopold reappeared and pushed the trunk to the door. The din woke
even the neighbor, who slept like a rock, and raising his hands to
Heaven, he cried, "Praise the Lord, that family of lunatics is leaving!"

Nannerl packed music in a small trunk and carried it down the
stairs, then went back up and got another, and then yet another;
Wolfgang, wanting to do no less, seized a large box, but his father tore
it from him, crying, "Be careful, my angel, please!" Anna Maria made
sure that the shutters were closed in every room, rearranged the cloths
that covered the furniture, then shifted them, then put them back as
they had been; she gave the apartment a last melancholy glance—
who could say when she would see her things again—closed the door,
and went down the stairs.

The boy darted in and out of the carriage, lay on the seats, opened
and closed the windows; the girl and the father settled the bags on the
back; the servant tied the instruments to the roof; and the reverend
couldn't wait to return to his meditations. As soon as Anna Maria
appeared, he traced in the air a large sign of the cross, reciting,
"Benedico vos in nomine Patris, et Filii, et Spiritus Sancti." And finally
the family climbed in and latched the doors, the servant bowed, and
the coachman whipped the horses, who took off with a whinny of
euphoria: Farewell, Salzburg! Great Europe, we are eager for you!

VIII.

It was a vis-à-vis carriage, of the type with two (very uncomfortable)
facing seats; on one side sat father and son, on the other, mother and

daughter. Now that the pilgrimage had begun, a sudden weariness replaced excitement, and Wolfgang rested his head on Leopold's legs while Nannerl sank into her mother's large, soft breast.

"Papa, is it true that I'll be able to try the piano?" the little boy asked, his voice already thick with sleep.

"What do you know about the piano?"

"Nannerl says it's much nicer than the harpsichord."

The girl pricked up her ears but said nothing, and Leopold spoke as if she didn't exist, caressing Wolfgang's head. "Your sister can say what she likes, but you don't have to listen to her. Guess who your papa will introduce you to instead: Johann Christian Bach. You know who he is, don't you?"

The answer came from the land of dreams. "The son of Johann Sebastian Bach."

"Excellent, my boy. He lives in London, which is far away, but perhaps we'll get there; and then he'll give you lessons in composition. He's an important man, and he can do a lot for your career."

Anna Maria hugged her daughter to her, and Nannerl abandoned herself to the warm, scented sweetness of that touch: she, too, would meet Christian Bach; she would show him her music, too.

The carriage had reached the outskirts of the city and was crossing a bridge over the river. There was no way its passengers could have glimpsed a small female figure half hidden under the parapet; perhaps Leopold might have recognized her, but just at that moment he drew the curtain. As soon as the coach had grown distant, the girl cautiously rose and, with an expression of suffering, touched her stomach, whose dimensions were now unmistakable. She settled on her head the tall wig, which she had put on with a macabre sense of ritual; she had even powdered her face and put on an old, low-cut lace-trimmed evening dress. Then she lifted her skirts and struggled up onto the balustrade.

From that moment she had no hesitation: she took a deep breath, filling her lungs, and jumped, turning so that she went headfirst. The flight was rapid, the thud muted, but the impact killed her instantly. Thus, in the muddy waters of the Salzach, ended the life of a voluptuous salon harpsichordist.

IX.

Nannerl saw only the Prince Elector's shoes, or rather the left shoe, for a greyhound had laid its nose on the right. It was some distance from backstage to the place of honor, but that shoe was as shiny as a dewy leaf, and the gold pin that clasped it seemed to emit light.

Maximilian III awaited the court concert with a welcoming smile on his perfect face, sitting deep in his armchair and occasionally leaning forward to pet the dog. A woman who resembled him, if a little older, sat beside him, with strawlike hair above protruding eyes of an indistinct brown: it was Princess Maria Antonia, his sister. She was magnificently dressed, and yet she appeared untidy.

On the stage, the chamberlain was ending his introductory remarks, while behind the curtain, Leopold was nearly having a heart attack. "I implore you, children . . . I implore you . . . Be calm, eh? You've got to perform well—and make a good impression for me." Meanwhile he smoothed his shirt cuffs and pinched the puffed sleeves. Anna Maria began to pull Nannerl's corset even tighter and the girl gently protested: "Mama, don't tighten it anymore. I won't be able to play—I can't even move."

"You'll manage if you stop being naughty!"

She turned, astonished, but at that moment the chamberlain came down from the podium, Anna Maria slipped into the audience, and Leopold mounted the stage.

"Good evening . . . Your Grace . . . magnificent Excellency . . . Prince! Good evening, illustrious ladies and gentlemen. I am happy and honored to have brought to this splendid court, into your enchanting presence, these spectacular prodigies—the Little Mozarts!"

The two advanced solemnly, clinging to each other like Siamese twins, with that soldier's march that their father had made them practice for entire afternoons. Herr Mozart wasn't aware of it, but the result was rather comical, and a few of the ladies in the audience hid giggles behind their fans.

"You will see what an incomparable talent is contained in the small body of this boy of only six, the future musical leader of the courts of all Europe: Wolfgang Amadeus Mozart! This girl is the most astounding harpsichord player you have ever heard, and she is only eleven years old: Maria Anna Walburga Ignatia Mozart!"

Maria Antonia whispered to the Elector: "Eleven? That girl is at least fifteen!" He tightened his lips in acknowledgment and nodded. In reality he hadn't heard a word: like many men contending with wives, mothers, or sisters, he switched off his hearing automatically when she spoke to him.

"And I, naturally, am the father, Leopold Mozart, vice kapellmeister at the Court of Salzburg, on leave at the moment, in order to promote my children's art throughout the world. We come now to the program: Nannerl will begin the evening by performing the First Sonata of Johann Gottfried Eckard, then Wolfgang will interpret a partita for solo violin by Johann Sebastian Bach. At the end of the concert I will be honored to accept any small token of your appreciation." He bowed, whispered to his daughter, "Now!" and hurried to sit beside his wife.

Wolfgang settled himself on a stool at one side of the stage, and Nannerl sat at the harpsichord. Apart from the Elector, who observed the two children with curiosity, the audience appeared indifferent; some repressed a yawn, others clapped their hands in a semblance of welcome.

Leopold felt as if he were sitting on a hot grill. He whispered to his wife, "Nannerl is growing like a reed. She's beginning to look too big. Soon you'll have to bind her chest."

"Goodness, there's time enough for that!"

"Let's hope."

Praying that everything would go well, Nannerl began the sonata, which was extremely difficult. Few musicians dared to perform Eckard's works, not wanting to risk embarrassment; but Nannerl's hands, with their strong, shapely fingers, independent of one another, seemed to forge the keyboard to their pleasure, rather than adapting to it. Her only problem was the corset, which was crushing her chest so that she could hardly breathe. It forced her to keep her back straight as a broomstick, which wasn't so serious, since even if she couldn't lean over, she could move to the sides; besides, the flapping of her wide sleeves was not an encumbrance and her arms could bend as they needed to. But that pressure on her chest made her short of breath and therefore nervous, and although the room was not well heated and her dress had a low neckline, she began to feel her throat, shoulders, and forehead burning.

Wolfgang immediately realized her discomfort. While continuing to play, she gave him a desperate glance, but how could he help her? He could hardly go over and loosen her stays. The sonata arrived at an extremely complex point in which the right hand executed a theme in the middle of the keyboard and the left jumped rapidly from one end to the other; Nannerl was gasping for breath, the heat was insupportable, and now, too, the *volants* of her sleeves had become a hindrance, a lock of hair was falling over one eye, and her entire body was sticky with sweat. She would have preferred a thousand times to be naked—yes, naked in front of the prince and princess and all the aristocracy of Bavaria. She couldn't care less, if only she were allowed to play freely! The right hand repeated the theme over and over, and the left went up and down, and, in a burst of anger, right in the middle of the passage, Nannerl raised her hands from the keyboard and there was silence.

A nervous sense that something was wrong spread through the room. Maximilian looked at Nannerl with a bewildered frown, while Maria Antonia whispered in his ear something that he (obviously) didn't hear; Leopold was glued to his chair, torn between fear that the concert would end in fiasco and his fundamental lack of interest in his daughter; Anna Maria was too busy scratching a spot off her skirt to realize what was happening; Wolfgang jumped down from his chair, not knowing whether to approach his sister or grab the violin and start playing, to distract people's attention.

But Nannerl surprised her audience by suddenly starting again, with torment on her face and her eyes narrowed in frustration. Skipping the repeats and variations, she reached the final notes of the piece, which ended in less than a minute, and then she ran into the wings without even taking a bow. Wolfgang followed her.

The applause burst automatically: after all, the show was over, or at least so it seemed—otherwise, why had that girl disappeared backstage? And quickly the clapping faded and the room filled with idle chatter. Some gentlemen stood up, in part to stretch their legs, in part to get a pastry from the buffet table that was set up at the back of the room; meanwhile, the stage remained empty.

Leopold began to boil: What was Wolfgang waiting for? The theater has precise rules; you can't cut off the emotional flow, or you risk facing an audience that will be hard to win back. And, as if to confirm his fears, the chatter increased and, with it, a lack of interest in the music. In a fit of anxiety, he jumped to his feet with the confused idea of improvising a speech; maybe, once on the stage, he would be able to find out what the devil his children were up to and take measures. There, that's what he would do! Excellent idea! He leaped onto the platform and began:

"Your Grace, magnificent Prince, esteemed public! I would be honored to call your delightful and distinguished attention to a subject that is surely of interest to you all: the technical preparation, achieved through methodical and careful study, of the two youngsters present here before you, or, that is to say, in the vicinity . . ."

The lecture was interrupted by a sound from backstage. It was the voice of the violin, which wound its way between the folds of the curtain, descended to the parquet, and then rose up to the vaults of the ceiling, filling the space with its fine, lustrous velvet.

"Exactly! Preparation without which the present performance would not be possible. Enjoy the rest!" And in a fraction of a second Leopold had returned to his seat.

The violin charmed the listeners like a snake in a basket. With suspended breath, they stared at the stage in expectation of the magician: and from the wings little Wolfgang emerged, giving sensual impulses to his bow and happily enjoying his enchanter's power as he walked about the stage playing, and behind him came Nannerl, her waist noticeably expanded, so that she was finally free to breathe. She held a flute, and at the right moment joined in, and the timbres of the two instruments, so light but so potent, mingled and echoed amid the vividly painted walls, moving in time; they excited their listeners, strangled them, blew life into their cheeks.

Leopold was fuming. Since when did his children and most promising students permit themselves to perform something that was not predetermined by him in every detail? But now the show had begun, and one never interrupts the show, so Herr Mozart had to submit to the artistic revolt of his children, trying to assume the air of one who knows everything because he has foreseen everything, including the unforeseeable.

On the stage, Wolfgang and Nannerl were improvising as they loved to do for themselves, without much structure and with the absurdity of genius. Playfully they shared forms and leaps of tone that no other could intuit, that passed from his mind to hers and then returned, as Nature willed. She abandoned the flute and sat at the harpsichord, then he abandoned the violin and she accompanied him as he sang, and then he sat at the harpsichord and she sang, accompanied by him. Lacking only the courage to rebel against her father's ban, she didn't touch the violin; but the ecstatic applause they received at the end repaid her even for that renunciation. And her joy was even greater when her brother, after bowing to the ovation, flung his arms

around her neck, crushing her in an enthusiastic embrace, and planted
a loving kiss on her lips.

X.

"It's true, Herr Mozart. What you said really is true. Nothing like it
has ever been seen, nothing even remotely comparable. I must offer
you the liveliest compliments on your children."

Maria Antonia stared at Leopold with her flat yet piercing gaze
and at the same time glanced at Wolfgang, who, perched on the arm
of a chair, was noisily eating a chocolate. The impudence of that child
annoyed her, while she inwardly approved of Nannerl, who nibbled a
tart without letting even a crumb drop; Anna Maria, on the other
hand, who, red in the face, did not dare even to touch the royal porcelain for fear of breaking it, was not worthy of her attention.

"I thank you from the bottom of my heart," Leopold answered,
putting down the plate with the piece of cake that he had barely tasted,
"but I would like to explain, if you will allow me, that talent is not
their only gift. Wolfgang and Nannerl are children of exceptional
character, accustomed to work and discipline. Without strict guidance, talent is in danger of being squandered; you, who are an illustrious musician, know this better than I."

"If I am illustrious it is due more to my position than to my
music," she said with false modesty, and bestowed on him a little
smile.

"I think it's time to play now!" the Elector exclaimed. He was not
taking any refreshment but wandered around the salon with his hands
clasped behind his back.

"Of course, Maximilian," said the princess. "Just wait, if you
don't mind, until we finish paying homage to the work of the pastry
chefs. You don't want anything to eat?"

He shook his head, left the group, and began to rub rosin over the bow of his cello. She, meanwhile, spoke kindly to Nannerl: "You are an extraordinary performer, my girl. Yes, extraordinary: Eckard himself could not play his own sonatas with such precision."

"You are very gracious."

"But how old are you, really?"

Nannerl glanced uncertainly at her father, who immediately intervened: "Eleven! I said so at the start of the concert."

"And I heard you, Herr Mozart, don't worry. I'm just curious to know when she will be twelve."

"Well, actually, that is, to tell the truth, next month."

"Ah, I knew it! And the boy, how old is he—eighteen and still small, thanks to a divine joke?"

"Of course not! Wolfgang is, that is, not six, but—seven last January, actually."

Leopold had not many times in his life come close to stuttering. But this was one of them. Anna Maria, still unnoticed, stared in wishful frustration at the pastries, unaware of the bad impression her husband was making.

"As I see it, Herr Mozart," Maria Antonia insisted with royal sadism, "you choose to lower the ages of your children to make them appear even more phenomenal! I would give you some advice, if you will allow me: forget it. The lie is believable in the case of the boy, but not of the girl, who seems even older than she is."

"Shall we play now?" the Elector interrupted, holding up the perfectly tuned cello.

"Really, Maximilian; right now, when the conversation is starting to get interesting?"

"Why, what are you talking about?" he asked, approaching.

"About this adorable girl. An exceptional player of many instruments, don't you think? If only she were able to compose, as we do, her talent would truly be complete. But, as it is . . ."

"Who says Nannerl doesn't know how to compose? She's way better than you!" cried Wolfgang, spitting out bits of chocolate every which way.

Leopold would happily have dug a hole in the floor that would swallow up his whole family, him first. "Son, be quiet, for heaven's sake. Excuse him, Your Highness, the child doesn't know what he's saying. I entreat you, change the subject."

"No, indeed, Herr Mozart, this particular subject seems to me of great interest!" Maria Antonia said, in annoyance. "So, young lady, what have you composed?"

Nannerl felt all eyes upon her, like rays of burning light. "My brother exaggerates. I've written some arias, a duet . . . but they're small things, not at all comparable to Your Grace's operas in the Italian style."

"What do you mean, you liar? 'Ah, Heaven, what have I done?' Is that a small thing?" said Wolfgang.

"Wolfgang, stop it," she murmured anxiously.

"Is that the title of an aria? Is there a cello part?" Maximilian broke in with interest, but this time, by contrast, it was his sister who didn't listen to him.

"You know what? She always carries all her music with her!" Wolfgang shouted in Maria Antonia's face. "She has a pouch hidden under her skirt. Come on, I'll show you!" And he jumped on his sister, immobilizing her, lifted her skirt, found the secret pouch among her petticoats, and removed the packet of manuscripts, which he threw on the princess's lap with a cry of triumph: "Look at that if you don't believe me!"

Leopold Mozart had gone from stammering to near-paralysis. His lower lip was contracting in uncontrollable spasms, and although he tried to make his vocal cords vibrate in some expression of regret, his throat appeared lifeless. Anna Maria had finally stopped gazing at the pastries and her eyes were fixed on Nannerl's legs, still indecently uncovered; Nannerl herself hadn't even realized it, too intent on observing her precious scores in Maria Antonia's wrinkled hands. Maximilian, too, was examining them, in a desperate search for something he could play at that moment, which finally he found: "*'Ah, Heaven, what have I done?'* Aria for soprano and strings. Is this what you were talking about, little boy?"

"Yes! Why don't we try it now?" Wolfgang burst out.

"Can you play the viola?" the Elector asked him. What a stupid question! He realized it immediately and continued rapidly: "Of course. Maria Antonia can sing, I play the cello, naturally, and the two violins—"

He broke off and turned toward Leopold and Nannerl. Her heart was beating so hard that her ribs could be seen rising and falling even through her dress.

"There doesn't seem to be any other solution! To you I leave the choice of who plays first violin and who second; but I would suggest, Herr Mozart, that out of gallantry and paternal love, you give first place to your daughter."

Nannerl looked at her father with feigned submissiveness, and her voice came out hoarsely, in a clever portrayal of distress: "In truth, my Prince, the violin is not an instrument for girls."

"Of course," Maximilian answered politely. "It's not right for a young lady to play the violin in public. But here we are practically family, aren't we, dear Leopold?"

Herr Mozart nodded with his eyelids, the only part of his body he could still control. Maximilian threw a precious Italian instrument toward him and only the fear that it would crash to the floor overcame his paralysis. Nannerl, her eyes shining with joy, took another polished violin from the Elector's hands and hugged it to her as one hugs a rediscovered friend. Maria Antonia began gargling to warm up her voice; she had the look of one of who, from the heights of magnanimity, is doing the masses a favor, but in fact she wasn't too secure about her sight-reading. Maximilian took his place, Nannerl distributed the parts, and while Anna Maria, finally ignored by everyone, could stuff her mouth with gelatins, the rehearsal began, and the composition of Maria Anna Walburga Ignatia Mozart echoed clear and proud through the rooms of the Castle of Nymphenburg in Munich!

My father, Leopold Mozart—what can I tell you about my father? I imagine you know him at least slightly, since you must have met him at court, and certainly you must have an excellent impression; he is indisputably a man of great intelligence, vast culture, and courtly manners; and I guarantee you, dear Armand, that he is capable of love, and that he loves his family intensely, but in different ways.

He married my mother out of love. More than anything he was fascinated by her natural vitality, which was something completely unknown to him; far from despising her unruly behavior, he observed it with patience and interest, even though at times he suffered from the effects of it. Then Wolfgang arrived, and he added to that vitality a sublime capacity for abstraction and a fierce imagination; and the boundaries of my father's world contracted, inevitably, to the relationship between him and his male child.

There is only one thing for which I cannot forgive Leopold Mozart: he so exhausted my brother that Wolfgang became ill—it's a miracle that he's so healthy and robust today. I was bigger and stronger, and was better able to withstand the discomforts of those journeys, the irregular meals, the endless series of performances; but as a small boy he had to endure typhoid, rheumatic fever, skin inflammations, and a number of minor ailments, from vomiting to recurrent headaches, not to mention smallpox, which, thank Heaven, we both survived. But nothing would sway Herr Mozart from his purpose, and the end of every illness was the beginning of a new activity, the preparation for a new and exhilarating success.

Because the European tour was a triumph! The concerts produced a lot of money; nobles and commoners both went wild over my brother's and my virtuosity, Wolfgang's fame was established, his musical culture became richer every day. I, too, nourished my soul on sights and experiences that in small, dull Salzburg I would never have known. But it wasn't enough

for my father, and we had to raise our sights and aim at London. And per-
haps he already had in mind the future, even more ambitious move: to
Italy. He would put up with the people of the south, whom he despised, in
order to bring Wolfgang to the land of opera and make him into a star of
the stage . . .

And for the journey to Italy, above all, I should be grateful to Leopold
Mozart; for it was precisely that journey that led, indirectly, dearest, to our
meeting. Consider then, Armand, that you should think kindly of my
father in a particular way.

XI.

At the center of the fresco shone a divine, half-naked coachman with
a gilded cloak over his shoulders that stayed in place despite the
speeding chariot. How many horses were there? Maybe two, one the
shadow of the other, but at that distance and with your head back it
wasn't easy to distinguish them. The chariot gleamed, but everything
around it was gray. Among some humbler figures at the base of the
painting were two women who seemed to be frowning, as if despite
their altitude they were not superior to human sufferings but, rather,
eager to descend and mingle. Nannerl smiled to herself as she imagined those maidens, in their flowing classical robes, circulating among
the noblewomen, with their elaborate, low-cut gowns, who crowded
the salon. She looked down and suddenly everything seemed to have
spots; this increased her sensation of being in an unreal place.

Versailles was more than a palace, more than a castle—it was a
city made for princes. Everything was excessive, from the enormous
park filled with bronze and marble statues and gigantic pools to the
vast buildings, their wide windows hung with lush draperies. The
walls of the innumerable salons were covered with plaster reliefs and
rose- and orange-colored stone; tall narrow-necked vases and busts of
illustrious whiskered men stood on pedestals, and beside doorways

were gigantic mirrors in ornate gilded frames. There was gold everywhere: gold statues, gold cornices, even the doors were of gold. And then the tapestries on the walls and the carpets on the floors, immense carpets covering surfaces as large as the main square of a normal city! On the hearths burned fires that could have swallowed up a herd of cows, and yet it was terribly cold: How could those ladies with their bold necklines survive the winters?

Herr Mozart, however, appeared confident that to be in such luxury made even him royal. Holding his son tightly by the hand, he proceeded with an air of satisfaction: "It was high time for a change of scene, after that rabble in the Paris streets. Don't you agree, my dear?"

Frau Mozart's mouth had been wide open, in amazement and fascination, for at least twenty minutes; her throat was dry, and she couldn't answer.

"*Superflua divitum, necessaria sunt pauperum!* Can you translate this axiom, Wolfgang?"

"The excesses of the rich are necessary for the poor," the boy answered, trying to free his hand from that of his father, who would not let go.

"Excellent, my angel. Unfortunately, this concept has at times been wrongly interpreted, to the point of leading certain depraved characters to appropriate for themselves the goods of others. Imagine, the Shah of Persia, a splendid country even farther away than England, was overthrown by a crazed mob, and his palace razed!"

Wolfgang managed to wriggle free and join his sister, who was trying to warm herself at the fire in one of the hearths, so close to the flame that she was in danger of burning her clothes; he grabbed her hand, which was softer than his father's and now warmer as well, and with her entered the room where they were to perform.

The harpsichord was practically invisible in that visual orgy, even though it was skillfully painted, gilded, and lacquered. It wasn't in a prominent position but, rather, half hidden among sofas, tables loaded with delicacies, powdered ladies and their courtiers—who seemed to have assembled there for anything but to listen to music. They chattered on and on, incomprehensibly, in their language that had so many vowels, concealing the smiles of their painted lips behind fans of feathers and fur, and nothing could make them stop talking: neither the *ahem*s of Leopold Mozart, nor the redoubled intensity of the four-hand piece that he ordered his children to play, nor the one they played with a cloth laid over the keyboard. And then, suddenly, a noble-woman entered through the archway and an apprehensive silence fell.

She was escorted by two imposing gentlemen beside whom she would have disappeared except for the obvious force of her personality; she must have been forty, and she bore the traces of a former beauty. The oval of her face, crowned by a jeweled diadem, was broken by luminous gray eyes, but too much rouge made her look like an old doll. A page rapidly approached Leopold and whispered to him to make the children stop playing; but the lady, with a majestic gesture, let him understand that she desired the contrary. She settled herself on a chair and sat there, proudly alone, with an air of appreciating the concert.

"Who is she?" Leopold whispered into the page's ear.

The answer had a tone of scandal: *"Monsieur, c'est la Marquise de Pompadour!"*

The name had no effect on the two children, nor did the sudden general interest in their performance excite them, for they were aware of its falseness. But Anna Maria gazed at the king's favorite with the scorn that is reserved for prostitutes, and when the applause broke out she felt a flare of rage as her husband headed straight for that witch and performed a spectacular genuflection.

"What you have seen is nothing!" Leopold exclaimed, spinning around and addressing the entire room. "The spectacle that you will witness in a few moments will leave you stunned. Would one of you, charming ladies, be so kind as to provide a melody?"

In response came a silence of unexpected embarrassment, punctuated by some murmurs and twittering laughter.

"Courage, ladies! I don't ask much—just hum a tune, however simple, even a nursery song. Incredible as it may seem, my little Wolfgang will instantaneously compose a fugue on that theme!"

The laughter increased, assuming a tone of mockery. Leopold turned to Madame de Pompadour with a smile that was intended to be appealing: "Marquise, won't you set an example for the court? It would be an indescribable honor for me."

She gave him a chilling glance, and the two gentlemen likewise stared at him with threatening scowls. He, undaunted, continued, though his voice was slightly less firm. "All right! I myself will break the ice. Here, let's see: in Augsburg, when I was a child, this lullaby was popular."

At that point the laughter grew very loud, and even the Marquise's lips parted in a silent sneer, revealing two rows of perfect teeth. Leopold stopped, finally speechless; he realized that all eyes were on the harpsichord, and what he saw when he turned to look filled him with humiliation: Wolfgang, with his head in Nannerl's lap, was sound asleep.

Madame de Pompadour, if she hadn't been Pompadour, would have bent double with laughter. Instead she proceeded calmly out of the room, with that spectral laugh cracking her face, followed by a good half of the audience. Just as it had arisen, the interest in the family of musicians evaporated. Only a few ladies dared to approach the little sleeper and caress his golden curls; Anna Maria couldn't repress a tender smile, but a furious look from the head of the family made her instantly think better of it.

"Take him to bed immediately!" Leopold growled at his daughter, and, with his wife on his arm, left the room.

XII.

If to get around within Versailles the nobles were borne in those chairs they called *chaises à porteur*, there was obviously a practical reason: the music room must have been at least a couple of miles from the entrance. Nannerl had to shake her brother and exhort him to walk on his own legs, for she would never have been able to carry him all that way; then, to get to the pensione Cormier, she had to ask for a ride in a carriage, because it was raining. The result was that, once they had reached the room, Wolfgang was as lively as a cricket. When she put the bed warmer between the covers, he was hiding under the bed; when she tried to put his nightclothes on, he evaded her with a silvery laugh, inciting her to follow him. "Let's have a trial! Let's say I stole a deer and you're the queen and you want to send me to prison!"

"Perfect," Nannerl said mockingly. "Dirty little thief, go to jail. Now get in bed."

"No, not like that! Let's have a real trial! You have to sit on the throne."

And he tried to push her toward a chaise longue, but she resisted. "That's enough, Wolfgang—if you don't stop it I'm going to go away and leave you."

"And I'll tell Papa you left me alone."

"If you try, I'll slap you!"

"And I'll tell Papa you hit me!"

She sat down and with a sigh of resignation recited: "The object of contention . . ."

"No, first you have to say the motto."

"Here forever happy are we."

"No, you don't understand. Real trials are carried out in Latin."

Nannerl looked at him with sudden bitterness. That rascal knew perfectly well that she had been forbidden to study the language.

"*Hic habitat felicitas,*" he pronounced, staring at her with an insolent little smile. "Come on, stupid, repeat."

She felt a tremendous desire to punch him, but with a heroic effort she restrained herself and was silent.

"*Hic habitat felicitas, nihil intret mali.* What in the world does it mean? Who knows? You don't know. You don't know because you have a head as round as a ball and completely empty!" And he pranced around in front of her until Nannerl angrily jumped up, extending her arms in a shove that she didn't intend to be violent but was. The child fell hard on the floor and hit his head.

He didn't cry. He looked at her with immense surprise, while she, terrified, knelt on the floor: "Wolfgang! Wolfgang! Did you hurt yourself?"

He said no, rubbing the sore place on his forehead. Everything vanished in an instant: excitement, the wish to play, the attempt to provoke his sister. She shed copious tears of guilt, and this left him even more bewildered. Then he stood up mechanically and insisted on getting into his nightclothes without any help from her; by himself he removed the heavy bed warmer, got into bed, and an instant before falling asleep gave her a warm smile of understanding.

Their parents found them like that, he in a deep sleep, she curled up beside him watching, with reddened eyes.

The night walk had made no dent in Leopold's bad mood. With a gloomy face he went into the adjoining room, sat down on the bed, and began to untie his shoes. Meanwhile Anna Maria whispered to Nannerl, "What happened? Did you quarrel?"

She didn't answer. She was listening with growing anger to the sounds her father made: a rustling of garments hung on the clothes rack, an indistinct muttering of disappointment for who knows what foolish reason, until she went to him and burst out: "Tomorrow Wolfgang won't play! Do you understand?"

"What's wrong with you? Be quiet or you'll wake him! Holy shit!" Anna Maria said, joining her.

"He's exhausted! He's not himself! He's always tired and sick, he's lost weight, he's not growing, and he has two black pouches under his eyes worse than yours. You can't make us perform like trained dogs every night. Wolfgang should go to bed early!"

Leopold, impassive, slowly continued to undress. He was now half naked, but he didn't care if his daughter saw him in that state; it was a way of communicating to her that her presence had for him the same value as that of a night table or a bedside rug.

"I will tell you one time only, Nannerl, and I will not repeat it," he replied in a low voice. "When you have your own children, you can bring them up as you see fit; for the moment it is I, I alone, who will make decisions for Wolfgang. He endures fatigue very well. Maybe it's you who are weak, and your thoughtless actions are the proof."

Furious, Nannerl pushed to the floor the rack on which her father had so carefully hung his clothes and returned to her brother, slamming the door behind her.

Anna Maria picked up the clothes and timidly added, "Leopold, perhaps the child is not completely wrong. She and Wolfgang both are rather irritable; maybe they are overtired."

"Nannerl is thirteen now—it is an ungrateful age," he opined, and turned out the light.

XIII.

Finally they were going to see the king of France! Lords and ladies swarmed like maddened bees in a huge room, at the center of which was a table so long that the ends vanished into the horizon, and so loaded with precious things as to make one fear it would collapse. Exquisitely painted porcelain plates were beautifully laid out on a tablecloth of white cotton tulle with lace insets, along with tall chalices engraved with the royal coat of arms, forks and knives with carved handles, carefully folded white napkins, carafes and bottles of the finest crystal, elaborate floral displays, and silver trays overflowing with fruit and brioches and cheeses. Towering candelabra with clusters of candles created that dim light that makes the face of every woman more beautiful.

Louis XV dined with the court one day a year: the first. The rest of the time, the inhabitants of Versailles had no right to look at the divine one while he ate like every other mortal. The *Grand Couvert* of the first of the year was a genuine occasion, a sort of prophecy foretold, and to Leopold's immense satisfaction, the Mozart family had been invited. And they would have the privilege of sitting beside the king and queen!

The babble of the guests who had assembled to obtain a place at the table echoed frenetically; as in the treacherous musical game, there were never enough chairs, and those who arrived late would miss their chance. The Mozarts would never dream of arriving late! Suddenly the pages closed the doors; only one tall, richly painted door remained open. In the silence, the women inspected their hairdos in the mirrors, and the gentlemen, the buttoning of their waistcoats, and finally, with the self-satisfied indolence of a peacock making the rounds, and flanked by imposing Swiss Guards, Louis XV appeared beside Marie Leszczynska.

Nannerl was disconcerted: the queen was a little old lady. She had white hair and gnarled, spotted hands, and a dress draped with cream-colored veils and with insets of white fur that made her resemble an overcooked meringue; she wore a sort of nightcap, also topped by a billowing veil, that was tied at her neck by a shiny ribbon. She descended wearily from the *chaise à porteur* and reached her place at the table, while the valets who held up her train were in reality arranged to hold her up if her legs should give way; finally, trembling, she sat down, heaving a sigh of relief.

It was obvious how much younger the king was. And seeing the wife, Leopold thought with secret lewdness that one could understand why he had spent his life looking for distractions. Marie was as hunched as Louis was proudly erect; he radiated the immodest and negligent air of one who can permit himself anything.

After the royal couple, the other diners were allowed to take their places, and Anna Maria, with Nannerl, sat beside the king, while at the other end of the table Leopold and Wolfgang were next to the queen. In a religious silence, the valets served the first course: *potage à la Regence,* a very fine purée of greens seasoned with a mixture of spices and dotted with choice early vegetables: the visual composition of intense earth colors and delicate pastel tints, not to mention the incomparable odor, made the guests salivate in an embarrassing and almost audible way. No one would have dared to start until the first delicious mouthful had reached the royal stomach. Extremely slowly, Louis XV tasted the potage, put down his spoon, wiped his lips with the napkin, then nodded his head in a sign of approval; relieved, the others imitated him, and a quiet tinkling of dishes and a subdued exchange of words replaced the reverent silence.

Wolfgang and Nannerl had been carefully trained: never address the royal couple, never! Unless you were directly spoken to, and in that case you were to respond with a low voice and bent head. Never serve yourself with your own hands, never chew with your mouth open, never drink before having wiped your lips with the napkin, never clean your fingers on the tablecloth, never pick your teeth with a knife or, worse than worse, your nails. Rigid as marionettes, the two children tasted the divine meal, which Nannerl found delicious and Wolfgang revolting, though he made an effort to hide it.

It was the gravelly voice of Marie Leszczynska that started the conversation. Behind the appearance of a foolish old woman, the queen had a lively mind, and if Madame de Pompadour was impossibly arrogant, she had simple and courteous manners.

"Monsieur Mozart, I am happy to meet you at last."

"If you please, Your Highness, it is an honor for me to sit at your side!"

"Your French is excellent—perhaps better than mine."

"Your Highness, please; you flatter me."

"Not at all. For me, too, it is a second language, so my judgment may be even more severe than that of a native speaker. And, I must say, your pronunciation and your choice of language seem to me outstanding. Are you also able to write in French?"

"Oh yes, if necessary. I was made to study it very seriously when I was young."

"So you must have translated personally your violin method."

Leopold looked at her with sincere surprise, and equally sincere gratification. "You have read my humble work, Your Highness?"

"I confess I have not. Music is not among my accomplishments—I would not have understood it. But I have heard it spoken of. I know that it has crossed the borders even of Russia."

"In fact, such a systematic treatment of the material had never been published."

"Do you intend to write other works?"

"I fear not, my queen. My present duties do not allow it."

"That is indeed a pity."

"Do you think so? I am convinced that a man must devote himself to the only activity in which he excels. And as the promoter of my children's career, and especially my son's, in all modesty, I excel."

The queen was silent while a waiter removed her empty plate and another took from a basket a bottle of Chablis and poured some into the wineglasses. Leopold feared that his proud estimation had irritated her and he was about to plunge into a thousand excuses when he realized that the waiter was about to pour wine for Wolfgang.

"No, not for the child, please!"

"Well done, Monsieur Mozart," the queen said with a benevolent smile. "In fact, take away all his wineglasses," she ordered the servant.

So she wasn't angry. While Leopold sighed with relief, the man hesitated before the child's bowl, which was still full to the brim. Wolfgang was squatting on his chair, looking down and pouting, prevented from protesting by paternal dictates and from swallowing that disgusting thing by his own palate. The waiter understood, winked at him, and Wolfgang's potage returned untouched to the kitchens.

"A life dedicated to one's children," Marie Leszczynska reflected aloud, sipping the Chablis. "Truly admirable, Monsieur Mozart. And also rare, on the part of a man. But tell me, what would happen if one day the children wanted to take paths different from those you have laid out for them?"

Leopold was no longer willing to risk contradicting her and answered as meekly as a lamb. "Once he is grown up, Wolfgang will be able to do what he wants, naturally. I offer him a possibility, no more; accepting or rejecting it is a matter of free will."

While he tasted the *croustades à la Saint Cloud,* the queen nodded, but her keen intuition told her that Leopold was lying.

At the other end of the table the situation was completely different. Philosophizing was impossible, since Anna Maria didn't know a word of French and had on her face the same expression as the mullet in sauce *cameline* that was lying on her plate. Nannerl, on the other hand, would have been able to start a simple conversation, but until the king had spoken to her, she was obliged to be silent; and Louis XV was not exactly a chatterbox, or at least he wasn't that day. Perhaps he thought that one's mouth should be used for one activity at a time. He barely moved his fork and knife, cutting his food into tiny pieces that he chewed with an air of utter concentration, as if it were an intellectual activity; his relationship with the external world was represented exclusively by slight nods addressed sometimes to one, sometimes to another of his guests, but never to Anna Maria or Nannerl. But the food was very good, and both happily gorged themselves.

"So, Monsieur Mozart, what might be your next move in promoting your son?"

"I intend to publish his compositions."

The queen looked with lively surprise at Wolfgang, who was at last contentedly chewing something that he liked: a *filet de bœuf* that the sympathetic waiter had already cut up for him.

"And this child writes music? I don't know much about it, sir, but I imagine that that is exceptional."

"Indeed, Your Highness. I intend to begin immediately to publish his works systematically, in such a way that a larger number of persons may become acquainted with his gifts. And naturally I have preserved his manuscripts in order, since there is no doubt, my queen, that one day they will be in great demand. I am preparing a splendid future for him."

"I know, I know, but now enough of this subject," she said, looking at the child with a maternal smile. "Let me hold this dear little fellow. May I?"

"Of course!" Leopold rose quickly, picked up Wolfgang, and placed him in the queen's arms. Torn away from that delicious meat, shifted from a comfortable chair to a slippery old lady covered with jewels, the child threw a glance of desperation at his sister, who was too far away and, in her turn, chained by etiquette, so that there would have been no way to intervene.

Marie Leszczynska had not only a keen mind but keen eyes as well. She immediately noticed the violet bruise on Wolfgang's temple, which someone had tried to camouflage with a layer of powder and hide beneath the elegant wig that he was wearing for the occasion.

"Oh, poor child. Did you fall?"

Leopold started. "How did that happen, Wolfgang?"

Nannerl, taking in the scene from the other end of the table, felt the food stick in her throat.

"Don't be shy; answer your father," Marie urged him graciously. "I give you permission to speak. And if the queen tells you to do something, you have to do it."

"Well, I—I hit the portable harpsichord with my head."

"Why didn't you tell me before?" the father said suspiciously.

"Because—because I made a scratch on the harpsichord and I was afraid you would get angry."

Leopold was justly incredulous. "You made a scratch on the instrument—with your head?"

"No, no. It's that when I fell I was holding the violin."

Leopold raised his voice. "And so you also ruined the violin?"

The queen laughed heartily, shaking and making Wolfgang shake with her. "Let it go, Monsieur Mozart. I assure you, you won't get to the end of it. I have had more children than you, and I am much older. You'll never know what really happened. And if you find that one of your instruments is damaged, what is the problem? You have it repaired. Now, little one, what would you say about tasting this *suprême de profiteroles à l'écossaise?*"

What that pyramid of sweetness had to do with Scotland is not known, but certainly it had something to do with gluttony. Sitting in the arms of the queen and eating from her plate while she cuddled him and caressed him, Wolfgang filled his stomach with chocolate, cream puffs, and custard, and then with strawberries and cream, and then almond-stuffed apricots, and finally the most delicious flavors of ice cream. And when the dinner ended and it was time to leave, his pockets were overflowing with candies of all kinds, hidden there by the loving and tremulous hands of the queen of France.

XIV.

Who had seen the sea? It had a strong odor, of salt; kitchen salt has no smell, yet the sea does. And it was so big it was frightening, and it moved on its own, pushed by an invisible power. It seemed possessed by a dark rage, eager to avenge some insult, in harmony with the leaden sky, which, at its signal, would descend to meet and mingle with it.

Wolfgang raced from stern to prow, looked out to observe the fish, lay down on the bridge to better feel the pitch of the small boat. Anna

Maria pursued him uselessly, with the constantly sharper sensation that her stomach had gone somewhere else, not the right place but higher up, in the direction of her throat, and that it was tying itself in knots. She took her husband by the arm and begged him to sit in the stern beside her, and not to leave her alone, at least for a few minutes.

"It's nothing, seasickness," Leopold declared. "Seasickness doesn't exist. You have only to concentrate on something else, and right away it passes. Pray. There's always a need for that: ask the Lord to grant us all good health."

Dragging a rope, Wolfgang darted past them and disappeared through a trapdoor. Frau Mozart sighed wearily.

"Let him go; don't worry. He certainly can't escape from here. Come, my dear, please."

Nannerl was alone at the prow, crouching on the bridge like a little Siren, letting herself be slapped by the wind. The English coast was already visible through the fog, and she wondered what that island was like, inhabited by such adventurous people, people who went boldly forth to seek glory and wealth in the farthest corners of the world. Their language was made up of words more familiar to her than Italian or French; but if it was true that the sun never shone, then what source of joy did they have?

She was joined by her brother, who knelt quietly beside her and in turn gazed at the distant strip of land. In harmonious silence, the two remained squatting beside each other, like two statues carved in the same rocky group, elaborating on their expectations for the London stay.

"What will Christian Bach be like?" Wolfgang asked.

Nannerl seemed to see him: he was a true maestro, a man who would be able to understand and help her as her father never would. "He must have . . . white hair, and big hands that are nimble and quick on the keyboard, and ink-stained. Also the keys of the harpsichord are stained, and he wipes them off himself, with a white cloth, and then . . . and then the pen that he uses to compose is one of those long silver ones. And he keeps the ink in a dark blue inkwell."

"I think he is better than Papa."

"That's obvious, Wolfgang! Is there any need to mention it?"

As for Leopold, sitting in the stern, his ears didn't burn, but something must have happened in his body, because he was paler than before. His wife serenely prayed: *"Sancta Maria, mater Dei, ora pro nobis peccatoribus, nunc et in hora mortis nostrae . . ."*

"Amen," he said, choking, and vomited into the sea.

It was another world! It wasn't Europe! All the customs, the objects, the behavior were different. The houses were low, of dark colors, gray, brown, even black, or the dirty red of unstuccoed bricks. In front of every building was an iron gate, to protect passersby from falling into the basements; every doorway led directly to a house. Buildings of apartments didn't exist: only many single houses next to each other, with rooms stacked three or four stories high. As a result, there were no internal courtyards: if Wolfgang and I had been born in London, where would we have placed the king's throne?

The rooms were small, which gave them the advantage of being very warm. The stoves used coal, not wood; wood was used, rather, for furnishing. Walls covered with wood, wood-beamed ceilings, even the floors that squeaked under your feet were of wood; the smell of pine was strong enough to make you faint. The windows were not wide, except those on the ground floor, which is called the first floor; and they had a strange system of sliding the windows open upward, so that they could never be opened completely; looking out, you were amazed by the view of streets swarming with an incredible mass of humanity.

Both men and women were tall, strong, and good-looking; blacks, Chinese, people of the lower classes mingled with the wealthy, and the latter did not consider this an insult or claim gestures of deference. They all seemed to be wearing costumes. The men's coats were long, reaching to mid-calf, and had tight sleeves that restricted their arm movements. The women never went hatless: they wore broad hats, round, with wide soft brims, tied behind, of shiny material or of straw, or of taffeta, and richly decorated with ribbons and trimmed with lace, bows, flowers, and sometimes even precious stones. The skirts were of linen, silk, cotton, fabrics from Persia and the East Indies, printed with little flowers or embroidered with delicate floral designs. Victoria, I assure you, would have been mad for those fabrics! The boys had short hair and felt caps perched on their heads, which they held on to with one hand when a sudden breeze threatened to carry them off. Then, one moment it was warm, and the next, cold air from the north lowered the temperature until your teeth chattered, and you'd want to go to bed immediately.

You might find yourself witnessing a quarrel right in the middle of a square: two men savagely beating each other—breaking teeth, cracking bones—while passersby ignored them, or stopped to watch as if at a stadium, or maybe they even joined in the fray. It could also happen that you would be accosted roughly by a stranger, because of your continental dress: we endured what to the English is the worst possible insult, to be taken for French! So my father brought us in a hurry to a tailor shop and had us dressed anew from head to toe. And so, proudly, in all things now similar to an ordinary local family, we mixed with the dust and smoke and were lost in the crowd . . .

XV.

"Herr Tschudi, I am honored by your welcome, and I must acknowledge, of course, that you are a skilled craftsman. And yet I confess to you that this new instrument—how can I put it? It doesn't convince me. An Italian invented it, right? It's time for that riffraff from the south to stop illegally trying to take over the music business."

"I understand your point of view, Herr Mozart. But may I be permitted to remind you that while the pianoforte was indeed invented by the Cristofori, it was perfected by Gottfried Silbermann, that is, a German—"

"Of course! And I am aware, besides, that Johann Christian Bach has already composed for the pianoforte. Make no mistake; I am, in all modesty, quite well informed. In spite of that, I don't think this instrument will have a wide circulation. One of those passing fashions that are gone as soon as they have arrived—surely you know what I'm saying?"

They were having tea in the workshop of the best-known maker of pianos. There was no habitation in London where the teakettle was not ready from morning to evening, and on every visit one was unfailingly welcomed with tea and buttered scones. And it seemed that the custom extended to craftsmen's workshops, or at least those that were doing well; and to judge from the fine Chinese porcelain cups and the heavy silver teapot, Mr. Burkhardt Tschudi was managing very well. He also had an assistant, a man in a white coat who was sitting calmly in a corner working with glue and file.

Nannerl couldn't wait to try the modern instrument, which had replaced the metallic and essentially tedious sound of the harpsichord with a completely new, much more expressive timbre, thanks to an ingenious system of levers and hammers. She was excited by the idea of investigating a broad spectrum of acoustic effects, depending on the intensity with which she touched the keys, from the delicacy of a light rain to the tremendous power of thunder, passing through a thousand intermediate shadings.

While the adults were conversing, she silently approached the magnificent instrument. Close up, it did not seem different from a harpsichord. It was of cedar, without decoration, and massive; it had a single keyboard, not the two, one above the other, that many harpsichords did. The moment she pressed her fingers to the keys, Nannerl felt the same emotion as when she had seen her newborn brother, and she realized that her life would no longer make sense without the pianoforte. Wolfgang joined her, mouth open in amazement, while she ran her hands up and down the keyboard, and crossed them, and then, still playing, stood up to see what the hammers were doing to the strings. She experimented freely, following only her own whim, instinct, passion.

"What are you doing—are you by chance improvising?"

It was the voice of Leopold. Mr. Tschudi looked at him with some disappointment, while Nannerl put her hands back in her lap.

"Girls should not give in to the wish for fantasy," Herr Mozart continued. "Eh! What would the world be if men did not take on the task of reining in feminine vanities?"

Anna Maria, who was adjusting a hairpin, stopped abruptly and tried to assume the air of a serious person.

With studied calm, Leopold put down his cup and wiped his hands and mouth with the napkin. "Very good! We have seen the instruments, and now I would say that we can go. Thank you, Herr Tschudi."

"Oh, so soon?" he said, unhappily. "We have some others upstairs. Don't tell me you don't want to see them! They are my best pieces."

"It would be very interesting, but you must understand that my son is wasting precious time that he should be devoting to practice."

"There is also a harpsichord upstairs. Wouldn't he like to try it out? It might, after all, be useful, in an educational sense."

Wolfgang's cry echoed amid the opened sound boxes. "Yes! I want to try playing both together."

"But of course, little one. My assistant will go with you."

Wolfgang darted away with the man in the white coat, followed by his mother and a resigned Leopold. Nannerl prepared to go with them, but Tschudi rapidly, furtively, closed the door to the stairs: "Come, play for me as you were doing before."

She glanced nervously at the door.

"Don't worry. They can't hear anything from upstairs."

"No, it's better if I go. My father will notice that I'm not there and come down."

"No one has ever played an instrument of mine as you did. Please, go back to it. Do this old man a favor."

Timidly, Nannerl sat down on the stool. She sounded some light chords, played a short scale, then a trill. Finally she let herself be possessed by a feeling of pleasure and at the upper end of the keyboard she spun a melody that contained echoes of treetops tossed by the wind on a beloved hillside near Salzburg, of the cool dampness of a cut bough, of the beating wings of a woodcock. She kept the volume low, fearing her father's ire, but there was no need; he was too much in the spell of Wolfgang's abilities, upstairs, and had forgotten her. And at the end, the old craftsman, with his faintly greasy complexion, gave her brief, emotional applause, the most gratifying she had ever received, and whispered a phrase that she never forgot: "Have the courage to fight for your dreams, little Miss Mozart."

XVI.

They had arrived. The Maestro lived in a four-story mansion with a green lacquered door. From above a long and oddly mobile nose, a butler as elegant as a lord gazed over the heads of the Mozarts and said only, "Follow me."

Pressing her scores to her breast, Nannerl felt her heart beating violently; a vise gripped her from the pit of her stomach to her throat, and she was afraid of stumbling on the steps.

"Welcome! It's a pleasure to meet you. How are you?"

"I am deeply honored to make the important acquaintance of the most esteemed and illustrious Herr Johann Christian Bach!" Leopold exclaimed, touching the Maestro's fingertips.

"Come now, there's no need to be so formal among colleagues. Frau Mozart, *enchanté*. Please, let me show you the way."

Above the majestic grand piano hung a portrait of Johann Sebastian Bach, with his severe, troubled expression and an enormous wig of white curls that hung down to his chest. The son, so different and so young, turned in a friendly manner to Wolfgang and Nannerl: "And here are the little Mozarts! The two prodigies I've heard so much about."

"And I've heard so much about you!"

"Silence, Wolfgang. Children should speak only if spoken to."

"No, no, Herr Mozart, let the little one express himself. So, what do you know about me?"

"That you are better than Papa! Nannerl said so."

A heavy silence fell. Bach, amused, said, "My dear girl, in art there is no established hierarchy, and it's certainly not a contest, that one can win or lose. But you, little boy, you must try to preserve this lovely impudence. If you can put it into your music, no one will be able to stop you."

"Impudence? I think that music is a matter of discipline," Leopold muttered.

"No doubt, discipline is indispensable. But it is only the means that allows us to express passion."

"As in the works of your father!" Nannerl interrupted headlong. "He was the first composer who—"

"Shall we get to the point?" And abruptly, and almost discourteously, Leopold offered Bach a bundle of scores. "These are Wolfgang's most recent compositions. I would hope that you might examine them as soon as possible, to assess the possibility of taking him as a student."

"Of course! I can even do it right away, if you have the patience to wait a little while."

"Pardon me . . . I have some things to show you, too, if you wouldn't mind: a lied with *basso continuo,* a duet, and even a cantata." With trembling hands, Nannerl offered her music to the Maestro.

"I'm impressed. So you, too, compose!"

"Let's not talk nonsense!" Leopold grew more and more nervous. "No woman composes."

"But I do—my scores prove it."

"Careful, Nannerl: this is the sin of pride! And as Saint Augustine says, *superbia parit discissionem, caritas unitatem.*"

"You call me proud? And making a show of your own learning—isn't that a sin of pride?"

Herr Mozart was dumbstruck, but only for an instant. "Be quiet, you foolish girl!" he shouted, his red face a breath from hers. He seemed ready to strangle her with his own hands.

There was a long silence. Embarrassed, Bach stared at the image of his father, as if looking for help. Nannerl held out the scores, but he didn't take them. She felt her mother grab her by the arm.

"Come, dear," she said, dragging her bodily. "Let's go in the other room, so Herr Bach can give Wolfgang a lesson; and then, if there's time, he will also listen to you. Come on, my sweetheart."

As they left the room, the fixed smile vanished from her face. "Your father is right—you really are foolish. Did you have to cause a scene in front of the gentleman?"

"I wanted him to listen to my music."

"You're a young lady. You'll never become a kapellmeister. Will you get that through your head? Papa has told you a thousand times."

"Are you taking his side now? Then I am telling you that to me it doesn't matter at all what Papa says! Or you!"

"Don't you dare! Holy shit!"

At that moment the butler arrayed like a noble entered with the never-failing tea tray. He looked at Anna Maria in shock, nearly dropped it as he put it down, and left.

"What a bad impression you've caused me to make!"

"Oh, of course. Now it's my fault."

"That's enough, Nannerl. You must stop using that tone." She took her by the shoulder and looked her in the eye. "Your father has arranged everything for our well-being: Wolfgang is the pillar of the family, and it is he who is to become a composer. We'll take him to study in Italy when he's older, and he'll become famous all over the world and we'll all be happy. Even you!"

"What do you know about what will make me happy?"

"And then we'll find you a husband. You'll have children. What's the use of all this passion for music?"

The half hour that followed was, for Nannerl, genuine torture. Through the closed doors, notes began to sound: Wolfgang was playing the pianoforte for Christian Bach. And meanwhile, flinging herself onto a chair, she waited in silence, doing absolutely nothing. Sitting on the sofa like a sultan, her mother drank tea and ate scones and tried to involve Nannerl in the feast, but her stomach had become a dry sack. She clasped her hands in her lap and began to twiddle her thumbs; suddenly exhausted, she leaned back and closed her eyes. Then she made an effort and got up. She went to the window and looked out, searching for any sort of distraction, but the room was at the back of the house and there were no passersby. Suddenly the music stopped; the door opened and Herr Bach appeared holding Wolfgang in his arms like an infant.

"Well, well, well, Frau Mozart! Do you know, it seemed to me that I went back many years? In your son I saw myself as a child." He put him down gently and suggested: "Now go to your sister. I must speak to Papa and Mama about your future."

Swifter than a gust of wind, Nannerl left the parlor, and Wolfgang trotted after her. "You know, he liked your cantata a lot. I told him that you wrote it, but he didn't believe me. He thinks I wrote it!"

"Leave me alone!" And she tried to go down the stairs but he held her by the skirt, giggling.

"Where are you going, you big goat? Want to play hide-and-seek?"

She slapped his hand, and he stopped short; she hurried down the stairs while the little boy stood there bewildered. "Nannerl! Why are you acting like this?" He tried to catch her, but she was already on the ground floor, heading down the hallway toward the door. She wanted to leave as quickly as possible, vanish, perhaps wander through the city alone, perhaps march to London Bridge and jump into the Thames.

"Nannerl! Here forever happy are we!"

She didn't turn.

"Here forever happy are we! Answer me!"

Nannerl shook the door angrily, but it wouldn't open. The stupid little wheels it rolled on were blocked. What a ridiculous system. Finally she succeeded, and was about to run into the street, but he reached her and pulled her hair: "Here forever happy are we! Now answer me, you bad—"

"I hate you!"

Was it my anger that made him sick? I fear it is so, Armand, and whenever I think back on the small, weakened body of my adored brother, of his face as it broke into a sweat again and again, his eyes without consciousness, I wish I could punish myself for the brutality that dwells in my soul, for those fits of fury that I don't know how to control, that I always become aware of too late. I promised you, my dearest, that you will never bear the brunt of this, but having reflected at length (because writing to you has led me to reflect), I have a fear of not being able to guarantee it.

I don't know from what deep place my anger comes, and I don't know what the causes are. I know only that it's sometimes difficult for me to understand the motivations of others, when they're different from mine, and that my first, instinctive reaction is, from the height of a nonexistent perfection, to judge their claims to be mistaken. However hard I've tried to correct this behavior, I am a prisoner of it. But I don't want to dwell on this matter. I wish rather to tell you, now, even if every single fraction of that memory is painful to me, of my little brother at the end of his life, and of how he came back from the abyss.

XVII.

The surgeon opened the wooden box to reveal, carefully arranged on the satin padding, a series of jars and sharp knives. He extracted a lancet for bloodletting, and with it made a horizontal cut in one of the child's veins, in the crook of his arm. Immediately the blood dripped into the bowl.

"How long has he been unconscious?" the doctor asked meanwhile, touching Wolfgang's forehead.

"Since yesterday morning," Leopold answered, weakly.

"And you called us only now? It's madness!"

"I told you! You never listen to me!" Anna Maria cried to her husband. He bowed his head and didn't answer.

Nannerl was curled up in a chair behind the bed, bent over a music book that she was trying to repair. But her hands trembled incessantly and the drip of Wolfgang's blood pierced her heart.

The doctor took a small bottle from his bag. "This is ground rhubarb, Madame. Mix a spoonful in a glass of wine and give it to him every two hours."

"I don't have any wine."

"Go and get some."

"Is it very serious?" Leopold whispered.

The doctor took him by the arm and walked him away from his wife. "If I were you," he murmured, barely audible, "I would give him the last rites. I'm afraid he won't last the night. I'm sorry."

Herr Mozart crumpled onto a chair, suddenly an old man. The music book fell from Nannerl's hands and she curled up into herself, shuddering in every fiber.

"What can be done we have done," the doctor said. "Now it will take the hand of God." He helped the surgeon gather up his equipment, and they prepared to leave.

"Wait, I'm coming with you. I'm going to find the landlord," said Anna Maria, and she, too, hurried out.

A moment passed that seemed to last an entire lifetime. Father, son, and daughter, in the same small space, were alone with themselves. Huddled in the chair, Nannerl went back in time in the darkness of her mind, to before her brother came into the world, a time when (as her mother told it) she had been a strange, introverted, mute child; only music seemed to exist for her, and even to that she came with a spontaneous, intense unconsciousness. Wolfgang, forcing her to see herself in him, had taught her to discover all that existed in the world, beyond her own small person; he, by being born, had saved her from a harmful isolation, and now it was up to her to save him. Suddenly she went over to him. His eyelids were shut; he was motionless, as if he had already expired. Oh no—too late?

"He's not speaking anymore. Papa, why doesn't he say anything?"

"I don't know," Leopold murmured, and just then he closed his eyes, covering his forehead, and two tears fell from his eyelids onto his chin and rolled all the way down to his throat.

The girl was astonished and filled with pity. "Rest, Papa," she said gently. "I'll take care of Wolfgang."

He collapsed on the bed and covered his head with the pillow, and slowly the sobs diminished.

In the silence, Nannerl timidly stretched out a hand and brought it to her brother's lips. His breath was weak, but it was there. Maybe his soul was already elsewhere; his face was lost in a disfiguring sleep, unhealthy and feverish, but some part of his consciousness must still be present, and she clung to that hope. She came close enough to feel his sticky warm cheek and whispered, with infinite tenderness, "And nothing bad will ever be . . ."

The child moved one leg, and the violin from which he was never separated slid from under the covers and fell, but Nannerl grabbed it just in time, before it touched the floor.

For a moment she didn't move. She looked at the instrument in her arms, then at her father: he was breathing rhythmically, asleep. She stared at little lifeless Wolfgang and began to pluck the strings, very softly, barely touching them, so that only he could hear.

With short, light notes she begged him to return from wherever he was. She implored him to leave the place where he had chosen to dwell because he was so extremely tired of a father who oppressed him, a mother who fussed over him, and a sister who accused him. She begged him not to abandon himself to the pleasantness of that place, but to make an effort to return, immediately, and she swore to him that she would never again be hostile, never again would they be divided, for together, the Little Mozarts were a force; while separated (there was no doubt), each would be inexorably diminished.

"Do you hear me?" Nannerl whispered, her eyes at last full of tears.

"You were a quarter-tone low." The voice was feeble but it was his.

"Are you better? Are you well?"

"You mustn't be afraid. I won't ever leave you."

She lay down beside him on the bed and embraced him with her whole self, holding him as tightly as she could. The child, in a hoarse voice, spoke again: "Your music is beautiful. Papa doesn't——"

"Shhh. Sleep, my king. Sleep in peace. Now we'll meet in the Kingdom of Back."

Intermezzo

Dearest Nannerl!

Your marvelous letters have made my stay in the Capital so much sweeter; I've had to leave only for short missions, lasting a couple of days, and I have always carried with me at least one, folded up inside my overcoat, near my heart, as once your music, too, was near your skin. Entering into your most intimate thoughts, and knowing your own particular experiences, makes me a man who has been granted a great privilege, and I will in every way try (I swear to you) to deserve it. Only now can I say that I begin to know you, my splendid one, and to understand you as others do not, out of narrow-mindedness or prejudice; and the deeper this knowledge becomes through your letters, the greater is my desire to see you again—a desire that, happily, will be satisfied in a short time!

The news is official: I am to return soon. I am unable to give you an exact date at the moment, but by the middle of next month I should be home. Then we will be able to meet. And I confess to you that mixed with the joy and the desire for that moment, which I have created in detail many times in my imagination, is a sort of fear. Essentially, the time we have shared until now has been limited to a few hours, and those spent exclusively in each other's company no more than two, perhaps even fewer. It's true that exchanging letters has brought our hearts closer, but it's also true that a part of me is frightened at the idea that in person everything might appear in some way different and surprising.

With this I do not mean to cast shadows on us—the opposite, in fact. I think it's the intensity of desire that makes this fear more intense, for the possibility that I glimpse in you and with you, my dearest, is so great that to lose it would be like losing life itself.

In apprehensive expectation, I offer you my most tender greetings

Until then,
Armand

Salzburg, May 30, 1777

My dearest friend,

I will be brief, very brief, swifter than an arrow, because today is mail day: Victoria is about to arrive and I want her to send you this as soon as the lesson is over. I can't wait to see you, Armand; I can't wait for that first marvelous moment to arrive. I can't wait to see myself in your eyes, to hear your voice, which makes everything vibrate. I imagine that the most obvious and simple thing is for you to come to our house. We won't be alone, it's true, but on the other hand I am tired of my subterfuges and do not want to provide my family with a motive for future reproaches; I have already suffered too many, believe me. And then what have we to hide?

Until very soon, Armand. I can hardly wait . . .
Nannerl

———

Vienna, June 10, 1777

My sweet Nannerl,

I have a date: June 22. Early on that morning, I begin my return journey, and on the twenty-fifth we will be able, at last, to see each other. The twenty-fifth of June! The day of our meeting! Two weeks from today, then; two long weeks during which I will greet every sunset with a heart filled with gratitude to life, since the end of the day bears witness to the passing of the time that separates me from you. The twenty-fifth of June, Nannerl! I want everything to be beautiful and right. I want to be able to express myself freely, in your sweet presence. I want nothing to disturb a moment that should belong to us two, and us two only.

For this reason, my dear, dearest girl, I would prefer not to see you in your father's house. Do you remember the day you brought me to the secret cellar of the Archbishop's palace, and Victoria played for the two of us, and there was no one else, and everything was in loving harmony? I confess that I have imagined a similar occasion. Like you, I naturally consider that we have nothing, absolutely nothing, to hide; but, on the other hand, I would like to enjoy your precious nearness in tranquillity, and with as little interruption as possible. The time will come when I will present myself to your family, and I will do so with immense pleasure, you may be sure; but at the moment I would rather spend some minutes, even a single minute if you prefer, listening to your words, listening to you and no other.

With fearful hope,
Armand

Salzburg, June 19, 1777

My dear, sweetly frightened Armand,

When I proposed that you should come to our house, I certainly didn't mean that you should present yourself officially to my father, announcing who knows what intentions. I assure you that I do not wish to jump immediately to conclusions, and that my most intense desire, for the moment, is to know you better—nothing more. I imagined that one day you might accompany Victoria to a lesson, that's all. Since you don't habitually frequent the salons of the fashionable world (I myself do so as little as possible), I thought that the lesson might be, so to speak, a substitute social occasion. I don't see many alternatives, apart from the cellar of the Palace, or the wood near the city where I go every so often to escape, or another meeting stolen in the heart of the night. But are not you, too, tired of that sense of something wrong?

With immense affection,
Nannerl

"Oh, you've come with your father! Major, what a pleasure to see you again!"

"Good day, Frau Mozart. I hope that my presence is not inconvenient. May I come in?"

"Inconvenient? But what are you saying? Come, come with me. Nannerl has just finished the other lesson. Perhaps you will even meet the student on the stairs. She is the daughter of that very sympathetic marquise, what is her name . . . Rinser, I think."

Snapping the fingers of her left hand as she searched her memory for the name, with her right, Anna Maria opened the door of the music room, saw Nannerl, and nearly fainted. Was that her daughter?

Her beauty had been multiplied ten times. She was wearing a pretty dress, clean and carefully brushed, not all wrinkled like the things she usually wore; it cinched her waist as it was supposed to and made her chest swell. Her hair was neatly gathered in a large bun on her head, which emphasized the oval of her face, while the two thick curls that fell on the nape of her neck seemed almost flirtatious. Her blue eyes seemed larger, and her cheeks were a lovely burning pink: Was it possible that she had put on rouge? And where had she gotten it? Stolen it from her, without a doubt! And why had she taken such trouble, if when she went to the places that count she got herself up worse than a nun? Struck by a suspicion, Frau Mozart turned toward Major d'Ippold, and his expression transformed it to a certainty: the man was as stupefied as she at the sight of Nannerl and, good heavens, was even blushing!

"Oh, then . . . ," she stammered, reflecting rapidly on what to do, "please, Major, come in. Maybe we should have some coffee now . . . I'll go . . . No, I'm not moving from here! Victoria, please, could you go ask Tresel to make some coffee?"

"I?" the student said, a little puzzled and a little fearful of encountering the Mozarts' fierce maid.

"Yes, you. Go on, dear. You, Major, sit here beside me, and you, Nannerl, opposite. There, good, like that."

"Mama, really; there is supposed to be a lesson here."

"Yes, but it's the last of the morning, isn't it? Surely we can allow ourselves time for a little chat. Isn't that so, Major?"

"Of course. With pleasure," he said, cursing the moment he had agreed to go to the Mozart house.

"You know what I am most sorry about? That my husband isn't home. He, too, would have been so pleased to meet you, I'm sure. But every morning he goes to court and . . . Oh, how stupid! Perhaps you two know each other already."

"Only by sight, Frau Mozart."

"Well, I suppose it's understandable. The work of a soldier and

that of a musician are very different! I imagine you seldom meet."
Then her tone became sharper. "But, excuse me for asking, Major, do
you intend to be a soldier all your life?"

"I confess that I don't understand the question."

"I mean, it's such a dangerous profession! And if one day you
should have children—that is, other children, apart from Victoria,
who is grown up by now—don't you think it would be more suitable
to assume less active duties? At the moment, you are always traveling,
going, coming, a mission here, a delegation there. It doesn't seem to
me a very stable life. I don't know if I make myself clear."

Just then, Wolfgang appeared in the doorway and started at the
sight of Armand. "What a surprise! Have you come to ask for my sister's hand? My father isn't here at the moment, but I would be happy
to play his part."

"Angel, don't make jokes. You are embarrassing Major d'Ippold,"
his mother said, contrite. "We are just exchanging some opinions."

"Why, what's embarrassing about a proposal of marriage? Oh, of
course, in this case the difference in age might be a little embarrassing, but apart from that, I would say we are within the rules. It's a little late for my sister, that's true. Twenty-six is more than old enough
to tie the knot! Luckily someone has decided—"

Nannerl jumped up. "Really, I must give Victoria her lesson, so I
will ask you to please leave. Major, forgive me, I couldn't imagine—"

"For your information," Wolfgang said, "Tresel has got Victoria
peeling potatoes, so you'll have to wait until she finishes the pile. And
it's quite a pile—I would say almost a mountain."

Armand, too, rose. "It is I who must go. Excuse me," he
announced with great politeness. "Your company is very pleasant
indeed, but I did not anticipate staying long, and unfortunately I cannot do so. I am truly sorry, but I cannot."

"Oh, what a pity," Anna Maria said, as he settled the collar of his
uniform. "And when will we have the honor of seeing you again?"

"The truth is that at the moment I cannot make any plans.

Tomorrow I go to Linz, and I will be there at least ten days. Then we'll see."

Nannerl had to sit down again. Her mother looked at her purposefully. "My goodness, it's a real problem. It's so difficult to cultivate a relationship at a distance. I wonder if it's worth the trouble." Then she smiled affectedly at the major. "In any case, if you find some time for us, you may be sure that this house is always open to visitors who have serious intentions. Serious and steady, am I clear? Please, come; I'll show you out."

"Thank you. Farewell, Herr Wolfgang Mozart. Fräulein Mozart, my compliments," Armand said, without even looking at her. He clicked his heels and went off toward the door.

Nannerl remained sunk in the chair, her heart in tumult. The efforts she had made to appear attractive now seemed ridiculous. She would have torn her dress to shreds, peeled away the stupid makeup, she would have yanked out the hairpins and pricked herself with them. But she let none of her agitation show.

Sadistically mocking, Wolfgang began to circle around her. "I am happy to discover, O my queen, that you are not made of ice, as you would like to make us believe—that you are even cultivating romantic proposals. Who ever would have thought?"

"Please go and call Victoria."

"Why don't you go? Are your legs frozen?" Then he brought his face close to hers, so close that he could have kissed her, and whispered, "Teaching seems to have brought you something good. Of course, that man is not exactly a boy, he doesn't have much wit, and he seems to have a big stick up his ass, but I acknowledge that he might have his attractions. You're sure that his breath doesn't smell?"

She didn't react, and he pushed on.

"How far do your fantasies go, Nannerl? There are things about life that you still don't know, that might even upset you. Think of nakedness, for example. Think of the skin free of its disguises. Not yours, I mean, but that of your man. Imagine him without the uniform, the horrible underwear he undoubtedly wears, lying on a bed on his stomach, and meanwhile you run your hand over his back, from the neck to the hips, in a slow caress in which you savor the curve of every vertebra, and the muscles next to the spinal column that form small strong hills, and slowly you go down, down, until you discover—what? The stick stuck up his ass!"

He guffawed coarsely, but, incredibly, even now she didn't react. Disgusted, he reached the door. "I was wrong. You really are all ice," he said, and he left her alone.

Salzburg, June 27, 1777

My dear Armand,

I am writing to you as always in the depths of the night, the third sleepless night after that unlucky day when you, consenting to my wishes, came to this cursed house. I am so tired my eyes are burning, but by now I know it's useless to try to sleep: I have risen a hundred times, tried to read, gave it up—I even thought of getting dressed and going out, of returning to the Residenzplatz, longing to find you beside the fountain. It's foolish, yes. I gave that up, too.

I don't know if I'll ever give this letter to Victoria to send, and yet I'm certain that it will be long and tortured, and that I will write and rewrite it many times. I have here before me your letters. They are more solid than the few memories I have of you, and they speak of you like an affectionate friend. And yet the thought of you, Armand, is colored not only by affection but also by pain: the pain of absence.

If I had known, dearest, that you were staying such a short time in Salzburg, I would certainly have agreed to meet you somewhere different from this house. And now it seems to me an outrageous crime that that time cut out for us two, which should have belonged to us alone, was ruined by those foolish interruptions that you, justly, would have liked to avoid. With my heart, with all my heart, Armand, I beg you to forgive not my mother, not my brother—since I cannot ask forgiveness for them—but me, and me alone.

I'm furious with myself, and not only for the mistake I made, but above all for the intensity of the love that I'm certain, absolutely certain, I feel for you. Maybe I shouldn't confess it so explicitly, maybe it's not prudent; some say that every relationship should be governed by calculation and cunning, in order to endure. But such attitudes, as by now must be clear to you, are not mine.

The thought of you runs tirelessly through my mind, beats on the walls of my skull, rebounds and sinks, and then quickly returns to start running again. During the day it seems to me that I am moving in water, and everything around me appears wrapped in a dense fog. I can't concentrate on the most banal activity, and, no matter how much I try to remove the thought, your face reappears continuously before me. I wonder if I will ever see you again. I hope with all my heart that I will. I pause to imagine what at this moment, this exact moment, you are doing. Even now, for example. I suppose that at this instant you are peacefully sleeping, and I want to believe that your dreams are tranquil and refreshing.

I have no dreams, Armand, only flashes of hallucination. My imagination gives life to actions that involve you, involve me together with you, and I am amazed. I see the moment when we meet, and I imagine my smile, and my calm gaze; a steadier smile and a steadier gaze, not subject to the changeableness of time. That smile I have already inside, in truth, and yet I must wait to let it emerge, for only in that instant will I be sure of it.

My dearest Armand, I beg you, don't turn your back on me, don't leave me to be consumed with remorse. Agree to see me again, only tell me where and when.

Yours forever,
Nannerl

From the house to the Residenzplatz, from the Residenzplatz to the house. It was the route that every night exhausted her legs and her spirit; yet she inflicted it methodically, like a rite of purification or an act of love turned inward that feeds on regrets. In the vain expectation of a response from Linz, in the overwhelming absence of news (why was Victoria so stubbornly mute? It wasn't like her!), Nannerl returned to the places that spoke to her of Armand and found a phrase of his or a gesture in every stone, in every statue, in every jet of water. She sat at the fountain, she wrapped herself in memories, she conversed with her lover in her mind.

Something woke her. A presentiment? Armand was entering the gateway of the Palace. Was it her imagination? No, the reality, the only one worth attending to! She hid behind the statues, her heart beating so hard it frightened her, and meanwhile the major dismounted his horse—oh how he dismounted his horse—took off his hat, smoothed his long dark hair, and adjusted the tie that bound the hat at his neck. While she devoured him with her gaze, Nannerl set off in the wake of a carriage, approaching closer and closer, until suddenly she was right in the center of the inner courtyard of the Palace, and there, in confusion, she stopped.

"Hey! Who's there?" a guard shouted, and he approached with thundering steps. She froze, and he stammered, taken aback, "Fräulein Mozart! What are you doing here?"

"The lady is expected by His Excellency!" Armand declared, joining them; he gripped the handle of his sword so hard that the knuckles stood out whitely. "I must tell you, Fräulein Mozart, that your appointment has, unfortunately, been postponed because our most esteemed sovereign has been called to fulfill an urgent duty without delay."

"Major," the guard objected, his whiskers quivering in bewilderment, "excuse me, but how do you know? You have just arrived."

"Out of the way!"

The man hastily withdrew. Then, still peremptory but quieter, Armand added, "Go to the cellar of the Palace; hurry! I will join you as soon as possible," and returned to the guardhouse.

Everything happened in an instant. *My God, what am I doing?* As she went along the corridor that led to the lower levels, Nannerl felt that she lived and died; she dragged her feet, she gasped for breath, she leaned against the walls. She wandered randomly through the deserted rooms, while the damp air saturated body and mind. Too much, she had done too much for a man who didn't deserve such efforts! She had exposed herself, had thrown herself at his feet, had let herself be trampled; rather, had induced him to trample her. She had begged him to love her; how can we ask someone to love us who fundamentally doesn't want us? That was why Armand had told her to go to the secret cellar. Because there, far from the eyes of leering soldiers or anyone else, he would tell her that he had been mistaken, that what he had declared in his letters was the result of a whim of which he had already repented; that she was not worthy of his attentions, that they would not see each other again. And, ugly as she was in that crisis, slovenly, pale, uncombed, she would have no way of getting him to reconsider! No, she had to avoid that torture. She turned back: she would cross the courtyard as quickly as possible and disappear, risk looking foolish in front of the whole corps of guards; but better the foolish figure than a pathetic scene that her pride could not stand. And yet if—if, on the other hand, Armand felt something for her, not love, certainly, love would be too much, but some sort of affection?

Suddenly she stopped, considering that there were a thousand innocent reasons for why he might have stopped writing: in a fit of jealousy, perhaps, Victoria hadn't sent him her last letter; or she had done so, but he had not had a chance to respond. What did she know, an ordinary girl, of the serious duties of an army major? And who was she to climb into a pulpit to judge a man's acts and make unwarranted assumptions? Not to mention that her letter could have been sent and not arrived, for the mail service was not infallible—not often, but every once in a while . . .

She made her way to a flight of steps and sat down. The steps were cut into the rock, uncomfortable and dirty; nevertheless she stretched out her legs and threw back her head and arms and remained like that, staring at the curves of the ceiling, drunk with conjectures. In her chest a whirling vortex of clouds colliding as heavily as bricks was making her feel sick to her stomach. Fearing she would throw up, she rose slowly and, in a dark cool passageway, took off her shoes and socks and lay on the ground with her legs vertical against the wall.

Skirts and petticoats fell onto her stomach, and the embroidered pantaloons slid down in a heap like an accordion. Nannerl paused to look at her legs (which she almost never did) and lightly touched them, caressing them. They were not ugly, after all; or perhaps it was the dim light that made them seem graceful, she thought. They were long, covered by an invisible down, with slender ankles between large feet and tapered calves, the kneecaps beautifully sculpted above the two mounds of soft flesh, connected to the big muscles of the thighs . . . Oh goodness, and what if Armand should arrive right now?

She got up and hastily tidied herself, smoothing her dress with her hands; she loosened her hair, then knotted it again, pressed the rebel curls behind her ears, ran her fingers over her eyes, her eyebrows, her cheeks, wet her lips, and straightened her shoulders; finally, with firm steps, she reached the door of the cellar and opened it.

The candelabra was already lighted. A man grabbed her from behind and covered her mouth with his hand and embraced her, with an arm around her breast that took away her breath; terrified, she wriggled free but then realized that she had nothing to fear. Armand let her go, and she turned and saw that he had a finger on his mouth, imposing silence on her after so much, too much, reasoning and recounting. And then, unspeakably slowly, he took her by the shoulders, bent his head, and placed his lips on hers.

It was a light kiss that left her dismayed. Was that kissing? But he did it again, and this time he parted her lips and became more ardent. She didn't know how to react. She felt Armand's mustache prick her, and his teeth bite her, and the wetness of mouths, and was not sure if it was a pleasant thing. The major realized it and took his lips away; he looked at her bitterly, perhaps in regret. Nannerl had a terrible desire to wipe her lips with her hand, but she thought the movement would offend him and overcame that urge. She wished also to ask for a mountain of explanations, but he preferred silence, and so she was silent. The thought of leaving passed quickly through her mind and quickly vanished. Just to do something, she took Armand's hand and, almost unconsciously, touched his nails with her fingertips: they were bitten down, cruelly, to the root. He immediately pulled his hand away.

"Forgive me. Please, won't you forget what happened," he murmured, and with disappointment in his face, he started to leave.

What? Risk everything to end in this moment? She had opened her heart, revealed her most intimate thoughts, to a man she would never see again? Oh no, it couldn't be. She stood before him and with an air of challenge rose on tiptoe and kissed him.

This time Armand did nothing. He held his lips half open, and meanwhile she pecked at them with hers, explored them, tasted them. Then she stepped back and began to caress them with her fingers, staring at them with curious eyes, pinching his mustache, touching his nostrils, following the dark profile up to his forehead, to the hairline, to the long hair behind that she loosened from its tie, and drew the face of the man over hers.

That was a true kiss. And each held the other's face, and hands caressed hair, and lips ran over chin, cheeks, forehead, and met for an exchange of breath that an exchange of words could never equal, and they could have continued infinitely, for they felt a wonderful, true intimacy.

The Journey to Italy

I have spent too many nights struggling between the phantoms of the day and plans, and memories, and regrets, but tonight it's not a painful anxiety that keeps me from sleeping, or a fear of having ruined everything; rather, it's an overwhelming joy, a jumble of images of a burning sweetness. And yet again the desire to write to you comes to me, Armand, not so much to put order into my mind's turmoil as to share it with you, you who are its cause and inspiration.

It was very late when I got home, after our encounter in the cellar of the Palace, and my family was already sitting at the table. It was all so different to my eyes. Time flowed peacefully around me, and I managed, for the first time, to take care of my own needs. I even found my appetite, which surprised those around me. And then

I asked permission to go to my room, and I shut myself in, and while only
a few hours earlier I had felt my limbs quivering with the need to act, sim-
ply to act, this time I lay down in company with the thought of you, in com-
pany with stillness and silence. The passing of the minutes caresses me,
does not wound me; life smiles at me, does not oppress me. And the circum-
stances that brought us together return to my mind.

I.

"Nannerl, you're purple. Try to calm down."

"Did you see how the singer is dressed? How can she control her
breath when her waist is strangled like that?"

"Where she can't go with her voice she'll go with her bosom.
Don't worry, my queen: the reason for her reputation isn't art but
what she has above the waist—in the front, to be precise."

"That's certainly no comfort to me!"

"She'll make an impression, you can be sure. And when the
applause comes, you will feel an emotion that has no equal. I guarantee it. Now give me that glass." And he took it out of her hands.

"I'm serious, though—no tricks: it has to stay a secret."

Wolfgang was sniffing the glass with a look of disgust. "What sort
of stuff are you drinking?"

He emptied it into an amphora, but she took another and gulped
it down, and the patricians of Salzburg doubled in number before her
eyes. Above them all towered Leopold Mozart, even taller than usual,
and with his features transformed into those of a grotesque god of the
underworld: Why had he come? Hadn't he said that he would prefer
to stay home and read, rather than put up with yet another entertainment? And yet there he was, conversing with Count von Esser, and
offering him a pinch of tobacco. Perhaps he had already asked him for
another letter of recommendation for Italy.

"Excuse me, ladies and gentlemen," Wolfgang announced at the center of the room. "I am sorry to distract you from your very important conversations, but if the moment seems to you propitious, we will start the musical entertainment."

He had remained short, and he appeared younger than his thirteen years, but he had a powerful voice and a forceful presence, and everyone hurried to find a seat. With some irritation, Herr and Frau Mozart had to take places at the back of the room.

"It is not for me to enumerate the vocal virtues of the celebrated Paulina Eleonora Gellert," he continued, while the soprano made her way to the front, preceded by her breasts, "or the pianistic ones of my sister, Maria Anna Walburga Ignatia Mozart, whom you all know well. I prefer to let my arias be interpreted by the two artists and to speak for me; I therefore confine myself to hoping that you will enjoy the show."

He returned to the audience amid light applause, and there was silence.

In all her eighteen years, Nannerl had never played so badly. Overcome by an inexplicable panic, made more acute by the alcohol, she couldn't control her fingers, which moved up and down the keyboard on their own; the notes were botched and hesitant. Luckily, the soprano sang well—in spite of the whalebone stays that had surely reduced her diaphragm to crumpled paper—and her jutting bosom and skillful gestures focused the attention of the entire audience. At the end, however, no one had time to applaud her.

"Ladies and gentlemen!" Wolfgang cried, jumping up onto his chair. "The author of the arias that you have just heard is not, in fact—me!"

The blood drained from Nannerl's face, and Paulina's bosom seemed ready to burst, indignant, from her dress.

"It's my sister who composed them: Maria Anna Walburga Ignatia Mozart! To this excellent musician, therefore, you must direct your applause, and not to me! Please, ladies and gentlemen: let the sound of your palms be at least equal to your pleasure!"

Scandal? Faint praise? Astonished ovation? Nannerl never knew what the reaction of the lords of the city was, for like a broken marionette she slid off the piano stool and fainted.

II.

"How long has this nonsense been going on?"

In the shadowy lamplight of the kitchen, Leopold's face was truly that of a god of the underworld.

"I told you, Papa, it was the first time."

"You be quiet! I want your sister to answer!"

"Wolfgang is telling the truth, Papa. We hadn't ever done it before."

"And whose idea was it?"

Nannerl was silent, uneasy, and her brother answered for her. "Truly, Father, it was mine."

"I told you to be quiet. Let Nannerl speak."

"Well, yes, it was Wolfgang who proposed playing my arias."

"And you should not have agreed!" he thundered. "So, you have continued to compose!"

"Well, yes . . . but only a few lieder, little songs . . . a quartet . . . But no one ever knew, Papa."

"A quartet? How the devil could you write a quartet without the least knowledge of counterpoint?"

This time Nannerl was silent for a long time. Wolfgang was dying to answer for her, but with a peremptory gesture Leopold ordered him to be silent.

"Well . . . the truth . . . the fact is that . . . Wolfgang gave me some lessons, every so often."

"What?"

"Nannerl didn't want to. I insisted, Papa."

"That doesn't count! She should have refused! And now you are to be quiet. Is that clear?"

Anna Maria came forward, timidly. "My dear, what happened is certainly very serious, but couldn't we discuss it tomorrow? We are all so tired."

"Our departure is approaching, and I have to make a decision of crucial importance. If you want to go to sleep, go ahead; the rest of us will not move. Now, Nannerl, I want to see the scores of all your music."

Hidden by her long skirt, the girl's knees seemed to give way even as she passed through the doorway, heading for her room. Her mother followed, carrying the candle and muttering, "Dear daughter, what is in your stubborn head? Why do you continue to challenge your father as if he were your worst enemy?"

"Wolfgang shouldn't have made that speech in front of everyone."

"Maybe so, sweetheart, but the more serious error was yours."

The old secret pouch was hidden under her mattress. It was threadbare by now, and so full of scores that it resembled a big brick covered with fabric. She carried it into the kitchen and handed it to her father as if it were a sacrificial lamb; and in Leopold's impatient hands it ripped completely.

He examined a couple of scores, then started: "I remember this lied! Wolfgang, it's yours. You submitted it to me some time ago!"

"Actually, Papa," Wolfgang said, "Nannerl composed it, not me."

Leopold's eyes seemed about to pop out of their sockets, the veins of his forehead about to explode. "How many times, you wretched children, have you tricked me?"

The children didn't dare respond.

"And I also remember this rondeau . . . and this duet? I even complimented you on the theme! What have you done, Wolfgang? Have you been continuously submitting to me your sister's music?"

"Papa, you left me no other choice," said Nannerl.

"I left you no choice but to make fun of me? Is that what you mean, you insolent girl?" He was shouting by now. There was no doubt that the neighbors could hear, and that those cries would be the subject of gossip for weeks.

A heavy silence fell, against which the strangled breathing of the head of the family stood out. His wife went to him, frightened: "My love, calm down . . . Don't get so agitated . . . Sit down, please." She led him to a chair, gave him something to drink, caressed his forehead without stopping until he seemed calmer.

"Just tell me one thing, Wolfgang," Leopold said in a rasping voice. "Has any music of Nannerl's been published under your name?"

"No, Papa!" she answered in a rush. "I would never—"

"Be quiet!" he said hoarsely. "I asked your brother a question, not you."

The boy was quick to respond. "Everything that has been published is mine, and no one else's."

"You're telling the truth?"

"Yes, Father."

"Are you sure? I cannot tolerate the idea that your work is spurious, do you understand?"

"I solemnly swear. And in any case, don't worry. I am the first to be careful about the integrity of my work."

That proud affirmation surprised Nannerl, but it wasn't the moment to comment. Leopold, for his part, appeared somewhat relieved.

"Now shall we go to sleep, dear?" Anna Maria said quietly.

The man didn't answer yes or no, so with gentle firmness she made him get up. He abandoned himself to the will of his wife and, exhausted, closed his eyes as she led him along the hall to the bedroom.

III.

The morning rays crept in obliquely through the window, which was wide open in spite of the cold weather, illuminating a group of sweaty men. Herr Mozart, looking for the best place to put the new pianoforte, kept changing his mind, tripling the work of the movers and surely causing them to curse to themselves; he refused to listen to suggestions from Wolfgang, who stood apart with a strange expression on his face. Nannerl paused in the doorway in amazement.

"You have made an excellent choice, Herr Mozart!" said a lanky young man. "It's the best of my pianofortes. It will give you the greatest satisfaction!"

"Thank you," Leopold answered, "but it will do so to my daughter in particular. She, in fact, is the one who will be using it." He pointed toward her with the sweeping gesture of a master of ceremonies.

"Fräulein Mozart, what a pleasure! I am a great admirer of yours: I've heard you play many times."

"My daughter is a fine concert performer, there is no doubt; but I am convinced that this piano will help give a more suitable order to her life. All right, there, in the center. That's perfect. Stop."

What sense did it make to buy a pianoforte on the eve of the sojourn in Italy? Nannerl searched her brother's gaze, but he seemed very interested in the mechanics and had stuck his head inside the piano case. The lanky man rushed over and kissed her hand. "Would you try it, Fräulein Mozart? Please, now, while I'm here?"

"Why don't *you* try it?" Leopold said suddenly.

"I, Herr Mozart? But I'm not a pianist. I've hardly studied. I'm a dilettante."

"Perhaps you know some of my son's easy pieces."

"Well, yes, actually. There is one, in particular. My poor grand-mother loved it and was always wanting me to play it. But I don't know if I remember it."

While the movers went off, surely to down a beer in some tavern, the young man placed two long, squarish hands on the keyboard and started a sonatina of Wolfgang's, which, however, he seemed to be playing with his feet. Wolfgang's expression was one of the most scornful in his repertoire, and Nannerl went up to her father timidly: "I'm grateful for the gift, but I don't understand."

He turned quickly toward the piano. "No, here it goes into the minor, you don't remember? Wolfgang, get the score so he can repeat the passage. It's in the third cupboard."

"I know . . . Where is that score," he said, opening the doors. He took out a folder that read in an elegant script "Pieces Composed at the Age of Eight" and quickly pulled out the right one.

"Do you mean that this is the original manuscript?" the skinny man asked, handling the page as if it were gold. "Would you sell it to me, Herr Mozart?"

"Why not, if you really want it. Give me a discount on the price of the instrument and we'll be set."

The man, intoxicated with joy, began to massacre the sonatina again, and Wolfgang couldn't keep himself from correcting at least the most glaring errors. Amid the repeating of notes, suffocated exclamations, and murmured excuses, Nannerl went back to her father: "Won't you explain to me what's the point of this?"

"Quiet, daughter—not now. Now I would like to listen to our friend."

"What is the point of a pianoforte?" she cried. "Certainly we can't bring it to Italy with us. Why have you bought it just at this moment?"

"You are not going to see Italy, daughter. You will stay in Salzburg with your mother and give piano lessons." He gave her a thin smile. "Haven't you always liked the piano?"

IV.

"Ask five florins a lesson, not one less, and insist on payment in advance. Look for pupils among the aristocracy and do it so that the word will spread as widely as possible. Every two weeks you will go to the posting station and send the money to me at the address that I will provide."

While Leopold dictated instructions to his wife, Nannerl, slicing cabbage on an old wooden board with a sharp knife, imagined that she was slicing up her father.

"Ah, and you had better find a servant. A presentable woman who can greet the pupils at the door and serve refreshments during the lessons. There has to be an aura of elegance and prosperity, because— remember this well, my dear—money calls forth money. Write that down, too."

Beside his sister, Wolfgang was contrite. "I'm sorry, Nannerl. I'm so sorry," he said in an undertone.

"Don't tell me you didn't know."

"No, I swear—"

"Don't lie to me!"

"Please, Anna Maria, don't make a mess of this," Herr Mozart concluded, then he turned magnanimously to his daughter. "Let's understand each other: you can keep part of the money you earn. Maybe you can buy yourself some pretty clothes."

Turning her back to him, she threw the cabbage on a plate and spat on it. Then she left the kitchen.

"Where in the world are you going, now that it's ready?" her mother cried.

"Leave her alone," Leopold said with an air of superiority. "She is stubborn, but at heart she isn't bad: it will pass."

He grabbed a fork, put a large forkful of cabbage in his mouth, and chewed energetically.

V.

For entire days she didn't move from her bed. Her hair loose on the pillow, her gaze dim, and her breath slow, she was like a wild creature in hibernation.

"Look at what I found," Wolfgang said, holding up under her nose an old parchment covered with scribbles. It showed a meadow with two trees, a castle with a crenellated tower, the sun partly concealed behind a cloud, a little lake populated by geese, and two human figures, one male, one female, with giant crowns on their heads. The whole picture was surmounted by a legend written in the uncertain hand of a child: "The Kingdom of Back."

Nannerl turned away. Wolfgang sat on the bed and placed a hand on her shoulder, but she didn't react. Then, resigned, he rolled up the parchment and placed it on the night table.

"I tried to persuade him," he murmured after a long sigh, "but you know perfectly well it's impossible. What was I to do? Refuse to go myself?"

He seemed to perceive in her a sign of assent, but it was only his imagination, because Nannerl did not move.

"I thought about it, but then I concluded that no one, in my shoes, would have done that. Think about it: Should I give up an opportunity so great for my career, for my very life? Not even you, in my place, would have—come on, admit it."

She rolled over, creating an abyss between herself and those words.

The boy then decided to be more honest. "I can't stay in this provincial place, Nannerl. Truly, I can't. Life here is nothing but a repetition of tired ballets for a crowd of stupid rich people. There is so much new music inside me—and I know that I'll only be able to pour it out in the freedom of the wider world."

Perhaps she had made herself temporarily deaf.

"Then there are some practical matters," Wolfgang continued, with a hint of shame. "The archbishop has refused to pay Papa for the whole time he's gone. And for my work at court I've never seen a florin, as you know. Italy is an expensive country, and absurd as it sounds, it seems that you don't get paid for concerts. Even if I were able to perform one of my works, I would get less than some ordinary tenor. In other words, Nannerl, we can't all four of us go. We wouldn't have enough to live on. In fact, the truth is that . . . that without the money you earn from lessons, Papa and I couldn't go, either."

What was all that talk of money? Nannerl seemed to be made of stone. If she was still breathing, it wasn't visible.

"Now I will confess something to you. If I revealed that those arias were yours—the ones that Paulina sang—I did it because I knew what would happen. I did it for you, Nannerl."

This time she turned abruptly and stared at him with wide-open eyes: this was a good one!

"It's true, believe me," he continued. "You have to stop hiding in my shadow. You have to become autonomous, compose in the light of day, have the satisfaction of hearing someone else interpret your notes. Ultimately, our leaving is a stroke of luck for you. From a distance, Papa won't have any way of controlling you; and now that the ice is broken, you can look for some nobleman to support you. Surely you'll find one."

Finally Nannerl opened her mouth, and her deep voice fell like lead on her brother's head: "So in effect you are going to Italy to do me a favor. Thank you, Wolfgang. Now I would like to be alone."

He rose in silence and went to the door. A moment before leaving he turned to look at her. "I'll miss you very much," he said with a catch in his throat. "I'll think of you at every moment. And I hope you'll think of me."

As soon as the door closed, she took from under the covers her scores wrapped in their shreds of fabric and hugged them to her.

VI.

Wolfgang wandered through the house. His hands were stuffed in his pockets and he proceeded slowly, looking down, kicking one foot with the other. His steps brought him to the kitchen; he leaned on the doorpost, not daring to go in, because his mother was busy taking little pastries out of the oven with the help of the servant she had just hired.

"Don't just stand there, Wolfgang," she called as soon as she saw him. "Come in! Look how well they turned out! Do you want to taste one?"

He shook his head and wearily went to the window that looked onto the courtyard.

"What is it, my angel: Are you sad? I know, you're thinking of your sister. Don't worry about her; in time she'll understand. Unfortunately, she has always been an egotist, that's the trouble."

"Egotist?" he repeated, bewildered.

"Of course, and not only that, she's as stubborn as a mule! Papa says it will be good for both of you to be separated for a while. And then, with Tresel's help, I will be able to teach Nannerl some housekeeping. Isn't it true, my dear, that you will give me a hand?"

The servant nodded with a kind of grunt while she tasted one of the pastries. She was a middle-aged woman of few words and of brusque manners; her smile was unknown.

"Oh yes, you'll see. Nannerl will become a fine housekeeper! Just like her mother, in all modesty."

"Madame," Tresel said, putting down the pastry with a look of disgust. "Is it possible that you added salt instead of sugar?"

"What?"

At that moment Wolfgang happened to look out the window and into the courtyard, the ancient seat of the Kingdom of Back, and gradually his eyes focused on his sister, who was intent on burning a pile of papers. She had lighted her pyre right in the center, where once the king's throne had been, and she was burning one page after another.

It was the manuscripts of her music. Methodically, and with implacable slowness, she took each page, set fire to one corner, and observed the flames as they licked the notes, colored them an irreversible brown, and transformed them into an intangible black dust. Only at the final instant, so as not to burn herself, she dropped the last corner onto the burning coals. Then she began again with a new page.

Wolfgang went down the stairs at breakneck speed. "What are you doing? Are you mad?"

"This is for Florence," she announced, throwing a sheet into the fire. "This is for Venice," she said, and tossed another. "And this is for Rome. Give my greetings to the Pope!" She threw the last pages onto the fire all together, so that the flames leaped up scarily. Wolfgang hurled himself at the pyre, trying to save what was salvageable, but the damage was done. He managed to pull out only one score; he threw it on the ground and stamped out the fire with his feet; the margins had been burned, but it was still legible.

"This one's safe!" he announced wearily. "The others I'll rewrite for you. I remember all of them."

"Don't bother. I would burn them again." On her face appeared a smile a million years away. "I will never compose again. Never, Wolfgang. I will be a provincial music teacher. Enjoy that money I'll be sending you."

And she sat down to observe the hypnotic dance of flames, as her brother watched in dismay. Tresel's impenetrable face appeared at the window, while the only surviving sheet of paper was tossed here and there by the wind.

VII.

Getreidegasse was paved with mud and ice, and mounds of snow were massed along the sides.

A carriage piled with baggage was at the door, and the coachman rubbed his hands, blowing on them with short puffs of breath, in a vain hope of warmth. Herr and Frau Mozart couldn't make up their minds to part from each other, and the Reverend Joseph Bullinger, who had already said a great deal, had nothing else to add and confined himself to looking at them affectionately. Wolfgang was inside the carriage; his nose and cheek were crushed against the window, making the expression of his melancholy unconsciously grotesque. His gaze was turned to the window on the third floor, his mind hoping that, behind the glass, his sister might appear, perhaps at the last moment consenting to say good-bye, with a gesture if not with words.

In the music room, Nannerl was far from the window. Shut up in a solitude that was to become her companion, she observed the shining piano as if it were an object whose value was insulting. She sat on the stool, arranged the folds of her dress, raised the lid of the keyboard, and pressed her fingers onto the keys.

She improvised, moving within a fertile land of fantasy where, guided by harmonic laws, she traveled naturally. Through rapid runs, frenetic yet orderly, and moments of stillness, through impalpable flights and long, dark decelerations; after a few phrases, she spontaneously added her voice, too. She didn't pronounce words; rather, she used her vocal cords like another instrument, which, in harmony with the one that her hands played but also in contrast, cried, breathed, and bent with the malleability that belongs only to flesh.

Her brother listened from the carriage, wishing he could reach the window and struggling not to cry, while the others paid no attention; only the reverend gave a sharp glance upward, a moment before pronouncing his blessing. And, meanwhile, Nannerl moved over the keyboard, eyes closed and mouth half open in a whisper, or half closed in furious vocalizing. It was as if she were playing a thousand times at once. It was her farewell to Wolfgang, and to music.

Leopold got in, the coachman cracked his whip, and the carriage, with a lurch, set off. It moved slowly down the street, and the boy, defying the cold, stuck his head out the window to listen as long as he could, but as the carriage moved away the volume grew fainter, until it became a weak echo that was suddenly, as the coach turned the corner, extinguished. And in the deserted street there was silence.

Nannerl stopped and laid her hands in her lap. She closed the cover and turned the key. The decision is made: I will never play again.

Every human relationship reaches a point where it cracks; the crack widens, leading, inevitably, to collapse. The process now was set in motion, there was no going back, and in some way I foresaw that my relationship with Wolfgang was, for the first time, in grave danger: I lost all interest in music, in people, in life itself, and remained unmoving in the expectation that the Kingdom of Back would be ruined, and that with it was annihilated not only the emotional terrain over which my brother and I had ruled undisputed and harmoniously but my very existence.

That's what I had become, my beloved, not long before I met Victoria and you. Alone, as I am today, when I must again resign myself to your absence, but also desperate, as today surely I am not, and thanks to you. I lay rolled up in the sheets and rose only when it was absolutely necessary. I closed the shutters, bound my head, and lay unmoving in the dark for hours; but as soon as I fell asleep, my legs contracted, my fingers curved and pressed the blanket as if it were a keyboard, and vague sounds came out of me, which woke me, disoriented and distressed.

During the day, Tresel brought me food, and I was comforted by the fact that she didn't ask me to be grateful. She entered quietly, removed the untouched tray from the foot of the bed, and replaced it with a new one; she didn't dream of feeling offended that her tidbits were so little honored. She didn't say a word, she didn't even look at me, and yet I felt that she understood and respected me. My mother's entrances were, on the other hand, an invasion.

VIII.

"Get up, my dear. It's not good for you to stay in bed all day! Is your headache gone?" Frau Mozart said brightly, caressing Nannerl with fingers sticky with flour and honey. She fluttered through the room. "I told Tresel to make you an omelet with jam. Are you pleased? Now let her bring it. I must admit that she prepares them well; they're almost like pastry. But she does waste ingredients, God help us! And we can't have that, unfortunately. Not for the moment, at least. But as soon as you begin giving lessons, we can allow ourselves some luxuries. Oh, here is Tresel. Come, come, dear, place the tray here on the bed. And now go and wash the dishes. Nannerl, my treasure."

She hadn't moved a muscle. Anna Maria sat beside her and sighed. "My treasure, my beautiful girl . . . you must eat something. Come, sit up." She approached the tray and glimpsed an envelope with writing on it set between the spoon and the napkin. "Look: there's a letter from Papa and Wolfgang!"

At that point Nannerl moved more than a muscle; but her mother was too busy tearing the seal to realize it. There were two sheets, one in Leopold's writing, neat and precise, the other in Wolfgang's, swirling and full of flourishes. Anna Maria seized the one from her husband: "I'm going to read it at the window in the parlor. Then let me see the other as well!" And she disappeared.

Nannerl sat up in a surprising rush, staring at the paper on the tray: it was folded many times so that it resembled a package. She unfolded it and discovered that inside was concealed a very small note, in minute handwriting. She jumped out of bed, dressed in a flash, hid the pages in her corset, and opened the door of her room. Abruptly she turned back to the tray, took two pieces of bread and stuck the omelet between them, making a sandwich, wrapped it in the napkin, and put it under her arm; she crept out of the room, hurried along the hall, grabbed a cloak, and, throwing it over her shoulders, left the house.

The streets were crowded with people out enjoying the warm day: ladies with entourages of children and nursemaids, girls half hidden by lace umbrellas, and even a few gentlemen accompanied by their dogs. Nannerl kept the hood low over her forehead and proceeded with her head bent, dodging the passersby and ignoring the few who recognized her and made a faint gesture of greeting.

In the time it took her to reach the woods just beyond the city, the weather changed radically. The first thunder could be heard as she was running along the path, lifting her skirt; the first drops fell as soon as she had climbed up to a large branch on the tallest tree. Sheltered by the leaves, she took out the larger piece of paper and unfolded it; she put back the small note and read Wolfgang's official letter, the one that his father had certainly read and that would also be seen by her mother.

Carissima sorella mia,

Thanks to God, we are in good health, Papa and I, and hope that you and Mama also are well. During the first stages of the journey we suffered from the severe cold, and the snow tormented us so insistently that I would be dead of exhaustion if I hadn't had the thought of you, Mama, our house, and our native land, now so far away.

I wonder how this period of solitude has been for you, and I try constantly to guess your thoughts and states of mind. I don't know if, dear sister, you have already begun to give lessons to the children of Salzburg; I imagine you in this new role to be as inflexible and as capable as our father, if he will allow me the comparison. In any case, I wish it were your words, and not just my imagination, that speak to me of you. I beg you, therefore, to answer this soon, and then to write whenever possible, which

*means every day there is mail. Never forget that you have a brother and
that he continues to love you sincerely.*

Wolfgang Mozart

The moment had come to seek a more effective shelter, for the
drops were intensifying and were so big that they hit the ground like
drumbeats. Nannerl slid down, holding on to the branches, ran rapidly
along the path, and crouched in a hollow beneath a rock. She took out
the small sheet of paper and prepared to decipher it, in the stormy
half-light brightened by flashes of lightning.

It was in Latin. Her brother had been clever: evidently he had
stuck it in the envelope at the last moment, before his father sealed it,
and if their mother had found it before Nannerl, she wouldn't have
understood a word, and would have taken it for some exercise that had
ended up there by mistake.

*Valde semper laetor quod te docuerim latinam linguam, qua
ita nunc possumus clam communicare.*

"I am pleased to have introduced you to the Latin language, since
it allows us to communicate in secret," Nannerl translated laboriously.

*Deditus sum ad parandos pro te aliquot modos de italica arte
musica.*

"I am preparing for you . . . some notes on Italian music." And
Mama said *she* was the one as stubborn as a mule! Wolfgang was
telling her that he had transcribed for her, secretly, some songs he had
heard sung by street musicians. What a strange idea! And he promised
to figure out a way of sending them without their father's knowing.

Nannerl flattened the sheet of paper and crushed it under a rock.

She opened the napkin, took out the sandwich with the omelet, and ate it greedily, covering herself with crumbs, then she wiped her lips with the back of her hand. She sat for a long time huddled in the shelter of the rock, waiting for the weather to clear. The falling drops created a carpet of sound. It was nice under there.

IX.

"Here they are!" Anna Maria cried as soon as she heard the knock at the door, and she pushed Tresel forward to open it. And entering her house, her own house, was Countess Katharina Margarethe von Esser and her daughter, the little countess Barbara.

This scion of the aristocracy was nine years old and astonishingly ugly: a squat, dark child with irregular features and clumsy movements. Although her mother took pains to clothe her in flowered dresses, and although the activity of dressing lasted at least an hour every morning, there was no way to make her appear pleasing. As a result, other gifts had to be emphasized: education, manners, and, naturally, musical knowledge.

"Countess Katharina, what an honor! Oh, what a lovely child we have here. You must be little Barbara. How adorable you are."

The child performed a sort of twisted curtsy, and the two women shook hands in an affected manner. "Come, Nannerl is waiting for you," Frau Mozart announced, almost dancing as she led the way to the music room.

Katharina von Esser lived on the basis of a solid moral principle: keep the conversation on a high level. She loved to swallow her words—she was able to do so at a matchless velocity—and she could converse on any subject, in any context, and even appear competent and knowledgeable. She had a phrase ready for every occasion, she fished out of her memory declarations she had heard who knew where or when, and even when she felt that she was on uncertain ground she always managed to acquit herself skillfully. She had a real talent.

"I am so eager to meet your daughter. My husband and I have heard her at several concerts, but we have never had occasion to see her close up. Isn't it odd? Reverend Bullinger assures me that she will be an excellent teacher, and I can't help but listen to the valuable advice of that holy man. To tell you the truth, my Barbara was already studying with another teacher, whose name, naturally, I will not mention. I will only confess to you, in all confidence, that I wasn't satisfied, for she is one of those persons who have no respect for their obligations. You know what I mean, don't you, dear Frau Mozart? Certain artists think that living in disorder makes them geniuses, but you know better than I that it is not at all true. Imagine, once we arrived at the teacher's house for the lesson, and she couldn't be found! She had left for somewhere or other, without even having the kindness to warn us. Scandalous behavior, to put it mildly."

At that moment Anna Maria opened the door of the music room and realized that Nannerl wasn't there. She went in hesitantly while the countess looked around with a questioning air.

"Please, make yourselves comfortable," Anna Maria said nervously, then added, a little harshly, "Tresel, serve the coffee. I'll be back immediately. Excuse me, Countess." And like a general ready to call the troops to order, she marched to the bedroom and opened the door.

Nannerl was lying among the pillows, her hair loose and uncombed and her clothes disheveled. On her face was an absent expression.

"What do you mean by this shameful behavior?" her mother hissed in annoyance. The girl, unmoving, said nothing, so her mother grabbed her by the arm and shook her violently. "We can't afford to make a bad impression like this! Hurry up and get ready and come out immediately. Am I clear?"

She received a weak nod in response, but it was enough. Anna Maria returned quickly to the music room; before entering she stopped at the door, took a deep breath, assumed a ceremonious air, and returned to her performance.

"Please, forgive us, Countess! Nannerl—well, Nannerl didn't feel well, and so she lay down for just a moment, but she'll be with us right away."

"Oh, poor girl, I'm so sorry. And what was her trouble, if I am not indiscreet?"

"Nothing serious, thank heaven, Countess. Every so often she has just a slight headache, that's all."

"I understand perfectly, Frau Mozart," Katharina declared, becoming serious. "When I was a girl, I had terrible migraines."

"Really?"

"Yes. And reflecting on the matter, which is certainly of great interest, I reached the conclusion that there is something painful for a woman in the passage to adulthood. Oddly, I was discussing this just the other day with our doctor, in anticipation of the shocks that even my Barbara will soon undergo, and for which I intend to be prepared, like every good mother. The truth, I believe, is that young men, as they grow, seem to expand. Don't you think, dear lady? It's as if the moment of puberty—forgive the bold term—projected them into life with increased vigor. It's easy, on the contrary, for a girl to withdraw into herself and suffer in silence; and it is only marriage, and, as a result, procreation, that lifts her out of this state and gives her the strength to go on. For me, at least, it was like that. And you how did you experience that phase?"

Anna Maria suddenly felt as though there were a void in her head—as if there were nothing but air in it. Since she was a girl, she had always had too much to do to have time to reflect on her own emotions. Only the rich have the opportunity of doing so, not people like her! Tresel saved her with a diversion, and her harsh voice was like the song of a nightingale: "Frau Mozart, would you like me to serve the *Gugelhupf*?"

"Yes, indeed! It seems to me just the right moment. Bring it now, with the server and the plates, please." And immediately she asked Barbara, turning on the charm, "Do you like *Gugelhupf*, dear?"

The mother answered, giving her a friendly smile. "It is her favorite cake, Frau Mozart. You have hit the mark."

"Oh, I am so pleased."

"Our cook always prepares it, for special occasions. On that subject, dear lady, I must compliment you on your maid. She seems to me a very serious, efficient, and courteous sort of person. These days it is so difficult to find good servants. You do agree? Imagine, at our house we've been having a terrible time with a maid. That barbaric girl kept some of the shopping money, and stole small amounts of change and once even a valuable ring. And yet she was recommended to me by my husband's family, with whom she had served for a good five years. I strongly suspect that there, too, she was constantly making off with something, and my mother-in-law never realized it, poor woman. On the subject of money—and forgive me if I allow myself to enter into the subject in such an explicit manner—how shall we arrange it?"

After a moment of disorientation, Anna Maria managed to stammer: "Well, the best thing would be to pay before the lessons—if possible, in a group of ten. The fact is that I have to send the money to my husband in Italy, and so, you understand . . ."

"There is no problem with that, Frau Mozart. As you can certainly imagine, I do not handle money, but I will send a man today to deliver fifty florins in cash."

The image of that sum made Anna Maria dizzy. She took a giant piece of *Gugelhupf* and swallowed it almost without chewing.

The chatter of the women had bored little Barbara to death, and she didn't like the cake, either, because it was different from the one that her cook prepared—too thick and too sugary. She had settled herself on a high chair and was swinging her bow legs, with a movement that progressed from idle to nervous, until she couldn't restrain herself and burst out, "Mama, can't we go?"

"My dear, don't be impolite. You must learn to mind your manners. You are about to meet your new piano teacher. Aren't you glad?"

"No."

"Frau Mozart, forgive her, please. After all, she is only a child and doesn't know what she's saying."

"But of course, Countess; don't worry about it."

With laudable patience, Katharina again spoke to her daughter: "One day you will thank me, dear. You don't understand now, and it's utterly natural, given your age, but music is an essential element of the education of a nice young lady."

At that moment Nannerl appeared in the doorway, weary-looking but dressed more or less suitably. As soon as she saw her, Anna Maria broke out: "I am sure that my daughter thinks just as you do. Don't you, sweetheart? Come, tell the Countess."

"Yes, of course, in a young mind music helps to develop the imagination."

"And for making a good marriage!" continued Katharina, victorious. "The best people adore girls who can play. Oh, I was sure that we would find common ground, my dear Fräulein Mozart."

Nannerl felt as if she had plunged to the bottom of the sea and that the three females before her had been transmuted into fish, or shrimp, or maybe octopus. A cold current was pushing her toward the countess-octopus, whose every tentacle was adorned with enormous bracelets down to the tip, and it forced her to bow in respect. From the pupil-octopus a hostile glance reached her, so she turned to observe those fixed and slightly veiled globules and imagined the invertebrate swimming away from the window, leaving an ink stain in her wake. But already she felt a tapping from the tentacles of the mother-octopus, which were pushing her toward the piano, and she was unable to resist; meanwhile, the voice of the countess-octopus resounded in a thousand cavernous echoes: "Come, Barbara dear, play for Fräulein Mozart. Let her hear how well you play."

There was no way out. The rite had to be enacted. The little countess sat down at the piano as if she were placing her head on the block; she tried to lift the lid of the keyboard, but it seemed to be jammed, so her nose wrinkled in bewilderment.

"Turn the key" was Nannerl's toneless suggestion.

The little girl found the key in the lock, turned it a couple of times, and raised the lid; she placed the protective cloth in a heap on one side, and then she played.

It was a simple passage, conceived for small fingers that had not yet reached a confident stage of autonomy, and so the right and the left were called on to move in unison; if one hand had to execute something more involved, the other stopped or held some long notes. Even a trained monkey would have been able to produce something recognizable, but Barbara was truly disastrous. Anna Maria, accustomed to rather different sounds, couldn't help realizing it, yet obviously she did not show it and affected a kindly sympathy. Whether or not Katharina was aware of her daughter's clumsiness was not clear; certainly her child's inclinations didn't matter to her. She cared only that she learn to play properly, behave properly, converse properly.

And Nannerl—oh, she was wounded by those horrible sounds as if by a punch in the stomach, and she realized immediately that there was no way to instill art in a mind that had so little desire. She turned her back on the Countess von Esser, to avoid displaying her state of mind, and, pretending to listen attentively, moved to the window that looked out on the street.

Among the passersby a young woman stood out, a few years older than Barbara. She was wearing a pretty dress, of a bright turquoise dotted with little flowers, and a hat with a white rose tied on by a blue ribbon. Without knowing why, Nannerl found herself staring at this anonymous girl, wishing to be in her place, far from this hair-raising recital, from her detested profession, free to wander the streets with a rose on her head.

Suddenly the girl stopped. She must have heard the little countess's performance and been at least as bothered as Nannerl. Following the sound of the instrument, she raised her head toward the window, a grimace of disgust disfiguring her gracious smiling face; the gazes of the two met and remained fixed on each other for a long moment.

X.

Hiding like spies behind the columns of the portico, Wolfgang and his father followed closely behind the carriage of Prince Michael II von Thurn und Taxis, the governor of Mantua. It had been Leopold's idea; he was determined to obtain an audience with his noble compatriot, who, to the humiliation of the proud Leopold, did not seem to take any account of him and his son. The day before, the two had gone to the princely residence to pay their respects; they had been refused on the grounds that the prince was too busy to receive them, and told to come back another time. Punctually they had appeared, but a valet declared that the prince had gone to Mass. Oh? thought Leopold. Then I will wait for you at the church door and follow you home, and we'll see if this time I do not succeed in seeing your fine aristocratic face!

While Leopold glanced pointedly at him and nodded to him vigorously to move, Wolfgang lingered, entranced by the architecture of that city on the plain of the Po, on a day without fog. He laid his hands on a column of the portico and the shiver of cold that he felt told him it must be marble. Then he looked up at the capital: it seemed familiar, like certain drawings in a Roman history book that his father had had him read. An Ionic capital, if he remembered correctly, simple but grand, with broad spirals on either side that stood out from the body of the column. It looked very old: Could it be genuinely ancient? Even the pilaster, if you looked at it carefully, had cracks and scratches over the whole surface and might really be from two thousand years ago. Wolfgang gazed farther down the portico and realized that the columns and capitals were all different, so they must have been debris, at least in part. But his meditations on the reuse of the remains of the Roman Empire were interrupted by his father, who grabbed him roughly by one arm and dragged him away: "Hurry up, for goodness' sake!"

They quickly covered the last stretch of roadway separating them from the prince's residence, for by now the carriage had a clear advantage over them, and they had no further need to hide. With one hand Leopold held onto his hat, which was not too solidly settled on his wig, which, in turn, was not well anchored to his head, and with the other he pulled the child, who was in constant danger of slipping on the pavement beneath the portico. Did Mantuans spread wax on the bricks of their outdoor parlors? As they hurried along, the two Austrians provoked smiles among the passersby out shopping, but they were oblivious and managed to reach the palace at the very moment that the carriage, having discharged its occupants, was turning to go back to the stables.

With a burst of speed, Wolfgang reached the guard booth, ready to be announced; but when he looked for his father, he realized that Leopold had lagged behind and was leaning against the wall, red-faced and gasping for breath.

"Papa, are you ill?" he cried in alarm, and returned to him. Leopold stood up, still panting.

"No, son, everything is all right. Let's go on."

He took a few steps, but Wolfgang stood before him with an almost tender smile. "If you present yourself in that state, the prince will have you beaten."

"Why? What's unpresentable about a little shortness of breath?"

"It's not that." And looking at his father he couldn't contain a smile: Leopold's wig had shifted backward an inch, leaving part of his grizzled head uncovered. Wolfgang adjusted it. "It needs a little powder, but at the moment that doesn't seem possible."

"Indeed. Let's go now," Leopold said gruffly, and presented himself to the guards with an air of superiority.

"Good day. Will you kindly announce to Prince Michael von Thurn und Taxis and his gracious consort that Leopold Mozart and his son, Wolfgang Amadeus Mozart, of Salzburg, have come here to pay their respects, as compatriots of the princely couple, less illustrious, of course, yet, like them, belonging to the Austrian Empire, which even in this province, certainly far away but not for that reason less glorious, shines and makes every aspect of its own high civilization shine."

As the guard looked them over from head to toe, a little smile emerged from under his mustache; he said something to another guard, who took a few steps into the courtyard to say something to yet another guard, who then disappeared into the palace.

Father and son could do nothing but await a response, stuck in a sort of limbo. On one side was the magnificent palace that had once belonged to the Gonzagas; on the other was the square traversed by peasants pulling carts piled high with goods. Not belonging at that moment to either place, Leopold, nervously, and Wolfgang, contentedly, observed the two worlds without really comprehending them. But suddenly the boy's attention was captured by a minstrel who, loaded with instruments, emerged from an alley and rapidly approached a doorway in a far corner of the square. He took a mandolin off his shoulder, banged the knocker against the door, and at the same time shouted toward the upper floors, gesticulating, with an impatient smile stamped on his face; he seemed a Bacchus of music, eager to throw himself into an orgy of notes that he probably couldn't read but that, simply, amused him.

"I really don't understand your passion for popular music."

His father's voice pulled Wolfgang out of his contemplation. He looked at him in some alarm, while Leopold continued, "I mean, Wolfgang, that stuff is certainly interesting; but once you've heard one song you've heard them all. Don't you think?"

"Yes, Papa," he answered weakly, "but what interests me isn't the technical part, but rather the energy that these people put into it."

"Really?" Herr Mozart interrupted, argumentative. "And yet, every time we meet a street musician you seem almost to be studying his nonsense; you seem to be engraving it in your mind with great care. Will you explain why?"

The arrival of a butler saved Wolfgang from the need to lie to his father. "Herr Mozart, unfortunately I must tell you that Prince Michael von Thurn und Taxis has some very urgent duties to attend to."

Leopold looked at him, deeply annoyed. He knew perfectly well that the life of a prince is seldom marked by urgent duties. "So he cannot receive us at all today?"

"Unfortunately, no, I am sorry," the butler said, colder than the columns of the portico. "I imagine you had better return some other time."

"Please convey to His Excellency our most respectful greetings," Leopold said between his teeth.

"It will be done, you can be sure. Good day." With not another word he turned his back and went into the palace, abandoning them there.

In great irritation, Herr Mozart took his son's hand and hurried off, crossing the square with long strides. The two thus passed the musician's door. From the window came a sympathetic chaos of instruments against which the singing of a female voice stood out: without appearing to, Wolfgang sharpened his ears and recorded it in his prodigious memory.

XI.

Katharina von Esser had invited Frau and Fräulein Mozart to a reception that evening in the heart of the fashionable world, and while Anna Maria was having her hair done by Tresel, Nannerl was still lounging in her housedress.

"You must stick your head out of your shell sooner or later, my dear. You have to meet new people, have conversations. You can't always be alone; it's not good for you. I'm only saying this for your own benefit."

"It's pointless to insist—I'm not going," Nannerl muttered.

"But your headache will pass, you'll see if I'm not right. Just get some air. You'll distract yourself and feel better right away. Have you had something to eat?"

She received a grumble of assent in response.

"Come now, put on your red dress. It shows off your figure so well. And a little rouge; you're whiter than a sheet. You'll see, you'll thank me."

"I'm not coming," the girl repeated, more decisively.

Frau Mozart sighed and inspected the work of her maid in the mirror: the arrangement was a success, but some pins seemed to be sticking into her head.

"Tresel dear, could you loosen them a little, up here? There's one that's going right into my head. All I need is for it to make a hole."

While the maid adjusted the hairpins, Anna Maria turned to her daughter in a placating tone. "We really can't go on like this, Nannerl. We have to develop some relationships, find new pupils. There still aren't very many, you know, and the fact is I can't do it all. Do you understand or not? You have to help me—you have to be there, too."

The girl looked at her sharply. "I said I'm not coming, Mama. Is that clear?"

"That's how you'll get a reputation for surliness. Holy shit! Where did that obstinacy come from?"

Just then there was a knock at the door, and Frau Mozart grew even more agitated. "Who in the world is that right now? Nannerl, you go; Tresel has better things to do."

Relieved by the interruption, Nannerl put on a dressing gown and went to the door; but what she saw when she opened it astonished her. Framed in the doorway, with an impertinent smile on her lips and a joyful light in her dark eyes, in a graceful purple dress and a hat to match, this one trimmed with a bunch of violets, was the girl of the white rose.

"Hello, Nannerl," she said as if she had known her from childhood. "Aren't you giving lessons today? That must be a relief. Your students are all so bad! How can you stand it?"

She must have been about fifteen, Wolfgang's age, and she exuded a lively good humor. She let out a silvery laugh, throwing her head back, then she took a score from her bag, which was embroidered in bright colors. "It's the First Sonata of Johann Gottfried Eckard, the one you performed in a concert when you were little. May I ask you to listen to it? I haven't played anything else for a month. I can play it from memory and even blindfolded, if you want!"

"Can you pay?"

The smile vanished and the brown eyes grew clouded.

"I can only give lessons to people who pay, because I have to support my brother's studies. If you can contribute, come back tomorrow. Otherwise, don't bother."

She closed the door and returned to the bedroom.

"Well, who was it?" Anna Maria greeted her, but she didn't answer; the red dress was now laid out on the chair, ready to be put on. Nannerl stared at it with mute rage; she would have happily torn it to shreds, if not for her mother's fury.

"At least it gives you some color. Tresel, come, do something with her hair. It's very late and we really must go. Do something quickly, but attractive, please."

The girl of the white rose, returning in disappointment to the street, surely heard Fräulein Mozart shouting, "I'm not coming! I'm not coming. Damn it, Mama, what language do I have to speak? You go alone!"

XII.

The dress was becoming, at least in style; but the flaming red color only emphasized her extreme pallor. Sitting on the damask sofa with a look of deep annoyance, Nannerl was a dissonant note in that universe of skilled conversationalists and expert entertainers, of subtle observations and secret understandings.

Anna Maria, on the other hand, appeared perfectly at ease, sitting at a card table with Katharina von Esser and two gentlemen; finding themselves on opposite sides in the game of *tressette* did not keep the two women, by now intimate as old friends, from conversing in a whisper.

"Why is your beautiful daughter sitting there all by herself sulking? Looking at her really makes me heartsick. It's a waste, a true contradiction of nature."

"Countess, thank you. Nannerl is quite pretty, in fact." Then on her face appeared a pained expression. "But she has such a terrible temperament. Poor girl."

"You know what I think about this, Frau Mozart. We must find her a fiancé as soon as possible. It's the best cure."

"Indeed! But I'm afraid she doesn't want to hear anything about it. Men don't interest her. There's nothing to be done about it."

"She'll change her mind, sooner or later, don't worry—all women like to be courted."

Throwing a card on the table, Anna Maria rested her eyes on Nannerl. A waiter passed by with a tray of glasses; she took one and swallowed the contents in a gulp. Frau Mozart sighed.

"I would like to believe you, Countess. But something tells me that my daughter will never find a man willing to put up with her."

"You mustn't give up so soon, my dear." Katharina's gaze, traveling above the cards she held in her hand, settled on an individual on the other side of the room. "I have an idea about the man for her," she continued in a complicitous whisper. "Look over there. Do you see him? His name is Johann Baptist von Berchtold zu Sonnenburg."

"Aristocratic?" Anna Maria said, with interest.

"Of course, my friend. Otherwise I would not have proposed him. He's a baron, very wealthy, with a number of apartments in Salzburg and Vienna, and also a house in the mountains that they tell me is splendid. How does he seem to you?"

Already Anna Maria saw herself dwelling in a luxurious mansion, surrounded by servants available to brush her clothes, shoes, even her nails, by cooks who at a nod would tempt her with the most refined pastries, by valets who would carry her from one salon to the other in *chaises à porteur* like those of Versailles. "He is . . . I would say . . . rather interesting."

"At the moment he has no one. Imagine, a year ago he was widowed, poor man, with four children to bring up, all boys. Isn't it sad when a child is reared by a crowd of governesses? I find it terrible, I must say."

"Yes, indeed, it's very hard."

Katharina laid down her cards and addressed the other players: "Gentlemen, would you mind a short pause? My friend and I have a certain matter to take care of. Forgive us, please. We'll be back as soon as we can."

The gentlemen nodded politely, and the two women crossed the salon like actresses on a stage. They took their time, partly to create a greater impact, partly because the countess was unsteady on her heels, which were too high; Anna Maria advanced in her shadow, but as soon as she was close enough to the baron to see his features clearly, she moved to one side and shamelessly examined him from head to toe, holding her breath.

Johann Baptist von Berchtold zu Sonnenburg was extremely handsome. Under thirty, slender, with long hair the color of grain that he wore simply pulled back, he had features so harmonious that they could have been lent, with advantage, to an Apollo. He had only one small flaw, as Anna Maria had to admit when he stood up, out of respect to the countess: he was short, as if the Creator had considered that such beauty in large dimensions would have been too dazzling, complicating his life.

"My adored Baron, what a pleasure," Katharina said, offering her hand.

"Countess, seeing you is always a genuine delight," he declared, without much conviction and looking around as if in expectation of someone or something.

"Do you know my good friend Frau Anna Maria Mozart?"

"*Enchanté,* Madame," he said, kissing her hand, and for an instant he was silent, observing her with an irresistible smile. His irises, ringed by long, thick, dark eyelashes, were of two different colors: the left was uniformly gray-green; while on the upper part of the right a blue patch appeared. "As you see, Madame," he declared in a clear, youthful voice, "I am shorter than you, and perhaps also than your daughter. Is the girl in question here, or do you intend to introduce me on some other occasion?"

"Baron, don't be mischievous!" said the voluble countess, and she turned to Anna Maria: "Baptist is an artist, you know. Just like your beautiful daughter. Who knows, maybe they would understand each other."

"What art does the young lady favor?" Baptist asked politely, looking up for a moment with those shining eyes of his.

Anna Maria dared to open her mouth: "Well, it's not a pastime but a profession, as a matter of fact. My daughter, Nannerl, is the best piano teacher in the city."

"Ah, but then I know whom you're talking about. I've heard her perform, with her brother! Dear Countess, this time you mean to assign me a musician as the mother of my sons? Well done—a true inspiration."

"I don't mean to do anything, dear Baptist," she answered, in some annoyance. "And in any case, I certainly don't have the power to choose for you what only destiny, and the divine plan, can arrange. I confine myself to smoothing the path to acquaintance of individuals whom my shrewd sensibility picks out as having some affinity, and not exclusively with a romantic purpose, believe me, but in order to widen the circle of my relationships, and of the individuals themselves. As I read the other evening in a French text that my husband obtained for me, nothing is of greater importance in this life than human contact: it is only through those around us, in fact, that we are able to achieve success, perform our duties, and obtain satisfaction. It follows that friendly relations should be cultivated and stimulated more than anything else, and it is undeniable that in that field, I possess a rare intelligence, or perhaps only good intuition. It is well known that those whom I introduce to one another habitually become at least friends, to their contentment and mine. And it is of contentment, dear Baron, that I speak: since it is absolutely certain, you must admit, that a new love would brighten your life, made unhappy by the misfortune that we all know and that I don't want to refer to explicitly out of respect for your feelings; it is absolutely certain, therefore, that love would genuinely brighten your life. You, dear friend, need to meet carefree young women who come to every occasion with a serene and positive attitude."

"Mama, I can't take it anymore!" The three turned toward Nannerl, who had joined them, paler than ever, stormier-looking than ever. "My head is bursting, and I'm tired. I want to go home and I will, with or without you!"

For a moment the baron looked at her with an ambiguous expression, amused by such unfashionable manners. Suddenly, he took a breath and declaimed:

"Oh, beautiful eyes, so weary and blue,
I, humble knight
With humble right,
If those eyes will consent
I, grateful and content,
Will carry them on my steed so white and true."

And he stood there, one hand raised in the air and the other pressed melodramatically to his chest.

A vaguely embarrassed silence fell. Nannerl looked at the man as if he were deranged, and even Anna Maria seemed somewhat taken aback. But Katharina, satisfied by what seemed to her an excellent beginning, commented, "Nannerl dear, our baron is a man worthy of the greatest interest. He has a unique gift, which he displays to everyone he meets: that of creating extempore verses of rare beauty, in perfect rhymes, sometimes alternating and sometimes in couplets. In short, he has just offered to take you home in his carriage, since you prefer to deprive us of your company. Is that not an unusually gallant gesture?"

Not satisfied, the man pressed on, in a thundering voice and with comically theatrical gestures:

> *"Not only to the dwelling of Nannerl,*
> *Who of all here is the most beautiful girl,*
> *Will I go, but further, mile after mile*
> *My humble carriage has the power*
> *To take that lovely, heavenly smile*
> *Wherever she likes, for hour upon hour."*

"Do you want only my 'heavenly smile' or can I come with my whole self?" Nannerl asked, in a sarcastic tone.

"Go on, go home, daughter," Frau Mozart cut her short. "I'll join you later. Please, Baron, take her driving as long as you like. And thank you."

XIII.

First, it wasn't even thinkable that a man so handsome could truly be interested in her; second, if he were, it would certainly not be manifested through bad poetry; third, while he was reciting, those eyes, unique in the world, bored into hers with such intensity that she felt naked, as she was in reality only twelve times a year, when she bathed. And so Nannerl avoided that contact, and ostentatiously examined the buildings that ran by outside the window of his luxurious vis-à-vis carriage.

> "Sadness now fills the simple heart
> Of this man, for too soon will we part,
> And th'angelic journey to solitude will yield.
> But surely you will not raise up your shield
> Against the darts of . . . of . . . Cupid. . . ."

The baron stopped and murmured to himself, raising an eyebrow, "Pity! I need a rhyme for 'Cupid.' "

"So you express yourself only in verse?"

"The truth is, prose is less congenial to me, Fräulein Mozart. The story is that the first words I uttered were in rhyme; and my mother, whom God has taken to glory, made me study poetry composition from earliest childhood, rather pedantically."

"If you have talent, why do you waste it like that?"

"Oh, so you think I'm wasting it?" he said, ironically. "Don't tell me that you don't like my verses, O lovely lady. My heart would break!"

"On the contrary, Baron, I find them enchanting, indeed!" she answered with equal sarcasm. "Spontaneous and not at all artificial—like a spring breeze."

"Then, if you will kindly consent, I will compose in your honor an entire poem: 'My Lady Nannerl in Springtime.' What do you think? Do you like the title?"

"Absolutely on the mark. It will make a great splash in the world."

"That is what I hoped to hear," Baptist declared. Then he became absorbed in thought, and suddenly said, "It's too bad your brother, Wolfgang, isn't here in Salzburg."

"Why?" she asked, surprised.

"Only he would be able to compose timeless music, to accompany the lines of my poem. Don't you think?"

"Oh, of course. He's the only one, no one else in the world," she said coldly and turned again to look out the window.

"May I ask you if you are in touch by letter? I imagine long letters between brother and sister. Is that not so?"

"Of course! Wolfgang writes me reams of letters. And some day or other I'll answer, don't worry. Any other questions?"

He was silent, more and more aroused by her rude manner, and meanwhile he imagined working his way under Nannerl's red skirt and the petticoats that were undoubtedly white and embroidered, and of caressing her legs with his hands and of tasting them with his tongue. Baptist was sure that if the mute anger of this young woman was transformed into sensual energy, they could lose themselves and their very identities; but the rolling of the carriage marked the passage of ill-spent time, and Getreidegasse came closer and closer.

"Do you like the mountains, Fräulein Mozart?" he asked suddenly. "I have a house on a lake, at Sankt Gilgen. Those who have visited me, I must say, have been delighted."

"I know Sankt Gilgen. It's where my mother is from."

"Oh, really? I'm so sorry I didn't discuss it with Frau Mozart. In any case, there will be opportunities: I could organize an excursion, as soon as the days are longer."

"Our maid is from Sankt Gilgen as well. The excursion, perhaps, could be made with her."

Just then, the coachman pulled on the reins: to Nannerl's great relief, they had reached their destination. "Baron, thank you for the ride. You have been extremely kind," she said with the barest minimum of politeness, jumping down and slamming the door. Then she leaned through the window to whisper to him: "Don't forget, write a nice poem. I'll be happy to hear you recite it."

He cried after her, "I'll come and see you tomorrow, if you're not

too busy," but Nannerl had already disappeared through the entrance-
way. So Baptist smiled and nodded to the coachman, and the rocking
of the carriage took on the rhythm of a violent imaginary embrace.

XIV.

The wide wheels of the carriage that bore Leopold and Wolfgang
out of Bologna produced a serene rolling motion. The carriage
belonged to Don Carlo Broschi, the celebrated Farinelli, who had
invited the Mozarts to his villa, a mile from Porta Lame. The man
who had performed in Vienna, London, and Madrid, causing hyste-
ria and madness—that castrato of unequaled range, breath, intona-
tion, agility, quality of timbre, and feeling—lived in retirement in a
small villa in the hills, in the shade of ash and mulberry trees.

Sitting opposite the Mozarts was a famous singer, Clementina
Spagnoli, known as La Spagnoletta. As usual, her neck was concealed
beneath a thick padding of shawls and scarves—she was terrified
by the idea that a dastardly puff of wind might damage her vocal
cords—but the adolescent daughter who accompanied her was
charmingly exposed, and while Wolfgang pretended to look out the
window, the corner of his eye was fixed on her immature breast, and
he was happy enough. No one said a word. La Spagnoletta was to perform the following day, and to converse would tire her voice; her
daughter was obliged by etiquette to be silent; Leopold was sunk in
his own inscrutable thoughts; and Wolfgang's could not be made public. The journey, in any case, was brief, and the residence that the idol
of Baroque music had had built for himself appeared at the end of an
allée framed by beds of cyclamens.

Farinelli was at the entrance, with his hands on his hips and an
oddly timid smile on his face. Wolfgang finally detached his gaze and
his thoughts from his carriage companion and turned them to the
singer. He must have been sixty-five years old, but he didn't show it;

he was tall, thin, and erect, and his hair was darker than Leopold's. He was a strange creature, like all castrati; he had soft fingers, narrow, slightly slumping shoulders, and a long neck, with no Adam's apple, like a woman's—or so, at least, one would imagine, for the neck was entirely swathed by his shirt collar. His legs were in a dancer's pose, the right in front of the left, with the feet slightly turned out, and he wore a silver redingote with the elegance of one who is used to wearing costumes onstage. As soon as the carriage stopped, he came out to open the door, and La Spagnoletta fell on him, letting her voice, incredibly, emerge, but in a cautious whisper: "Adored maestro . . ."

The house was a jewel, beautifully frescoed and adorned with works of art that Farinelli had acquired or received as gifts. A broad carpeted staircase led to the first floor; in the center of a vast salon stood a billiard table, and on the walls hung portraits of the kings of Spain, Sardinia, and Asturias, and even a pope, all of whom had been Farinelli's patrons. And yet there was nothing ostentatious in the exhibition of those trophies, and Don Broschi, showing them to his guests, seemed almost apologetic. His collection of musical instruments, too, was precious: different viols and numerous harpsichords built in various countries of Europe. While Leopold observed them with a critical eye, Wolfgang, for once, seemed barely interested in musical matters; the girl in the low-cut dress was, for him, much more fascinating. Standing beside her mother, who allowed a haughty boredom to be manifest, for she had already made this visit several times, the girl was reserved, fanning herself a little. Her golden-brown hair was gathered on top of her head, leaving bare the white nape, with its furrow; two locks of hair, artfully curled, fell from her temples to her shoulders, undulating in the wind made by the fan, and Wolfgang imagined touching them with a caress or even a kiss.

To his great surprise, the girl suddenly made a half turn, closed her fan, and stared at him, as if waiting for him to speak. Wolfgang was embarrassed. He had almost resolved to follow the adults into the next room, but she spoke to him: "Is it true that you're only thirteen?"

He didn't answer.

"Do you speak Italian?" the girl asked.

"Yes, of course."

"So is it true that you're only thirteen?"

Before replying he looked at the door. "Actually, I'm two years older, but don't tell my father I told you."

"Why should I?" she said, as if insulted.

Wolfgang felt her physicality emerging from her clothes like a magnetic wave. She, on the other hand, seemed to be studying him with scientific attention.

"Is it true that you are writing an opera for the Royal Ducal Theater of Milan?"

He limited himself to a nod.

"How did you get a commission like that? I mean, you're only fifteen! And besides, what makes you think you can do it?"

He smiled to himself, not at all annoyed.

"You'll be working with people who are at least twice your age," she went on, shrugging. "In my opinion they'll take advantage of you and you won't get a word in."

"Do you also study singing?"

"Are you serious? I hate music."

Not even that heretical statement made her less attractive. "Why?" he asked.

"For my mother the theater has always counted more than me. The only thing that's important to her in life is to put on a nice costume and hit her high C. How could I like the opera?"

At that moment, as if she had been summoned, La Spagnoletta appeared in the doorway to command her daughter to join the rest of the group; she did so not in words, of course, but with a gracious wave of her hand. The girl repressed a sigh of boredom, took Wolfgang by the arm, and led him through a small room with tapestry-covered walls, a corridor crowded with grandfather clocks, and a room that held a collection of ceramics, until, finally, they reached a salon from which there was a splendid view over the roofs of Bologna. Farinelli's most beautiful harpsichord was set up there, and yielding to Leopold's entreaties, he was preparing to display for his guests his mythic voice. On a stool near the window sat an aged man who wore the habit of a Franciscan. He greeted Wolfgang affectionately. He was a true crowned head of music, and not just Italian music: Father Giovanni Battista Martini.

"Do you know him?" the girl whispered to Wolfgang, surprised and a little irritated by the position that this boy from Austria was gaining in her territory.

"He's the best maestro I ever had."

"Big surprise," she commented. "He's the best there is."

Everything possible had been said of Farinelli. That his voice made the orchestra players lose their concentration and caused his fellow performers to go out of character, that he loved women and also men, that he could make the most mediocre melody beautiful. This superhuman could range over three octaves as if they were one, could produce two hundred and fifty notes in a single breath, was able to hold a high note—vibrating, precise—for an entire minute. But all this when he was young; and both Wolfgang and Leopold strongly doubted that the old castrato was still able to astonish.

They were both mistaken, and grossly. Sitting at the harpsichord, which he had named Raffaello Sanzio, and accompanying himself with his slender hands, he held his chest erect to fill his expansive lungs, and his control of that breath was magisterial. From Carlo Broschi's throat came a ribbon of pure silver, now dark, now bright, exploding in fireworks of harmonics in the center of the salon; his face was one with silver itself, and his entire body became an instrument. It was like seeing a cello, an oboe, and a clarinet combine and become human and gain even a soul, and sing it. Farinelli did not indulge in virtuosities like a nostalgic lion, but every embellishment was sober, necessary, and perfect, and every passage was incomparably natural, incomparably moving.

The Mozarts sat openmouthed, Father Martini listened with a far-away smile, La Spagnoletta affected a complicit appreciation, and her daughter had started fanning herself again, serious as the Sphinx.

"Nannerl should be here," Wolfgang said softly to himself, sadly.

The girl heard him. "Who's this Nannerl?" she whispered in his ear, distracting him from listening by the warmth of her lips.

"My sister."

"And why isn't she here?"

"She stayed home so that I could go," he murmured.

"Good for you, then. Where's the problem?"

Maybe she wasn't completely wrong. The boy was silent and closed his eyes, letting the art of that marvelous interpreter permeate his entire being. Then he reopened them and gazed at Farinelli and at Father Martini, one a performer and the other a spectator. There they were, two men of a similar age, two equally superior minds, two equally simple persons. Perhaps it was age that made those two great men so without egotism, so modest and reserved. In the end, Wolfgang reflected, an old man has experienced and overcome problems that young men struggle with, and no longer has anything to prove. Far from the distracting tensions of daily life, he's not blinded by the need to prove something, and is able to grasp only what's essential in everything. To an old man, basically, nothing at all matters, not even dying, if he has lived well, and this is what makes him great.

"When I'm old I want to be like them," he said in a low voice.

The girl replied after a moment. "I want never to be old. I want to be at most my mother's age, and that's it."

"I, on the other hand, yes, I want to become old, very old. And you know what I'm going to do? I'm going to go and live in a house in the country, like this, maybe even in Italy, maybe even around here. And it will always be open to my friends, who'll be able to come whenever they want. And we'll talk about art, if we feel like it, and then we'll make music together."

"What a bore! Luckily I met you as a young man," she said, and staring straight at him she placed a hand on his thigh and intimately caressed him. He let her do it, happy and unmoving, with his gaze fixed on the wall and his lips parted, until Farinelli's aria reached its climax in a piercing sharp, and then he abandoned himself. Fortunately his agitation could be read as musical rapture.

XV.

This letter did not contain secret messages in Latin, or at least so it seemed to Nannerl; her mother had opened it and Nannerl had offhandedly asked if that was all. Receiving a somewhat bewildered affirmative answer, she had dropped the subject and had gone to the woods to read the letter in peace.

Cara sorella mia,

I beg you to forgive me if I write only a few lines, but I am composing furiously and I always have my music in my head, nothing else. Besides, you are incredibly lazy in answering me, and as you can easily imagine, writing to an absent correspondent is even more laborious. Anyway, I hope that God is keeping you in good health and letting you enjoy the good weather, which in this part of the world already has a luxuriant splendor, but that in dear old Salzburg, too, will soon shed a warm light on those woods that you love more than any other thing or person.

Wolfgang A. Mozart

She had to read it a second time and then a third. She couldn't believe that it was so cold and subtly accusing. Suddenly she heard a movement in the leaves, as if an animal were hiding in the bushes; she turned her head but saw nothing in particular, so she went back to the letter.

Between the lines, her brother was accusing her of being without feeling, egotistical; and in relation to the barrier that had always existed between them and their father, he seemed to be shifting dangerously to the other side. This allusive manner was not like Wolfgang; his mocking joy had disappeared, replaced by resentment. What should she have done to keep his affection? Write boring letters telling him about her flat, dull existence, so that his should appear even more interesting, between a concert and a theatrical opening, a triumph in the press and the ecstatic reception by an audience? Maybe she could illustrate for him in minute detail the pedagogic progress of Barbara von Esser or tell him how her mother dragged her through salons full of empty-headed people, from whom he himself had fled without a second thought.

"Look, Nannerl: they are blue like your eyes. I chose them one by one, thinking of you."

She started and almost fell off her branch. At the base of the trunk, standing in a ray of sun, with a smile on her lips and a necklace of gentians in her hands, was the girl of the white rose.

"How could you take the liberty of following me?" Nannerl said, as soon as she recovered from her astonishment.

The girl didn't answer. With care, she arranged the flowers around her neck and then climbed the tree to deliver the gift personally; that is, she tried, for in fact she wasn't very agile. She kept tripping on her lace skirt, and her delicate hands couldn't get a grip on the bark. Nannerl's irritation rose.

"Go away! Go away, I say."

But the girl had decided not to move, and with an extreme effort managed to reach the base of the big branch on which her favorite music teacher was perched. There was no way of escape for Nannerl, so she slid along the branch and hazarded a long leap to the ground.

Too long. She landed awkwardly on a rock, twisting her right ankle outward, so that she fell and rolled over, moaning. She sat up, took off her boot, and touched the instep of her foot, her face contracting in a grimace of pain.

"It's my fault," the girl murmured, tumbling down out of the tree, with her dress dirty and slightly torn by her unusual adventure; but the necklace of flowers remained intact.

"Don't worry; it's nothing," Nannerl said, and supporting herself with her hands, she stood up, keeping the injured foot raised. She tried to move a few steps, but it was a bad twist, and she found it impossible to put any weight on the leg. She stopped, exasperated.

The girl approached without saying anything. Gently she took Nannerl's arm and put it around her own shoulders, then placed her arm around Nannerl's waist. Nannerl didn't resist.

"Lean on me. Come, let's see if it works."

The two took a few slow, cautious steps.

"What's your name?" Nannerl asked.

"Victoria."

"Victoria, you mustn't pick gentians. They are precious flowers and should be left to grow in peace. Remember that."

Holding on to each other, the two began their slow descent down the hill.

XVI.

The old harpsichord of the Mozart house seemed to groan with joy at the return of hands that could make it sing: impetuous and decisive, precise and passionate. At the keyboard, Victoria's languid grace disappeared completely and she was transformed into a visionary being, in a rapture of creation. She played the First Sonata of Johann Gottfried Eckard, that sonata that only a fool would have put on a concert program, and Nannerl listened to her interpretation, so similar to her own of long ago, while sitting on the sofa with her ankle on a stool and her face relaxed in a radiant smile.

"Whom have you studied with?" she asked as the last chord faded in the air.

"With my mother."

"I'd like to meet her."

"She would also like it, you can be sure; but it's impossible, unless you go and see her in Paradise."

"I'm so sorry," she whispered, stricken.

"It happened a long time ago. I can speak of it easily now, though for my father it remains a taboo subject." Victoria went over to the piano and caressed the polished wood as if she wanted to embrace it.

"We also had a harpsichord and a piano, but then Papa gave away everything. He said that the instruments reminded him too much of Mama. And that if she had not been so obsessed with music when she was alive he could have had more of her company."

"How do you manage to practice?"

"There's a worthless old instrument in the cellar of the archbishop's palace. A broken harpsichord, with a couple of missing keys; but it can still get out the notes." Then she lighted up with enthusiasm. "This piano is something else completely, of course. It's new, isn't it?" She turned the key, raised the cover, took off the cloth, and eagerly looked at the keyboard. "I'm sure it has a splendid tone. May I hear something?"

"I don't play anymore."

The cold statement seemed absurd to Victoria. "What do you mean? Why?"

"You play it."

It was an order, and welcome. The girl sat down and immediately started Eckard's sonata, which on that malleable instrument assumed a completely new character; inexperience led her to "pound" a little where there was no need to, however, so, with a patient sigh, Nannerl rose and, hopping on her good leg, joined her and, while she played, began to instruct her with increasing passion.

"Don't move suddenly to the forte. You have to increase the intensity little by little . . . again, Victoria . . . not too much. Don't lose the character of the piece. Very good. Now lighter . . . Do you hear how the harmony changes? You have to bring it out."

The two didn't hear an imperious knock at the door. When Tresel opened it, standing before her was an imposing man of around forty wearing an impeccable uniform and highly polished boots; a large sword hung from his belt and, as was customary among military men, he didn't wear a wig, but his long hair was gathered at the nape and held by a tie. He wasn't handsome yet he had a shadowy attractiveness that might be fascinating to women. Not to Frau Mozart, however, who, arriving, looked at him in bewilderment: What in the world did the man want? Was he there to arrest her?

"Good morning, Madame," he declared firmly. "I have come to get my daughter."

"Would you introduce yourself, Herr . . . ?"

"D'Ippold. Major Franz Armand d'Ippold, in service at the Court of His Excellency the Prince Archbishop. I have reason to believe that my daughter is in this house without my permission."

"Really?" Frau Mozart answered, with some irony. "If you would like to make a tour of inspection, go ahead. I give you permission."

Armand heard the sound of the piano from the music room and marched in that direction.

"But really! Sir, Major! Where are you going? I wasn't serious. Tresel, do something!" She hurried along the corridor, followed by the maid. "Listen to me—my daughter mustn't be disturbed when she's working!"

The officer opened the door, and as soon as she saw him, Victoria took her hands off the keyboard. "All right, let's go!" he ordered, as if he were speaking to a recruit.

For an instant they were all silent. Victoria started to get up, but Nannerl stopped her. "Excuse me, but why do you want to take her away?" she asked the unknown man, defensively.

"It's a question that is no concern of yours, don't you think?" he answered coldly.

"You don't want Victoria to play?"

"It has nothing to do with you, I repeat. And in any case I have no intention of wasting money on music lessons."

"I don't want money to teach Victoria."

"That will be something to discuss later," Anna Maria put in, but no one paid attention. In the silence Armand stared at Nannerl, impenetrable and fierce. Then he said, "And why, may I ask, would you give my daughter lessons for nothing?"

"Because she has talent! A rare, genuine talent! And not to develop it would be a real crime," she said, approaching him, limping, supporting herself on the lid of the harpsichord. "You don't know what it means to have talent and not be able to express it. You haven't the least idea! You can't let your daughter become an unsatisfied woman who destroys her soul in silence, in bitterness, in senseless obligations, who ends up hating herself and whoever comes near her. You mustn't do that, do you understand? It would be worse than a crime, it would be a sacrilege!"

This passionate outburst left the women astonished, while the officer curled his lip in a sneer of sarcasm.

"A sacrilege, you say? An act against God? Well, God has taken away from my daughter something much more precious than 'talent'!"

His gaze darkened, and pain was clearly legible on his face; but immediately he shook himself and, ending the matter, said, "Victoria, let's go. Out of here."

This time Nannerl didn't have the energy to restrain her, and she went to her father with downcast eyes. "Please forgive me for the disturbance, Frau Mozart," Armand said coldly. "I guarantee you, in any case, that my daughter will never set foot in this house again. Never. Good day."

He clicked his heels and crossed the hall with measured steps.

Tresel opened the door, and just before Victoria went out Tresel took Victoria's hand and for a fleeting instant held it.

There is no need, my love, to tell you what happened after our first meeting, since you know already in every detail; but by now I would find it hard to give up this habit of telling you my story, and also myself. It doesn't take more than a couple of hours away from my sleep each night, don't worry; and it adds so much to my waking hours, in terms of understanding and tranquillity. It's a place that's mine alone, ours alone, a place that I guard jealously and that sometimes reminds me of the old imaginary kingdom that you, too, through my thoughts, have visited. It's the only expedient that allows me, right now, to preserve my closeness to you; for even if I shouldn't say it, Armand, my love, my dearest, I miss you, I miss you tremendously and wish only for your return.

Every one of your departures provokes in me the same violent cycle of emotions. First, I have a strange jolt of pride that leads me to think: basically I have no great need of him. I can do without him from time to time; indeed, this is a precious chance to practice my autonomy; and it will make me appreciate even more the moment when, at last, we will be together again. Then five days pass, inevitably five days exactly (and I always realize this afterward), and I am assailed by a dark dissatisfaction that has a single cure: your presence.

As if that were not enough, the approach of another separation increases my sense of abandonment. My mother and brother will soon be setting off on tour, and God knows when I will see them again. It will be a long journey, which my father has organized in every detail and which will take them first to Munich, then to Augsburg (where they will stay with my uncle and my cousin Thekla), Mannheim, and, finally, Paris. Oddly, both of them embark on the new endeavor unwillingly, as if they had some idea of calamity. Wolfgang is eager for the opportunity, but he would like to travel alone; imagine, to avoid having Mama with him, he proposed that I should accompany him! She, on the other hand, is not sure she can replace my father in the practical matters, nor does she know how to manage her headstrong son. But so it is: Herr Mozart arranges and the rest of us can only submit.

I will therefore continue, my beloved Armand, to fill the physical space between us with paper, and characters, and ink stains, and some tears, and with warm laughter at my awkwardness—mine, not yours—since I've begun to suspect that I am a master not of music but of insecurity and embarrassment.

XVII.

Nannerl was completely hunched over behind a cart piled with caged chickens. She was crouching down, her shoulders bent and her head low; she clutched a score in one hand and with the other pulled Victoria by the skirt. "Look out; they'll see you."

Victoria was beside her, also partly hidden by the cart, but she was peeking out perilously to check the doorway. "Don't worry, Nannerl. Do you think this is the first time I've done it?"

"If they discover you, they'll also discover me; and what will I say to them?"

"They won't discover us," she declared arrogantly, then she saw something and shuddered. "Now!" And she sneaked in front of the cart.

Nannerl hesitated. The chickens cheeped.

"What are you doing? Come on!" Victoria grabbed Nannerl and pushed her toward the gateway; at that moment a grand carriage was entering, distracting the guards. Rapidly they slipped inside and crossed the inner courtyard, straight to a small warped door that opened onto a corridor; this ended in a flight of stairs, which descended into a dark, cool chamber. Nannerl followed Victoria, her heart in her throat.

"See how easy it is?"

Leaning against a wall, Victoria was laughing, while Nannerl struggled to compose herself. "I would never have thought of entering the palace this way."

"Want to say hello to the archbishop? Maybe he'll invite us to stay for dinner."

"Don't be silly, Victoria. Where's the cellar?"

"And you relax. What a bore you are. Over here, come on."

The palace basement was a maze of tunnels. The two passed through an archway and descended a narrow spiral staircase; Nannerl had to be careful not to hit her head. They traversed a long corridor, went through a doorway to a straight, steep flight of stairs, and finally arrived at a door that Victoria opened with a solemn air.

It was impossible to see anything. With assured movements, the girl lighted the candles of a candelabra, one by one, and Nannerl began to distinguish the outlines of old furniture, piles of unused dishes, stacks of paintings, even an old rocking horse. What was the archbishop doing with a rocking horse? And then headboards, a broken mirror, a box of doorknobs, everything covered by a thick coating of dust; and finally the harpsichord, protected by a white cloth that in that jumble seemed to glow with its own light. Victoria took off the cloth and folded it carefully, then she lifted the lid of the keyboard. Nannerl still seemed dubious.

"Calm down; no one can hear. I've come here millions of times and my father has never found out. And anyway, the archbishop has just sent him to Linz, on one of his missions."

"All right," Nannerl answered, and placed the score on the music stand. "It's the great Bach, Johann Sebastian, of course—certainly not that clown who lives in London. Go on, and pay close attention to the different voices."

Victoria looked at her in astonishment. "What? I'm to sight-read it?"

"Of course. You can do it, believe me. Have faith in your capacities. Don't ever let yourself be conditioned by those who underestimate you. Never."

"I understand. But why don't you let me hear you, at least once?"

In response she received an exasperated outburst: "Because I don't play anymore! I don't play anymore, Victoria, won't you understand that? Look. I've let my nails grow."

And she showed Victoria her hands, which were not those of a pianist. On the palms there were calluses, the result of climbing trees, an activity no longer followed by warm-water soaks and softening creams; and her nails were long, but like those of a wild animal, not of a cared-for lady—uneven, broken, worn here and there, even a little dirty. Unthinkable for such hands to play.

Victoria seemed to grow sad, but she said nothing. She sat down, placed her hands on the keyboard and her eyes on the staff, and timidly performed the passage from Bach. Nannerl stood next to her and began instructing her.

"Very good. You have to move ahead with your eyes. Ahead of the notes you're playing. What you read has to be different from what you're doing. Learn to let your thoughts run on two parallel lines, and yet with control over both. Continue like that. Now you are the master of the piece."

While the girls nourished their souls on music, on the upper floors of the palace preparations were under way for the more earthly nourishment of His Excellency. On the table in the middle of the kitchen lay five loaves of crusty white bread, just taken from the oven; one of the chickens that had offered shelter to the two intruders had had its neck wrung, and the cook Claudia had plucked its feathers skillfully. The cook Gunther, her husband, was preparing to make the archbishop's favorite soup, *Gulaschsuppe,* with beef, lard, onions, and spices. The boxes of vegetables were piled on the floor next to one wall, and he, a robust man, picked them up all together to place on the work surface, but the action had an unexpected result. Just behind the pile was a hole in the wall—not very big, a couple of inches or so across—and as soon as he removed the box the distant sound of a harpsichord could be heard through the hole.

Gunther stopped, speechless, staring at the strange phenomenon. Claudia, however, throwing out a handful of feathers, said nonchalantly, "What are you surprised at? It's Major d'Ippold's daughter, isn't it?"

"Ah, yes," the man said, hitting the palm of his hand against his forehead, and prepared to weep over the onions.

Suddenly the sound stopped. In the cellar Nannerl had exclaimed, "What are you doing? That's an F-sharp!"

"It wasn't bad," Victoria answered. "In fact, it's much better than the F-natural, in my view. Besides you said it: I'm the master of the piece."

"I didn't tell you to change the notes. You can't allow yourself to alter the choices of the author. You haven't the least right!"

"Let's go on. It's not so serious."

"No, it's fundamental. You're an interpreter, no more. The value of your art is in rendering as best you can the art of someone else. That's it." Then she added, in a lower voice, "You don't have the slightest idea what it means to compose."

Victoria stared at her. "Why, do you?"

Fräulein Mozart didn't answer. She indicated a point on the score and said darkly, "Start again here."

Victoria insisted: "So, do you compose or not?"

"I said start again from here."

XVIII.

For the shopping, Anna Maria gave Tresel some coins and with those demanded that she acquire smoked meat, sausage, and high-quality game. Most of the time the maid was forced to choose old chickens, which she masked as pheasant using a flood of spices. As she was filling her basket with chives, cumin, and paprika, she realized that she was being followed. A little hat crowned with a tuft of daisies emerged from the potato stall; and as soon as she turned in that direction the hat disappeared. Tresel wasn't alarmed. She calmly chose a big head of garlic, added it to her basket, paid, and moved to another stall; then she thought again, turned back, asked for a sprig of marjoram, and when she raised her head from her purse, she found Victoria's childish face before her.

"Nannerl composes. I know she composes. And you know something, too, don't you?" the girl demanded.

The servant made a half turn around her and continued choosing carrots and onions.

"Do you understand? So, you have nothing to tell me?"

Tresel sniffed an onion to see if it was fresh.

"And then, why did she stop playing? Every time I ask her to let me hear something, she invents an excuse. Once she said it made her ankle hurt!"

The servant decided that the onion wasn't fresh and moved on to another stall.

"Do you have a tongue? Answer me!"

And so it went, through the whole market, the whole way home. Victoria followed her, entreating, wheedling, and Tresel went straight on with the energetic step of a woman from the mountains, her arms filled with baskets.

"In my opinion she wrote it all, the music she makes me study. It's true, right? She talks a bunch of big names—Eckard, Schobert, Bach. But in my opinion it's all hers. Can you understand what I'm saying, or do you speak only the dialect of Sankt Gilgen? Tell me something, please, Tresel! I just want to understand, I want to help her!"

They had now reached the house. "Come," Tresel said, finally. Then she went in and disappeared up the stairs.

Victoria looked around: there was no one nearby, apart from a young woman walking on the other side of the street with a newborn sleeping in her arms. Her father wouldn't find out. So she hurried up the stairs.

From the ground floor the labored sound of the piano could be heard. Tresel gestured to her to be quiet, and she opened the door without making any noise; she put down the shopping baskets and went along the hall on tiptoe, making sure every so often that Victoria was following with the same caution. The door of the music room was closed; Nannerl was giving a lesson to some aristocratic young lady, and on a sofa outside, a lady and a little girl were waiting their turn. The child looked at Victoria and smiled.

The journey ended in a room so small that it barely contained a bed shorter than normal and a night table, nothing else. Tresel opened the drawer and from a false bottom took out a sheet of music paper inscribed with handwritten notes. The paper was smoke-stained and the edges were scorched.

"It's true, Nannerl wrote music," she admitted. "But then she burned all her music. Only this was left." And she showed it to Victoria, who held it breathlessly: it was an aria for a soprano. The title said: *"Vane son tue parole, vano il pianto"*—"Vain are your words, vain your tears."

Tresel immediately, jealously, took it back. "You didn't see it," she said sharply. "You know nothing. And if you really want to help her, don't torture her anymore!"

She put the score back in the drawer and, with her head, invited Victoria to get out of the way.

XIX.

The target was large, and it showed a rather risqué scene, painted in bright colors. In the middle of a lovely grove of trees, a man had been caught by the painter in the act of preparing to take care of his needs: his pants were half down and his pink buttocks were in evidence; his face, turned back toward the observer, was immobilized in a slightly embarrassed yet jolly expression. The players passed the guns back and forth and took shots, and the feathered darts stuck in the canvas; those who hit the buttocks got the highest score.

Fräulein Mozart made one bull's-eye after another, and the assembly of aristocrats was delighted, whereas she, without a word to anyone, continued to shoot, aiming at the target with great concentration. The other guests were gossiping, as usual. What else could one do? Three boys between four and six were romping about in a game of war, totally ignored by the company, while a fourth fair-haired child, barely a year old, slept in his nurse's arms. The buffet was abundant, worthy of the villa of a baron: cooks, waiters, designers had worked for weeks on the preparations for this little party, whose purpose was for the baron to see Nannerl again.

"You have no idea what I had to do to get her here," Anna Maria whispered to Katharina, with a beleaguered air. "I dragged her by force."

"My dear, the important thing is that she came. You'll see, our friend will succeed in making some progress, sooner or later . . . It just takes a little patience."

A small round of applause broke out in Nannerl's direction as she hit the pink buttocks yet again. She acknowledged the applause with a small bow and loaded the gun again, while the baron moved to her side, assumed a pose, and began his jesterlike recitation:

> *"The huntress Diana took aim!*
> *And like her target my heart*
> *Is pierced, and for her longs, aflame!*
> *Alas, cruel maid . . ."*

Here the font of inspiration dried up, perhaps because of a sudden self-critical impulse, and he stopped. The guests took it as a pause for effect and stood with bated breath; Nannerl, however, appeared completely uninterested in the poetic act and continued to hit one bull's-eye after another. Anna Maria poked her with an elbow, then with great affectation pleaded: "Herr Baron, continue, please! Your poetry is so delightful."

Immediately Katharina echoed her, smiling at the guests: "These marvelous verses—you know he improvises them? He pulls them as if by magic from his wonderful mind. Isn't it astonishing?"

"Oh yes, everything here is astonishing," Frau Mozart said, hinting as she eyed the rich furnishings of the salon. Then she poked her daughter again with her elbow and growled, "Will you stop it?"

The silent challenge caused Baptist to return to his Muse. He came so close to Nannerl that she could smell the odor of his body and, in a low voice, uttered in her ear:

> *"This dark scowl, alas, escapes me*
> *But the lion's heart that roars so fiercely*
> *has gentle depths, I know . . .*
> *And there we will go . . ."*

The baron took a deep breath, readying himself for the coup de théâtre he had arranged, and offered:

> *"A sole desire from my heart flows:*
> *That in counterpoint to my verses may*
> *Celestial music be made, and so . . .*
> *And so . . ."*

"The rhyme's not coming—too bad," he mumbled, smiling under his mustache at the situation and at himself. He went to the other end of the salon, which was bigger than the Mozarts' entire apartment, and under the fascinated gaze of his guests grabbed the corner of a cloth draped over a large object and pulled it, uncovering a pianoforte. For an instant he was silent, wondering how Nannerl would take this provocation, and then, like a gallant courtier, he called upon her: *"Mademoiselle Mozart, jouez ce petit piano pour moi! Je vous en prie."*

Among the guests rose a murmur of surprise, a rush of fans and oblique smiles. Katharina exclaimed, "Oh yes, dear Nannerl, play for the baron, do be good." Then she turned to the others haughtily: "She is my daughter's teacher, did you know? An exceptional teacher. Under her guidance, Barbara has made great progress."

Anna Maria addressed Nannerl with less benevolence. She kicked her in the shins and hissed: "Put down that dreadful gun and go and play!"

Finally Fräulein Mozart stopped aiming at the painted buttocks and turned to face the room; but she kept the gun balanced on her shoulder, so that through its sight passed an array of the nobility of Salzburg, who amid little laughs and murmurs of fear tried to get out of the way. Then, rapidly and silently, like a goddess of the hunt, she crossed the room, reaching the baron, who was raising the lid of the piano; in a flash, she shot and hit him right in the buttocks. The feathered dart remained fixed in his redingote, to the silent dismay of all present and above all Anna Maria, who thought she would die.

She then raised the gun aloft exultantly and declaimed:

"Baron, my heart may grieve
That my shot had success.
Take it as you would believe,
As anything but a yes."

With a masculine gesture she tossed the gun randomly into the arms of one of the guests, reached the door, and fled.

XX.

The journey from the far south took place in an unbearable heat that made one's clothes stick to one's body. Leopold had decided to hire for himself and Wolfgang a light, half-open carriage, of a type widespread in Italy but uncomfortable for long journeys, the so-called *sedia*. It had only two wheels, was drawn by two horses, and could carry two passengers at most, sitting at the front and poorly protected by a folding top. It was, however, a fast carriage, and Herr Mozart hoped to cover the distance from Naples to Rome in a single day.

Exhausted by the heat, the horses galloped laboriously on the rough road, foaming with sweat, and the coachman whipped them without pity. The carriage swayed incessantly, the trunks anchored to the front bars jolted up and down, the noise was exasperating, and the air that beat on their faces, burning. The father was weary, the son nervous.

"Wouldn't it be better to make the journey in stages, in a comfortable carriage?" Wolfgang said, raising his voice to be heard over the din.

"It would cost more," Leopold answered.

"What?"

"It would cost much more!"

"Sometimes I don't understand you, Papa. With all the money that comes from home, we still have these problems?"

He leaned back without answering. The boy took off his shirt and with it dried his forehead and chest.

"You are in danger of getting sick if you do that, Wolfgang. Try to relax and think of something pleasant."

Pleasant? What was pleasant in Wolfgang's life? All his habits had changed. He looked on life with arrogance, pushed by a father who devoted all his energies to him and demanded the same of others. He was getting used to thinking that this was right: that the entire world should revolve around his matchless talent. Yet apart from the applause and the praise he received, he couldn't picture any particular pleasures.

"What are you thinking about?" he asked his father.

Leopold's mind had turned to Anna Maria, but he didn't want to divulge this, so that his own homesickness wouldn't weigh on his son.

"I'm thinking of when we arrive at the inn, of the good plate of rice and roast chicken we'll have prepared for us, and the comfortable bed we'll find."

"That's all?"

He lowered his head, ashamed, and his son understood his words from the movement of his lips. "I'm thinking of Mama, Wolfgang."

A woman? In the life of young Mozart there was no woman as important as Anna Maria was for Leopold. His sister by now seemed lost to her own obstinacy, and the Italian girls who had introduced him to sensuality had been mere extras; as soon as he became close to one of them, he left that city for another. And then the singers were old, the nobles seldom interesting, the servants forbidden by his father.

Like a blow from Heaven, in an instant everything changed, and those thoughts ceased to make sense. All Wolfgang knew was that an enormous force was pushing him out of the carriage, and an opposing force, his father's hand, was restraining him. The *sedia* was tilted frighteningly to one side, dragged downward by the collapse of one of the horses, who was neighing desperately and writhing in a powerful swell of muscles. One of the trunks crashed to the ground and fell open, the contents scattering in front of the carriage. The coachman tumbled onto the grass and disappeared in a ditch. And then silence.

His father's terrified eyes, inches away, were examining him. "Are you hurt?" he asked. Wolfgang shook his head. Leopold, not satisfied, checked his son from head to toe, testing his limbs, but the boy wriggled free in irritation, jumped down, and reached the edge of the ditch. The coachman was a little banged up, but essentially unhurt. Cursing in his incomprehensible Italian, with its heavy Neapolitan accent, he climbed up toward the road. Wolfgang found a long branch and held it out to him, and grasping that, the man managed to climb out.

"Now what?" Wolfgang said, dazed, looking at the twisted coach with his father still inside, the horse striving to get up, the other horse pawing nervously, his trunk smashed open on the ground.

In response, the coachman yelled what must have been a series of insults at the animal, then he grabbed it by the bridle and helped it to its feet; luckily nothing seemed to be broken. Wolfgang began to gather clothes and objects and stick them in the trunk. He picked up the bag with his underwear, then his beautiful gilded tailcoat with polished buttons, all dusty (he noted with disappointment). He shook it out, folded it carefully, and put it in the trunk, and started to collect books and papers, which were lying within a radius of a few feet. But when he returned to the trunk he noticed something odd: on the gilded tailcoat there was now a dark stain. He realized that a sticky liquid was dripping from the carriage, looked up, and with horror saw his father trying to stanch a large wound on his shin.

"How did that happen?" he cried, and leaped to his father's side, almost afraid to look at the cut, with its ragged, uneven edges, and so deep that the white of the bone was visible.

"It's nothing, son; don't worry," Leopold answered. "Find the medicine bag."

The coachman also came over, and shook his head grimly, as if looking at a man condemned to death. Wolfgang shoved him aside frantically, opened his father's trunk, and took out the case that held ointments and bandages.

"Here it is! What should I do?"

"Nothing. Let me do it. Don't be upset, really, Wolfgang. It's not serious." He took a white cloth, tore off a long strip, and bound his calf tightly with it. Immediately the strip became red.

Wolfgang couldn't be still. "It's my fault. If you hadn't held on to me . . ."

"Let's not talk foolishly, son. It's fine. With this bandage I can get to Rome, and there we'll find a doctor."

"If we had taken a better carriage . . ."

"Enough now, Wolfgang. There's no point in recriminations. Try

to be practical, for once!" Then, more calmly, he spoke to the coachman in Italian. "Antonio, are you ready?"

The man nodded, but he was still scowling.

"Wolfgang, have you got everything?" Leopold asked again.

"Yes, everything," he murmured submissively. Then he closed his
father's trunk and fastened his own to the front bars. Antonio took his
seat, called to the horses, cracked the whip, and they started off again.

The carriage moved along the road at a more prudent pace and
slowly disappeared around a bend. But something was left behind: the
transcriptions of songs for Nannerl, the folded sheets now mingling
with dust.

XXI.

She had had a discussion with her mother that morning; that is, Frau
Mozart had performed a polemical soliloquy and she had been silent,
trying to let the reproaches slide over her. But the bad mood lingered.
On the way to the Residenzplatz, she was thinking that this surprise
visit to Victoria's wasn't a great idea after all. The procedure for
secretly entering the Palace, which she was used to by now, suddenly
seemed childish; and what purpose did it have, ultimately? To finally
teach someone who was worthy of it? So what? At that moment she
would have preferred to flee to the old tree, in the hope that her sense
of oppression would evaporate in the fog or be dissolved by the rain.
A downpour, a thunderous cloudburst was what it would take. And
instead in the streets an irritating quiet reigned and the few passersby
seemed to be walking on tiptoe, or on a gigantic mattress, and stamped
on their faces were foolish smiles.

There was only the sound of heels clacking loudly behind her, a
solitary pair, echoing up to the tops of the buildings. He or she who
was moving with such determination had first appeared with a muted
tolling, which had increased in volume and then opened up into a

broad spectrum of resonances. By now the individual was close, and Nannerl was almost certain that it was a man, because of the compactness of the sound, which couldn't be coming from the spool-like heel of a woman's shoe. To find out, she turned, and her heart skipped a beat as she recognized Major d'Ippold.

Quickly she turned toward a shop window, pretending to be interested in the pastries on display, and waited for the oblivious man to pass her unobserved. As he came even with her, she stole a glance at him. In profile, his features seemed to be carved in marble, and over his shoulders he wore a cape that rippled as he walked, softening his gait. The uniform was laced tightly, emphasizing his powerful build; the buttons gleamed and so did the sword, which was partly hidden by the sash; the boots, whose broad, low heels had produced that resonant sound, shone as if just polished. The officer was clearly headed to his duties at the Palace.

Perhaps she wasn't meant to see Victoria today. Perhaps it would be better to postpone it and run off to the woods; she had only to make a half turn and go up the hill. But that man who was walking in front of her, so erect and vigorous, provoked in her a feeling of spite: giving lessons to his daughter under his nose would be a sweet revenge, for Victoria and also for her.

She let Armand gain some distance and then she followed him through the narrow streets. At the corner of the Palace she stopped, cautiously, and waited until he went though the gateway; then, as if very naturally, she walked toward the center of the square, pretending to be in search of a cool spot near the fountain. She sat on the edge of the basin, half hidden by the grand sculptures, without losing sight of the entrance to the Palace.

Finally a sign of life: a boy approached the gateway pushing a wheelbarrow full of fruit. He was too small to hide behind, Nannerl thought; a coach with an escort of soldiers would have been better. She moved toward the boy anyway, following a diagonal that made her course less obvious and her face less recognizable to anyone strolling near the square. Meanwhile, the wheelbarrow was proceeding into the inner courtyard. Suddenly the boy clumsily, or perhaps tripping on a stone, let the cart tilt, and some fruit rolled onto the ground. With an effort, he tried to reverse the error by stretching out one hand, but that was worse: the wheelbarrow went off-balance completely and overturned, and the inner courtyard of the Prince-Archbishop's Palace resembled the market square.

All the guards, not to mention Armand himself, turned toward the boy in irritation. Nannerl immediately took advantage of this and sneaked toward the warped door; but as she opened it, she was again invaded by a sense of spite and turned, recklessly, to look at Major d'Ippold.

Their eyes didn't meet. He, in fact, was leaning over to pick up the fruit, as if it were the most obvious and normal thing. The guards observed him rather stiffly, but after a few instants, like good subordinates, they began to imitate him; and meanwhile he, tranquil, went on picking up apples and pears and putting them in the wheelbarrow and into the grateful hands of the incredulous boy, perhaps also saying a few kind words that Nannerl couldn't catch. When the wheelbarrow was full again, Armand gave the boy a pat on the head and watched him go off, shaking his own head with a smile that made his features more pleasing. Then he said something to the guards, turned, and went into the Palace.

Continuing to challenge fate, Nannerl made no move to go through the door and remained in that position, her hand resting on the doorknob and her gaze on the courtyard. There was nothing more to observe, but the eyes of her imagination perceived a scene of such indecency that it made her sweat. She and the officer were alone in a room, not very big, maybe a kitchen, pleasantly cool, with a window divided in fourths by a wooden frame, and half closed. Armand was sitting on a straw seat and she was sitting on his lap, legs astride, with his arms around her. Her very soul was crushed by the contact between their two bodies, and her consciousness was free to expand

and to vanish through an opening that had been created at the top of her skull; but she held on to him and, concentrating all her senses on him, was sure that he would keep her from exploding.

The daydream lasted less than a second. She immediately chased away the fantasy, opened the door, and ran along the corridor. From there she went down the flight of steps and arrived at the little room.

Oddly, she hesitated for a moment while deciding which direction to take; perhaps her senses were still in disarray. Then she made up her mind and descended a stair that in fact didn't seem that familiar. But when she reached the bottom she thought she knew where she was; she walked decisively along a passage and down some stairs, yet finally had to conclude that she had never been there. She retraced her steps, or so she thought, but found herself in an equally unfamiliar place. There was no doubt: she was lost.

On one wall was a lighted torch stuck in a bracket. She took it out and tried to get back to where she had started, but suddenly, frighteningly, she came face-to-face with a man, his arms full of brooms: it was Gunther, the cook.

"I'm sorry," she mumbled, already imagining herself dragged in chains before His Excellency. "I don't . . . that is, I mean that . . . really I am here because . . ."

"That way, Fräulein Mozart," he said calmly. "The last door on the left, then down the stairs."

Bewildered but certainly relieved, she followed his directions and found herself at the top of the steep flight that led to the door of the cellar. Already the sound of the harpsichord reached her in a confusion of echoes, the notes bouncing off the walls of the stairwell. Suddenly Nannerl recognized a certain passage and was horrified. Victoria was playing, and singing—something for which she had no talent—an aria for soprano that carried Nannerl back a hundred years: to a time when she was little more than a child, at the end of the European tour, and was composing vocal music with the complicity and secret support of Wolfgang; a time before the departure of her brother, which had marked a turning point in her existence, before she had learned to confront loss, solitude, bitterness. But it wasn't possible that Victoria knew it!

She took the final steps on tiptoe and held her breath as she opened the door, praying that it wouldn't squeak. It didn't, and at the far end of the basement room was the harpsichord, illuminated by candlelight, and Victoria seated, her back to her, intently singing in her chirping voice. Nannerl approached stealthily, while a sense of intrusion into her innermost self increased. She came very close, so close that she could touch Victoria, or even strangle her. And on the music stand she recognized her old score: the edges were scorched, and it was blackened.

Violently she pushed the girl aside, and Victoria fell to the floor with a cry of fear; then Nannerl seized the sheet of paper and looked at it, stunned. It was her "Vain are your words, vain your tears." Her manuscript, the real one, beautifully copied in her hand, with that small erasure on the last beat because she had not felt like transcribing the whole thing from the beginning.

She spoke in a half-whisper, bewildered. "What are you doing, Victoria? Playing with my life, behind my back?"

Victoria was still in a heap on the dirty floor, breathing hard, and for a moment she didn't have the strength to speak. Then she said weakly, "Forgive me, Nannerl. I wanted . . . I wanted to surprise you."

"Who gave it to you?" she asked, still stupefied.

"I stole it from Tresel. I'm sorry, believe me, Nannerl. I didn't want to upset you. Your music is beautiful."

"My music is dead!" she cried, and ran away, up the stairs.

XXII.

The armor around her heart was molded, cast, and ready. And that day, rather than throw it aside and leave herself open to hope,

Nannerl put it on, bolted it, and barred for a long time the door to her dreams. She hugged the score to her, creasing it carelessly. She walked with determination, yet without a goal. From the Residenzplatz through the narrow streets, from the city's center to the outskirts, and then again to the center, her eyes red but dry and a lump in her throat that would not dissolve. She bumped into more than one passerby and didn't bother to apologize. Someone shouted a mild insult at her, but she couldn't hear. In her mind a raucous symphony sounded, a collection of orchestras superimposed, each going its own way, at high volume—an intolerable cacophony even for an untrained ear.

She found herself on the road that led to the hill outside of town, and her legs went up the slope like an athlete's. Nannerl ran, she ran for hours and felt no fatigue; she didn't take the path but went deep into the undergrowth. Her dress caught on brambles and tore, branches slapped her face, her neck, her arms, scratching her, yet she pushed on, heedless.

It had already been dark for a while when she got home. Frau Mozart, who had been waiting for her anxiously, opened the door and, seeing her so upset, couldn't repress a cry of fear.

"Good Lord! What happened to you, child?"

She didn't answer. She didn't have the strength. Slowly, she scraped the dirt from her shoes and plucked the leaves from her hair.

"Where have you been? Are you all right? Do you have a headache?" Her mother assaulted her with questions, while she, mute, turned her back and went to her room.

"Nannerl! What's wrong? Dinner's right here, it's still warm . . ."

Finally she said wearily, "I'm not hungry," and continued walking.

"But you can't go to bed on an empty stomach," Anna Maria insisted, running after her. "You won't sleep well, you know." On the dresser halfway along the corridor stood a vase of roses with stems so long they practically grazed the ceiling. "Look how beautiful they are!" she fluttered, in an attempt to cheer her. "They arrived just this afternoon, with a note so sweet, in rhyme; and guess who sent them to you? Baron von Berchtold zu Sonnenburg. You see, he is still interested in you, in spite of your rude behavior."

In answer, she received a slammed door and a key turning in the lock.

Finally, she would have at least a few moments of peace. Nannerl pulled the aria from her corset and undressed, tugging at her torn dress, piling the petticoats haphazardly, kicking off her shoes at the foot of the bed, ripping out her hairpins and throwing them on the floor along with a few strands of hair.

At that moment Wolfgang, too, was in a bedroom: that of a modest but comfortable inn. He was playing the violin for Leopold, who was lying in a chair, in pain, with his leg bound and resting on a stool. Frau Mozart knew almost nothing of the accident; her husband had not told her that the wound was infected, the leg swollen, and that at night his forehead was burning and he kept breaking out in a sweat that was not caused by the hot Italian summer. He was haunted by a fear of its getting worse, and only Wolfgang, who could make the violin sing like no one else, managed to give him some solace.

"That theme is really original," he said weakly. "When did you compose it? I can't remember."

The boy stopped playing and looked affectionately at his father. Then he said vaguely, "A few years ago . . . but actually I don't recall exactly when, either." Then he put the bow back on the strings and took up the melody of "Vain are your words, vain your tears." To make it his own, he changed a note every so often.

Nannerl was huddled under the sheets unable to sleep. She lay on one side, her arms squeezing the pillow, her jagged, yellowed nails scratching it. Her toes contracted spasmodically, and her eyelids kept opening and closing as if she had a tic, and then opened into darkness.

Suddenly she rose and in a single rapid movement seized the score and ripped it to pieces.

At the same instant the sound of the violin broke off in a harsh sound. "What happened?" asked Leopold.

"A string broke . . . how strange."

XXIII.

Tresel didn't say a word, but that was normal for her; it was much less so for Victoria. She entered the Mozart house as if the floor were burning and stood there, head bent, playing with the wristbands of her dress; Tresel's stern silence made her feel even guiltier. Tresel would have loved to slap Victoria's shameless little face until it turned purple, but a servant can't do such things, so she turned her back and went to the music room.

Nannerl was busy choosing some easy pieces for her students. She looked thinner, or perhaps it was only the eyes sunk in their sockets that made her face look wasted, made her seem much older; pale, jaws clenched, she looked almost like the Leopold of earlier days. She looked up as Tresel entered and understood who had come to see her. She said only, "Let her come in. Thank you."

"Shall I bring something to drink?" Tresel asked, somewhat sharply.

Nannerl shook her head. "She won't stay long."

Tresel went out, leaving the door open, and indicated it to Victoria with a gesture that was almost rude; then she returned to the kitchen to prepare the liver dumplings, happy to be out of the presence of that little hussy.

With an effort, Victoria peeked in and then slowly entered. She stood with her hands clasped at her waist, mortified, under her teacher's angry gaze; she had composed a litany of apologies, but at that moment she forgot them all.

In any case the silence didn't last. "It's ridiculous for you to come here!" Fräulein Mozart said to her harshly.

The sentence struck Victoria like a whip; in a second her eyes filled with tears, while her lips trembled. She turned and was about to go and never return, but Nannerl spoke again: "We can't risk having your father discover us!"

She froze. What was that plural? And then, what would her father discover?

"I've prepared a program of study for you," Nannerl continued, in the same inflexible tone. "It's a concert program. We'll meet in the cellar, a week from today."

And she pointed to a bundle of scores on the piano.

The tears welled in Victoria's eyes even more abundantly as she stammered, incredulous, "What? What did you say? A concert?"

Nannerl didn't answer and didn't change her expression. Victoria frantically dried her face, laughing and crying at once, then suddenly darkened: "But—where? No one knows me. No one would give me a stage."

"You take care of studying. I'll take care of the rest."

The girl approached her, trembling, and in a whisper asked, "Have you forgiven me?"

"Go!"

So Victoria took the scores and skated lightly along the corridor, her heart hammering madly.

The moment she was alone, Nannerl melted in a tender smile. Tresel, on the other hand, grinding liver in the kitchen, groaned in annoyance when she heard the door close.

XXIV.

The cellar looked different. Most of the dirt was gone and the jumble of furniture had been piled against one wall. The harpsichord had been placed in the center and there was an open space around it, which allowed Nannerl to walk in a circle, listening to Victoria, instructing her, and sometimes interrupting her with the brutality of a slave driver.

"No! Stop. They're triplets! Concentrate!"

Victoria repeated the passage once, and another time, and then yet again.

"There, that's better. Go on like that. Forget you have two hands. You have ten fingers, and they are all independent. Let them run. Faster! Even faster! You have to work hard, Victoria, or you'll remain a talented unknown."

The girl's forehead was pearled with sweat. She went on playing ardently, eyes closed, as if in a trance.

In the kitchen the hole in the wall was free of impediments and the sound of the instrument cheered the cooks, who were busy preparing the archbishop's afternoon coffee with his favorite sweet, *Zwetschgenknödel.* Gunther was making the pastry and Claudia was patiently pitting plums and stuffing them with lumps of sugar; their gestures kept time to the music, and they were very quiet. But suddenly the music stopped and there was no sign of its starting up again. Puzzled, they went to the hole, his hands white with flour, hers black with plums. What in the world had happened?

Nannerl was devoting some minutes to style markings. She was sitting beside her student, who was shaking her hands and trying to relax her aching wrists, showing her the music for a new piece.

"As you see, this is a minuet," she said. "So when you play it try to imagine the dancers bowing. You have to picture their light, graceful movements, so as to be refined and delicate yourself."

She rose and turned her back to the harpsichord so that, unable to see Victoria, she could concentrate on the sound. From the first notes, however, the girl launched into a mellifluous interpretation, with languors and endless rallentandos that would have left the dancers with their feet in the air for an impossible length of time. Nannerl listened to her, suffering silently, and just then feared she had made a mistake. Maybe Victoria wasn't ready for this venture. Maybe her decision had been hasty and incautious.

"I said to be gentle, not mawkish. You're worse than a society doll. You should take that damn rose not just off your hat but out of your head! Do you understand what I'm saying?"

Victoria nodded, discouraged.

"Now start again. Respect the notes, respect the style, and behave like a real musician. Because that's what you are now!"

Victoria began, and after a few moments Nannerl calmed down; she had exaggerated her tone, but perhaps it had been useful in some way.

In the kitchen, Gunther and Claudia had abandoned the *Zwetsch-genknödel* and were happily dancing a minuet. As they took each other by the hand, flour mingled with the pulp of plums, and though their aprons were hardly fit for a ball, their red faces expanded into wide smiles that an elegant ballroom would never have known.

XXV.

"Papa says that his leg isn't giving him any more problems," Anna Maria said, scanning a letter from her husband. "He says that it was really nothing and that now, in effect, it's healed."

"Good for him," Nannerl commented calmly, while Tresel poured boiling soup into her cup. Mother and daughter were sitting at the table, and Frau Mozart had several times exchanged her spoon for the magnifying glass that helped her read; she resigned herself to giving up her soup and devoting herself exclusively to reading.

"Yes, but he's not telling me everything. I mean—if it were serious, do you think he would tell us?"

"I don't have the slightest idea," Nannerl replied. Then she thought about it for a moment. "Probably not. He wouldn't want to worry us."

"There, you see? You've said it, too; it's serious!"

"No, I didn't say that. Calm down, Mama. In any case it's no use torturing yourself. Whatever has happened, from here you can do absolutely nothing about it."

"You certainly know how to comfort a person!"

"He's the one who wanted us to stay home, right?" she said, shrugging her shoulders and raising her eyebrows and the corners of her mouth.

"It's pointless to talk to you," Anna Maria declared in irritation, then she took the cup in her hands and swallowed a mouthful of soup that burned her esophagus. "Tresel!" she cried. "Good heavens, didn't you let it cool a little before serving it?"

"Frau Mozart, it was you who told me to hurry."

"It's true," Nannerl added. "You said you were hungry."

"What's wrong with you two? Are you in league against me?" Frau Mozart was about to launch into a string of remonstrances when Nannerl cut her off with a surprise announcement.

"Mama, I almost forgot to tell you. I've decided to give a concert at court." Then, very calmly, she took the spoon, filled it with soup, blew on it, and swallowed.

Frau Mozart's face was miraculously, suddenly transformed. Her eyebrows widened, her pout dissolved, her lips relaxed, and, her eyes alight with excitement, she exclaimed, "At court? You, sweetheart?"

XXVI.

The news spread rapidly through Salzburg. The good people of the city waited impatiently for the *rentrée* of Maria Anna Walburga Ignatia Mozart, Anna Maria had transformed the bedroom into a dressmaker's atelier, and, meanwhile, Victoria was practicing secretly ten hours a day; she no longer felt pain in her wrists, and between her knuckles small, round, powerful muscles had developed.

"Oh, it looks wonderful on you," Frau Mozart said happily, arranging the muslin around the neckline. "You are really a fashion plate, Nannerl, dear. When you take your bows everyone will see how lovely you are! Isn't it true, Tresel, that she looks like an angel?"

The servant, pouring coffee into the cups, let out a monosyllable open to various interpretations.

"Now make a nice curtsy, a preview, just for me," Anna Maria said and stepped away, admiring again the costly work of the dressmaker, which squeezed the girl's bust like a trap and at the waist opened out over the hips in a puff of yellow taffeta dotted with flowers, and then fell to the floor in an exultation of flounces. To encourage her, the mother clapped and said, "Come, my love, place your hands on the sides of the skirt, lightly, then cross your feet and bend your knees just slightly. And don't forget: smile."

Nannerl followed the instructions with scant interest, remaining as stiff as a pole, but in any case the whalebone stays would have impeded any attempt to bend.

"No, dear, that won't do. You look like a sack of potatoes. Watch me." She positioned herself and then performed an elaborate bow, with a wide smile that, more than anything else, made evident the lack of a pair of premolars. "Luckily you still have all your teeth. Come, try again and let me see them."

With appreciable effort Nannerl repeated the bow, obviously holding her breath, and even managed to smile.

"Excellent, sweetheart. You're a wonder. The baron will die when he sees you."

"Let's hope it happens before he leaves home, so he'll stay there."

"Oh, come. He wouldn't miss it in any case. Or who will read the famous poem?"

Nannerl looked at her. "What poem?"

"The one he wrote for you, you know? 'My Lady Nannerl

in Springtime'! He's supposed to recite it at the beginning of the concert."

"And who gave him permission?" Nannerl asked with some irritation.

"The master of ceremonies, of course! Countess von Esser told me that his proposal had been accepted immediately and with great enthusiasm. It seems odd that you don't know anything about it."

Nervously Nannerl began to take off the dress, and Tresel went to help her.

"And to tell you the truth, there are a couple of other things that seem to me a little odd," Anna Maria continued, scrutinizing her daughter, but she was busy fighting with the laces and didn't notice. "First of all, why haven't you complained that the bust is too tight and you won't be able to play?"

The question left Nannerl nonplussed. She murmured, "Really, it's not so tight."

"Heavens! Only a few years ago you would have been complaining endlessly! And then there's another thing I don't understand."

"What's that?" she asked, somewhat tense.

"Why in the world don't I hear you practicing? I was expecting you to shut yourself in the music room for weeks at a time, and yet you haven't been playing at all."

Instinctively Nannerl hid her hands behind her back, just under Tresel's nose, as she was busy unlacing the corset. With a strained smile she said, "What's the matter, Mama, are you afraid I'll make you look bad?"

"Oh, not at all. You were always wonderful, and you will be again this time, I have no doubt." She went to her and caressed her cheek. "Do what seems best to you, you're the musician, and I don't understand anything about it. Tresel, did you put on the water for the bath?"

"Yes, Frau Mozart, some time ago. Do you want me to check it?"

"No, dear, I'll go. You help Nannerl take off all those things, and hang them up neatly on the mannequin, please." She disappeared through the door. Nannerl, staring out the window, stood still as Tresel undressed her. With surprising audacity, a swallow landed on the windowsill and chirped merrily, but she, absorbed, didn't even hear it. The skirt was spread on the chair, the bustier laced around the wooden torso, the petticoats hanging on hooks, when she heard Tresel's harsh voice.

"You're fond of that girl, eh?"

Nannerl shook herself and looked at Tresel in bewilderment.

"Try to be a little fonder of yourself," the servant said, then brusquely handed her a dressing gown and went out.

XXVII.

The Knights' Hall at the Palace was overflowing, and the final latecomers hurried up the grand staircase in a swish of skirts and clicking of heels, as a few three-cornered hats, slipping out of the careless hands of the owners, rolled down the steps. The local nobility had turned out in its usual fashionable rivalry, in an orgy of colors bright enough to wound the optic nerve. Even Anna Maria, as the esteemed mother of the performer, had been busy: she wore a wine-colored dress embroidered with silver, with a wide neckline adorned with ribbons and braid. It was impressive, but a mere rag compared to the superb toilette of Katharina von Esser, in bright pink with orange insets, the skirt draped with lace and supported by panniers so broad that she had to perform complex maneuvers to get through doorways. The task had been completed, however, and she had spread herself out on a sofa intended for three, occupying it entirely. To speak to her in confidence, Frau Mozart was forced to stand behind her.

"I've already received five new requests for lessons," she murmured in excitement. "You see, Countess? Five, even before the start! After the concert it will be at least three times that."

"My dear, are you really sure it's a good thing?" Countess von Esser asked, pretending to enjoy the perfume of the flower—artificial, of course—that was sewn onto her glove.

"Well, of course. Why, don't you think so?"

"My friend, I can understand the needs of your family, but I wouldn't like Nannerl to be transformed into a sort of vestal of music. At this rate she is in danger of being occupied night and day with her pupils, and completely neglecting her social life. Let's be clear: the baron's patience is not infinite, and if Nannerl insists on refusing him, which sincerely grieves me, we must bow to the inevitable and go in search of someone she likes. Otherwise, we really are in danger of having her beauty wither in solitude. Don't you think?"

Frau Mozart nodded silently as she observed her daughter, who at that moment seemed farther than ever from romantic proposals: she was talking, in fact, with the Reverend Joseph Bullinger. The two were standing near the platform on which the harpsichord stood, and the man of the church had placed his large hands on her shoulders affectionately.

"I am so happy for you, my dearest girl," he said.

"Really, Father?" she said, lowering her head.

"Oh, of course! I was afraid that you had abandoned your gifts forever, and that made me profoundly unhappy. Let me tell you one thing, Nannerl, please. Sacrifice is not always a meritorious act and meant for good; it is so only when it makes us genuinely happy: *quo veraciter beati esse possimus.* And self-punishment has never made anyone happy, my girl."

She was evidently uneasy, and he thought it was because of his preacherly tone.

"You're right; I shouldn't speak to you like that just when you are about to perform. I should be happy for you, and express my good wishes and no more than that. But the truth is I've thought about you a great deal, and until now I haven't had an opportunity to speak to you. I've seen you rather seldom in church."

"It's true, Father, and I'm sorry."

He stopped her with a gesture. "You mustn't ask pardon of me. And in any case I'm certain that from now on things will change. A return to performance is like coming back to life for you; I read it clearly in your aspect and in your more tranquil movements. Now, that's enough. I'm going to sit in the first row. And my attention, my dear, will be all on your art."

He embraced her, and she hid her tense face in his ecclesiastical robe. As soon as he moved to go and take his seat, she turned her back. Her guilty gaze rested on a small door behind the stage, then on the proudly garbed audience assembled there for her, and, finally, on her mother, who, seated in the middle of the room, gestured encouragingly toward her—poor woman. The prince-archbishop had settled himself on the throne, a shriveled old man of power, and inclined his head toward her, the performer, with a benevolent air; beside him was Major d'Ippold, a robin redbreast in his uniform. He, however, avoided looking at her, ostentatiously, perhaps still harboring ill feelings toward her. And if everything went according to plan, the major really would detest her; he would want to run her through with his sword . . . But the chamberlain had already taken his place and was introducing the program. The evening's entertainment was officially beginning, and it was too late for second thoughts. So Nannerl drew up her courage and, in a silence charged with expectation, mounted the stage beside Baron Johann Baptist von Berchtold zu Sonnenburg.

The poet held in his hands a creased parchment, and his magnetic eyes had lost much of their usual mockery, which made him even more handsome. Nannerl sat in a chair at the side while he prepared to make public the verses he had written for her and, with them, the violent attraction he felt for her. He unrolled his parchment and began to read with a surprising lack of inflection.

"My Lady Nannerl in Springtime

Winter are your hands,
locked promises, motionless, tenacious.
Summer is your voice
Of vibrant, quiet gold, and unexpected thunder . . ."

The baron's voice was a steady sensual whisper. Nannerl listened to him, struck in spite of herself by verses so unlike the ones she was by now used to.

"Autumn is your hair,
soft and loose, warm in color.
Springtime is your face,
its fresh scents, a tender glow."

He stopped and rolled up the parchment. The audience remained in bewildered silence.

"That's it, ladies and gentlemen," he said.

There was faint, polite applause; hands clapped without conviction, while a perplexed murmur of voices arose. The only one who exhibited no sign at all was the archbishop, for he had fallen asleep and was snoring lightly.

Katharina nodded to Frau Mozart to come to her. "My dear," she whispered, "I fear that the baron has gone mad. I've never heard anything so awful, without even a rhyme! Maybe your daughter is not completely wrong in refusing him. That man must be mentally unstable."

On the stage the unstable man had gone over to Nannerl, and she was looking at him in a new way. She offered him her hand without even thinking about it, and he took it and, kissing it ardently, noticed the long, uncared-for nails. His expression became skeptical and perplexed: How could Nannerl play, with those claws? They would get caught between the keys and break off; and surely the fingers could not run swiftly nor the pads have the proper sensitivity. She guessed his thoughts, pulled her hand away, and said, "It's time, Baron. If you don't mind . . ."

With those eyes of different colors, Baptist gave her a puzzled look and went to sit in the audience.

Slowly, Nannerl reached the instrument. She raised the lid. She turned to the audience and for an instant didn't move. She distinctly felt her heart beating against her chest; she breathed through dilated nostrils. With all her soul she prayed that things would go well. With all her soul she asked forgiveness for the lie she had told. With all her soul she tried to convince herself that she was acting for the good. After all, what had the Reverend Bullinger said? Giving to our neighbor is a good thing when it makes us happy. And this particular gift had made her happy, up to that moment; and would make her ecstatic, if only God would help Victoria not to be overwhelmed by emotions.

"Now!" she cried, and disappeared into the wings.

The little door at the rear opened and Victoria appeared; in a fraction of a second she had sat down on the stool and was playing intently. But the first part of the piece was drowned out in a roar of dismay, an outcry on the part of counts, dukes, and marquises (on occasion they could become a mob of fishwives). Katharina, however, was openmouthed, mute, and Frau Mozart's head was spinning. The self-discipline of Major d'Ippold vanished in an instant, and in a fury he headed toward the stage, ready to drag his daughter off; then, realizing that he would only create a scandal, he returned to his seat near the throne, but he was on burning coals.

Victoria played with determination and passion; the audience seemed to inspire rather than intimidate her. Nannerl, in the wings, had fallen to her knees and was listening, not looking, and all her mental energies were directed to her student, and if she could she would have urged her on aloud, as she did in the cellar. She would not have interrupted her, however, because there was no need. It was going well. It was going well!

Victoria's father, on the other hand, seemed about to explode. Forced to be still, forced to hide his rage, he squeezed his eyelids and, in an attempt to calm himself, breathed as deeply as he could. And one of those deep breaths struck into his consciousness the memory of she who in life had been so obsessed by music, too much. To the point where she taught her daughter to play even before teaching her to speak. To the point where she was always at home playing and never went out into the light of the sun, so that every time he returned from a mission he found her more haggard. To the point where she died practically on the keyboard, because she had wanted her deathbed to be placed beside the instrument. And yet that vivid memory in Armand was not of death but of life. In Victoria he saw a spark of the woman he had desperately loved, and not only in her body but in her habits, perhaps for the first time; and only in that moment did he understand why his wife had loved not only him but also the piano. Because to penetrate a sheet of music and make it a living thing must be intoxicating. Because to perform in public, something that Monika had seldom been able to do, must be even more exalting: one became a channel of universal emotions capable of transforming an audience into a mass of vibrant humanity. And that was exactly what his daughter was doing at that moment. Armand's eyes shone, and the officer who had never wept in his life was in danger of doing so in front of his subordinates, his superiors, and the archbishop (who, however, continued to snore placidly).

But he did not dissolve in tears, because there was a thunderous ovation, a deafening clapping of hands, a wild mix of cries and praise. "Brava! Bravissima!" And his daughter was sitting with her hands in her lap, she, too, dazed by acclaim that perhaps she thought she didn't deserve. Suddenly the usual Victoria returned, his lively and impulsive girl who was nevertheless timorous and fragile. The spectators rose and applauded her, even Joseph Bullinger, even Frau Mozart, if only in imitation; even His Excellency's two cooks, at the back of the room, jumped up and down, trilling with joy—the least astonished and the most excited.

The noise woke the archbishop with a jerk that banged his old bones against the throne. "How did it go, Major?" he mumbled. "Did Fräulein Mozart play well, as she used to?"

Armand hesitated, embarrassed, and the chamberlain came quickly to his aid: "Very well, Excellency! The public is very satisfied, as you can see for yourself!" And so the decrepit ruler applauded the blurry figure on the stage.

Victoria rose and, rather than move to the front of the stage and thank the audience, went to her teacher in the wings.

"How did I do? How did I do?" she repeated.

Nannerl smiled, filled with emotion. "Very well. No one missed me, Victoria. Be proud of yourself." The girl impetuously embraced her, but she pushed her gently aside. "Come, come. Go and take your bow. You have to be polite to your public." Then her expression became ironic. "But if you don't feel like curtsying, forget it. Believe me, it's not important."

Victoria hurried to the center of the stage and at her appearance the applause grew louder. Nannerl, invisible to the crowd, looked at her affectionately, and for the first time in years felt a peaceful warmth envelop her soul.

Suddenly a hand rested on her shoulder. She turned and was startled at the sight of Armand, whose proud features seemed to have cracked and whose eyes were surprisingly bright. The man said nothing and his emotions were not plain. Of one thing Nannerl was certain: there was no trace of hostility.

"Major, I'm sorry," she murmured, staring at those brown irises, which were large and set in a network of veins. "I didn't want to cause suffering . . . If I had known . . ."

"Call me Armand, that's all," he said, and his face opened in a faint smile. While in the hall the applause continued, the two couldn't take their eyes off each other, bound by an intense, impalpable current of desire and dismay, until a voice startled them.

"I beg your pardon . . . Oh, have I ruined the mood?"

A young man wearing a large plumed hat had come upon them from behind. He planted himself there, staring at them with mocking intrusiveness, while Nannerl turned to one side, confused; she felt her cheeks burning and tried to hide her blush.

"I would like to speak to you, miss, if you don't mind," the young man said. "Or maybe kiss you, seeing that the one who is here, so to speak, doesn't dare. But I don't know if it's suitable. Let me think . . ."

Suddenly he brought his mouth to Nannerl's ear, so close that she could feel his breath, and whispered, "Here forever happy . . ."

"Wolfgang!" she yelled, and embraced him violently. The plumed hat fell onto the stage and rolled down into the first row, as she hugged her brother so hard that it hurt; the contact with his now-adult body seemed to her so strange, but more intense was the joy of having him near.

Armand went silently away. Brother and sister remained enthralled, mute. It was a long embrace accompanied by the fading, finally, of the applause.

Mademoiselle Jeunehomme

I.

"Who was that man in the uniform?"

"No one."

"He must have a name, this no one!"

"What difference does it make to you, Wolf-gang? He's the father of my student."

"So, do the fathers of all your students look at your ass?"

Her brother was very changed. He was still shorter than she was, as he always would be, but he had grown a lot; and apart from that, his manner was very physical, his language was crude, and in his behavior toward her he swung between fierce possessiveness and malicious disparagement. He dressed with extreme care and powdered his face and his hair; he walked proudly along the street, gratified by the reverential greetings that the people of Salzburg addressed to him and his beloved father. Leopold leaned on his wife's arm, a few steps behind; he limped slightly and used a cane. He complained that his leg remained sensitive to changes in temperature, but he did it only to win extra attention from his wife, for in effect he had recovered.

"Italy is full of mediocrity and corruption," he sighed, sitting at the table of the inn beside his son. "To make it possible for Wolfgang to work I had to maneuver in some repellent games of power. I'm glad to be free of them."

"What do you mean?" Anna Maria protested. "In your letters you said it's a marvelous country."

"It is, certainly, but I fear one has to have been born there to deal with its complexity."

At that moment Wolfgang slipped one hand under the table, laid it on Nannerl's thigh, and squeezed, in a gesture between lechery and mockery, and at the same time he whispered, "I love you. I love you so much I'm asking for your hand, and when I have it—I'll put it on my ass!"

She freed herself from his grasp and murmured, "I see the trip was bad for you."

"Oh, I wouldn't say bad. I sank into abysses of lechery. Shall I tell you about it?"

"Children, don't whisper at the table," their mother interrupted. "What were you saying?"

"I was complimenting her on . . . Victoria. That's the girl's name, isn't it, dearest sister?"

"And who is this Victoria?" Leopold asked.

"My student who performed the other night."

"Ah yes, Victoria d'Ippold," he said, nodding. He looked only at the son beside him and the wife opposite; it was as if Nannerl were not present. Who knows, maybe looking diagonally was hard because of his leg. He leaned his head against his chair back and let his memories flow. "That girl's mother was an excellent harpsichordist. I heard her a couple of times, years ago, in private concerts; then she stopped performing because of her uncertain health. Her husband never recovered from the loss. A very sad story."

"So that man in uniform is free!" Wolfgang exclaimed, winking at Nannerl. "And he might even be attractive, if only he were twenty years younger and removed the stick he's got up his ass."

She looked at him furiously while Anna Maria giggled. "Come, don't use bad language, angel."

But he went on. He put his hands around his mouth to create a kind of trumpet and lowered the volume: "The ass beheld by the stick, the stick stuck up the ass . . ."

"Stop it, please," Nannerl hissed, and he said, "I just want to know what's been going on in my absence, since your letters left something to be desired."

"Oh really? Shall we talk about your transcriptions, then?"

"Now stop that, will you! Oh shit!" Anna Maria cried, and raised a hand as if to hit someone, but the host arrived with a carafe of wine and she pretended to be brushing off a fly.

Herr Mozart took a swallow of wine and appeared to appreciate it. Then he clicked his tongue and turned to Nannerl, staring at the glass against the light ostentatiously. "I have only one question. Does Major d'Ippold pay regularly for his daughter's lessons?"

She answered firmly. "So far I've been teaching her for nothing. Now we'll see."

"We'll see—who, dear child?"

"The d'Ippolds and I. Why, does it have to do with anyone else?"

"Yes, of course. As long as you live in my house, you will do as I say."

"As long as I'm the one who's getting paid, I'll do what I think is right!"

Leopold began to get irritated; with clenched fists, he stared at the empty plate in front of him. "Very well. Then you will stop giving lessons completely. Since there's no longer any need. I will return to work and something remunerative will be found at court for Wolfgang. Today I will write to the families of all your students to let them know that you are stopping. Are you happy?"

"But, really, my dear. It would be a pity, don't you think?" Anna Maria intervened timidly. "The two of us have managed, with some effort, to create a position for ourselves in the fashionable world, and it would be a shame to throw it away."

"Now that Wolfgang is here in Salzburg, he will provide us all with a position in the fashionable world. And without the least effort."

The young man seemed satisfied with the direction of the discussion. He took one of Nannerl's hands and touched the ugly nails patiently. "Sister, I think you should reflect on what our dear father says. If you stopped teaching and started giving concerts again, wouldn't that be better?"

"I am a mere provincial music teacher. Have you forgotten?"

"Oh, time passes . . . And we have both grown up. You are better than anyone I've ever met, and even that Victoria is only a dilettante compared to you. You know what I'm going to do? I'll write a concerto for piano and orchestra, just for you! Wouldn't you like to be the first in the world to play it?"

"It would be an incredible honor," she answered with a sarcasm that didn't touch him.

"Shall we order?" Anna Maria urged in a cheery voice and nodded to the host. Then she turned to her husband entreatingly: "My treasure, don't make decisions in a hurry. If Nannerl has given a few lessons without pay, the rest has gone according to your plans, I assure you. She is the best teacher in Salzburg, and her students can be recognized by their taste and the precision of their touch. This is what all the nobility say."

"Who have not heard her play for years," Leopold grumbled.

"And I have my doubts that someone who never plays knows how to teach."

"Theoretically I agree with you," Nannerl declared. "But every rule has its exceptions; and once upon a time you yourself called me exceptional. If you no longer think so—anyway, it doesn't much matter to me."

"Sirrrr!" Frau Mozart cried. The man arrived with a large tray, and the scent of Wiener schnitzel calmed them.

II.

The door of the dark, deserted cellar opened and Victoria's slender silhouette appeared. In the silence she lighted the candelabra and advanced, carrying with her a tremulous sphere of light. Behind her was Nannerl. Protected by the obscurity, she dared to touch the arm of the man who stood uncertainly on the threshold, for he had never been there and was afraid of violating a sanctuary.

"Come," she said gently.

Armand entered and closed the door behind him. That storeroom piled with dilapidated furniture seemed to him truly a sacred place, transformed by the women into a practice room. His astonished gaze traced a circle and stopped on the harpsichord.

Victoria was already on the stool, and Nannerl went to sit beside her. And under the guidance of her teacher, the beloved student began playing a Bach sarabande.

It was a slow dance, in a minor key, composed of broad chords that progressed with poignant mastery and trills that suspended the harmonic resolutions, holding off relief in an unbearable delay. Armand went to the instrument, listening, careful not to make the least noise; he observed, rapt, the faces of the two women, that of Victoria abandoned; Nannerl's more vigilant. Then he walked around the instrument and placed a warm, protective hand on the shoulder of each of them.

Anyone who had seen them would have thought of a small, loving family group. Victoria appeared unaware of the paternal gesture and continued to play calmly, repeating the piece again and again, in an eternal da capo; and each time, she entered into the spirit of the composer more fully and added something of her own in a slight pause or an accent of feeling. Nannerl was, on the other hand, profoundly disturbed by Armand's touch and was thankful that he couldn't see her flaming face.

Slowly the man's hand moved from her shoulder to her neck and then her cheek, and stopped there to savor the contact of her skin, which had grown damp. Breathing through her mouth, then holding her breath, Nannerl closed her eyes and bent her head slightly, enjoying that caress. Eyes closed, she slowly raised her arms and placed her fingers on the keyboard. Softly she caressed the keys while Armand caressed her, without pressing, without her nails touching the ivory and the ebony, without creating the slightest sound.

III.

Those were her hands! Long, appropriately for a tall girl, rounded and strong, with broad fingertips, nimbly producing a succession of notes astonishing for their rapidity and yet their precision. They were hers, Nannerl's. But they were not hers. She was relegated to the audience like an ordinary spectator, and the pianist, known throughout Europe, had attracted to the theater not only the aristocrats of the city but those of the neighboring principalities. And she was good, oh she was good! Her technique was enough for two, and her capacity for emotion, and her interpretative imagination. This is playing! One cannot play better than this. Nannerl saw herself on the stage, the herself she could have become, if only . . . If only what? The young woman even looked like her. Her hair was the same gold color and was done in a style Nannerl liked. Her complexion was pink and white, like hers. In profile, the tip of her nose turned down slightly, just like hers. And the dress was perfect for a concert: it was the one she would have chosen, not too tight in the waist, the sleeves short and not puffed, not too elaborate, because the performer wants to be remembered for her music, not for her wardrobe. And now the concert is over and the pianist rises and bows. Even the bow is perfect. No simpering curtsies or inappropriate batting of eyelashes. Only a measured nod of the head, hands joined at the breast: this is how to say thank you. And then the artist leaves and doesn't return, in spite of the prolonged applause: this is how we keep from confusing ourself with the image others have of us.

"So, how did she seem to you?" Wolfgang asked, rising from his chair and unfurling his legs.

"You want the truth?"

"Obviously."

"I don't think I will ever have the courage to perform after seeing her. Tonight I've had the confirmation that I'm not worth much even as a pianist."

"Do you expect me to contradict you and comfort you?"

"Not at all, Wolfgang."

"Just as well. In any case, if you think you're not worth much, you're not. And as for courage, you've never had any. You've always been towed along behind someone else."

She didn't have time to respond, for Leopold took his son by the arm and led him away. "Into the dressing room. We have to do a little public relations." He turned to his wife and daughter. "Would you like to come, too?"

"If it won't disturb you," Nannerl said angrily.

Herr Mozart ignored the combative tone and hurried on, talking to Wolfgang. "You should write a concerto for this Frenchwoman: it would be an excellent investment in the future."

"Why not? I think it can be done," the young man affirmed, while on his lips appeared a wicked smile. "You know what I hope, more than anything? That she's not as masculine as her name. It would be a real waste, with those long legs."

"Think about paying her some compliments on her artistic gifts and don't worry about the rest." He stopped at the door of the dressing room, made sure that his family looked presentable, assumed an obsequious air, and then knocked.

"Entrez, s'il vous plaît," said a clear voice from inside.

Upon opening the door, the Mozarts were assailed by a profusion of heady scents. The dressing room was overflowing with roses, freesias, lilies, carnations, camellias, arranged in jars, baskets, Chinese vases; bouquets had been placed on the shelves, on the chairs, even on the floor. The artist greeted the new arrivals with a gracious gesture of her arms similar to the opening up of a flower, and Wolfgang felt drawn to her full, shining lips like a bee to a pistil.

Leopold kissed her hand and said in his impeccable French, *"Je suis enchanté, Mademoiselle Jeunehomme."*

"Which in my language means 'young man,'" answered the pianist with a beautiful smile. "Isn't that funny?"

"Your *charme* is delightfully French, my dear mademoiselle. And your fame is certainly inferior to your art."

"Oh, thank you. I know you, too, of course, by reputation—and your son the prodigy." Her eyes were as green as a new shoot and she fixed them on Wolfgang's; he was pervaded by a sexual energy that left no doubts about the femininity of Mademoiselle Jeunehomme.

"It is you who are the prodigy," he said gallantly. "Your fame is certainly inferior to your . . . beauty."

Nannerl had stayed in the doorway, stiffly, and her unease increased as she watched her brother take one of Mademoiselle Jeunehomme's hands and place it on his heart.

"Do you hear these heartbeats?" he said. "During the concert they were in unison with your fingers, as they are at this exact moment."

"Oh how sweet . . . You have a poetic soul, dear Mozart."

"Especially when it's useful," Nannerl said in a whisper, but she was heard. Her parents gave her a furious look; Wolfgang, however, didn't lose his composure.

"Mademoiselle, this is my dear, adored sister, Maria Anna Walburga Ignatia Mozart. Forgive me, ladies, if I neglected to introduce you. Nannerl is also a musician, did you know?"

"Yes, of course," Mademoiselle Jeunehomme answered arrogantly. "I was told that you, too, used to play a little, at one time. Now you teach, yes?" And receiving no response, she again turned her leaf-colored eyes to Wolfgang. "So, my dear, when will you make a nice journey *à Paris*?"

"My brother has already been to Paris," Nannerl interrupted, offended. "We played together for your king, if you don't mind."

The pianist seemed hugely annoyed. "I know. A thousand years ago, if I'm not mistaken, or thereabouts. My dear Walburga, you must understand . . ."

"Nannerl."

"All right, Nannerl, then. You must understand that times have changed. I realize that for a person who lives in a small city, and is merely a teacher, this isn't easy to comprehend; but the world of music is constantly evolving. One doesn't always have to be in the service of some ruler. It's more of a risk, of course, but if things go well, the personal satisfaction is unsurpassed. Am I right, dear Mozart? Wouldn't you like to live in Paris, or even Vienna, I don't know, writing music on commission and not being anyone's slave?"

Leopold was getting alarmed. "Forgive me, Mademoiselle, but it's not clear to me what you're getting at."

"Only to say that a career like that is possible, provided—"

"Provided?" Wolfgang urged her on, curious.

"You have the right contacts. That's all." And she smiled at him again.

He devoured her with his eyes. "Contacts of what type? Close contacts, perhaps? My sweet 'young man,' the idea of close contact with you is delightful."

This game of seduction was at its peak, and the two seemed to be alone in the room. Leopold and Anna Maria felt they were extraneous and so did Nannerl, but she refused to accept it.

"This discussion of contacts is interesting," she declared in a sharp voice. "Now I can see how Mademoiselle has gained her reputation."

Mademoiselle Jeunehomme turned suddenly. "What do you mean?"

"Love for music, of course, but above all for musicians. And for impresarios, patrons, theater directors—who else? Maybe even some governors. A life of love can smooth the path of a career."

"Get out of this room!" the Frenchwoman screamed.

Leopold became a monster. He chased his daughter to the door and gripped her forearms with such force that they turned pale. Meanwhile his wife entreated the pianist: "Mademoiselle, for pity's sake, don't be offended, forgive her—Nannerl didn't mean what she said."

"Out of this room, is that clear?"

"Wait! Please, wait just a moment!" Wolfgang cried in his powerful voice. They fell silent and looked at him. He appeared the least upset; in fact, the situation amused him hugely. "I have a proposal. Why not transform this quarrel into something more interesting?"

"What do you mean?" the pianist asked suspiciously.

"Mademoiselle, I believe that there are duels more productive than verbal ones. And rather than waste a competition with great dramatic potential, I would suggest transferring it to the stage: organizing, that is, a public contest on the piano—between Fräulein Mozart and Mademoiselle Jeunehomme!"

"What a stupid idea!" Nannerl burst out, and tried to free herself from the grip of her father, who restrained her.

The other, however, began to show some interest (if only to oppose her). "A competition between two pianists? It might be interesting. Of course, it would get a good audience."

"Especially if they played your music, Wolfgang," Herr Mozart suggested.

"That doesn't seem necessary, Father. Maybe I could write an introduction, a divertimento, say—a light piece to open the evening."

"And you would perform it yourself, on the violin, with a small orchestra."

"Whatever you think."

Leopold pondered. "Mademoiselle Jeunehomme against Fräulein Mozart. It sounds good. I see it already on the posters."

"I agree!" the Frenchwoman declared. "From my viewpoint, it can be done."

"Perfect!" he exclaimed, in great satisfaction. "How long will you be in town, Mademoiselle?"

"At least till the end of the month."

"The end of the month? I don't know if the theater still has a free night. I'll go and speak to the manager right away."

"Tell him that you're a friend of Countess von Esser and have him give you a discount," Anna Maria whispered.

"Brava, dear wife." And finally he let go of Nannerl's arm, as she preceded him to the door, calling back to Mademoiselle Jeunehomme, "You'll compete by yourself!"

And she vanished into the theater.

IV.

"Did you see what character she has? That's why she plays so well. I wish you had her determination."

"I've thought about it some more. She's just a megalomaniac with big hands. She can roll out a thousand notes in a single minute, but it's pure exhibitionism."

"Keep your voice down," Wolfgang said. The last spectators, leaving, passed the sister and brother putting on their mantle and overcoat. He took her hand and led her away from the door. "If you think you're better than she is, show it."

"But why? Why do you see life as a competition? I have no desire to play 'against' someone."

"With someone, against someone, what's the difference? In my opinion it's simple: you're afraid of losing."

"That's not true."

"Are you sure? Now you live shut up at home, giving lessons to a few girls who don't even know what a note is. You don't do anything else. You don't play anymore, you don't compose. In my view that's the attitude of someone who has a tremendous fear of confrontation."

"It's thanks to the money of those girls that you went to Italy to lead a life of pleasure! So you should speak of them with respect. And of me as well."

"Respect for those people? But are you crazy, Nannerl? And in any case I've never asked you for a thing."

"In words, no, but maybe by your actions you've claimed a lot. And what have you given me in exchange? You couldn't even send me transcriptions of a few songs!"

"Be honest, please. You would have burned those, too."

"You know something? I might have. And you know why? Because it doesn't make sense for me to persist in writing music. No one will publish it. No one will sing it. Who in the world would it matter to?"

"You. Isn't that enough?"

"But I . . . I can't do it anymore by now. I don't have any skills. I've hardly studied at all."

"You know whose style your arias resembled? Antonio Salieri's. Isn't it enough for you to be like the director of the Italian Opera in Vienna?"

"Wolfgang, be serious. No woman composes."

He shrugged his shoulders. "Remember Maria Antonia, the sister of Prince Maximilian? The one who sang your 'Ah, Heaven, what have I done?' in the voice of a cat whose tail is being pulled? Well, she writes operas in the Italian style, right? So there's at least one other in the world."

She was silent for a long time, then she murmured, "You compare me to the sister of a prince? Weren't we the king and queen?"

V.

Countess Katharina Margarethe von Esser was in a bad mood that afternoon. Perhaps she was beginning to realize that her daughter played just as badly as she had at her first lesson. At home she insisted that she practice, and while Barbara obeyed, as soon as her mother left to go visiting, she slammed down the lid of the keyboard and moved on to games that were more fun. Her father had given her a mechanical duck that could squawk, smooth its feathers, peck at its feed, eat it, and even eliminate it; she adored this duck, and fed it cakes made of mud and raisins. Then there was her favorite among her ten dolls, the doll as big as she was, which could wear her clothes, the velvet and brocade skirts, the hoods and hats for going out—but she was inanimate and would never be able to play an instrument, lucky her! For the little countess, the day of her lesson was torture, and she would have done anything to avoid it, but parental dictates were not to be discussed, and so she rebelled by playing even more clumsily than she could, in the hope that her mother, sooner or later, would give up.

Nannerl seemed incapable of listening to her. She was sitting on the sofa beside the countess and, while Katharina nervously fanned herself, her face appeared lost in thought. She could no longer identify her own feelings, which changed continuously between frustration and satisfaction, resolve and a terrible sense of impotence. These were bitter thoughts, so she preferred to keep herself busy with practical duties and work, and avoid them; but if work was fruitless, as in the case of Barbara, she plunged inevitably into an abyss of depression and felt that her life had no meaning.

Suddenly the door opened and two people came in laughing loudly: Wolfgang and Mademoiselle Jeunehomme. They were elbowing and shoving each other, clutching their stomachs in hysterical laughter provoked by who knows what. The presence of Nannerl and the two visitors did not restrain them but, rather, seemed to increase their hilarity. Barbara stopped playing with an uncertain look, and even the countess's fanning missed a beat.

"Excuse me, dear sister." As he spoke, Wolfgang couldn't stop howling. "I'm so sorry, Countess, it's just that . . . that . . ." He was suddenly silent, and placing his hands on Mademoiselle Jeunehomme's hips, he pushed her out of the room. Trying to suffocate a laugh that came out through his nose with a piglike sound, he addressed Barbara: "It's just that we wanted to compliment you on your outstanding musicality."

Then he went out, banging the door.

Katharina's mobile jaw was paralyzed. It was clear as day that the two had been making fun of them, and if good manners had not prohibited her she would certainly have run after them and insulted them. It was Nannerl who tried to get to them: she jumped up and went to the door, opened it, and saw the two at the end of the hall, arm in arm, mocking her, imitating her.

She went back into the room and crossed it rapidly, then turned back, angrily wringing her hands. After a moment Barbara, to whom the interruption hardly mattered, burst out, "What should I do, start again?" Nannerl, continuing to pace, didn't answer, and so, grunting, she began again.

The child's hands seemed to play against each other rather than together. Undoubtedly she did it on purpose. And those two were surely listening, and continuing to mock her and, above all, her teacher. Wolfgang and the Frenchwoman were insolent, cruel brutes, but they were right. Barbara had one indisputable ability: to reduce a small graceful piece of music to something inelegant. What the author had intended was unrecognizable once it passed through her hands. Why was she, a Mozart, forced to endure such an insult? Not one, but a long series of insults. Teaching might make sense in some cases, but otherwise it was pure humiliation, of her professionalism and of her talent; and it was a lie that everyone accepted. Her students in general had little aptitude, and she knew it but couldn't say so to them; even her mother realized it but would never say so, and the parents of the girls themselves were aware of it but kept up the pantomime as a matter of form. And meanwhile Barbara continued to pound on the keys, making sounds that were increasingly intolerable. Now she was playing very loudly, maybe to attract attention or maybe because that was her particular way of mocking the situation. Well, the little countess was the only worthwhile person in that bunch of hypocrites. She hated music and didn't pretend not to. She came only because her idiot mother made her, and she wouldn't dream of letting her think she liked it. She, too, was a victim, just like Nannerl. She had to help free Barbara from her yoke. She had to do something for her at least.

"Good Lord!" Fräulein Mozart cried with as much voice as she could. "You are hopeless, Barbara. You're hopeless for music. You must stop coming to lessons. It's just a waste of time."

The little countess, for the first time since she had known her, smiled at her with immense gratitude and at that moment managed even to seem pretty. Katharina, on the other hand, deeply offended, took the child by the hand, dragged her away, and left the Mozart house, firmly intending never to return.

VI.

"What's between you and that Frenchwoman?"

She had burst into the kitchen, where, by the light of a lamp, in the middle of the night, Wolfgang was transcribing scores. The young man glanced coldly at his sister.

"Nothing. And anyway, what's it to you?" Placidly, he dipped his pen in the ink. "Oh damn, I've made a blot. Would you hand me a clean rag?"

She approached, restless. "Where's the blot?"

She looked at the manuscript, but didn't see it. She saw instead a piano part written in the elegant hand that she knew well and that resembled hers so much, with those slender brackets on the left side of the sheet of paper and the whimsical inclination toward the right of the bar lines. Then, on the upper line of the staff, she could make out a mass of notes, short, close together, which continued for many beats, delineating a section that was complex and intended for effect: a passage for a real virtuoso.

"What are you writing?" she asked, vaguely alarmed.

"A concerto, as you can clearly see. For piano, of course, and then strings, two oboes, two horns. As its title it will have the name of the artist who will perform it in front of six hundred people. Or even more, maybe, let's hope. 'Jeunehomme Concerto.' Don't you think it sounds good? Papa likes it a lot."

She froze, then turned her back and went out. He shouted after her, "Didn't you say you don't want to play anymore? What am I supposed to do, Nannerl? Stop composing to imitate you?"

VII.

In fact there were more than six hundred people. What is more enticing than a local star who writes a concerto, and conducts it, for an international star? All the people of Salzburg identified with Wolfgang and were proud of him and, therefore, of themselves. The foyer of the theater was overflowing, and a frenzied crowd was pushing its way in; a pair of guards was ready to bar the doors to limit the flood. The canniest headed immediately for the orchestra to assure themselves of a seat, and those who could not resist a few moments of gossip were irritated, because the others stepped on their toes. Everyone was there: nobility, bourgeoisie, a few politicians, musician colleagues, amateur players, instrument sellers, the directors of rival theaters, a small group of military men, and then Katharina von Esser, Johann Baptist von Berchtold zu Sonnenburg, the Reverend Bullinger, and even Armand d'Ippold with Victoria.

But Nannerl wasn't there.

Leopold and Anna Maria, clinging to each other, made their way through the throng; he was in the grip of uncontrollable anxiety, as if the concerto were his. "I'm going to make sure that everything is in place. You stay here," he ordered, and disappeared into the hall. Frau Mozart, disoriented, looked around in search of a familiar face; everyone seemed taller than she, and she could distinguish only imposing wigs, necks covered by long hair tied with ribbons, and broad shoulders adorned with insignia. Suddenly a gap opened in the crowd, at the end of which she saw Countess von Esser, with her husband, the count, and another aristocratic couple. Katharina was wearing one of her magnificent outfits, a *robe à l'anglaise* of an ample cut but with narrow panniers: the last word in fashion. Anna Maria, who was wearing the same wine-colored dress she had worn at the court concert, felt she made a poor showing, but she knew that her friend was indulgent toward her lack of means and, with a big smile, joined her. That smile vanished immediately.

"Where is that rude daughter of yours?" the countess addressed her. "Did she stay at home to wallow in her spiteful behavior?"

Frau Mozart tried to ask for an explanation, but her throat was dry. The count looked at her haughtily. "Is this the mother of that Nannerl?" he asked.

"Yes, exactly," the countess said, and turned to her friends. "That woman's daughter is an extremely vulgar girl. She treated my Barbara in an unforgivable fashion, and in front of me! The only thing to say is: those of ignoble birth act ignobly. Let's go, my dears, it's time to take our seats."

And she went off without a glance.

Anna Maria froze as the crowd hurried around her and the foyer emptied. A sensation of humiliation and dismay pressed against her eyelids. She saw a chair and collapsed into it, trying to get control of herself; she took a handkerchief from her purse, closed her eyes, and daubed at them, smudging her makeup. The first thing she saw as she reopened them was a pair of shapely masculine legs sheathed in breeches hemmed at mid-calf by a narrow ribbon. The man knelt down on one knee and took her hands. It was Baptist.

"Your daughter has nothing vulgar about her, Frau Mozart," he said warmly. "And those of noble birth are worth very little, believe me. Nobility can be bought, and genius cannot: that is innate and touches the elect few. And your daughter is among the elect. You know I'm right."

Anna Maria was in danger of bursting into tears again. "Yes, but Nannerl must correct her behavior once and for all. She must, damn it! She mustn't always be so hard with people, or she'll create an emptiness around herself. She'll be a lonely, bitter, mean old maid."

"No, Frau Mozart, don't worry; that will never happen."

"On the contrary. And what if I were not here, what would become of her? I could drop dead unexpectedly for some reason. It could happen anytime, even soon."

"What are you saying, Madame? You are so young!"

Anna Maria touched his carefully shaved cheek in an impulse of maternal gentleness, and whispered, "Baron, you would be the right man for my daughter. It's a real pity."

Then she rose and went wearily into the hall.

She was greeted by the noise of the instruments tuning up, quietly, each on its own. There was not a single empty seat, and people were standing crowded along the walls, but luckily her husband had laid his coat over two seats in the front row. Leopold was on the stage giving some hysterical advice to Wolfgang, who, however, appeared calm and self-assured. An oboist called to him with a question; he went over and pointed to the score with an air of encouragement, then firmly, kindly, pointed his father to his seat.

The moment had arrived. Herr Mozart took his place beside his wife. The musicians stopped tuning their instruments, and silence fell on the audience as well. Mademoiselle Jeunehomme entered, sat down confidently at the piano, bowed her head briefly in concentration, then looked expectantly at the maestro, and Wolfgang, with a decisive gesture, gave the beat.

At the same instant, in the Mozart house, the key clicked in the lock of the piano lid, then dropped on the floor, and was lost under the instrument. The score of the concerto was ready on the music stand; an illicit copy made by Nannerl in secret.

Fräulein Mozart is alone in the music room, as bright as day in the light of lamps and candelabra; she observes her hands, whose nails, finally, are cut short—and she plays. There is no one around her. She can do it. Her family and the entire city are at the theater. No one will ever know. Not even Victoria. Not even Wolfgang. And not Mademoiselle Jeunehomme.

The two pianists play in unison. With the same mastery and the same passion. The same abandon and the same control. The same sweat dripping from pale foreheads onto the keys. The only difference is that Nannerl is alone, while the other is followed by a rapt, attentive audience that sometimes bursts into warm applause in the middle of the piece. Because it's surprising, the "Jeunehomme Concerto." It's something that has never been attempted before, and Nannerl is aware that she would never be able to write such innovative music. But play it, yes. The piano is the protagonist from the opening bars. It plays a dialogue with the audience, creating a counterpoint that excites, a dramatic contrast that draws one into the heart of the action as soon as the curtain is raised. And then that series of embellishments that her brother has set out unequivocally, leaving nothing to the fancy of the interpreter, the most original trills and cadenzas that have ever been imagined; and the second movement, slower and of a shadowy beauty, with passages that seem inspired by a recitative in opera; and, finally, the fast-paced rondeau, with its disconcerting, restful minuetto right in the middle, an oasis in the heart of pure frenzy . . .

And Mademoiselle Jeunehomme makes a tiny stumble. It's strange; maybe she's tired, maybe she had to learn the part too quickly, maybe deep down she's irritated because she would have preferred to elaborate the cadenzas by herself, as she has always done. It's an almost imperceptible mistake, but Wolfgang can't help noticing and can't suppress a grimace. She sees it and becomes more nervous and stumbles again, very slightly. Wolfgang begins to be seriously worried. Even Leopold notices. Let's hope the audience is not aware.

Nannerl, however, proceeds with mastery; she resolves every passage brilliantly, expresses every shade with the power of repressed passion that is just waiting for the moment to burst out. She is no longer herself, no longer the hard, bitter young woman; she is again capable of creating and being moved, of touching the center of her own humanity and making it vibrate, and connecting it to the divine that is in us. But suddenly, unexpectedly, she takes her hands off the keyboard; looking around, she perceives her own anguished solitude, her silence. She jumps up, hurries to the house door, and runs like the wind.

It's far, but she covers the distance in a few minutes. She hasn't put on her wrap, but she doesn't feel the cold. She runs fast, faster and faster, frantic, panting, holding up her skirts, and meanwhile in her mind the orchestra resounds, and it's she, not Mademoiselle Jeunehomme, who is playing the concerto. There is no one in front of the theater, and the door is open. She crosses the foyer, her heart in her throat, just in time to hear the final chords of the rondeau and see the entire city jump to its feet, in a crash of applause and a deafening roar of acclaim.

At that moment, Maria Anna Walburga Ignatia Mozart ceased to live. And, indeed, she might have been a soul without a body, since no one noticed her. She felt minuscule, a nullity, an insect to be crushed underfoot; every man, woman, and child was turned to the stage, shouting, "Brava! Bravissima!" at the Frenchwoman and, "Bravo, Maestro!" at her brother. And she, what was she doing, down in the orchestra? She advanced a few steps, in the confused purpose of jumping onto the stage, but just at that moment her brother and that other woman took each other by the hand and bowed, together: a graceful, harmonious, affectionate bow.

It was the last image she took in before her vision darkened. She turned around and left the hall, dragging her feet, and meanwhile people went on clapping, ignoring her, and she repeated, in a whisper, "Now it's my turn . . ."

The foyer was deserted, and her steps became more and more hesitant. The mirrors on the walls reflected her image into infinity, blurred, distorted, grotesque, until she saw nothing anymore and fell, inert, on the floor.

The applause faded, and the spectators prepared to go home; but first, Armand reached Nannerl. He fell to his knees beside her and laid his head on her chest to listen to her heartbeat, then his fingers on her mouth to feel her breath, and then, not satisfied, he touched the veins of her neck. Reassured, he stopped to steal a glance at that lovely face, defenseless now, the eyes closed, the features relaxed and the lips parted—free of that uselessly severe expression that she loved to put on.

Then the major took Nannerl in his arms and carried her off. No one was in time to see them. Only Baptist: who followed them with his gaze as they went along the deserted street, under a crescent moon.

VIII.

A few drops of water on her forehead, and her eyes opened in the darkness; a shiver ran through her entire body in spite of the cloak that enveloped her—a rough cloak, it must not be hers. She realized that she was lying on the steps of the splashing fountain in the

Residenzplatz, and that her head rested on something solid yet soft; she opened her eyes and recognized Armand's face above her and that the something solid were his thighs.

She sat up with a start.

"Be careful, Fräulein Mozart—don't make sudden movements," the major said solicitously.

What time was it? How long had she been unconscious? What had that man done to her?

"Would you like me to take you home?"

She shook her head.

"Would you like me to bring you some water?"

"Please, be quiet," she murmured, and pulled the cloak tightly around her, curling up her legs. The major nodded; he stopped asking questions and did not even look at her. He sat still, beside her, and she felt that she could not do without that quiet, substantial presence.

After a long silence, she murmured, "Did you like the concert?"

"I'm sorry, I didn't hear you."

She turned to look at him. "I'd like to know if you enjoyed the concert."

"Victoria wanted to go at any cost, and I went with her," he said, shrugging his shoulders. "According to her, the music was marvelous, but the pianist played some wrong notes."

"That's impossible. Victoria must be mistaken," she said submissively, losing her gaze again in the deserted Residenzplatz.

"Nannerl, I don't know if I can ask you, but why did you come only at the end? Was there some problem?"

She seemed not to have heard the question. Her hands were clasped around her knees, and suddenly he took one. It was freezing. "Are you cold?" he asked.

The gesture moved her and she liked it. The major's hands rubbed her hand; their touch was perfect, and they warmed it pleasantly. Nannerl offered him her other hand. The man's fingers seemed to sink into hers and his palms were just the right size to envelop them, like a glove. She had never felt anything like that. She had held the hands of her brother, of her mother, she had taken in hers the hands of her students to examine them, gentlemen had kissed her right hand out of politeness, but that touch, that touch was something utterly different. There was no sweat or sensation of stickiness, no harsh friction or excessive softness, but her skin and the major's seemed made purposely for that mutual contact, seeming to provide for each other nourishment and strength. Who knew if he felt the same sensations. Nannerl lowered her eyes onto that grip and for the first time could observe the man's hands. They were not much bigger than hers; the palm was strong and broad, naturally, but the fingers were not especially long; and the fact that Armand had almost no nails made them shorter. Was it possible that he cut them so close to the root? No, he bit them, out of a nervous habit; this must be the explanation. And not only the nails were cut off, but the skin around them had been pulled away cruelly, leaving red patches and ugly furrows where the flesh of the fingertip should have been pink and healthy.

He had an impulse of shame. "You must be warm by now," he said with some anxiety, and crossed his arms.

"Now it's you who is shivering."

"Not at all. I'm used to the cold. Would you like to go home?"

"What was your wife's name?"

The man stiffened even more and was silent for a long time. "Monika," he murmured, turning his head.

"And what, exactly, did she die of?"

He rose, annoyed. "I think it's time you went home. Your family will be concerned."

"I don't care."

"What would you like to do? Stay here all night?"

"If you don't feel like keeping me company, go on. I can't force you to stay. Besides, Victoria must be worried." She held out the cloak.

With a sigh, he sat down again and the sword he wore at his side hit the step.

"May I see it?" she asked after a moment.

He unsheathed it cautiously and showed it to her, holding it flat. It shone in the moonlight like a mirror.

"Have you ever killed anyone, Major?"

"It's not something to boast of."

"Then you have."

"It's obvious, don't you think? Why are you asking these questions?"

"Doesn't Victoria ever do that?"

The man's expression brightened. "You know her. More than anything, hers are demands. And to her credit, I should say that she always manages to get what she wants, one way or another."

"Does that come from her mother?"

"Please, Fräulein Mozart, I don't wish to discuss that subject."

"I understand. I'm sorry."

Another long silence intervened, but it was less communicative.

"I've never been to your house," Nannerl said timidly. "Where do you live?"

"Not far from here."

"And when you're away, you're not worried about leaving Victoria by herself?"

"My colleagues watch over her. My daughter doesn't take a step that they don't know about."

Nannerl smiled to herself, thinking of Victoria's maneuverings to enter the Palace right under the nose of those colleagues. Then she said, "Victoria wants to be a concert pianist. And I think she has the talent and the perseverance. Don't you?"

"And you, on the other hand, why do you no longer play?"

She had never initiated a game like this: a subtle pricking, with a sort of conscious pleasure, a push, maybe to induce a reaction that might expose the other, maybe just to see where one would end up. End up? Is there something toward which things inevitably tend?

"I think you're right—it's time to go home," Nannerl said and started to rise.

He jumped to his feet and held out his hands in a gesture of protection. Laboriously pushing herself up from her heels, and trying not to trip on her dress, she managed to stand. She was at the top of the steps and he at ground level; it seemed natural to keep moving and so find herself in his arms. They held that embrace for a long time, and though between the two bodies there were many layers of fabric, the thick material of the uniform, the rough stuff of the housedress that she hadn't had time to change, they gave each other warmth, and each felt the beating of the other's heart, and Nannerl knew that a place nicer than that chest did not exist in the world.

"You don't have to come with me," she said, detaching herself and setting off rapidly.

"You don't want my cloak?"

She turned with a half smile. "How would I explain it?"

As she disappeared into a narrow street, Armand reflected that that girl was exceptionally strong and free. A pity that he was about to undertake a long mission to Vienna. Perhaps he could correspond with her, using Victoria as a go-between.

Bitter Interlude

Salzburg, July 23, 1778

Armand, my love,

Never in my life, never, did I want to write this letter, and I've put it off for a long time, occupying myself with a thousand things, even those that I habitually avoid, and those that are not my responsibility, delaying the moment when I would again have to plumb the depths of grief, and feel it more intensely, and draw you, too, into it.

My beloved mother is no more on this earth. A mysterious illness took her from us in a foreign land. We couldn't even have her remains; not even a final caress was granted us, or a final look at the broad face, the smooth forehead, the large, soft body of my mother. The last image I have is of a woman unhappy to leave us, a woman getting reluctantly into a carriage, perhaps aware that she will not return. My mother didn't want to go to Paris with Wolfgang, but in this house, what my father arranges is not discussed.

Do you know what she said to me a moment before closing the window of the carriage? "Don't behave foolishly with the major." Yes, Armand: the last time I heard her voice, my mother spoke to me about you. But what did she mean? Why didn't I ask her then? I'll never know what she meant. Never.

I do know that the moment I heard the news will remain burned in my memory, extended like a rallentando before a da capo, and that it will never stop hammering there painfully: my father staggered and nearly fell, and the Reverend Bullinger had tears in his tired old eyes, and I was in the doorway listening to their whispering, and thinking, It can't be true. My mother died in Paris? And of what, my God, did she die? An internal fever. What is that, an internal fever? An antispasmodic powder was administered, which did no good; two bowlfuls of blood were drained, which didn't get rid of the fever. She died, unconscious, in my brother's arms, the arms of one whom she brought into life. She died as a light dies. Is it really true?

Who was more like me than my mother? Once I would have said Wolfgang! But not anymore. Now that she is no longer among the living, I feel lost and incoherent, as if I could be carried off by the first gust of wind, a tree whose roots have been treacherously pulled out by an evil spirit, a lump of flesh and bone at the foot of that tree, tossed out among the rotting leaves, a rotting leaf itself, and like a leaf, unable to move by its own will.

Your
Nannerl

Linz, July 30, 1778

My sweetest girl!

I shed every tear with you, and urge you to weep, to cry out loud if you feel the need. It's not true, my beloved, that tears are useless: if they were, God would not have given them to us. They are the heart's blood; their flow is synonymous with life. Reading your letter and thinking of your suffering, I myself wept. Now, please, my love, my adored one, grieve with every fiber of your body and soul; sink into the cold mud of sorrow and let it dull you and, yes, immobilize you; then, when you have done so as long as you need to, begin to live again, in the certainty that your good mother would want that and nothing else.

A thousand anguished questions crowd your mind at this moment, I'm sure; I can almost hear them, and I can almost hear your painful search for an answer, the only just answer, the only one that calms you, the only one that allows you to transform your grief into a weapon that can strike, as you have been stricken. Should your father not have sent Frau Mozart to Paris? Did your brother, when she became sick, give her proper care? Could you yourself have opposed your father, though you have never succeeded before, and persuaded him to give up this foolish plan?

Do not indulge in this harmful exercise, my love, I entreat you! My experience of mourning has taught me that no one is responsible. Those who are responsible do not exist, Nannerl. Believe me, my love. Therefore let the painful questions form in you; don't resist, because to combat them can reinforce them. Only, do not seek answers, and in that way, gradually, I guarantee, you will no longer hear their voice.

Maybe each of us is born with a destiny already written, and maybe the death of your good mother has a beneficent purpose in the cosmos that our small minds cannot discern. Be sure, in any case, that she is observing you from Heaven, and that if you are happy she is happy with you; be sure that your mother is beside you at every moment, a loving, invisible presence, watchful and blessed.

Lovingly, your
Armand

———

Salzburg, August 7, 1778

My dearest,

I thank you for your wise and thoughtful words. I have your beautiful letter with me at all times, folded up carefully between the stays of my corset, and in moments of dark despair, in the moments when everything appears empty and meaningless, I read it again, and I embrace it as I would embrace your warm hands. I thank God every day that I met you, Armand. I cannot imagine what my life would be if I hadn't.

Do you think, my beloved, that one can age ten years in a very short time? I fear that that is what is happening to my father. His gestures have become slow, as if controlled by an internal force, and if he takes a step he seems about to fall down; more than once he would have if Tresel or I hadn't been there to catch him. His walking stick has become a necessary support, and it makes a rhythmic, spectral echo through the house (since he stubbornly refuses to go out). He is bent over, like a plant in arid soil, dried up like straw, and his skin has turned gray. He seems lighter, and I know that if I had to, I could carry him without much effort. Complaining of pains in his stomach and in his bones, he does nothing but sit in his chair with a blanket over his legs; he shuts himself in his room and remains motionless and mute for whole days.

Our acquaintances, as soon as the news spread, hurried to visit: the von Essers (the Countess momentarily forgot to hate me and was sympathetic), the Marquis von Rinser (the affectionate father of one of my students, who brought sweets and a basket of flowers)—even Baron Johann Baptist *von Berchtold zu Sonnenburg offered his condolences (his unhappiness, I must admit, was genuine)—but my father wouldn't see anyone. His reaction is really worrying, and I wouldn't have expected it. We are always confident that we know those dear to us thoroughly, but human nature is surprising, don't you think, my love?*

The plan of our life together, Armand, must necessarily be put off. I can't leave my father alone now; I have to wait above all for my brother to return from abroad, and until my father recovers, at least a little. At the moment my place is beside him, and my duty is to take care of him, comfort him, make his life less painful, if possible. As soon as you return, my love, we will, of course, see each other; you will continue to visit this house, and my father will be glad of your presence, I assure you. But for the long-desired epilogue of our love, or, rather, its long-desired beginning, you and I will have to wait again.

Yet the waiting will be sweet, I hope, and not keep us from imagining a time of arrival, a simple religious ceremony, a small, welcoming house where we'll live, you and I, a new family, with Victoria.

Yours more than ever, and forever
Nannerl

———

Linz, August 15, 1778

My beloved,

I've had some news that I hope will cheer you: my duties in the Army may change! I will speak to you in person about the details as soon as possible, but I want you to look forward to it from now on, incorporating it into your images of our future. A position is now being created in which I will no longer be subject to frequent journeys and postings and missions and legations far from home, far from you and from my Victoria; it involves, instead, duties based in Salzburg! You're happy about it, aren't you?

In such circumstances, dearest, our wait will even be more than sweet;

it will be the spice that adds flavor to the meal; it will be (if you allow me an incursion into your territory) the suspension of the harmonic resolution, which, the longer it is wisely delayed, the more satisfying it is to the listener when it does arrive. How do I know these things? And if I told you that Victoria sometimes instructs me? You will be able to do so yourself one day, when we live together, if you want; provided you don't find it humiliating to transmit a crumb of your knowledge to a tone-deaf officer . . . That same man who from this moment swears, adored Nannerl, to love you and protect you every day that comes, and to make you happy as you deserve. To be with you, my love, to be two will be to be infinite and expanded, and to be deeply rooted in the fresh, fertile earth; do not fear— no evil spirit will treacherously dig up the roots, because I will fight it and will win. Ours will be an infinite companionship, an infinite sharing, an infinite linking of thoughts and communion of breath.

Already I see the moment when all this will begin—not tomorrow, my love, but soon. And already I see it . . .

Part Two

The Gallant Officer

I.

Six months before the marriage that was never to be celebrated, Victoria was clambering up the narrow stairs, her pianist's hands carefully lifting her skirts with great care, to reveal delicate blue silk shoes decorated with fake pearls. She reached the landing and straightened her dress, which touched the ground on all sides, including the front, and which that night she would put back in her wardrobe after meticulously brushing it. Then, just as she seized the knocker and prepared to strike, a force pulled it back, the door opened, and like a hulk emerging from the stormy seas, Father Jakob appeared.

"Fräulein d'Ippold, what a pleasure to meet you

close-up," he began, analyzing her aspect with a grimace of irritation. "It has been reported to me, with great courtesy, that my church is not worthy of your musical art."

He was an unctuous priest, who was continuously adjusting his collar, and when he wasn't doing that he was rubbing his hands or ruffling the pages of a worn, well-thumbed Bible that he always carried with him. He shouldn't have taken such poor care of the word of the Lord, but in his opinion that untidiness presented public testimony of how often, and in whatever situation, he consulted the sacred pages.

"Oh hello, Father," Victoria replied uncertainly. "Is it you, then, who is going to officiate?"

"In person. Even if the ceremony, unlike those that I usually perform, will be rather brief: with not many guests, almost all of them soldiers, besides, and no music."

"Perhaps you don't know that the organ is not my instrument. I've never understood anything about pedals."

"So Fräulein Mozart told me."

"I'm preparing a small concert for the wedding reception, and it wouldn't be right to play everywhere."

"This, too, was explained to me in abundant detail. In any case, I don't have time to discuss it further. Your father is inside waiting for you. Good-bye."

He marched past her, trampling the hem of her skirt, and went down the stairs as if he were descending into Avernus.

Many times Victoria thought back on that encounter and wondered whether, if she had complied with the urgent desire for spectacle of that shepherd of souls, it would have been better for all concerned; but it was only an idle exercise (as she later reflected), since the past cannot be rectified, and it's better to concentrate one's energies on the present. As soon as she heard the thud of the street door closing, she went in. The apartment, empty of furniture, had a pleasant smell of paint, and the noise of every footstep echoed from the floor to the walls; so she proceeded on tiptoe, following the voices, and reached the fiancés just at the entrance of the special room.

"I'd like this to be yours," Armand said to Nannerl with some hesitation, but as soon as he saw his daughter, he seemed comforted. "I hope you like the flower patterns on the walls. To me, the whole is altogether like a garden. Your old harpsichord would go perfectly in the center, I think. Herr Mozart has said that we can take it."

"And why not put it in the parlor, next to the piano?" Nannerl asked, in bewilderment.

"Because you'll need a quiet atmosphere, to . . ." He hesitated and looked at his daughter a second time, in search of support, but she didn't help. "To compose," he burst out, quickly adding, "If you want to, my love. What I mean is that, if   if you ever decided to go back to it, this would be the right place."

Nannerl immediately changed the subject. "Tresel is returning to Sankt Gilgen. She wants to live with her son and grandchildren, and it's also time she retired, poor woman. We'll have to find someone else. Where's the maid's room?"

"Next to the kitchen," Victoria said. "And when does Thekla arrive?"

"In time to be my maid of honor. Anyway, she'll write, certainly, to let us know the date."

"You mean your cousin also knows how to write?"

Nannerl did not appear amused. "She's not a genius and she understands nothing about music, but she's not bad," she said. "Do you have some reason for resentment that I don't know about?"

"Not at all! But Thekla is very different from you, I must say. She doesn't even seem related to you."

"Nor do Wolfgang and I seem so anymore, if it comes to that," she murmured. "Here's our room! Isn't it, Armand? Or is this Victoria's?"

"You two decide. I like them both. This is noisier, but it's certainly bigger."

It was also the more beautiful, and here the painter had been

particularly inspired. The vaulted ceiling was sky blue, with a scattering of soft clouds like cotton; a group of plump putti seemed about to
throw down handfuls of flowers and cover the three of them with
petals. The walls were a milky white, and in the corners the artist had
demonstrated his real talent, drawing bunches of climbing vines
sprinkled with roses but no thorns; the floor was the color of a green
meadow, making one wish to take off one's shoes and go barefoot.
Nannerl went to the center and turned in a circle, her arms locked
tightly around her: Why had Armand brought up that subject? Better
not to think about it or risk discussing it. He was here, in his eternal
uniform, and she couldn't wait to tear it off him and pinch and caress
and bite the solidity of his body. And soon, in that very room, or the
other, she would taste the earthly delights that take place between hus-
bands and wives. Only at that moment would she truly begin to live.
How long would she live still? Another thirty years, perhaps. She had
spent half her time on earth in attempts at affirmation, detachment,
evasion: the new condition that was opening up to her was not a flight
but an initiation.

From the window came the sound of an approaching carriage.
The room really was noisy, and at that moment Victoria hoped that
Nannerl would choose it. But she said nothing, opened the shutters
and looked out: along the river a royal carriage proceeded, large and
decorated with gold, drawn by six horses, preceded and followed by
a troop of guards. Princess Maria Antonia, sister of Maximilian III,
was making an official visit to Salzburg.

Armand came over to her. "There is an editor . . . who would like
to publish your music."

II.

"You have to find the courage to expose yourself or you'll never know
if you're really worth something," Wolfgang said, jumping about the

parlor of the Mozart house. "It's time, Nannerl, it's time to let your creativity emerge. The conditions are all in place!"

"I don't want people to be able to buy my music," Nannerl said. "It's as if they could look inside me."

"Nonsense. You really wouldn't like to know that someone, somewhere in the world, is interpreting a piece of yours?"

"I don't need that sort of banal satisfaction. It's not for me."

"Really? Dear sister, you can fool yourself as long as you like, but you don't fool me: you're just afraid that someone will tell you your music isn't any good."

Armand stepped forward, showing off his diplomatic skill. "Excuse me, that's not possible, do you think, Wolfgang? Nannerl's talent and your teaching cannot but produce excellent results."

"My teaching? Ah, then I am to help her compose! You've organized everything, eh, Colonel d'Ippold? Your friend the publisher, the mentor . . . I really am ecstatic—you're the man with marvelous schemes," he declared, while his gaze turned sardonic. "It must be an effect of the stick you've got up your a—"

"Will you stop it?" Nannerl burst out.

"I humbly beg your pardon. I didn't mean to insult your fiancé; besides, he knows how congenial he is to me." He turned and stuck his tongue out so that it touched his chin; it was seen and, to keep things peaceful, ignored. "In fact, he is the perfect man, I daresay," he went on, wandering about the room. "He loves you, he respects you, he stimulates you, he prepares the ground for you—and by the way, dear future brother-in-law, what is the name of this publisher?"

"Alois Flatscher," Armand answered in a low voice.

"Flatscher? Odd, I've never heard of him. Whom has he published?"

"Various authors. In any case, if you don't mind, I would prefer to take care of the matter myself, in all its aspects, except the musical, of course, which I leave to you two."

"Well, whatever you like," Wolfgang said, shrugging.

"Thank you very much. And now would you mind leaving us alone just for a moment?"

"Oh, you want me out of the way? No problem, I'm going!" he said with mock disappointment, reaching the doorway in a single leap. An instant before going out, he turned: "If you kiss and start slobbering, just remember to clean up."

And he slammed the door.

In the silence, Armand sat down beside Nannerl. Defeated, hurt, she murmured, "I haven't composed for years. I wouldn't even know where to begin."

"Write music for me: it would make me happy and proud."

This alone might impel her to let what was buried in her, that special part, reemerge. Tempted, she said, "Yes, but what kind? Something for piano, or arias, or what? Could I speak to him, this Herr Flatscher?"

"There's no need; and be certain that whatever you write, he'll publish it."

"But why would he publish my music? What does he know about me? He's never even met me."

"Don't worry about that," he said gently. "You write what you like, what you've always loved. An opera in the Italian style is always popular; you could attempt that."

"A whole opera? I could never do it."

"Why not? You have talent, and passion, and intelligence. You're just as good as that Antonio Salieri who is so talked about, believe me!"

III.

Cousin Thekla from Augsburg was neither pretty nor distinguished nor refined. She was, in fact, excessive in every aspect, even more than Wolfgang; but she was liked by others, thanks to a knowing, childish cleverness. She leaped down from the carriage, threw herself on her cousin, and enfolded him in hands, feet, arms, legs, and knees, kissing his forehead and his hastily shaved cheeks; bits of beard pricked her lips, but she didn't mind at all and continued to plant kisses while he, half suffocated, laughed.

"Wolfgang! I'm so happy happy happy to see you again! You, more than anyone: you know you're my favorite, little Wolfgang. Don't be offended, uncle."

In the doorway was Leopold Mozart, limping and bad-tempered. "I've been waiting three hours for you," he burst out in a cracked voice. "Did you stop to play along the way?"

"Forgive me, please, dear, kind uncle," she answered, embracing him so enthusiastically that she was in danger of breaking his ribs. Suddenly she detached herself and cried, with a hop, "Where's Nannerl? I have to show her my maid of honor dress!"

Fräulein Mozart was at the window, and she gazed at the scene without seeing it; she didn't look out, she didn't move the curtain aside or make any gesture of greeting. She had in her hands a large volume; she held her place with a finger. It was a volume that had been read, reread, and underlined, not by her but by her brother; amid the words, musical lines had been inserted with examples of harmonic solutions. She opened it and attentively reread a passage, then, thoughtfully, closed it.

IV.

"Why isn't your congenial fiancé here at the concert?"

"Because I asked him to stay home, and his daughter with him."

"You told him not to come? And he agreed without protest?" Wolfgang asked, widening his eyes.

"He, yes. Only Victoria expressed some objections."

"I must correct myself: Armand is not the perfect man but the perfect imbecile. He does nothing but indulge you, even when your requests are ridiculous!"

"My relations with him don't concern you."

"But your behavior does, if you don't mind. Can you explain what annoyance the d'Ippolds would cause you?"

"The same as you. Go sit down and don't bother me."

"Do you think you'll arrive at a spiritual state if you listen to the princess's arias in solitude? Relax and enjoy the evening, Nannerl. It's the best way to get something productive out of it."

"I will as soon as you get lost!" she burst out, then went to the table where the refreshments had been laid out, took a glass of wine, and drained it in two gulps.

The most eager spectators began to disappear in the direction of the *salone,* a procession of bright fabrics that narrowed into a funnel to pass through the archway and then scattered among the rows of seats. Timidly, Fräulein Mozart crouched in the shadow cast by a column: in front of her she could see a section of the audience, and right at the back, on the dais beside the archbishop, was Princess Maria Antonia, looking just as she had when Nannerl had met her at the court of Munich—perhaps she was even wearing the same dress. She didn't seem at all aged. She was surely one of those creatures who when they are young seem old, arousing the pity of their peers and the desperation of their mothers; yet at a certain point they stop, and while for everyone else time runs inexorably onward, their faces show not a wrinkle more than they did in youth. Perhaps only a little arthritic, she waited for the evening in her honor to begin: a selection of her arias was to be interpreted by a singer who, once known above all for her breasts, had, as these grew old (since she was of a normal species), shrewdly replaced them with a refinement of her artistic gifts: Paulina Eleonora Gellert.

Suddenly Nannerl found herself completely alone, while the last few spectators went to sit down, and holding the empty glass, she began to walk in front of the doorway, which a page would soon close. Servants were clearing the remains of the refreshments, like stagehands who pick up the props in the interval between two acts;

they knew her and paid no attention to her, and this pleased her. Slowly she went over to the table and, noticing an untouched glass of wine, exchanged her own for it. "To your health," one of the servants said, in a friendly manner.

From the entrance to the concert hall the page called to her: "What are you doing, Fräulein Mozart? Would you like to come in or not?"

She looked at the waiter timidly, as if with the air of asking advice, but he shrugged. Then she went to the page and offered him the glass: "Would you like it?" Without waiting for an answer she thrust it into his hand, to his astonishment, and went into the music room.

She remained standing at the back, against the wall, for the entire concert. She saw her father in the first row turning to look for her, and her brother, sitting beside Thekla, gesturing to her to join them; but she ignored them. She didn't know the princess's arias, since she had never heard them and the scores were not in circulation; they had never been printed, and this was their first public performance in Salzburg. At first it seemed to her that they were nothing special, and rather than listening she smiled to herself at the soprano's affected movements; but gradually she was able to abandon her critical attitude and let the sounds take possession of her, and she began to appreciate the freshness of the melodies and the rather clever fusion of music and words. Suddenly she opened her purse, took out a notebook and pencil, and quickly made a note; as she listened, she chewed on the end of the pencil, and then, with an automatic gesture, she went on writing, with increasing excitement, until, by the end of the last piece, not a single line was left blank.

She put the notebook in her purse, hurried out of the hall even before the applause began, and sped home. Her heart felt light and her lips softened in a gentle smile. It seemed to her that she had become a girl again; it seemed to her that she could be a girl again, if only she wanted to, if only she were allowed to touch again lost emotions. It was no more than a small action of the mind, an action as simple as snapping your fingers, and much more pleasant; and if she had known that it was so simple and pleasant, she wouldn't have wasted years of life in—no, in fact nothing, nothing had been wasted. From that moment on every past experience would be transfigured and reinvented because, as her brother rightly said, the time had come to let her creativity emerge.

She took off her coat, grabbed a candlestick, and went rapidly through the dark rooms; she stopped at a door, knocked, and whispered, "Are you still awake?"

She burst in before getting a response. Tresel, the ancient and tremulous Tresel, was in her nightgown, sitting on her bed.

"I want to compose an opera," she announced. "A whole opera! *The Gallant Officer*. I'm going to dedicate it to Armand!"

In a deep voice, the servant commented, "It's about time." Then she lay down and put out the lamp.

V.

The truth was that Tresel had never really liked the d'Ippolds, and didn't look favorably upon the marriage. Until the moment she left the Mozart household, she continued to work with the stubborn energy of a far younger woman; she cleaned, shopped, cooked, and washed the clothes. One laundry day she spoke openly to Nannerl. The cauldron was filled to the brim with hot, cloudy water, and using a big wooden spoon, she pushed the gray clothes toward the bottom and dragged them up, and again crushed them down to the bottom. There was an odor of dirty water, of boiled staleness, and the steam lay on her white hair and further reddened her red-veined cheeks. Under her armpits were two dark stains, and from her forehead, from time to time, a drop of sweat fell into the pot, mixing with the old odors of her masters, and to Fräulein Mozart it seemed that she herself was in the big pot, mixed with the sheets, and that, with that spoon, the servant was beating her.

"I know what you think," she stated. "That, considering the daughter he's got, he must not be much of a man. It's true, right?"

Tresel ran the back of her gnarled hand over her forehead and returned to mixing.

"I forgave Victoria long ago for stealing my score," Nannerl insisted. "It's an old story. Have you not yet forgotten it?"

Tresel confined herself to shaking her head lightly, as if before a child too silly or too stubborn to understand the most obvious thing. Then she stirred up the coals, because the fire was slowly going out, and cautiously took a little water out of the vat, which she would use for the next washing or for the bath. And meanwhile she murmured, "You're wrong. The girl is the least of my worries."

"Then, what's wrong?"

She gave her a swift, penetrating glance. "He's not the man for you. That's what's wrong."

"But what do you know about it? You hardly know him!"

The maid ended the conversation by turning her back: if Nannerl didn't want her opinion, she shouldn't ask for it. Nannerl, however, circled around her: "You can't leave me like that. If you begin to say something, you have to finish—is that clear?"

"What do you love about him?"

"A lot of things."

"No, on the contrary. One only: the fact that he is unhappy."

"What do you mean, Tresel?"

"Just that. The solitary warrior, the dead wife, a man who goes away and you never know if he'll return. All nonsense. It shouldn't be grief that leads you to a man but joy. Now, go on, for goodness' sake, or I will never finish this laundry!"

VI.

There was a strong core in Nannerl, at least at that time, in her chest; you could compare it to a pulsing sphere or a giant bubble; that core was present in every circumstance, and contained her true identity. If she became conscious of it and let the original melodies enclosed in it emerge, she felt the flowering of an emotion so overwhelming that it broke down every certainty that bound her to life; so she tried to take refuge in roads already traveled, in predetermined designs, and yet, obscurely, she knew that an attempt so inauthentic was destined to fail. And so she wasn't satisfied with what she created, and found confirmation that what she created had no value and she, as creator, even less.

Nannerl rose in the night, walked around the instrument, sat down, and tried incessantly, uselessly, to settle that inner conflict. She examined the notes she had made at the princess's concert and compared them with her work, asking herself what, precisely, was imperfect in it; perhaps that passage . . . She played it with her left hand, rewriting swiftly with her right and filling the piece of paper with marks; then she took another sheet and began again, changing something, changing many things, changing everything, and finally, in a burst of anger, she scribbled all over it and left the music room.

The solution must be in one of those treatises of Wolfgang's. Or perhaps, rather than of a solution, one should speak of comfort, since Nannerl desired above all some authority to tell her that she was proceeding as she should. She went into her brother's room, rummaged among his books, found one that seemed relevant to her case, and began to read it avidly, in the light of the lamp. But gradually she began to feel sleepy, more as an escape from torment than as a real physical need; and as she turned the pages she wondered if it would not be better to put it off, and yield to that oblivion.

Father, son, and cousin came home from the Palace very late. "Luckily there was the reception," Thekla burst out, taking off her coat, "otherwise the evening would have been as dull as a funeral. But why did Nannerl leave? I mean, she should come and have some fun with us, until she's married!"

"She'll have fun afterward, you can be sure," Wolfgang said, and the two laughed maliciously. Thekla's laugh was a sharp, skull-piercing "Heh, heh, heh."

"Silence, children. Respect the sleep of others, and mine above all," Herr Mozart said, and went to bed.

As soon as he turned the corner, the position of the two cousins became more intimate. Wolfgang slipped an arm around her waist; she placed one hand on his buttocks, and thus entwined, silent and furtive, they reached Wolfgang's room. Light filtered out from the half-closed door; he opened it softly and was greatly surprised to find Nannerl asleep on his table, her face resting on locked arms, her back rising and falling in the regular rhythm of her breath.

"What do we do now?" Thekla whispered. "Damn your sister!"

"Go to your room," Wolfgang said. "I'll take care of her."

"Come on; you promised to spend the night with me."

"We can't do it every night; it's not prudent, pretty little cousin. Go on, go to beddie."

He gave her a kiss on the lips, and she, growing passionate, pushed her tongue deep in his mouth and lowered her hands along his body; but he jumped back, stifling a laugh, and sent her off with a pat on the rear.

When he turned, his heart skipped a beat: his sister, sitting straight up against the chair back, was staring at him unkindly.

"I ought to keep a catalogue of your conquests," she said. "But this is unforgivable. Never touch her again, if you don't want Papa to know, and also uncle."

And she left the room. Wolfgang snorted: how predictable!

VII.

"May I come in? Herr Mozart, I've brought your fruit salad."

"What did you put in it, Tresel?" he wailed in response.

"Only apples and pears, as you asked."

"And how much sugar?"

"Two spoonfuls, as usual."

"It's too much, for goodness' sake. Don't you know sugar can go to your head?"

Periodically Leopold went to bed complaining of nonexistent troubles and tormenting Tresel with obsessive requests for food: for that alone, she couldn't wait to return to her village. Once, the broccoli had kept him from sleeping because it was too heavy; another time it was the chicken breast that caused his insomnia, and the evening infusion mustn't be too strong or, because of a supernatural bond between the herbs and his knees, he wouldn't be able to walk correctly.

With a glance of understanding at the servant, Nannerl took the bowl. "Let's put it here on the table, then if you get hungry we'll see, all right, Father? Thank you, Tresel. You can go."

And Nannerl began reading again, as he closed his eyes and prepared to listen. It was a historical essay, ponderous and monotonous as water dripping into a basin, and Nannerl's low voice made it, in part intentionally, soporific; in a technique that was by now well practiced, she gradually slowed her diction, made her voice softer, and even pretended a yawn so that her father might be induced to imitate her, but that day he was in a strange mood, and certain small movements of his hands and nervous contractions of his lips signaled that he hadn't the least intention of sleeping. Nannerl was impatient, eager to go and work on her opera, so when she finished the long, eternally long, chapter, she laid down the book and with a discreet rustling of skirts tried, very quietly, to leave the room.

"Who will write the requiem for my funeral?" Herr Mozart muttered suddenly.

Nannerl turned. "What did you say, Papa?"

He opened his eyelids and looked at her: "For my funeral I want a proper requiem!"

"But why are you having such gloomy thoughts?" she said calmly, returning to his side. "You'll live to be at least a hundred. You'll see. You'll bury me, Wolfgang, and our children, if we have any."

"I want you to compose it."

She didn't know whether to laugh or take him seriously. "But, really, wouldn't it be better if Wolfgang did it?"

"No. You have to do it."

Having spoken he reached out his arm, took the bowl of fruit, and ate it with the greed of a child. Nannerl looked at him in astonishment while the old man swallowed the fruit and noisily drank the juice and licked the last grains of sugar from his fingertips, and then she rushed out and closed the door and had to lean against the wall.

VIII.

" 'I am grateful for your hand'—the melody of this aria is remarkable, Nannerl. Fresh, immediate, and with a passage of restlessness that emerges here, in the central part, to dissolve in the joy of a surprising finale. Compliments."

"Thank you, Wolfgang," she said, continuing to transcribe.

"But who wrote the text?"

"I did."

"What do you mean?"

"I wrote it. I wrote the words and the music together."

Wolfgang was silent for a long time. Her face was bent obstinately over the scores, and the scratching of pen on paper was the only sound in the room. Then, staring at her, he asked, "Do you intend to write the whole libretto?"

"I've already done it, in part."

"And—don't you think that's too ambitious? I think you should demonstrate your compositional ability, not literary. It's an entirely different skill."

"I couldn't find a libretto that satisfied me."

"But what is the subject of the drama, if I may ask?"

"The subject is Armand."

After another, very long silence, he said, "It seems to me a little thin."

"To me, however, it seems more than sufficient! And in any case, Wolfgang, I want to talk about composition, not dramaturgy, if you don't mind."

"At your service, my queen," he said with a sneer, and threw the scores down in front of her. Then, in a torrent, he spoke: "Let's start with this aria: it's the only one in which you haven't drowned in the myth of your own perfection. Because your problem, Nannerl, is that you don't accept your mistakes, or those of others. You personally never make any, or at least so you think; and if you made one, you would try to forget it."

She glanced at him coldly, but he was concentrating too hard to notice.

"Maybe the subject inspired you, or belongs to you more than others," he continued, "or maybe when you wrote it you weren't asking yourself anxious questions; or for an instant you forgot yourself, thank God. In fact, this aria is good because it's sincere and technically imperfect."

"Where is the flaw?" she exclaimed.

"There, you see? You have to understand, Nannerl, that the search for perfection leads nowhere. You have to write in a more mindless way; or be clever, if you like, but imperfect. You have to stop wasting your days staring at the wall and the white sheet of paper overcome by the pressing fear of not succeeding, because the truth is, Nannerl, that if you forgot your fear you would work better, and much faster."

She felt terribly tired, suddenly, and no longer knew what to think. It was true. She, too, particularly liked "I am grateful for your hand," and couldn't figure out the reason. "And what about the rest?" she asked weakly.

"Precise, faultless—and rather obvious. You remember what Christian Bach said?"

The notes swam before her eyes.

"He said that technique is the means, not the end; it's what allows us to express passion. I see here only technique, Nannerl. Your passion isn't there. Where did you put it?"

IX.

Victoria had been bold. She was wearing the short costume of an Amazon, and the strap of the quiver over her shoulder separated her breasts to unusually provocative effect; her father wasn't at all happy about it and had tried to send her home to put on something more chaste, but she paid no attention to him. There were hundreds of guests at the party, and not all were in costume, but there was no one who didn't wear at least a mask; and concealing their identities, the people of Salzburg, the nobility and the bourgeoisie, could play at not recognizing one another, at courting the wrong person, to then be undeceived and retrace their steps, with pretended, amused outrage. Armand, however, wore neither costume nor mask, in order not to seem ridiculous in the eyes of his colleagues or himself, and in his impressive colonel's uniform he skirted the dancing area on the arms of his women, moving almost in time with the music.

Withered as a fruit forgotten in the sun, Katharina Margarethe von Esser followed them with a scornful glance.

"So the young Amazon is the famous d'Ippold girl," the count whispered.

"Yes. But she is too attractive to be a pianist, don't you think, my dear? Men look at her rather than listen to her, and women, too, but with less pleasure."

"Apart from Nannerl Mozart. That girl is her protégée."

The countess stared disapprovingly at the Marquis von Rinser, who had just joined the conversation and therefore aborted her very interesting disquisition on the differences between the sexes. "Please, do not utter that name in my presence. I say no more."

The count began hinting vigorously to the marquis that he should drop the subject, but Rinser, because of the amount of alcohol he had drunk, was oblivious and asked, "Why not? Nannerl is a fine teacher."

"Oh, do you think? I found the exact contrary, to tell you the truth. And I speak from experience, since it is certainly not my habit to express judgments not supported by concrete facts. If I hadn't personally been the witness, not to mention the victim, of a serious breach of manners on the part of that woman, who deserves to spend the rest of her existence in a place where she can do no more harm, I would never permit myself to say what I say, dear Marquis. It's sufficient to know that my Barbara has refused to get near a keyboard, thanks exclusively to that so-called fine teacher, and that any hope of giving my daughter a proper upbringing has been thwarted, and forever. Further, I will tell you that, in my infinite generosity, I had found for that woman, whose name I continue not to mention in order not to waste my breath, a suitor of high quality, a man of our milieu (here, too, I name no names, but out of discretion); and she, without the least respect for me or for him, rejected him, and in a rude and vulgar manner. And now she is going to marry that wretched man she found on her own; not that the celebration of a marriage not arranged by me is in itself a problem, but I am certain, absolutely certain, that my good, dear friend Frau Mozàrt, who unfortunately is no longer with us, would not have approved of that marriage. And I am even more certain that from Heaven above, where Anna Maria is, she looks down at her daughter and her heart swells with grief for yet another blunder that that girl is about to commit. I will conclude, Marquis, by calling your attention to the ancient Roman costume that the person in question is wearing: don't you think, really, it is a genuine insult?"

Rinser went off muttering who knows what, his head in a whirl, and collapsed in an armchair.

Meanwhile the ancient Roman was alone amid the crowd, and uneasily she observed Wolfgang and Thekla, shepherd and peasant girl, transform the *contredanse* into a ballet of rustic seduction and disappear laughing through an archway. Armand had been taken off by a captain, and Nannerl's father was reclining on a sofa, among the cushions, a look of annoyance on his face. She decided to get him something to drink and, passing a trio of red-faced men, approached the refreshment table.

"You're getting all that money for a copper-plate printing?" said one of the three. "My dear Flatscher, you make me think I'm in the wrong business!"

"With all due respect," the other answered caustically, "you continue to work in fabrics, and I will stay in publishing. It will be better for us both."

Nannerl quickly turned back. "Excuse me, are you Herr Flatscher? Alois Flatscher, the publisher?"

"You are not only rich but famous, too, it seems," the dry goods merchant said, giving him a pat on the stomach. "So, am I right or not, to say I've done the wrong thing in life?"

"Stop it and go to hell!" Flatscher exclaimed. Then, politely, he kissed the hand of the unknown woman. "Alois Flatscher in person, at your service. Compliments on your costume, Fräulein, I would say that it is scrupulously faithful to the images that have been handed down to us."

"Compliments to you . . . that is, I meant . . . thank you. I am Maria Anna Walburga Ignatia Mozart. I was so eager to meet you."

"I am almost . . . almost beginning to envy you, too, Flatscher," said the third man, with a sneering laugh.

The publisher seemed not to understand why that girl was giving him such a radiant smile.

"You don't know who I am?" Nannerl asked. "And if I say to you *The Gallant Officer*, nothing comes to mind?"

"Please forgive me, Fräulein, but I'm afraid I don't know what you're talking about."

"But how is it possible? Colonel d'Ippold says that you are eager to see the manuscript." She looked around. "He was here himself, a moment ago."

"Ah, the colonel. Of course. Frankly, what I am eager to see is the last installment of the money he owes me."

Nannerl was speechless.

"Quite a man, that army officer," Flatscher said to the other two. "He spends a fortune to publish the first opera of his dear fiancée. He's bankrupting himself, literally, I'd say, eh?"

"Now I'm beginning to find you repellent," the merchant said. "You publish amateurs for a high price?"

Suddenly the noise of the room became painful to Nannerl's ears and her ego. She left the three businessmen and leaned against the back of a divan, then looked around, in every direction, in search of her fiancé; he wasn't there, nor could she see anyone of her family, only a formless herd of multicolored strangers, a crowd that was diverse yet all the same, which made her feel more alone than if she had been in a cell. There he was! She made her way, pushing and shoving. She wanted to speak to him right away, but as she drew closer, she saw that the officer was short with white hair—he was another colonel, not he, not her man. Suddenly a group of revelers carried her away into a new room, and then another; a girl in an Oriental costume took her by the hand and dragged her, laughing and shouting, and she was too weak or too defeated to resist, and suddenly she was in an empty room and didn't know where they had all gone; she couldn't even hear the music of the orchestra that would indicate the way back. She wandered through deserted rooms filled with furniture, pictures, and carpets, all different; she opened door after door—how could she be lost? There—a corridor with a door at the end, and that door will lead to the ballroom, directly or not. It must be so. She opened it . . .

A man and a woman were making love. Or something like that, something she imagined was making love. He was almost completely dressed. A shepherd. It was Wolfgang.

Too caught up, neither he nor the girl—Thekla, certainly—noticed her, and she stood on the threshold, disturbed and fascinated, curious and horrified, and hadn't the courage to leave or to make her presence known. This was sex? It seemed something clandestine, rapid and stolen. The two were lying on a chaise longue. Thekla's face wasn't visible. Nothing of her was visible, for he was on top of her and covered her with his body and his cloak. Only her voice could be heard. They were not words but sighs that were exactly in time with the thrusts of her brother's groin. But they were strange sighs—were they pain or pleasure? They seemed muffled—could he possibly be covering her lips with his hand? That would be cruel! He wasn't sighing, no; he wasn't emitting sounds, but the fascinating movement of his buttocks and thighs continued, an impetuous motion, a desirable motion. Enough. This is morbid. She had to go right away. And as she was thinking that she had to go, she went in, whispering, "Wolfgang, Thekla . . ."

It wasn't Thekla's face beneath Wolfgang's, or the costume of a peasant girl partly covering the body. The costume was that of an Amazon, and the face was Victoria's.

"No!" Nannerl cried. "No, Wolfgang!"

Wolfgang jumped up, away from his lover, and as she stood up, they both awkwardly adjusted their clothes. That silence, that tragic silence was more deafening than a full orchestra. Nannerl was transformed into a statue of wax; Victoria and Wolfgang waited for a reaction from her, a terrible reaction, which inexplicably didn't come. She was trembling, her lips parted, but her gaze, fixed on them, didn't see them, because she no longer saw anything around her.

Then, light as a leaf, she turned and went out of the room. She closed the door carefully, until the latch clicked, and with her open hand she lightly caressed the knob. Then she smoothed her ancient Roman costume with delicate touches and began walking. When she was halfway down the corridor she saw a butler passing. "Excuse me," she said. Her voice was that of a child. "Could you show me the way out, please? I was following an engaged couple, but I lost them."

The butler led her, and she went straight home, without saying good-bye to anyone. She fell into her bed, stunned, and fell into a long, heavy sleep, which left her bewildered in the morning, and in the grip of a strange anxiety.

X.

Victoria, too, crept home that night, tore off her dress, and crushed it in the bottom of a drawer. She took a cloth, dipped it in the basin, and scrubbed her chest, arms, and legs; the rough gestures scratched the skin and turned it red. She got in bed and a moment later heard her father returning from the party. His steps, his movements, were hesitant. His silhouette appeared in the doorway.

"What happened, Victoria?"

"I don't feel well, I'm sorry," she murmured.

"You all disappeared suddenly."

"Nannerl brought me home, then she left."

"She came with you here alone?"

"Yes . . . My head is splitting . . . I can't even speak. Every sound is like thunder."

He approached on tiptoe and said gently, "Can I do something?"

"No, thank you. I'm sure I'll feel better tomorrow."

"Rest, then," he said, and closed the door.

She didn't rest at all. To say that she was sorry is to say nothing; Victoria was filled with shame, imagining a grim future in which Nannerl would never speak to her and, on the other hand, would tell Armand everything. He would be furious and would insist on a reparatory marriage . . . Marry Wolfgang? Would it be a good thing for her to marry a man of his type? Faithful he would never be, nor stable, and she strongly doubted that he would be able to guarantee her a solid future. The foolish thing she had done was taking up space inside her, invading her; her whole self was one with that foolishness, and in anguish she brooded that nothing in her life would have meaning from that moment on, neither her affections nor her music.

The following morning she waited until Wolfgang went to his work at the Palace, then she knocked at the door of the Mozart house, trembling and confused from her sleepless night. Nannerl was in her room trying on her wedding dress, and greeted her with a meek smile.

"Oh Victoria! What did you do in the end, last night? I didn't see you. Did you go home early?"

She was silent, uncertain. She looked around. There was no one there but the two of them. So she said, "What do you mean? You know perfectly well where I was hiding, and with whom."

That happy and childish expression didn't leave Nannerl's face. "Do you like the dress? It's pretty, isn't it? The flower pattern must be to your taste, I imagine. And also the color: it's a beautiful shade of green, just as you would like," she said. She spun in a circle, and the train twined around her feet. With an air of amusement she bent down to disentangle it, while Victoria couldn't understand if she preferred to be silent or was making fun of her.

"Nannerl, I have to talk to you," she murmured.

Nannerl looked at her in silence, with an air of momentousness, and sat down on the bed, taking care not to muss the dress. "And I need to talk to you, in fact. I've already discussed the matter with Wolfgang, which is proper; but, apart from him, with no one else. At the moment I would prefer that only you, my brother, and I know about it, since the matter concerns us three most of all, and only we can understand it fully; your father is also involved, by force of circumstance, but only indirectly."

"Oh, thank goodness. Then you don't intend to tell him?"

"Well, he will have to know necessarily: it was his initiative."

Confused, she stammered, "What are you talking about? What initiative, Nannerl?"

"Publishing my opera!" she said, radiant. "I've finished it—finished—and I really am satisfied with it! I still have to revise many parts, of course, and I suspect that the last part, in particular, will need quite a few corrections, because I worked on it with less intensity."

"Nannerl, please! Why do you pretend not to understand?"

She seemed wounded. She sighed, a short, deep sigh, and asked, "Aren't you happy for me? I hadn't written a note in ten years, and you have been insisting, all of you, and finally you convinced me, and now that I've done something, won't you enjoy it with me, and Wolfgang, and your father?"

"Of course. This isn't what we have to talk about now, you and I, but about last night. About what happened."

"Why, what happened last night?" she asked, genuinely surprised.

"You know very well!"

"No, I have no idea. What should I know?"

"Stop this! You saw it yourself!" Victoria cried, exasperated, seizing her by the shoulders and shaking her.

Nannerl freed herself with a look of annoyance. "Don't wrinkle my dress," she said, and smoothed the sleeves. "I really don't understand you. Why are you being so rude? Why do you have to make me worry, anyway?" Then she called Tresel to help her undress, and the girl left the house, more bewildered than when she arrived.

XI.

It wasn't long before she discovered that she was pregnant, or, rather, that she became certain, since from the beginning she had felt it, or feared it, or thought she deserved punishment. And yet in that moment a sense of hope took possession of her, and in her thoughts the punishment was transformed into a sweet reward. The family that for her was Music, that had changed her, made her an artist, would welcome her into it through a bond of blood; now it belonged to her, on her own account, that family, and not only through the second marriage of her father. She would give Wolfgang a son and

Nannerl a nephew, living proof of the creative capacity she had acquired, and a marvelous exchange for the supreme gifts she had received from them.

In this state of mind Victoria waited for Wolfgang at the door of the Mozart house. It was a luminous morning, and when he appeared at the exact center of the arched doorway, his redingote carefully buttoned, a bundle of scores under his arm, the sun struck his slightly protruding blue eyes, and he stopped for an instant to adjust the brim of his hat. To marry him, at that moment, seemed to Fräulein d'Ippold more than desirable. She would be able, surely, to transform his barbaric impulses and direct them toward the good; she would tolerate his excesses, in the knowledge that with the passage of time they would diminish; she would understand his lofty soul and enable him to express, for the joy of all, the best of himself . . .

He set off along the sidewalk, concentrating on some melody that he was revolving in his mind, and as soon as he saw her, he stopped. He didn't seem pleased. "What do you want?" he murmured warily.

Victoria gestured to him to be quiet and persuaded him to retrace his steps; the two young people went back through the entrance, into the courtyard, and stopped at the base of the grand stairway. The vaults above them amplified every sound, and she had to lower her voice to a faint breeze that she blew into his ear so that the news would not rise to the top floor of the building.

His reaction, however, was thunderous. Wolfgang burst out laughing. Victoria felt ill treated by his raucousness, multiplied as it was a hundred times by the reverberation; he made no attempt to stop but seemed amused by his own laughter, and its echo. Gradually, his hilarity subsided, and he looked at her, finally still.

"I understand, and I feel for you," he said. "But why, may I ask, are you telling me?"

And he burst out laughing again, but this was a lighter and more circumspect laugh. He kept staring at her, sneering, waiting for some response, shielded by his amusement. Since Victoria couldn't find the words, he continued, "I mean, my friend—we both know perfectly well that we are not the first, for each other, and not the last; what I mean is, in essence, *mater semper certa, pater incertus*—oh, sorry, maybe you don't know what that means."

"I don't know Latin, but I know that," she said, offended.

"Then you also understand that no one on this earth can declare that I, and I alone, am the cause of your condition. And to look at you even now, dear Victoria, even now that your aversion toward me is clearly legible in your dark gaze, even now, I say, you are so pretty and pleasingly alluring that it's hard to believe you aren't available to anyone who asks."

Her right hand flew out and delivered a strong and powerful slap, but he massaged his cheek with a composure that was more irritating than his insults.

"What do you want me to say?" he continued, disdainfully. "That I love you and wish to marry you? It's not so, unfortunately. And in any case, even if I loved you, certainly at the moment I don't intend to saddle myself with a wife and child—assuming it's my child, which, I repeat, I don't at all believe."

"It is so, however, and you know it very well!"

"Are you telling the truth? Who in the world would confirm that there was a relationship between us? You say so, but, as I've already said, your word has no great value. Furthermore, I affirm the contrary, and I am, of course, more credible; besides, we have never been together in public."

Not wanting him to see her cry, Victoria turned and ran breathlessly up the stairs, stumbling again and again on the damn lace of her dress. She heard him shouting after her, "Forget it; it's completely pointless!"

Then, with the scores under his arm, Wolfgang started off again toward the Palace; but he no longer felt like laughing, and no more notes lodged in his mind. His step became irresolute, and as he parted from Victoria the guilty thought that he had abandoned her took shape in him. On the other hand (he made an effort to reflect), the idea of making official a bond that, while fun for them both, had been only a game without rules was completely ridiculous; and it was even more unacceptable that the consequences of a folly committed consciously by two should weigh upon him alone. It wasn't impossible that that had been Victoria's aim from the first moment: to snare him and then arrange things. That was not how Wolfgang imagined his life, certainly not as the prey of some calculating whore. Now on the threshold of adulthood, he had very different priorities: to assert his matchless art freely in the world; every interest or insincere affection or distorted and unhealthy sense of justice had to be sacrificed in this pursuit. This was the essence of the matter; and his father, besides, would unconditionally approve such reasoning. And so any vexing sensation of having committed an injustice was buried again in the place from which it had emerged unbidden, and Wolfgang's walk became decisive again, and the road to the Palace appeared to him downhill.

XII.

Tresel opened the door and at that moment, at the sight of Victoria, guessed what had happened. Mute as always but, for once, less severe, she accompanied her to Nannerl, who was gathering up her scores in a large folder on which appeared, in swirling letters, the legend *The Gallant Officer*. Then she closed the door and disappeared.

Fräulein Mozart glanced carelessly at the sheets of paper. "Hello, Victoria. Would you mind, as soon as you can, delivering the folder to your father? I would have called a messenger, but since you're here . . . And I, forgive me, I'm too tired to go out. I've been working every night, until last night, and now I've had enough—I'm really anxious to be free of this opera and move on to another. I'm already thinking of my next work, you know? Who can say if this man Alois

Flatscher will be interested in publishing another. I am so curious to meet him, for I haven't yet had the opportunity. Sometimes I try to imagine what sort of man he is, my patron, but I can't imagine what he looks like or what he's like. Have you ever seen him?"

The young woman stood silent, in the doorway, trembling and in tears. Nannerl looked at her finally, and in an instant her expression became surprised and pained. She ran to her: "Who hurt you?"

"Wolfgang."

"What did he do to you?" she cried angrily. "Tell me!"

She was too upset to explain. So Nannerl made her sit down, called Tresel and asked her to prepare a tisane, then gave Victoria a handkerchief and waited patiently for her to calm down. Meanwhile she placed one hand on her knee and moved it back and forth, patting her lightly and affectionately as one quiets the crying of a child.

Victoria at last managed to unburden herself, and as she explained the reason for her suffering, and the injustice she felt had been inflicted and the sense of impotence that suffocated her, Nannerl observed her with a grieving and understanding look. Victoria told her everything: how the seduction between her and Wolfgang had developed, how he had both repelled and attracted her, and the series of secret rendezvous—whose very secrecy was exciting—they had had, reaching an intimacy that she had been unable to stop. And then the epilogue, and his indifference and scornful rejection.

When she finished, Nannerl said nothing but poured the warm tisane into the cup, handed it to her, and made her swallow it down to the last drop. Then she poured the other and sat with the cup in her hands, savoring the warmth it gave her, and without taking her gaze from the liquid, she said, "Victoria, for once I agree with Wolfgang. I don't think, for your own good, that you should get married and have a family."

To Victoria it seemed that the world was turning upside down. No, this was not reality.

"If you did," she continued, very serious, "your career as a pianist would be dead. What goal have we worked for in all these years? To make you a good little wife? If I had known that was your aim, I certainly would not have devoted my energies to teaching you. If that was always your objective, in effect, you should have told me the first day."

"Nannerl, I'm pregnant! Pregnant! By Wolfgang. Will you understand?"

"Maybe it's you who won't understand. Maybe it's only a small female problem . . . It happens. It's a very common thing."

"Your brother and I have had a relationship!"

"Maybe. But it could also be—forgive me—that you exaggerated his interest."

"But you saw us together! You saw us the evening of the masquerade. You opened the door and we were there and we were—"

"Why do you lie, Victoria? What is your purpose? I don't know what you're talking about, and frankly I'm tired of listening to all this nonsense." She put the cup down and rose. "Now do me a favor: go home and play through the program for the wedding reception. Go over every piece carefully, and if you have questions, make a note of them. Then tomorrow at this time come back here, and after clearing up your questions we'll try a rehearsal: just as if it were the day of the concert, without my interrupting you. Go on now and try to calm down."

XIII.

The church was cool and smelled of incense, and the few faithful prayed silently, kneeling before sacred images and gazing at them in yearning and fear, or hunched in meditation on the wooden benches. Victoria alone was speaking. She had burst into the confessional and a river of tears and words flooded that wooden cage; she herself was in danger of drowning, but she held on to the priest as if to a raft. Her eyelids were swollen blisters, the skin thin, reddened, and they seemed to have swallowed up her eyebrows. The tear ducts, exhausted, released a burning liquid, and her shoulders heaved as she strangled her sobs.

She told him everything, without reserve, from the evening of the fête; of the betrayal of Wolfgang and even worse that of Nannerl, who knew everything but persisted in an absurd, incredible lie. He imposed on her fifty Our Fathers, fifty Ave Marias, and a week's fasting, then let her go; she flung herself onto a bench, not at all relieved, and kneeling amid the veiled women recited prayers. She didn't realize that she had been observed.

Katharina von Esser had gone to church to deliver a generous offering (in exchange, certainly, for a prominent plaque that would make her generosity known). She stopped to observe Victoria with malicious interest, then, when the priest came out of the confessional, went over to him with a broad smile. It wasn't Reverend Bullinger, who was too old now to practice, but the acid-tongued priest who was to celebrate the marriage: Father Jakob.

XIV.

"Hello, my love," Nannerl said with a playful lightness that was reminiscent of her mother. In the small room with the floral walls she settled the scores on the shelves and carefully ran a cloth over the white keys of her old harpsichord. No longer empty of furniture, and smelling now of wood, wax, and fresh laundry, the apartment on the Salzach was ready, and awaited only the wedding day, when the new family would go and live there.

From the doorway, Armand stared at her strangely, as if trying to grasp some meaning in a gesture, in the tone of her voice. Then, silently, he sat down at the instrument.

"Would you like me to give you a lesson?" she asked, smiling.

For a few moments he kept his eyes lowered on his own hands as he picked at the nails, which he had long ago stopped biting for love of her. So, as she continued to putter, he looked at her again and said, "Last night Katharina von Esser came to see me at the Palace."

"Oh, really? Why in the world? What did she want?"

"The truth is, to tell me something that she had learned in various indirect, not entirely clear ways. In any case, what she said concerns you and me personally." He jumped to his feet and went toward the door, as if in search of light; the small room had only a little window, high up and facing west.

"What is that scheming woman sticking her nose in now?"

"You're right, she is a disagreeable woman, and I assure you that I long to keep my distance from her. But the fact is, in a difficult situation, the countess, without even intending to, has done me a great service."

She started to say something, but he, with a curt gesture, put a finger on her mouth: "Be quiet and listen."

She stood beside the harpsichord, speechless.

"At this moment I find myself, dear Nannerl," he said darkly, weighing his words, "with a daughter who is pregnant by someone who doesn't want to marry her and, what is perhaps worse, with a betrothed who knew that she had been seduced and was silent."

"What do you mean?" she murmured, in dismay.

"Do you want me to repeat everything? I see no need for that. You have got the idea—of that I'm sure. What I urgently need to know is if what the countess says is true."

"It's all false!"

"You don't know how I hope you are being honest, Nannerl. On the one hand, I think, it's plausible that Countess von Esser has invented everything for some malicious purpose of her own; but why, explain to me if you will—why would Victoria support her hypothesis?"

"What does Victoria say?"

"That you saw her with him. That—just to be absolutely clear— the night of a masked ball that I don't even remember the details of, you surprised my daughter as the victim of the lustful desires of a certain man . . ."

"It's not true!"

"And you have behaved as if it were nothing; and what is more serious, what I cannot accept, Nannerl, is that you didn't tell me, her father! You should have informed me instantly."

"But none of it's true, I swear!" she cried desperately.

"Why do you insist?"

"I'm not lying, Armand!"

"So it's Victoria who's lying? And why do you think she would do that?"

"I don't know. There must be a reason, yet I don't see it . . ."

Nannerl was agitated, like a windup toy whose mechanism is slowing down. Flailing, she flattened herself against the wall, just opposite her old harpsichord, and suddenly Armand went to her and took her face in his hands. With immense gentleness he whispered, "Nannerl, please, enough. Don't you understand yet that we have to rewrite everything, you and I? My daughter, my own daughter, is in danger of ending up in a convent, or worse; and I can't let that happen. I have to devote my life to her, dear Nannerl, and her alone. Because, distracted by my love for you, by my egoism, I didn't protect her as I should have. And now how can I even think of having a new family with you when I have to take care of the one I have and have always had?"

He took his hands from her face slowly, as if in a last caress, and said, "I didn't come to tell you that we can no longer marry, because that's obvious—beyond discussion. I'm here because, my sweet Nannerl, I want to keep a good memory of you. More than anything now I want to know why you said nothing to me."

The mechanism suddenly wound down, in a convulsive shudder that shook her limbs. She turned red and began sweating, and an infinite weariness took possession of her so that her legs gave way and she crumpled to the floor, sliding along the wall.

He took her in his arms and carried her, trembling and weeping, to the bedroom and laid her lovingly on the bridal bed. Then he closed the curtains, and a restful shadowy light filled the room. For a long time Nannerl lay curled up, and her lips let out only a long sob, while her closed eyes, little by little, saw again an unacceptable memory. And meanwhile Armand held her in his arms, and slowly the ice inside her melted.

"Yes, it's true," she murmured finally, finding words again. "It's so—it happened. There was a long corridor," she continued laboriously, "with hunting scenes on the walls, it seems to me, and a door at the end. I opened it and found Wolfgang and Victoria . . . in a situation that I would never have expected to find them in."

"Go on," he urged her kindly.

"At that moment, Armand, at that exact moment I understood that our marriage was in danger—that what I had longed for my entire life had been destroyed in an instant. And I felt as I did when I was a girl, when my brother left for Italy, or even earlier, when my father forbade me to play the violin. Yes, I felt just the way I did then: prevented from grasping happiness by someone else's actions. But this time it was worse, because with all my soul I had hoped to redeem that pain in a life with you. And then—I don't know how it could happen, Armand, but I swear it happened—then I forgot it completely. And now . . . now there's another memory that is coming out."

She sat up. She was no longer trembling. She looked her betrothed right in the face and murmured, "You paid to publish my opera. You paid a fortune—is that true, Armand?"

He assented, bowing his head.

"I met that man, and he told me. I had also forgotten that."

"I shouldn't have done it. It was a foolish mistake."

"Oh, I felt so humiliated."

"Not only for that reason, Nannerl. Because being with you, in time, I entered into a game that was completely wrong, in which only your fulfillment counted."

"But I wrote the opera about you, for you."

"Exactly. You wrote it for me, and I wanted to publish it for you. But together, in common, we made nothing, and never could have."

"You still don't want to marry me?" she cried. "But I'm not guilty. I had truly forgotten everything, truly."

"You think that I don't want to marry you to punish you? It's not that, Nannerl. Now, rather, it seems definitively clear that we have nothing, absolutely nothing in common."

"How can you say that? We have loved each other for years."

"I came to you with the intention of saving you, of perhaps making up for the mistakes I made with my first wife. But I'm unable to; it's evident. And you, for your part, came to me in the hope that I would save you. We have failed, Nannerl. We have to accept it. Now we are two strangers, nothing else. And I cannot have a stranger near my daughter. You understand, don't you?"

He seemed to her suddenly a different person, and in anguish she tried to see again the Armand she knew and the self that had been together with him. But he was not willing to go back.

"Perhaps you don't understand," he continued in an affectionate tone. "No, maybe it's impossible, unfortunately. Because you, dearest Nannerl, have never created anything. You have no children and you brutally killed your musical soul. You don't have a solid moral center, and it's perfectly logical that you don't, since you've had no models to help you. I couldn't have saved you, ever—only you could, if only you had wanted to. But in this effort no one, not even the next man I hope you love, can replace yourself."

Nannerl felt her body become vapor and disappear, and in its place she felt a void, a black, empty void that sucked in and swallowed up everything around her and turned her to dust.

"I will ask for a transfer to Munich, far from these troubles, and I will take Victoria with me. As soon as possible, she will go back to giving concerts, and perhaps lessons, too, like the ones you gave her. She will be grateful to you for that teaching; and I am, too, Nannerl, with all my heart. Let us part now."

XV.

Salzburg had never seemed so alien to her. No longer did any corner of those streets belong to her, those buildings made opaque by the cloudy, cold day, as if they had been soaked in a dense, sticky liquid. The idea of returning to the wood, to seek the comfort of her tree, didn't even occur to her. She headed toward home, but her steps, with a will of their own, followed a convoluted, tangled route, so that more than once she found herself at the same intersection vainly trying to figure out where she was. Finally, without knowing how, she reached the street door, and then the foot of the stairs; but halfway up, she had to sit down on the steps to quiet her breathing. Her legs hurt as if she had run for miles uphill, and when she opened the door she wished only to sink into her bed and remain there for the rest of her life.

In the music room she found her father and brother. They were engaged in a serious conversation. Herr Mozart was dictating, and Wolfgang diligently took notes. A mirage of resolve drew out her last ray of energy.

"It's all ready," she said from the doorway in a distant voice. "Everything is set: the church, the new home . . . But the marriage that must be celebrated will not be mine. It will be Wolfgang who marries, and he will marry Victoria."

The two men were silent. She went to her father, sitting in the chair with the old blanket over his legs; she arranged it carefully, knelt, took his gnarled hands, and said, "Wolfgang seduced her. You perhaps will not believe it, but I know for certain, because I saw them together. And now he must repair the evil done, as soon as possible, before the news spreads—"

He said gravely, "It has already happened, Nannerl. The rumors have just reached this house."

"What have you heard, then?"

"Many things about your dear Fräulein d'Ippold and her promiscuous ways."

Then Nannerl hid her face in the fleshless legs of her father and abandoned herself to grief. She became a knot of suffering, clinging to the man who should have been with her, on her side, she was sure of it; and she implored him to show his love, at least this one time, when it seemed most important. "Please," she sobbed, "don't you, too, give in to this deception."

He was embarrassed. "Daughter, stop it. You know what I think about tears."

"You must help me—what is right must happen. Wolfgang behaved terribly with Victoria, with Armand, and with me, too, and he cannot escape unharmed."

"Wolfgang will leave tomorrow for Vienna. I have arranged all the details. He must get away from this nasty little scandal and find his way in a capital of great Europe, where finally his music will be able to take flight."

"Enough of this! Enough, father! You push Wolfgang to seek success only so that you will be able to redeem your own mediocrity!"

They were all struck dumb, and suddenly Nannerl noticed the ticking of the clock and the aching of her knees on the floor, but she couldn't get up. Herr Mozart slowly turned his head, his mouth twisted in disgust. Then he moved the blanket to one side, rose, pushing himself up with his arms, and walked to the door, leaning on his cane. There he stopped.

"You have taken down all my instructions, Wolfgang?" he asked, impassive.

"Yes, Papa."

"Very good," he answered, and disappeared through the doorway. Stunned, Nannerl rose from the floor and sank into the same chair.

Her brother shook his head in her direction: "My compliments. If you want him to hate you to the end of his days you have achieved your purpose."

He went to sit beside her, and she felt her heart beating very slowly, a tired piston in time with the pendulum of the clock. After a moment she said hoarsely, "How could you do this to me, Wolfgang?"

"If you're referring to your Victoria, I assure you that I didn't mean to harm her or you."

"But you did, and now you abandon us—how can you?"

"My music needs other horizons, Nannerl. Haven't you understood that yet? I have to free myself, finish something grand, I have to say everything I still haven't been able to say because I haven't had the opportunity. Otherwise, dear sister, I am in danger of coming to the same end as you."

"And what is that? Tell me, please."

"Poor in spirit, a slave of your victimhood, and forgetful of your talent. The queen I loved is lost."

He rose, took a folder of scores, and held it out to her. "Your *Gallant Officer* is the mirror of what you have become. The music is just decent, in fact, neither good nor bad. I would have preferred it to be worse rather than of such mediocrity. But the text! Oh, the text, Nannerl. The text is an outrage. With an irrational faith in your abilities, which alternates with the low opinion you have of yourself, you wanted to tell the story, too. And what has come out is a shapeless construction without the least spark of humanity. You intended to tell the story of your life, I imagine; but of life you know absolutely nothing because you have never lived, and you don't even know it. You could have done great things, but you weren't capable of them."

"Then go, go to Vienna!" she cried, tearing the folder from his hands. "Go on, try to get free of us. But one thing is certain: you'll never succeed. You'll never have lasting success. You'll be surpassed by mediocre people. You'll never even earn a living, and you'll die poor and alone!"

XVI.

With a wild light in her eyes, she walked, staggering, hampered by her skirt, her shoes, the cobblestones; the people she met made a wide circle around her as if she were mad. And perhaps she really was—or was about to do a mad thing.

She reached the bridge over the Salzach and stopped in the middle. There was no longer anyone around, so she leaned over the parapet and watched the water flowing, like life, which flowed around her, she who had always been unmoved. She lifted her skirt and with a great effort, hugging to her breast the folder containing *The Gallant Officer*, climbed up on the balustrade.

She stood there a long time, eyes closed, hanging on to a pillar, letting the breeze run over her skin and blow through her thoughts as well, emptying her mind. Then, with a resolute gesture, she untied the ribbon around the folder, opened it, and turned it upside down into the river.

The pages made a sinuous flight, like lazy birds pleased with their own wings; they scattered like confetti and, like confetti, gained meaning by being thrown. They landed on the water, floated there for a while, became soaked, and then disappeared, forever, amid the waves.

One score only Nannerl could not bring herself to throw away, and she kept it in her arms, folding it against her chest. It was the only aria that Wolfgang had not despised: "I am grateful for your hand."

I Am Grateful for Your Hand

I.

"What in the world is she doing in there all the time?"

"Nothing, Herr Mozart."

"What do you mean, nothing? Try to be a little clearer, Tresel!"

"It seems to me that I have been. She does nothing. She lies on her bed all day, she doesn't speak, and she never moves."

Nannerl's anguish spread through the Mozart house like a silent shadow, which Herr Mozart could no longer ignore. He had imagined that sooner or later his daughter would take up the ordinary activities of any individual, but that moment was slow in arriving. Thus he sometimes found himself pacing near her room, trying to catch some sound from inside, and finally even putting his ear to the keyhole; but he heard absolutely nothing, not a cough, not a rustle of limbs amid bedclothes.

He rose from the table, irritated, and, even forgetting to lean on his cane, he reached the small room that led to Nannerl's. On the floor outside sat a tray of food, almost untouched, which he moved aside nervously with his foot. The idea of opening that door repelled him slightly, but curiosity and some ancient trace of responsibility dominated. So he placed his clawlike hand on the knob, turned it, and pushed, but nothing happened.

"Tresel!" he shouted. "She's locked herself in!"

"What can I do about it?" the maid said, joining him.

"Bring me the big key ring."

"But if the key is in the lock on the other side, Herr Mozart, surely you won't—"

"Bring me the keys before I kick you."

Sighing, the servant returned with a bunch of keys on a large ring. "Here, see if there's one that works."

He grabbed the bunch, chose one, stuck it in the lock, and met resistance.

"Herr Mozart, I told you—"

"Be quiet. If you open your mouth you're making a big mistake."

Angrily Leopold attacked the lock, sticking in one key after another and twisting the knob, and from time to time he pounded his fist on the door and yelled, "Nannerl, do you hear me or not? What do you think you're doing? Nannerl! Open the door immediately or I'll have to call a locksmith." And just then he heard, on the other side of the door, the ricochet of a metal object on the floor. "You see?" he said with a victorious air. "I've got the key out!"

"And I'm pleased," Tresel commented, impassive.

"Now let's see if I can . . . make the lock turn. There, I've done it, we're there!"

He opened the door and saw nothing, because the room was darker than a moonless night, but a stink of airlessness and sweat and excrement in a chamber pot somewhere in the room hit his sensitive nostrils and went to his head.

"Good God, Tresel! Don't you clean this room? Don't you ever change the sheets?"

"She won't let me," she answered tonelessly.

Cautiously, Leopold walked to the window and opened it, and thus he could see what remained of his daughter: lying on the bed on one side, unmoving, with the covers pulled up over her head, wrapped up as if in a cocoon.

"She's alive, Herr Mozart, don't worry. Of course, she's not very well."

"Take away that disgusting thing," he ordered, indicating the chamber pot. "And stay out for a while."

Warily, he approached the bed. By now he was certain: his daughter was seriously ill. Who knew what had happened in that stubborn head to make her sleep continuously, night and day, and eat almost nothing, and not even wash. Wolfgang had left for Vienna—well, three weeks earlier. So it was a little less than a month since she had buried herself in that room. And then, good heavens, Colonel d'Ippold had sent back the linens, the old harpsichord, and even some pieces of furniture, and it was all piled in the parlor, blocking the way and the view, in the useless expectation that Nannerl would decide where to put it. One couldn't go on in that way.

"Daughter, it's time you got out of this bed. Roll up your sleeves and start doing something useful in the house."

No answer, no sign of having heard.

"Nannerl! It's time to show a little willpower and overcome this ridiculous laziness. Come on, you must get up."

"I'm cold," she murmured.

"What? You're cold? Well, that's not surprising, if you never move."

"I hurt everywhere."

"It's because you never get up, for heaven's sake. At this rate your blood will stop flowing."

"It would be a great relief."

"What did you say?"

"The idea of death comforts me, Father. I would like it to come soon; I would like to take my life myself. But I am so inept that I would fail at that, too. Why don't you do it?"

"That's enough of this nonsense. Get up, right away!"

"You think you can force me? Go away and close the window," she said, and covered her head again with the pillow.

Gnashing his remaining teeth, Leopold resigned himself and returned to the parlor (failing to close the window, out of spite). With his limping gait, he began pacing from one side of the room to the other, hitting the floor with his cane, obsessively following the outline of the uneven tiles. He had an invalid in the house, he thought with anger and impatience. It wasn't enough to have lost his wife, and that his son was called to seek success elsewhere, and that the servant was soon to leave, abandoning him to unknown hands. Now, added to his troubles, was an unmarried daughter possessed by melancholy specters, who persisted ardently in her inner suffering and would not emerge from her state. Maybe he should call a doctor or find her a place in the hospital; maybe she needed a specialist to take care of her day and night, full time. Yes, that was the practical solution; he had neither the tools nor the will nor the desire to care for her. Of course, it would be a great expense.

"Herr Mozart?"

He turned in annoyance. Tresel had finished clearing up and had taken off her apron and cap.

"What in Heaven's name do you want?"

"Herr Mozart, if you don't mind, I have an idea."

"Since when do illiterates have ideas floating around in their heads?"

With equal impertinence she sat down right in front of her master, who remained standing. "I would like to take Nannerl to Sankt Gilgen. I would like to have her at my house."

"Why?"

"The mountain air will do her good."

"That's it?"

"What else should I tell you?"

Leopold was silent for a long time. A thread of interest brought him a few inches from the servant. "And, if I might ask," he said, "how long would you keep her?"

"How should I know? Until she's recovered."

"I would like to determine an exact date; after all, you would certainly want something for her maintenance, and I think I had better calculate the costs."

"Don't worry about it. It won't take much money."

"Truly? Well, basically that's secondary. What counts is that my dear daughter should get away from the places that represent so many sad memories for her, and so—so yes, I think that ultimately, in spite of everything, your idea isn't bad. Give me the address so that I can write to her now and then, and see that you make her answer every so often. Come on, get the bags packed."

II.

"Do you want to eat?" was the question, always the same, and Nannerl's reply was always "No, thank you, Tresel." So the old woman withdrew into the dark space of the ground-floor window and prepared the meal for the large population of her house, except the guest. Nannerl stayed outside in the noon sun—with a white parasol carefully arranged to shelter her head—her eyes closed and her thoughts more inert than her body. She never went far from the large farm building—just a few yards, to the bench surrounded by tufts of grass and flowering plants; the town that had given birth to her mother and to the old servant didn't interest her, nor did she feel pressed to make friends with Tresel's descendants, from her son Martin to the daughter-in-law with the lame leg, to their children and the children of their children. She had never found herself in a dwelling so crowded, and every so often, when the children tumbled about her too noisily, she found herself wondering who in the world had wanted her to go and stay in that chaos. But they all left her in peace each day; they asked no questions and made no claims on her, and the pale, luminous beams of the sun had begun to warm her soul. No part of her skin was exposed directly, but one day, just as an experiment, she cautiously took off a glove and stretched her hand outside the cone of the parasol's shade.

The light made her flesh appear even whiter, and the skin of her palm and of her emaciated fingers seemed to be made of many infinite hollows, which could be filled with light and warmth. In those hollows was the vital substance of life, she imagined, and it spread from one finger to the next (for they were communicating) like an ointment, and from her arm to her shoulder; there it stopped, however, because the ointment was not inexhaustible. So now Nannerl thought of pulling her sleeve up above the forearm to expose it to the sun and let it, too, enjoy the warm massage; but to do it she would have to put the parasol down and leave her face uncovered. It was too great a risk. Not knowing what to do, with one hand holding the handle and the other in the border area between light and shadow, she managed to stick the parasol between her head and neck, quickly pushed the material of her dress up above the elbow, and courageously extended the limb into the sun.

First she was cold. The skin, unused to the air, was covered with tiny hills, one for each hair, and the rays wounded it. The warmth came suddenly, like a slap; it didn't spread through her body but stayed on the surface, biting her. Suddenly she closed the parasol and placed it on the bench beside her, and untied her hat. As she took it off, some locks of hair remained tangled in it, and she freed them impatiently; then she uncovered the other forearm, took off the glove, placed her open hands on the bench, and threw back her head, eyes closed, to face the sun.

She seemed to feel its weight. Her eyes seemed to be rotating, radiating concentric waves, like a rock thrown into a lake. Stirred by that internal movement, Nannerl listened to the rustle of the wind, a distant meowing, the hooves of horses beating on straw, and she felt herself part of an organism made of mountains, and meadows, and warm light, making life possible; her own organism did not differ from the larger one, and now she felt herself swell with air, and deflate, and swell again, and grow strong from the fascinating contractions of her heart. The apparent immobility of her flesh was no longer a renunciation but a recharging—the vigilant stillness of one who, in waiting, becomes.

"What did I tell you?" Tresel said to her son, from the window. "It will pass, finally."

III.

Her face was peeling and red, and the shadowy light of the hearth had begun to feel confining. She was restless indoors, unable to accept her condition of inactive guest; everyone was very busy during the daylight hours, but there didn't seem to be a suitable task for her. Tresel absolutely would not let her clean or cook. She allowed her to make her own bed in the room on the upper floor that she shared with a couple of kids who slept like logs (thank Heaven!), but, otherwise, the old woman considered it absurd that she whom she had served for years should now serve her. "I've always done it myself" was the recurrent excuse. Or "You're not capable!" And Nannerl, who although she felt at home in that household as she never had in the Mozart house, couldn't resign herself.

She went out into the courtyard with an old hat on her head, to keep the sun off her already sunburned nose, and for a moment thought about splitting logs, but the idea of accidentally amputating a foot discouraged her. Then she thought of making a neat stack of the logs lying in a heap in a corner; she unpiled them one by one, then invented an orderly and efficient arrangement (she thought, with great satisfaction): the first layer perpendicular to the wall, the second parallel, with a distance between one log and the next of exactly three inches. When she reached the fifth row her head was spinning a little, but she thought it was from the lack of physical exercise and how little she had eaten, and, unalarmed, she kept going. Halfway through the eighth row, she had used up the logs. Not satisfied, she stood up to see if there were others in the courtyard or the fields, so that she could finish the prodigious sculpture; but at that point she became extremely dizzy and, panting, she prudently sat down on the construction itself, which collapsed with a crash.

"Come with me," Martin said, looking at her as one looks at a half-wit, holding out his hand. Tresel's son was short, but he had strong arms and was only a little more talkative than his mother. He didn't lead her inside to recover, or give her time to catch her breath, but without releasing his grip he dragged her along the rocky path that led to the stable. "If you really want to be useful," he said, "you can take care of Ebony."

"Who's that?" she asked breathlessly.

"A horse, obviously," he answered, as he pushed her through the stable door and then toward the narrow stall of a filly, who greeted them with an angry neighing and retreated. Flattening her ears back, she pawed the ground and showed her teeth. Despite her name, only her mane, muzzle, and the area around her eyes were black; she had a grayish coat and a squat, ungainly body with a disproportionately large head.

"Why in the world did you name her Ebony?"

"She was black when she was born, like a raven, a real beauty; but when she grew up she played this trick. She's certainly not a pure-bred; I have no idea who got her lustful beast of a mother pregnant!" Nannerl blushed violently while he, with utter naturalness, continued: "And she also has quite a character, to tell you the truth. The owner foisted her off on me because she shied all the time. No one wants her around." And saying, "Good luck!" he went off.

"But what am I supposed to do?"

"Curry her!"

And he disappeared, swallowed up into the light of the stable yard.

Disoriented, Nannerl looked around: all the horses were dozing or eating quietly; only Ebony was beating her hooves on the ground, and the dark-circled eyes, which stood out against the ash-colored coat, watched her sullenly. She was supposed to take care of this hostile beast! That Martin was astonishingly rude, to think that she was at his service. Helping in the house was one thing, but to be ordered about by an ignorant despot was another. Her father, Herr Leopold Mozart, was sending a mint of money to the family to pay for her stay. Nothing else was due them, unless she herself chose to do something for her own pleasure.

She abandoned the filly and, with lowered head, retraced her steps, wrinkling her nose at the foul smell; she reached the stable gate, which Martin had left open, and imagined his mocking expression when he discovered that she had been unable to do the job. She stopped. After all, what else did she have to do in this remote place? She had no wish to read; she hadn't brought many books, and in the house there was not even one. She had read the most recent letter from her father and was not in the mood to answer. After all, if she thought about it, in the past she had done things more arduous than curry an ugly, capricious horse. She turned, settled the hat on her head, and called, "Ebony!"

A few sleepy sounds responded. The one addressed, hidden in her stall, was silent.

"Ebony, now I'm coming to see you and I'm going to take you out and curry you. Whether you like it or not."

The other horses slid past her gaze as she cautiously approached the filly. The warning seemed to have disposed her favorably, or perhaps Nannerl's deep voice had recalled to her some mysterious memory.

The two studied each other for a long time, motionless and watchful. Nannerl stood twenty paces away. The horse looked at her, then turned her head slightly, pretending indifference, and then looked at her again, ears straight and eyes so dark against the gray coat that they were like the eye sockets of a skull. When Nannerl advanced two steps, however, Ebony let out a strange whinny and flattened her ears like a cat.

"I know you don't like me. I'm sorry, I really am, but I confess that I don't like you, either. If no one else likes you, why should I?"

A strangled sound came from the horse; she shook her mane and scraped the straw with her hooves.

"Now I'm moving another step closer. Look at my hands: they're empty. I have nothing that can hurt you. Besides, I don't see why I should. Believe me, you're not that interesting to me."

She advanced very slowly, and Ebony remained motionless, a bundle of combativeness dangerously ready to unfold and expand. Nannerl kept getting closer and closer, and very gently placed her hand on the stall door.

"Now I'm going to open it," she said, while out of the corner of her eye she looked at the stable gate, which was still open: and if Ebony should escape? "I'll open it," she repeated, a little hesitant, "so you won't feel like a prisoner in here." Slowly she lifted the latch, with her head slightly lowered so that she could still see the horse, and pulled the gate toward her until it opened. Ebony snorted and moved her head up and down, as if nodding, but it was unclear whether she really approved of the operation.

So Nannerl backed up and said, "Come."

The horse didn't move.

"Come on," she repeated, trying to assume a benevolent tone, and at the same time terrified at the idea that the filly would take off into the stable yard. Ebony seemed to think about it, then, with a sudden leap, she covered the ground between herself and Nannerl, who, frightened, started but kept her feet planted. The filly didn't move, either, and showed not the least intention of fleeing but, rather, had an air of wanting to test this bold human being, and herself.

For some minutes, it seemed, nothing happened. Nannerl could feel on her face the breath of those large, distended nostrils, and now and again she looked at the eyes, just as large, over which the dark lids rapidly rose and fell, and she thought that she, too, had that unconscious habit; and she, too, at that moment was breathing through dilated nostrils, while her lips were locked between her teeth in an expression of fear. She relaxed her mouth and chin, and in a flash understood intimately the condition of this horse that no one wanted anymore, who had been ruined growing up, who angrily pushed away anyone who approached to help her. With genuine kindness she murmured, "May I touch you?"

She heard the sound of the tail swishing against the flanks, but otherwise the beast didn't move a muscle. Timidly she stretched out an open hand and placed it on the horse's muzzle, and with a firm caress reached her cheek, which she scratched vigorously.

Ebony liked this. She stood without moving, enjoying Nannerl's attentions. From the cheek she moved to the neck, and began scratching Ebony with two hands; she felt the horse grow less tense as her muscles released, and it seemed to her that she even felt the animal's frightened and hostile thoughts vanish. Fräulein Mozart felt like laughing with joy, so she did, only holding back a little in order not to disturb the horse. Surprised by this unmotivated happiness, she asked herself how many other times in her life she had felt this way: surely her own character had been naturally joyful, and something, some internal weight, had always suffocated it.

"Let's go outside, Ebony," she exclaimed, and took her by the halter and ran outside with her. She tied her to the wall with a long cord and told her to stay still and be good, while she brushed her back, picked up her hooves and cleaned out the dirt, oiled them to soften them, and then amused herself by combing Ebony's tail and her curly mane. Meanwhile she never stopped talking to her, in a way that she never would have to a person, any person.

That night Tresel's *Frittatensuppe* seemed to her worthy of the palace of Versailles, and she filled her bowl twice, and would have done so a third time if she had not feared being impolite. She took only a single helping of the boiled meat, but after they were all served she asked politely if she could scrape the bottom of the pot; and when Martin's lame wife arrived with the apple strudel, she couldn't even manage a taste because, with her head on the table, a child among the children, she had gently fallen asleep.

I V.

"Do you know how to ride?"

"Not very well," Nannerl said, squinting into the light at the boy in the saddle of a beautiful horse, its coat truly a glossy black, with reddish highlights. He didn't belong to Tresel's family. His attire and his accent said that he was of the well-to-do class.

"I can teach you, if you like," he proposed.

"Why would you do that?"

"Because I'm good! My father brings me here every summer to practice, and now I can ride any horse, on any sort of terrain."

"Oh, really? Then you must know that someone who knows how to do something well doesn't necessarily know how to teach, and vice versa."

He wasn't offended, or perhaps he didn't understand. "Is that your horse?" he asked, observing Ebony, whom Nannerl was leading around by the bridle to stretch her own legs and to make the horse stretch hers.

"Not exactly. Let's say I take care of her. Come, Ebony, move along. What are you doing just standing there?"

"Her name is Ebony? Ah, then I understand. I know the owner. He got rid of her like a piece of garbage. In my opinion, of the two, he is the real beast," he declared, jumping down easily from his horse and tying him to a fence post with a lead. Then he joined Nannerl and, observing how meekly the filly followed her, said, "She likes you."

"How do you know?"

"I know horses. She likes you, and even more, she'd like to take you out. If you want I can teach you to ride her."

"Ride her? Really? They say that she always shies."

The boy shrugged. "What does that have to do with it? With someone like her owner, I would shy, too. Come on, let's saddle her."

"What? Now?"

"Or when, may I ask? Where can I find a woman's sidesaddle?"

"I don't even know if there is one."

"Of course there is. Martin!" he shouted toward the stable. "Nannerl wants to learn to ride. I need a saddle."

"You know Martin?" she asked, bewildered and, even more surprised, exclaimed, "And how do you know my name?"

Suddenly the boy was silent. He turned red and assumed the unmistakable look of someone who has been caught out. "After all," he stammered, "who doesn't know your name? You're Mozart's sister."

"Oh . . . I see. And what's your name?"

"Vincent."

"And what is your family name?"

"Ma-a-a-rtin!" he shouted even louder. "Please, the saddle!"

Martin was just arriving with a pile of leather and cloths and straps in his powerful arms, and even a stool. "Excellent!" he said. "I need someone to make this filly run for me, otherwise she'll get fat, and then all she's good for is the table." He put everything down beside the fence and went off.

Vincent grabbed the blanket. "First this. The rest I'll explain as we go along. I would do it for you, but I can't reach."

"How old are you?"

"Ten."

"You seem older."

"That's what everyone says. Now the lamb's wool, and then the saddle. Put it like this, with the straps on top, then let them hang down the other side, grab them from beneath, and fasten them tightly around the stomach. Don't be afraid to pull hard; you won't hurt her. I don't know if Ebony is used to being ridden sidesaddle, but we'll just go at a walk. Now the bridle."

"So you are not from Sankt Gilgen. Where are you from?"

"Why do you ask?" Vincent demanded with some alarm.

"You said you come here in the summer," Nannerl said, fastening the chin strap. "During the rest of the year where do you live?"

"Ebony is ready! Perfect! Let's put the stool here. Now climb up and sit in the saddle," he ordered, and pushed her next to the horse.

Hesitant, Nannerl put one foot on the stool, and it wobbled. Vincent settled it more firmly. She again put her foot on it, stood motionless for a long moment, observing the horse's muzzle, then she stepped back and leaned against the fence.

"Are you afraid?" the boy asked, without a hint of mockery.

"It's not a matter of fear," she answered bluntly. "But I think that at my age it's too late to learn new things."

"Do you want me to mount her and show you how it's done?" She said nothing, and Vincent approached the horse, who immediately whinnied and moved to one side (since he had skillfully led her to do so). "You see?" he said indifferently. "Ebony wants you, not someone else. You try, and if you don't like it you can get off, all right?"

Nannerl looked toward the far end of the stable yard. Martin was standing in the doorway of the stable with his hands at his side and an expression of challenge on his sunburned face. Vincent was chewing a blade of grass with affected nonchalance, and even his horse seemed to be betting on the rider's ineptitude. So, in a flash, she found herself mounted on the filly.

"Brava!" the boy burst out. "Now keep your right leg on top of the horn, and put the left solidly in the stirrup. Take the reins and give a little tap with your heel."

Ebony didn't move.

"Another tap, a little harder. She has to understand that you want her to go."

Nothing: she stood like a rock. Then Vincent hopped over and gave her a good whack on the rear, and she took off at a gallop.

"Pull on the reins! Pull on the reins, Nannerl!" he cried, frightened, while even Martin came running, but she was too occupied with trying to keep her balance to follow their advice. Luckily the gallop wasn't out of control, so she quickly managed to find her seat. She pulled on the reins, and Ebony slowed down.

The horse settled into a slightly hesitant walk, as if displeased with her indecisive rider and waiting for a new, clearer order. Nannerl tried to perceive her movements and adapt to them, and slowly she moved one hand from the reins and placed it on the horse's neck, caressing her and whispering gentle words. Martin and Vincent were standing outside the enclosure, holding their breath, giving her orders that she didn't hear. As Ebony walked in a large circle, Nannerl felt the horse bearing her weight and was sure that she wasn't offended by it, that, rather, she felt the presence of the rider as a complement of her own forces, not always necessary but compatible if present. Nannerl swayed at every stride, watchful but not rigid, soft but not completely yielding; and she understood that this graceless horse could help her perceive reality from a different perspective. In fact she was already doing it, for Nannerl had never been so high up and in motion; riding was not like being in a carriage, which she would have had no idea how to guide. Her adherence to the body of the animal became a silent mutual accord, and Ebony was transformed into an extension of her, and she into an extension of the horse.

When she dismounted she was sweaty and her eyes shone; she wanted to take off the saddle and bridle herself, and afterward she brushed the horse and rubbed her down with tripled affection. She led her back to the stall, took leave of her with a long caress, and that night couldn't close her eyes, excited at the thought of how much she still had to discover, together with Ebony.

V.

With infallible aim, the pebbles hit the hole at the center of the gnarled knot on the trunk. One after another they entered the cavity and disappeared, until the protuberance was filled; then Nannerl cut a small branch from the tall trunk she was perched on and, with it, emptied the hole, and a hail of stones fell on the mantle of leaves covering the ground. Not far off, in the shade of a leafy branch, Ebony seemed to become alert, but Nannerl didn't pay too much attention. She picked up the slingshot, loaded it, pulled the string, and let it go, and again the pebble sped docilely into the hole. Intently she stuck her hand in the bag to get another, but the horse began to whinny and pull at the lead, so she parted the leaves to see what was agitating her and made out the profile of Vincent approaching on horseback. She secured the slingshot to her belt and slid quickly down the tree. She did not want the boy to view her from below and see her undergarments.

"I came to check your style," Vincent said with a cheerful expression that made his childish features even more attractive. "Martin is a great trainer of horses but not of riders. In my opinion you need some correction."

Nannerl didn't smile, however. She turned her back with a long sigh of annoyance. She untied Ebony and went off with her along the path, on foot.

"Did I disturb you?" Vincent called after her, and when she didn't answer he followed and joined her. "I'm sorry. I didn't mean to. If you don't want to ride we can do something else."

"You are very kind, but it doesn't seem to me that I asked for your company. I would prefer to be alone."

"But don't you get sad always being by yourself?"

She kept going.

"My father and brothers are having a picnic at the lake. Would you like to come and have lunch with us?"

"I can't," she said. "If I'm not back, Tresel will worry."

"I know! So I told her that you would be with us."

Nannerl pulled the lead and stopped. "What in the world do you want from me?" she burst out. "You should be playing with children your own age, instead of always following me. I'm grateful, believe me, that you taught me to ride, but that doesn't give you the right to treat me like a friend. And it may be true that you gave me the idea, but otherwise I learned by myself. I don't owe anyone anything, not even Martin. All he did was give me some advice when I asked him. I don't need an intrusive little boy around who thinks he can organize my days. Now go away and don't come back. Do you understand?"

Vincent seemed to crumple in his saddle, while the corners of his mouth curved down, his forehead wrinkled, and his green eyes were hidden under long, thick lashes. He turned and galloped off.

"Wait!" Nannerl shouted, immediately sorry, but he speeded up, and she was left with an intense desire to slap herself. To make a child cry! Perfect! It was the only thing missing from her list. Why did she always realize her mistakes too late? And what was the source of this rage, which always exploded unexpectedly and always against the most unsuitable object?

"Ebony, we have to follow him," she murmured nervously, but she didn't know how to get into the saddle; obviously she didn't have the stool with her, nor was there a fence in sight, nothing that could help her up. She walked as fast as she could, but her pace could not match the horse's, and their progress was awkward. Suddenly she came upon a crumbling wall on one side of the path; maybe it wasn't high enough, but it was better than nothing. "Now you have to help me, Ebony," she said decisively and settled the horse beside the wall. She climbed up, hoisted her skirt, stuck her left foot in the stirrup, and with a great effort managed to lift herself, turning in the air so that she fell heavily onto the saddle. Ebony snorted and staggered, but otherwise didn't seem to disapprove of the strategy. Vincent was no longer to be seen, nor could the sound of his horse's hooves be heard; he must have taken the path to the lake.

"Now go!" Nannerl cried, and gave Ebony a heel and the whip, and away they went along the path. She ducked to avoid the branches, in the uncomfortable position required by the sidesaddle, with both legs on the left, and at that moment she wished she were a man so that she could control the horse's movements properly and ride with greater freedom. At the summit of the little slope that led down to the lakeshore, she stopped abruptly and in the distance saw Vincent amid a small group of people, all men, and as many horses. She straightened her skirt and proceeded cautiously and slowly, and realized that the boy was recounting something to his audience. No doubt he was talking about her and her rude behavior, and yet he wasn't crying, nor did his attitude seem offended. Three of his listeners were boys, while the fourth, presumably the father, had long blond hair gathered at the nape. Vincent pointed to her and the man turned and rested two magnetic eyes on her, one gray, one blue: it was Baron Johann Baptist von Berchtold zu Sonnenburg.

VI.

"Welcome, Fräulein Mozart," Baptist began tranquilly, showing the same irresistible smile of nine years earlier. "Hermann, help her down," he said to his oldest son, a youth who was an exact copy of him. "We have bread and butter and some *Würstchen*—just a small snack, I'm afraid, but the wine is good and they tell me that you eat rather sparingly."

"Who tells you?" Nannerl said, heedless of Hermann's arms reaching up toward her.

"Tresel, naturally."

"And how do you know her, may I ask?" she demanded through clenched teeth.

"Sankt Gilgen is only a small village: the sound of a fart echoes from one end to the other even before one has finished producing it."

The boys giggled, while Nannerl said, sharply, "I didn't recall, Baron, that your poetic eloquence could reach such heights."

"You, however, are exactly as I remembered you, Fräulein Mozart: full of enchanting sarcasm."

"I haven't missed our skirmishes at all. I have no more desire to compete. And I've realized, besides, that showing one's anger is completely pointless, not to say damaging."

"You think so? I wouldn't be so sure of it. In any case your anger never bothered me: it was only a habit, identical in that sense to my couplets. Now will you get down, please, from that nag?"

Nannerl wished with all her heart that Ebony would rear up and shatter that perfect nose; but the damn horse seemed to enjoy the attentions of the baron, who was idly patting her flanks. Should she turn and flee? But where? It seemed to her that she was in the middle of a conspiracy in which all of them, from Tresel to the fair-haired child now observing her with an irritating little smile, were trying to push her into some unclear territory. Alone against this mass of manipulative humanity, she decided to join the game and carefully jumped to the ground.

"Compliments on your dismount. Now, boys, get things ready," the baron ordered, and pouring her a glass of red wine, he led her to the shade of a beech. "Sip it slowly, not all in one swallow, the way you like to drink: it's quite strong."

"What do you know about what I like?"

"Not much, in truth. Lately I've led a somewhat retired life, more often here than in Salzburg, and very seldom in Vienna. The aristocratic world began to bore me. Ah, just for your information: I'm not married."

"Well, neither am I," she murmured.

"I did know that. Katharina von Esser told me. Rather, to be precise, she wrote me."

Nannerl began to regret not having fled.

"Her letter," the baron continued, "had a triumphant tone. Even the handwriting—full of capital letters, as if it were an ode carved in marble, with a few spelling mistakes here and there, but one can't ask too much. In essence the countess announced that you, Fräulein Mozart, were again a free woman, and she let it slip that she deserved much of the credit, and proposed that I should court you again. Something that I never did seriously, as you know, and I have no intention of starting now—don't worry."

"Then why did you come? Because you feel sorry for me?"

"Should I feel sorry for you? Why?" he asked, widening those unique eyes. "Because of that dark, melancholy expression? On the contrary, you have my most complete approval: you don't hide behind a frivolous manner but show your feelings in a genuine way. And as far as I can deduce from your complexion, you don't hide under a parasol, either. And in that, too, you have my total approval."

"Baron, I would like to know why you looked for me."

"It wasn't me. My son Vincent is the sole maker of this delayed meeting. I hope that confession doesn't offend your self-esteem."

"I don't have much left."

She didn't utter too many other words. The butter seemed to her rancid, the bread dry, and the *Würstchen* stringy. She drank three glasses of wine, but that didn't help her forget herself. She returned home at a walk, slow and sad, with an irritating sense of alienation from Ebony, who was stubborn and wouldn't go into the stable.

Nannerl tied her up outside the stable, then went to her room, fell onto the bed, and stayed there, practically inert, for a week.

VII.

"Why, may I ask, must one show gratitude to one who offers us a hand?" Baptist said, opening the door.

Under the sheet, Nannerl half opened her eyes, then slowly uncovered her face in confusion: the baron, dazzling in his hunting clothes, was holding a piece of paper with the look of one who has just read a colossal bit of nonsense.

"Are you mad? Go away!"

"Not before you have explained the meaning of these verses, O sweet Fräulein Mozart. The poetic image is excellent, I won't deny it, and the inspiration seems to me utterly genuine. Yet I really don't understand why, in this life, one would need to rely on the help of a person one doesn't even have the courage to look at."

"Get out of here now! And give me that score!"

"I would be interested in hearing you sing it. Maybe the notes give the text a meaning that can't be grasped from reading alone. I've studied music some, but as a mere amateur, and certainly at first sight, I wouldn't be able to penetrate this little creation. So I'll confine myself simply to reciting:

"I am grateful for your hand
And like a girl remain
beside you: knowing that,
I have no need to turn
My gaze upon you . . ."

"Tre-e-es-el!" Nannerl shouted, trapped under the sheets. She was wearing a loose, old-fashioned nightgown and beside the bed sat the chamber pot. She stuck out an arm and quickly shoved it in the nightstand.

The baron gave a faint, careless smile. "Spare your precious vocal cords, Fräulein Mozart. I can tell you that there is no one in the house. Tresel is out shopping. Martin is struggling to train that bad horse. Speaking of which, in recent days Ebony has regained her proverbial hostility. No one has been able to approach her."

"But there's always someone here. Help!"

"Whoever is here, I assure you, doesn't care about my scandalous presence with you. Maybe they don't even think it's scandalous."

He closed the door and didn't open the shutters, but with sure, quick movements lighted the lamp on the night table. He wore a long coat, white trousers, and riding boots, and his body, though not imposing, was perfectly proportioned: his shoulders were broad and rounded, and one could imagine the powerful muscles of his chest.

"So?" he said, staring openly at Nannerl's legs wrapped in the covers. "Do you want to explain the meaning of this composition, or do you prefer not to? I don't understand how we can expect someone else to grant us permission to live, or help us to do so by offering us a hand."

"You yourself, Baron, are here to offer me help," she said argumentatively. "Isn't that true?"

"No, certainly not. I don't intend to rout your hypochondria or sweep away your gloom. In fact, I'm somewhat fascinated by it."

"You said you had no interest in me."

"I might have lied," Baptist said, and held the score up to the light. "I would get rid of any concept of salvation or gratitude for it. So the first line has to be completely rethought. Not to mention the stale image referring to an infantile need for protection. The second line, too, I'm sorry, must be thrown out. But the next, 'knowing that, I have no need to turn my gaze upon you'—that perception is admirable, in my opinion. Visual contact with one who is beside us may be unnecessary, provided it is dictated not by fear but by a mutual awareness.

Also language, in that situation, may be superfluous. There, maybe I've got it. 'In your silent consent I rejoice . . .' "

"It doesn't fit the music," Nannerl said curtly.

"There are more syllables than there should be—you are very right, Fräulein Mozart. But fitting it to the music is a job we could do later. Let's try to see, now, if we can rework the whole without distorting the original. All right?"

"As you like."

"Thank you. So: "In your silent consent I rejoice, I remain'— certainly not 'like a girl.' What nonsense. We have to get to the exact opposite concept, my friend: the one who chooses to be at our side does not try to help us, or make us, so to speak, better by offering us a hand, but, on the contrary, welcomes us and praises us for what we are, and that attitude makes us free. Now I need an animal."

"An animal?"

"Yes, something that represents freedom, to put in place of the word *girl*. Don't bring out your nag, please."

Nannerl sat up nervously, barricaded between the pillows and the sheets. "I don't know. Nothing occurs to me."

"Come to think of it, the idea of the animal is poor. What would you say, rather, to a reference to Roman history?"

"Such as?"

"You know what the Romans called the slaves who bought their own freedom? 'Freedmen.' We could use the term.

> *"In your silent consent I rejoice*
> *and a freedwoman I remain*
> *beside you: knowing that,*
> *I have no need to turn*
> *My gaze upon you . . ."*

"How does it seem to you?"

"Without rhyme or reason."

"Life is often without rhyme or reason, Fräulein Mozart. Now take off that sheet."

"What?"

"Take off your covers, show me yourself. Just for a moment. I swear that nothing bad will happen."

She yelled, "Get out, right now!"

"Let me admire you. Just as you are, in that nightgown, which may be a little too small."

"I will not!"

"Reflect: there's no point in being stubborn. Sooner or later you'll have to get out of bed, and I won't go before that. For instance, you might need to use that object that you quickly hid in the night-stand. Would you like me to watch you performing the act or let my eyes enjoy your legs, which are nice even if they're wrapped in the finest cotton?"

"I won't take the covers off, Baron. Leave this room . . . please."

"That polite tone doesn't suit you, Fräulein Mozart. It's just an inauthentic and clumsy attempt to get me to yield. So I won't." And, very calmly, he sat down on the floor beside the door.

"Then I'll go."

"As you like."

"Hand me that robe, please."

"Again the false gentility? You won't achieve your goal that way, Nannerl."

"Give me the robe, for Heaven's sake!"

"There, now I recognize you. And in that case I might agree to some of your requests, even the most bizarre. But at the present moment, unfortunately, I find myself in a rather uncomfortable position for reaching the object, which is obviously closer to you than to me."

In fact, the robe was hanging on a stand at the foot of the bed. Biting her lips, Nannerl kicked at the sheets, which were tightly tucked in under the mattress, wrapped herself like a mummy, got to the robe, and put it on, over the sheets.

Baptist burst out laughing, like a boy, throwing his head back and half closing his eyes. But when Nannerl's bare feet passed in front of him, he stopped and couldn't keep himself from touching one. They were long and very white, the blue veins prominent, and the big toe oddly shorter than the others. He let his hand slide over the cool skin until he felt the thick material of the nails, and it seemed to him that Fräulein Mozart shivered and that she slowed her walk slightly, before disappearing onto the stairs.

VIII

With some apprehension Nannerl observed Vincent approaching Ebony, who, shut in her stall, was rolling her eyes and pawing the ground with her hooves.

"What's wrong with her, do you think?"

"I don't know. Maybe she is seriously crazy, or maybe just a bit capricious. One would have to mount her so she can find some relief by walking."

"I don't have the nerve anymore."

"But you've got to try. She's always been good with you. The only person who can make her recover is you."

"Martin trains her almost every morning, and he was born among horses. Who could do it better than he?"

The boy grimaced. "Don't say this to anyone, but I really don't like the way Martin treats animals. He's too quick with the whip."

"How do you tame a horse without it?"

"There's no need to frighten them; they're natural cowards. They have to trust their rider, not do what he wants just to avoid punishment."

Nannerl opened the gate and went into the stall. The filly stopped pulling on the rope, but her flattened-back ears gave her a hostile appearance.

"Ebony trusted you, and I think she still does," Vincent declared. "You'll see, after the first round she'll be as docile as before."

"Then maybe you should do the first round."

He laughed. "In that case we'd have to saddle her twice. Unless you want to try riding like a boy. But I would advise you not to do too many things at once. And how could you, with that long skirt?"

"All right. Let's lead her outside," she said, taking the rope and setting off through the stable. Ebony was so impatient for the sunlight that Nannerl had to hold her back forcefully.

The wind shook the treetops, which perhaps was obscurely threatening to the horse. Pulling hard on the lead, she escaped into the stable yard and stood at the end, near the fence, at the farthest point from the woods.

"Let's saddle her there, if that's what she wants," Vincent proposed. While Nannerl put on the saddle, he patted Ebony on the nose and spoke calmingly to her. When the horse was ready, her gaze had become mild again, her ears relaxed, and her tail swished against her flanks in a movement that seemed merely lazy. Maybe it was also that the wind, for the moment, had ceased.

The boy went to get the stool and placed it on the left. "Now get up. Try to avoid abrupt movements, and don't be afraid. If you're tense, she'll feel it and she'll be tense."

Nannerl climbed cautiously into the saddle, anchored her right leg on the horn, and took the long crop from Vincent, who handed it to her skillfully, without alarming the horse.

She started off at a walk, and slowly went halfway around. It was all absolutely normal. With her whole body Nannerl followed the swaying of the animal, feeling her placid and even bored movements.

"You see?" Vincent exclaimed. "Keep on like that, then we'll try going faster."

Was it the stirring of a leaf? A passing chicken? A sudden gust of wind? No one ever knew what startled the horse: she swerved violently, trying to free herself of her rider.

Miraculously Nannerl managed to stay in the saddle. She regained her equilibrium, gripping the reins and biting her lips so hard that they bled. Meanwhile the horse stopped in her tracks, abruptly pulling her head and neck down in a movement foreshadowing serious trouble.

Beside the fence, Vincent had stopped breathing. In the softest possible voice, he said, "Nannerl, you'd better get off now."

She was too frightened to do anything.

"Get off, right away," Vincent repeated, a little louder.

"Can you do something to soothe her?" she gasped, holding desperately to the reins

"No. Let go and get off, calmly."

To resist the horse's angry maneuver, Nannerl clutched the reins, and the more she tugged on them, the farther down Ebony lowered her head and neck, wrenching Nannerl's shoulders.

"Let go and get off!"

"I can't!" she cried, in a panic.

The boy ran toward her, and he saw clearly the horse's eye staring at him with hatred, a moment before she bucked.

Ebony took off at a gallop, twisting wildly, planting her hooves on the ground and raising her rear to the height of an adult man, kicking hard, and then arching her back one, two, three times, until Nannerl was hurled away like a broken doll and flew, spinning, into the center of the stable yard, where Vincent reached her, screaming with fear.

IX.

"We could take her to my house. She would be cared for there day and night," said a male voice, clear and in some way familiar.

"Better not move her," said another, unfamiliar voice.

"Her father should be notified."

"There's no hurry. We can very well wait a few days." This was a female voice, hoarse and resolute: certainly Tresel.

Out of the din rose the anguished crying of a child. Nannerl blinked her eyelids and felt a piercing headache, and realized that it was difficult to move her neck.

"She's awake!" Vincent cried, jumping up next to her, and his eyes, swollen with tears, searched for hers.

"A good sign. Out of the way, little boy," said a corpulent man with eyeglasses on his nose, picking him up and moving him aside. He leaned over her. "Fräulein Mozart, can you hear me?"

She tried to nod but immediately felt a stabbing pain in her head.

"Don't try to answer. You've regained consciousness, and you'll also regain your strength, I assure you. Unfortunately, to judge from the bruises on your forehead, you must have hit your head. Now let me examine you and make sure that you didn't get any other injuries, and you try to let me know if it hurts when I touch you."

"Should we leave, Doctor?" asked that male voice, coming now from the door.

"It's not necessary, Baron," he said. "You can stay." Slowly and with intense pressure he felt one leg and then the other, from the ankle to the groin. "Everything all right, Fräulein Mozart?"

She nodded; it was barely perceptible. The doctor conscientiously went over her arms, her ribs, and her stomach, and finally appeared satisfied. "As I thought," he declared. "At the moment the regulatory fluid can't be released by the brain in the usual way, and as a result the muscle fibers don't contract and expand as they ordinarily would."

"What does that mean?" asked Tresel.

"That there's nothing serious, apart from the blow to the head. She'll have to be utterly quiet. For today don't give her anything to eat, and starting tomorrow she can have liquids, but don't force her if she refuses."

Vincent ran to her side. "Nannerl, forgive me," he murmured, while his green eyes filled with tears again. Raising a hand to touch his cheek, she tried to smile at him and opened her swollen lips to say something that no one could hear.

"Don't try to speak!" the doctor interrupted. "Ladies and gentlemen, she must be kept as tranquil as possible. You had better leave. You, especially, little boy. Out!"

"My son and I will stay and watch her," Baptist said, with equal firmness, and he settled himself in a chair by the bed, getting the child to sit in his lap. Then, in a gentler tone, he added, "Tresel, go on. Thank you, Doctor. We'll take care of the fee later."

The others left the room, without another word.

In the silence, Nannerl closed her eyes again and concentrated on her breath, trying to maintain a regular rhythm and imagining the painful point on her head gradually dissolving, like a hill of sand washed by ocean waves. The man and child beside her seemed to be caressed by the same wavelike motion, and they breathed in harmony with her, except that Vincent every so often blew his nose and stifled a sob. It seemed to her that she saw Baptist affectionately embracing his son, and she heard him whisper, with immense tenderness, "It's not your fault . . . it's not your fault . . ."

X.

"My poor wife never liked Sankt Gilgen. She said that she hadn't married me to end up in a prison. She felt comfortable only in Salzburg, where she could go to the theater and the parties, visit her friends— and she literally adored Vienna. She would have liked to move there, but I abhor big cities, and was always opposed. It's strange. At a distance of years, I begin to think that we weren't very well matched. We married too young to realize what we were doing; and we did it essentially to please our families. I brought the noble title, and she a stream of money. Put like that, it seems rather squalid, but I assure you,

Fräulein Mozart, that Johanna and I truly loved each other. We were the same age and had been friends since childhood. To get married seemed to both of us utterly natural. You understand what I mean, don't you?"

Lying among the pillows, Nannerl assented weakly. Baptist was wandering about the room with his hands in his pockets, and sometimes he seized from the night table her hairbrush or the jar of hand cream, examined the item attentively, and then put it back.

"There, good: limit yourself to nodding or, if it's really necessary, denying. Speaking isn't allowed. Too tiring. So, as I was saying, I loved Johanna deeply, and when she died I was overwhelmed by grief. It was a little over ten years ago, in early spring. You will agree that no season is suitable for death, but spring even less so. Yet, with the passing of time my wife has become a loving memory that at times emerges spontaneously, but which I can also summon for myself. Above all, I've learned to appreciate how much good I got from that marriage, and I assure you it's a lot. Starting with my sons."

"May I ask how she died?"

He was silent for a moment, reflecting. "Six words, seventeen letters, among them seven vowels. From now on that's the most I will allow you, O my sweet convalescent." Then he moved closer, and with a sad, serious expression said, "She died giving birth to Vincent."

"Oh God. I hope he never finds out."

"Actually he already knows, and always has. I told him myself, when he was very young."

"I must say, Baron, I find that cruel."

"But don't you think it would be worse if he had learned it as an adult, and from someone else, and in the wrong way? The world of the nobility is teeming with poisonous tongues, as you well know: imagine my boy now twenty, and one fine day Katharina von Esser comes along and for who knows what ridiculous reason lets fall the valuable information, which now leaves an indelible mark on his consciousness. That, in my opinion, would be cruel."

The light from the half-open window illumined Baptist's face fully, and in the sun's rays his right iris, the one flecked with blue, seemed almost transparent.

"It's shocking," Nannerl murmured, "how certain people are able to ruin the lives of others."

"Spare your resentment for more worthy targets, Fräulein Mozart. The countess is one of the most fragile people I've ever met."

"I certainly wouldn't call her fragile."

"Katharina has an absolute need to control the lives of others, since she has no control over her own."

"What do you mean?"

"It will seem like gossiping, but—it's the truth. The count, her husband, has always betrayed her, with whatever skirt he finds in the neighborhood. The convents of the principality are home to his many conquests."

"Oh. I see. But still I can't feel pity for that woman."

"You are not required to," he said and smiled at her, coming even closer to the bed. Then politely he asked, "Would you mind if I sat next to you?"

"Of course not—please."

Baptist sat on the edge of the bed and reached out to close the door a little. A ray of light rested on Nannerl's legs, hidden by the covers. He ran his gaze over her body, from the bottom to the top, and stopped finally to observe the golden hair scattered on the pillow and on the shawl, fastened at her breast by a cameo.

After a moment she murmured, "Do you still write poems, Baron?"

"No, these days I merely demolish those of others."

She laughed lightly. "I don't believe you. I'm convinced that you still do it yourself."

"Would you like me to recite 'My Lady Nannerl in Springtime'?"

"No, please," she said laughing harder. "Although I sincerely appreciated that particular homage. By the way, I don't think I ever thanked you."

"You can do it now, Nannerl," he said, and suddenly took one hand and brought it to his lips. She held her breath, while the beating of her heart accelerated madly. "Please, Baron, please, no," she whispered, withdrawing her hand.

"Forgive me. So, the poetic vein. The answer is yes, I have continued to amuse myself. It's purely a matter of fun, though: I have never recited my verses outside the family circle, nor have I ever had the desire to offer them to a publisher. I have no ambition to be anointed a poet. And, frankly, in my opinion, fame brings only annoyance. Nobility gives me enough already."

"Do you know any of your compositions by heart?"

"All, Fräulein Mozart."

"Recite one for me."

"What would you say to a fable instead?"

She looked at him ironically. "Do you intend to treat me like a child, Baron?"

"Preserving certain childlike traits can be a good thing, I think." His gaze was lost on the white wall, and with a nostalgic smile he said, "So, I'll tell you the story of a small animal covered with spines that hadn't been happy for a long time."

Nannerl raised her eyebrows. "So you're really going to do it?"

"Don't speak. It's tiring. The little animal had been sick for a long time and couldn't even move its paws. It had never loved deeply and had never completely opened up. It was pretty to look at, and various male hands were eager to touch it, but it didn't consider itself worthy."

"Please, Baron . . ."

"Let me continue. One day, from among the spines, the hedgehog saw a hand that appeared more interesting than the others and, rolling cautiously, it approached. It began to open up to see it better and, slowly, opened up completely, presenting to the hand of the man its most secret and vulnerable part, its soft, fuzzy stomach and its soul, allowing that hand to touch all its imperfections. The hedgehog became very vulnerable; it grasped the hand tightly. In that one hand, the hedgehog forgot all others, other masculine hands that were certainly warmer and more enveloping. The hand walked about; the hedgehog crept after it."

Vaguely uneasy, Nannerl pulled up the covers, and the cameo on her breast disappeared under the white of the sheet.

"Then the season changed, and the hedgehog became as brown as the foliage of a plane tree in November. The hand of the man changed, too, and from round and warm it became skeletal: the flesh disappeared under the dry skin, and the skin fell off in flakes, revealing a tough soul. And with anguish, the hedgehog saw that the hand's desire to dig among its spines had died, for that hand was certain by now that it knew every hair on the hedgehog's stomach. So, considering itself exemplary in its own perfection, it began to insist that the hedgehog become worthy of it. The animal was imperfect, not unfit: it couldn't run like a hare or fly like a butterfly or sing like a cicada, and it wasn't dazzling like a rooster or mysterious like a cat—but how can one compare, may I ask, a cat to a hedgehog?"

He stopped looking at the wall and fixed his eyes on hers. She would have liked to look away but his eyes attracted hers like a magnet.

"But the hand of the man was ruthless with the hedgehog's stomach. It scratched it and made the blood flow, and then humiliated the hedgehog and left it alone. Its little heart was invaded by a great anger, and it closed up again, depriving the world of its savage beauty. In its isolation, it tried with all its strength not to think anymore of that hand, but the truth is that it didn't succeed."

Nannerl had to blink her eyes. She seemed to feel a massive weight on her forehead, and her breath was short.

"Who can say if it had been right to offer itself with such generosity, baring its imperfections, so as to rouse the desire to make up for them. Perhaps that hand had acted with absolute honesty, with its own peculiar way of loving. Maybe it wasn't able to love. Or maybe it just didn't love the hedgehog. The creature found no answers. It didn't understand, but it was aware of that—and one who knows that he doesn't know has his life in his own hands."

The tears ran freely down her cheeks, hitting the sheet like a gentle rain. With a slow caress, Baptist wiped them from her face, then tasted their salt on the tips of his fingers.

XI.

In an instant Ebony had escaped. All Martin's skill had not been enough to stop her. He had taken her out of her stall to clean it, and as soon as they reached the stable yard she tugged so unexpectedly and so violently on the rope that he fell hard on the ground, while she galloped toward the hill.

Sitting on the bench, hot, Nannerl stared at the sundial on the wall, and it seemed to her that the shadow never moved. Martin had gone in search of the filly and hadn't returned. The baron was offering her a glass of cool water, which she kept refusing. She rose, took a couple of steps, and sat down again. She crushed the grass with her shoes and then tore a handful out of the ground and threw it. Finally the sound of a gallop could be heard, but of one horse only, and at the end of the gravel road Martin appeared. He dismounted, tied his horse to the gate of the stable yard, and came toward the house.

Nannerl ran to meet him. "Did you find her?"

He went right past her with a grim face and headed straight for the door.

"Where are you going? Did you find Ebony or not?"

He went into the house, took a key from a drawer, and put it in the lock of a large wardrobe.

"Can't you answer me?" said Nannerl, joining him. "What in the world happened?"

"Calm down," Tresel ordered, wiping her hands on her apron.

"Martin, would you like me to call some of my men?" Baptist asked, with an odd expression on his face.

"That would be very kind, Baron," he answered. "They'll have to dig a hole and throw her in. It can be done there, in the place." Meanwhile he took a gun from the closet and quickly assembled it.

"Do you want to go right away?"

"As soon as possible."

"Is it far?"

"Not very. Halfway between here and your house."

"Then I'll come with you. Ammunition?"

"In the back, on the left."

Tresel had already taken the case from the closet and handed it to her son.

"You'll kill her?" Nannerl asked, breathless.

Martin didn't even look at her. "I should have anticipated it and brought the gun, instead of having to come back." He slung the gun over his shoulder and left the house.

"But why?" she cried.

"Do you want to come with us, Fräulein Mozart?"

She felt as if she were choking. Baptist and Tresel stared at her, at once decisive and grim. "All right," she whispered, and the baron took her by the shoulders and they ran to his horse. "I'll carry you behind me. Don't worry, the horse is used to it." He mounted easily, freed the stirrup, and held out his hand. "Come on, Fräulein Mozart, a good jump. Then grip the horse's back hard with your legs and hold on to me."

Nannerl found herself in contact with the body of the horse, behind the saddle, and her legs were spread and half uncovered, but there was nothing to be done. She put her arms around Baptist's broad chest and her head against his back. She felt perfectly secure.

"Are you ready?"

A weak assent and they were off, following Martin, who was already in the distance.

The horse ran furiously and yet the jolting was gentle, and Baptist went with him and she with Baptist. She tried not to resist the motion but to follow it, to stay one with the rider, as if drawn by the irresistible wave of a flood; and she tried to hold in thoughts of the consequences and drive out the fear of falling, the fear of that solid, muscular body to which she clung, and the terror of what would happen to Ebony. The path among the trees narrowed and Baptist shouted, "Get down with me!" She bent over him, crushing her breasts against his body, the branches slapping her, and suddenly the path opened up and they were in a broad clearing.

The pace slowed to a light trot, then to a cautious walk. It seemed to her that Baptist stiffened slightly, and the horse stopped.

"Are we there?"

He murmured, "Poor beast." Nannerl stretched her head out beyond his shoulder and so doing, she saw the horse.

She was trapped in a hole, covered with saliva and foamy sweat. Her eyes were bulging out of their sockets, and unearthly sounds came from her.

"You have to get down first, Fräulein Mozart."

She slid to the ground. Martin was already loading the gun. Both Ebony's front legs were broken, and they seemed to emanate a bony whiteness of death. She was suffering terribly, and she shook her big head and tried to move, and the more she moved the more pain she felt, and the more pain she felt the more she cried out.

"I'm sorry, Nannerl," said Martin, "but it happens. Even if her legs could be fixed in some way, her life would be terrible. The best thing is to end her suffering immediately."

With a wild look, Nannerl placed herself between him and the horse. "Wait—I'll do it."

He continued to load the weapon. "But if you don't know how to shoot . . ."

"I want to be the one to do it."

"You risk hitting her without killing her. Get out of the way."

"I think we should let her do it," the baron said quietly. "Give her the gun, Martin."

Nannerl took it in two hands. It was massive and heavy, and she thought that to pull that trigger she would have to use four fingers, two on each side. Next to her, Martin shook his head and Baptist looked at her silently.

She raised her arms until she had Ebony's eye exactly in the gun sight. Her hands were steady. In an instant she could destroy the life of this beast, who was already destroyed. In an instant she saw herself again in the courtyard of the old house on the Getreidegasse throwing her manuscripts onto the fire. In an instant, exactly as it had been then, it would all be over.

"I can't," she whispered. "Baptist, you do it." She gave him the gun, he took aim, and the next minute Ebony was dead.

She turned her back. "Now take me home. Please."

XII.

She lifted the latch and went into the stall. Her hands were clasped behind her back and her head was bent. Her feet sank into the straw, and she thought of nothing.

"Are you sure you're all right?"

"Yes, thank you, Baron," she answered without looking at him.

"You had begun to call me by my name."

"Really? When?"

"Before. Anyway, you can call me whatever you like. Even by my full family name, if you have enough breath."

She gave no hint of a smile. She began to walk slowly along the edge of the walls with her head lowered.

"Would you prefer to be alone?"

"I don't know."

"But you don't mind if I stay near you."

"I don't even know that."

Baptist closed the latch and went in. He, too, began wandering through the narrow space, without ever losing sight of Nannerl and always keeping a distance of a few feet between them. They seemed separate yet linked by an invisible bar, and the fulcrum of the bar was the center of the stall.

Suddenly he consumed that distance and pushed her against the wall. He pressed her shoulders against it, sank his face into the hollow of her tanned neck, and breathed in its odor. Then he fell to his knees, raised her skirt, and rubbed the top of his head against her pubic bone.

"Someone might come," she whispered.

"I closed the gate. If anyone opens it, we'll hear. Only the horses know we're here." And meanwhile he went on rubbing his forehead against her thighs, and a thousand odors hit him: the freshness of undergarments, the dustiness of the flounced skirt, the enveloping scent of her.

"Lie down," he said.

He took off her shoes and stockings and reached his fingers under the cotton of her long culottes, touching the pale, tremulous skin, and the more she let go, the farther up he went, stopping at the hollow of her knee and on the soft flesh of the inside of the thighs. He tasted her with his tongue and even his teeth, letting his warm breath inflame Nannerl, then he had her lift up her hips and in a quick move he took off the culottes.

Slowly he approached her face and touched the skin of her eyelids, which she immediately closed; he persuaded her to let her head fall back, and with his open hand caressed her from the knee to the groin and down to the other knee, and then again to the groin. He, too, was lying on the floor of the stall, facing her, and he put his arms around her thighs, and rested his head on her stomach, and for a long moment was absolutely still, breathing deeply over her. Then he opened his mouth and tasted the flavor of her, and while she held her breath and trembled, he pressed with the most pleasurable force, and from his throat came low, vibrant sounds. She raised herself on her elbows and looked down, and saw the face of Baptist mingled with her sex, and his blond hair spread on her stomach, and the sight increased her piercing euphoria. Unable to hold herself up she fell back, and just then her limbs tensed; she stopped breathing and squeezed her fists.

Baptist waited until the wave was spent, holding her tight in his arms and stretching out his hands to caress her breasts. Then he lay on top of her and began gently kissing her face, her half-closed eyes, and her parted lips, from which her breath came short and fragrant, and slowly he penetrated her.

That was the movement of hips and thighs she had seen Wolfgang making with Victoria, but to receive it—oh, to receive it was a completely different thing. Baptist raised himself slightly, and then pushed deeper and deeper, and gradually became fuller inside her, and she expanded and welcomed him joyfully, completely. She put her legs around him and began to move with him, and realized that this increased her pleasure, so she moved more forcefully, and realized that it increased his pleasure. Then she wanted him to stop and lie on the straw in her place and she was on him and took him back inside her, then she began to raise and lower herself and go back and forth in a crescendo, and meanwhile she entwined her fingers in his and never let her eyes leave his. Sometimes she slowed the rhythm, to savor this precious time, then again accelerated, and he followed her and guided her, with his hands wrapped tightly around her hips. Until neither could any longer resist the force that sweetly swallowed them, an explosion that, starting at the point of contact, radiated outward, dissolving the bodies of the two lovers, and their very identities, outside of that place, outside of time.

Lying on the straw in their close embrace, Nannerl and Baptist lay still for a long while, with hearts pounding at unequal rhythms, like elements of a single system, different and essential to each other.

XIII.

A slovenly servant wiped her runny nose on her sleeve, arranged the knot of her apron on her lower back, and knocked three times on the bedroom door.

"Excuse me, sir, may I enter?"

As she anticipated, she received no answer. Interrupting the master's little nap was a suicidal act, but what else could she do?

She knocked louder. "Sir? Herr Mozart?"

She half opened the door, just in time to hear a shout: "What the devil do you want, you idiot?"

Quickly she went to open the shutters. "Sir . . . I'm sorry but you must get up. There's a visitor for you."

"And who might that be?"

"A very distinguished gentleman. He's waiting for you in the parlor."

"What do you mean? Didn't you tell him I don't receive anyone at this hour?"

"Yes, but he said that it's very important, and that he won't go until he speaks to you. Look, he gave me his visiting card."

Leopold took the card from the girl's dirty hands, held it away from himself just enough so that he could decipher it, and on his face appeared an expression of satisfaction. "A baron? What in the world does he want? All right, bring me my scarlet jacket and go to the kitchen and prepare some refreshment."

"What shall I prepare it with? The noodles left over from lunch?"

"Coffee and tarts, idiot!"

"What shall I make the tarts with? You won't let me buy anything."

"There must be some bread, surely? Slice it and butter it."

"There's not even any butter."

"Invent something, you imbecile. Use your brain. Get going!"

Wandering among the dusty furniture of the room, Baptist searched for traces of Nannerl. Above an old harpsichord hung a painting that depicted the whole family: her father held a violin and was leaning on the case of a piano, while her mother, of whom Baptist had a vivid memory, was shown in a painting within the painting; she must by then have gone to a better life. Brother and sister were seated at the keyboard. Nannerl's hair was done in an imposing and artificial style, bound at the top with a reddish ribbon from which a large tassel dangled. Her lovely face seemed to disappear completely, and her expression had something timid and sad about it. The celebrated Wolfgang did not seem much happier, but a greater resolve showed in his features; and if Nannerl touched the keys with some hesitation, his fingers reached out to dominate them.

"Good evening, Baron," Leopold began, and, eying the card, added, "von Berchtold zu Sonnenburg." He came toward the baron leaning on his cane. Under the scarlet jacket he had buttoned the waistcoat wrong, and from under his wig sprang a tuft of white hair. "Your family is known to me, naturally, and yet I don't recall ever having met you in person."

"No, in fact, Herr Mozart," Baptist answered with extreme politeness, shaking Leopold's hand. "On the other hand, I had the opportunity of meeting, some years ago, the late Frau Anna Maria and also your daughter, Nannerl."

"Neither of the two is present in this house, for very different reasons. Of the death of my wife you have had news, I see, while at the moment Nannerl is outside the city."

"In Sankt Gilgen. I know."

"You know?"

"Yes, Herr Mozart."

"And how is that, if I may ask?"

"Because I have lived in that village for some time; and in fact I have had occasion to see Nannerl more than once in the course of the summer."

"Oh, really? Then perhaps you can tell me something about her." In a tone of resentment he added, "Recently her letters have been rather scarce."

"That is exactly why I am here, Herr Mozart. Nannerl has charged me to inform you that she does not intend to return to Salzburg."

"May I?" the servant chirped from the doorway, bearing triumphantly a tray with two cups of coffee and slices of black bread on which she had smeared some dubious substance. "Here's everything: spoons, sugar. Would you like me to bring some milk, sir? There is half a jug left."

"Get out!" Leopold shouted, and she disappeared in a flash. "Baron, I fear I have not correctly understood your declaration," he whispered with increasing nervousness. "Since when does my own daughter engage a perfect stranger to bring me a message from her? And then, what a message! I sent her to the village so that she could recover from a serious affliction, whose causes I am not about to explain to you, but at this point I am forced to consider that the mountain air has made the affliction worse. Nannerl must be out of her mind by now!"

"It may be," Baptist said calmly, "since she has consented to marry me."

The stick fell out of Leopold's hands and rolled to the baron's feet. He picked it up. "Sit down, Herr Mozart. You seem to need to."

He accompanied Nannerl's father to the sofa, while the old man stammered, "But how . . . what . . . marry? And I . . . I didn't know anything about it?"

"I understand that it might seem to you a rather sudden decision, but I assure you that it has in fact been very much thought about and properly motivated. Need I add anything more?"

Leopold cast a sidelong look at this fine-looking man with the eyes of a serpent. He spoke with an intolerable self-assurance, and even with a sense of pity! With tight lips he said, "It seems the idea that I might deny my consent hasn't even occurred to you. And if I did so?"

Baptist didn't lose his composure in the least. "Are you not pleased that your daughter will become a baroness, Herr Mozart? I confess that it surprises me: I would have bet on the contrary."

"No—that is, yes . . . Really, the fact is that—you understand, I should have been informed of the matter with some advance notice! It isn't right for a father to be cut out of a deliberation of such importance. Also, to tell you the truth, there are some things that you probably don't know, and of which I alone can inform you."

"Oh, indeed? Do so immediately, please."

"Yes, but don't stand there, Baron. Have a cup of coffee and some tarts," Leopold said unctuously, considering that the shoes worn by this man must have cost as much as the floor they rested on.

"Thank you, but I must refuse: I don't drink coffee, and in any case I dined just an hour ago. Tell me, then."

Herr Mozart took a long, deep breath, and with the grim expression of one who announces a catastrophe, he stated, "Nannerl has no dowry. All my earnings, the family savings, the very proceeds of her lessons have been used up in supporting the studies of my son. Apart from some extra linens for the house, and a few pieces of furniture—which in any case it would be in bad taste to reuse—I have nothing, nothing to give her, do you understand?"

"And so?"

"I mean only that . . . that marrying her includes accepting a responsibility, not only for your wife but in some way for the entire family. I, a poor old man, am in danger of being left here, completely alone—in short, I thought it was my duty to let you know about the situation in its entirety."

"I am grateful for your conscientiousness, but don't worry: I will provide thoroughly for Nannerl and the children I hope we will have, since my means allow me to guarantee a comfortable life for those who are dear to me"—his gaze was fixed on the worn upholstery of the sofa—"and only those who are dear to me," he concluded with a polite smile.

"Oh, well, I understand."

"I am delighted. The marriage will be celebrated in Sankt Gilgen, in exactly fifteen days, in the church of Saint Giles. The guests will be only those who are indispensable—and yet they are not few, between Tresel's family and the sons of my previous marriage."

"What? The servant will be there?"

"Yes, of course. I will arrange to put at your disposal a carriage, Herr Mozart, so that you may be present and then brought back here, to your house, after the ceremony."

"All right, Baron," he grumbled.

"You may call me Baptist, if you like. As far as your other child is concerned, however, I'm very sorry, but I'm afraid I can't make the same arrangements, for obvious reasons of distance."

The old man shook his head. "In any case, I don't think Wolfgang would move from Vienna." Then, growing animated, he continued: "His latest opera was a triumph, did you know? And you will understand that to abandon the field at the peak of success, even for a few days, might be an irrevocable mistake."

"The concept is perfectly clear to me. Still, I imagine that Nannerl would like to tell him the news. Would you be kind enough to provide his address?"

"Please, forget it. I will write to him." He lowered his voice and, with the air of one who is revealing a painful secret, added, "The relationship between my children is almost nonexistent now. At one time they loved each other dearly, and today they hate each other."

"I wonder why," Baptist said in a firm voice.

"Who knows?"

"Precisely: Who knows?" he repeated, then calmly retrieved his hat. "At this point I would say that we can end our meeting. I will let you know the details of your transportation to Sankt Gilgen."

"Thank you."

"Not at all. My respects, Herr Mozart."

"Wait, Baron—that is, Baptist!" He stood up and hobbled to the door. With an attempt at a smile he said, "Would you accept that old harpsichord, at least? It has a certain value, and my daughter was very fond of it."

"Frankly, Herr Mozart, I don't think it would interest Nannerl anymore. Let's leave it here. It goes very well under the painting."

The Break

I.

Snow in the mountains, on the trees, snow icing the lake, snow even on the entrance drive.

The carriage stopped at the gate and a woman with a haggard face and wearing no makeup descended. She straightened the folds of her fur, which gleamed in the sun. Then from her purse she took a muff, also of fur, and put her hands inside. Breathing in the cold air she approached the iron bars and looked up at the roof of the villa, where a chimney was spewing smoke with a cheerfulness that was utterly out of place.

She went through the gate cautiously, leaving dainty footprints on the white ground, and passed a man who was intently hammering on a wheel. She gave him a vague nod of greeting.

"Would you like me to announce you, ma'am?" he said.

"I would prefer not," she replied, and instead of going to the door, she slowly approached a window. With the muff, she cleared a square of frost, breathed on it, again wiped it with the fur, and tried to make out what was happening inside.

"Excuse me, but what do you want?" said the man at the wheel, coming up to her. "Tell me your name immediately!"

With sad, dark eyes she looked at his face and modest clothes. "All right, I'll knock," she said. She went to the door and rapped twice. A cheerful din escaped and some scattered cries, and yet no precise sound.

"They can't hear you," the man said. "You have to knock louder."

So she raised the knocker and let it fall with a deafening thud and, when nothing happened, did it again and yet again, in a repetition that became more and more exasperated. The man observed her uneasily. Finally the door opened and a young man appeared with a child on his shoulders; the two of them emanated a palpable, irritating joyfulness.

"Oh, how nice! We have guests," the young man began. "What may I do for you, ma'am?"

"I would like to speak to the baroness. Is she home?"

"Who are you?"

"Victoria d'Ippold, now Paumgartner. Your mother and I know each other well."

"Really? Well, Nannerl isn't my mother—she's the woman I chose for my father," he explained happily, and managed to kiss her hand without letting the child fall. "*Enchanté*. I am Vincent von Berchtold zu Sonnenburg. And this is Jeanette, my little sister. Jeanette, say hello to the lady. Come in, if you don't mind, we'll show you the way. It's a great pity you're married, Madame. I certainly would be inspired to court you."

In a large room with a pillar in the center a lively disorder reigned.

Tables, sofas, and floor were littered with toys of every sort: a tricy-
cle with a horse's head; a dollhouse with furniture; various wax and
porcelain dolls dressed up in brocade, muslin, and lace; a mechanical
creature in the guise of a painter; and a giant marble chessboard, complete with pieces at least a foot tall. And yet there was not a single
instrument, not a drum, not a bell, not even a fife.

"Who's here?" a deep voice called down from the floor above.

"Are you presentable?" Vincent said. "Anyway, it's a woman,
don't worry."

With her heart in her throat, Victoria, standing at an angle at the
foot of the stairs, listened to those impetuous footsteps without looking up; then they ceased, and an astonished silence forced her to turn.
Nannerl gripped the banister with two bare arms, and her chest, fuller
than Victoria remembered, was animated by anxious breathing. She
was forty but seemed younger than Victoria, and her cheeks glowed
like those of a girl interrupted in a game. Her hair had been hurriedly
gathered up by two combs at the top of her head, and curls, still blond,
fell to the soft curves of her neck and shoulders, rising and falling
with her breath.

She said nothing. She descended the last steps, staring at Victoria
with those blue eyes that no longer seemed severe, and as her lips
parted in a smile, she embraced her warmly. Victoria was unable to
yield to the embrace, and she wished not to be there, not now, not for
this reason. Nannerl released her and caressed her face and kissed her
and sought in her features the memory of too many years of separation, murmuring, "Victoria . . . dear Victoria . . ."

Victoria had to push her away brusquely. She cleared her throat
and said, "Please, send the child away."

A hint of fear then appeared on Nannerl's face. She looked
at Vincent, who went upstairs without a word, holding his sister by
the hand.

"Let's sit down, Nannerl," Victoria said.

Nannerl took the doll clothes off the sofa and piled them on the floor. She sat on a pillow, restless, her hands on her knees—practical, rough hands, no longer the lords of her body. "Tell me, please."

"It's about Wolfgang."

II.

The door opened and Nannerl, frantic, ran out. A strange lament came from her mouth, her throat, her chest, and her brain, a visceral sound of animal grief. The man with the wheel heard her, saw her, started, and stood with his hammer poised in midair. She ran along the drive, reached the gate, seized it, gripped it as if to break it, then opened it and went into the woods; she stumbled and sank in the snow, staring at the sky and wishing it would crash down on her head.

"Go after her!" Vincent cried, darting outside, followed by Victoria. "I'm going to call my father." He got on his horse and went off at a desperate gallop, while Victoria struggled along the drive, picking up her skirts and her fur, and looked around for Nannerl. She saw her crouched at the foot of a tree and, reaching her, was about to grab her, but she jumped up and continued on with agitated steps. Victoria, trying to keep up, was gasping, "Nannerl, please, stop."

"Tell me more. When did it happen?"

"December fifth. They buried him the following day."

"How did you find out?"

"My father was on a mission to Vienna. He saw the bier coming out of the Palace."

"How did it happen?"

"He'd been ill for a long time, but no one knows what it was. The doctors didn't know."

Suddenly Nannerl stopped and grabbed her by the shoulders. Shaking her, she cried, "I knew nothing, nothing, do you see? Does it seem to you possible?"

Her voice echoed among the mountain peaks and gradually faded.

For a moment Victoria thought Nannerl would lose consciousness, but instead she ran off among the trees repeating, "Go away. Leave me alone."

III.

"I'm sorry, Baron, but should someone go and look for Nannerl in the woods?"

"No, certainly not, Frau Paumgartner. If my wife doesn't want company, no one should impose it on her."

"But the cold is terrible."

Playing a game of chess with himself, Baptist didn't answer. For a good half hour he had been playing with those big pieces; he moved one after careful consideration, then, in no hurry, he rose, went to the other side, thought about it, and moved another, then returned. Victoria no longer knew what to think.

"I wonder how you can be so calm."

"I could not be," he said, and at that exact moment the door banged and Nannerl burst in, crying, "Baptist, I've decided: tomorrow I'm going to Vienna."

Seeing her, Victoria felt her heart contract with pity. She was trembling, and her teeth chattered, and it seemed that her body was drawn toward an abyss that she was desperately trying to avoid. Her wild stare had nothing human in it; she was no longer herself, neither the loving woman Victoria had just had time to see, nor the inflexible girl whom years before she had loved. From her wet, snow-stained skirt, spots dripped onto the floor, and she crossed her arms over her chest, gripping herself with pale fingers. She had a swelling on her cheek, as if she had run into a tree or as if, unable to bear the pain of her soul, she had hit it.

"I'm going to Vienna," she repeated. "I have to understand, Baptist.

You will tell me it's useless to ask painful questions and search for answers, but I must try. You will tell me I should resign myself to fate, but I cannot! You will tell me that those who are responsible don't exist, but I must understand if somewhere, in fact, they do."

As she spoke, from the upper floors came Vincent, and then three more young men, and beside one of them a young woman with an infant in her arms, and then the girl Jeanette, and a boy a little older. Vincent carried a blanket, which he unfolded and placed around Nannerl's shoulders, and then he gently drew her to the hearth.

"I have to go alone, Baptist," she continued. "You will tell me that someone should come with me, but this concerns me more than all of you, and I must face it in solitude. You will tell me that now I should go to bed and weep until I cannot anymore, and then begin to live again, but you know perfectly well that I am not capable of that! You will tell me that it's hard for me to leave here, that I do not go willingly even to Salzburg—imagine Vienna. But now I feel, I feel it, that I must force myself. I must come to an understanding of what has happened. And it's not a punishment. I need it, Baptist!"

He had remained sitting at the chessboard, and Victoria seemed to see a tear shine in those special eyes of his. Then he rose and in a clear voice said, "I will go and give the orders to the coachman." As he passed Nannerl, he caressed her swollen cheek, and went out.

IV.

By late evening Nannerl had calmed a little. Wrapped in a blanket and sipping hot broth from a cup, she let Victoria rub her legs with aromatic oil.

"When I heard that Wolfgang was getting married, I was completely indifferent," she said, "as he was, I imagine, at the announcement of my marriage. For some time our father functioned as a

go-between, through those long-winded letters of his, telling Wolfgang about my family life, I suppose, and me of his successes. He also
sent me some copies of his scores, which I haven't even looked at."

"You never play?"

She gave a tired smile. "Have you seen a piano in the house?"

"No—and I wonder how it is that you feel no desire to touch a
keyboard, at least once in a while."

"And yet it's so, Victoria. And it's not a bitter renunciation, I assure
you. I would need too much practice by now to recover from that inac-
tivity. Besides, I doubt whether I would entirely regain the agility that
distinguished me, or my precision of touch. Sometimes it occurs to me
that I could play again, and we'd only have to bring in a piano that is
in one of our apartments in Salzburg. But it would be a lot of trouble;
and then I forget about it, and so I've let it go completely."

Victoria compared her own well-cared-for hands with Nannerl's.
"But, then, what do you do with your days?"

She smiled more openly. "With this house, with my husband, with
his children and ours—don't you think that's more than enough?
Jeanette is a special child. I'm having her study Latin, and then
she teaches me, can you imagine! And my little boy is lovable and
brilliant."

"Then you haven't introduced music to your children, either?"

She sighed. "Stop, Victoria, please. Long ago I stopped feeling
tormented because certain people urged me to do something that they
considered right for me, and that I really didn't want to do. You, and
your father, and Wolfgang—more than anyone, Wolfgang." She
interrupted herself and again whispered the name of her brother, then
suddenly hid her face and burst into sobs.

Victoria felt completely impotent. She placed a hand on Nannerl's
head, but it went unnoticed while she moaned, "I never met his children, nor he mine. I never saw his house in Vienna, nor did he ever
come to this place. I have used every ounce of my energy in hating
the memory of him."

"When were you last in touch?"

"Five years and five months ago. Wolfgang sent me good wishes for my name day. I wrote to thank him—and then nothing." She dried her tears on the blanket. "The intensity of my grief is disconcerting to me, because when our father died I felt nothing."

"Is that possible?"

"Nothing, I swear to you. Neither regret nor a sense of loss. Rather, perhaps, a trace of satisfaction—though it's cruel that I say it and even crueler that I felt it." She put on her woolen stockings, ending the massage. "You know what my father said just before he died? He begged me to reconcile with Wolfgang. And I didn't. And now I know it was just to contradict him. Oh Victoria, I can't wait to go. I must mend this break."

"Excuse me . . ."

Baptist was at the foot of the stairs with a book under his arm and a lamp in his hand. "I would like to remind my gracious consort," he said with a slight smile, "that this is our last night together for who knows how long, and it might be polite on her part not to let me sleep in solitude."

She smiled at him in return. "I'll join you soon."

"Good. Good night, Frau Paumgartner," and he vanished into the darkness of the staircase.

For a few moments the women were silent, both wondering if it was the moment to end the conversation. Then Nannerl said, with a certain hesitation, "You, too, are married."

"Yes, to a musician."

"Really? That must be a wonderful union. And the child," she added, looking away, "well, you know what I mean . . . is well, is in good health?"

"It's a girl. Yes, she's well. And my husband is an excellent father to her."

Nannerl nodded, deeply comforted. Then she asked, "Have you had other children?"

"We would have liked to, but it didn't happen unfortunately. In any case, it would be difficult to reconcile my concerts, and above all the lessons, with a houseful of children."

"How many students do you have?"

"Twenty-six."

"My goodness. So you must teach every day, for at least five hours."

"Every morning I practice myself, and afternoons are for the students. Two of them," she continued with tender pride, "have already performed in public."

"It seems that teaching is satisfying for you," Nannerl considered, with some surprise.

"I try to be a teacher worthy of what I had."

Another long silence fell, then Victoria murmured timidly, "We could go part of the way together tomorrow."

"A brief part, of course, before separating."

"How long do you think you'll stay in Vienna?"

"I haven't decided yet," Nunnerl answered, getting up and wrapping the blanket around her legs. Then she went to a window that looked onto the back and with a sort of reverence opened it, defying the cold. "Come," she said, and pointed out to Victoria the snowy hills illuminated by the moon, and meanwhile she murmured, "A thousand times I have leaned on this windowsill wondering which direction Vienna was, in which direction I should turn my gaze, to imagine being close to my brother. I indulged in the certainty of a common feeling, that he thought of, and sometimes even dreamed of, me. And I was sure that in the end we would find each other, that, as in our childhood, a rhyme would be enough for us to be in harmony again."

She stopped speaking, sensing a presence behind her; it was a child in a nightgown. "Jeanette! What are you doing awake? Come upstairs right now!" Nannerl exclaimed, quickly closing the window and freeing herself from the blanket. "I'm sorry, Victoria, I really must go. Do you know how to find your room again?"

"Of course; don't worry." As she watched Nannerl go toward the stairs with the child, she said, "I like the name Jeanette. You chose well."

She turned, smiling. "Oh, thank you. Baptist chose it, in fact. And what is your daughter's name?"

"Nannerl."

V.

"Baroness, we've arrived!"

The coachman had to call her again. She was lying amid the cushions that she had arranged on the seats so that they made a kind of lap in which she could curl up, huddle; she heard that male voice and the tapping on the window, but they did not seem to be addressed to her. In her mind she was elsewhere, in a dark room, at Wolfgang's deathbed.

Her sick brother did not have compresses on his forehead or arms wounded by bloodletting or strange equipment and tubes around him. He seemed only enormously tired, barely reacting to or interested in the world. He was lying on one side with the sheet twisted to cover his mouth, and his eyes, bulging, stared at the walls. Nannerl was sure that he could hear and understand in every detail what was happening but did not wish to influence the course of events. Around him appeared other personages, somewhat obscured: Herr Mozart, above all, who, seated in a corner, observed the scene as if it were merely a plot of his devising; and then there was Constanze, Wolfgang's wife, who, wearing something loose-fitting, was sitting on the edge of the bed caressing him with inappropriately sensual gestures. A doctor hovered in the room as well, and, like a bad actor, kept repeating the same line, in search of the proper tone: "The poor young man is done for, and we must hurry the end, so as to keep him from needless suffering." And he poured a beverage into a cup: a fast-acting poison.

Wolfgang downed the liquid, as if obeying fate, as if resigning himself to an unjust punishment that he was too tired to defend against; but at that exact moment, Nannerl knew, with utter certainty, that it wasn't the end and that his condition wasn't irrevocable. He was merely oppressed by a deep melancholy, which every man, if he wants to, has the power to survive; but perhaps this perception had arrived too late, and the hidden director had already brought the drama to its end.

She approached the head of the bed: Wolfgang was still lying on his side, with a veiled gaze. And he was alive. Was it possible that the poison had not taken effect? Possible that the father, having figured out the trick, had exchanged the liquid for a glass of water? She grabbed her brother's hands and uttered the ancient formula for harmony, but he made no response, and Nannerl couldn't guess his thoughts.

"I'm ready, Sebastian," she said, shaking herself. She felt extremely weak. The cold air didn't revive her but made her long to get back in the carriage and go home. What a macabre idea to go and see Wolfgang's tomb. Why had she asked the coachman to take her here? Once she found the stone, was she going to try to talk to a marble plaque? Her brother was not in this place; no trace of his consciousness could be found on this earth. What remained of him? To what purpose had he been born, lived, and died, at only thirty-five?

"Would you like me to accompany you, Baroness?"

She shook her head and held out an arm to keep him away. The gate squeaked as she opened it, and she was in the cemetery of Sankt Marx, as if following the will of someone else.

A dense fog had lodged in her mind. A void made of too many thoughts, which led her to wander aimlessly among the iron crosses arranged in neat rows, the bunches of frozen flowers in opaque, dirty jars, until she saw a caretaker shoveling snow, and dragging her feet, she approached him.

"Excuse me, could you please tell me where I might find the grave of Wolfgang Amadeus Mozart?"

"Wolfgang who?" he asked, sticking the shovel in the snow and resting an armpit on it.

"Mozart! You don't know him?"

The man snapped his fingers. "Oh yes, that poor musician. They dumped him in a pauper's grave."

"A pauper's grave?" she repeated, breathless.

The caretaker played with the shovel, observing Nannerl cynically; he seemed struck above all by her expensive clothes. "Why—do you want to go there?" he said, sneering, and without waiting for a response, he set off. "You know, at the moment I didn't understand, but now I remember clearly. The wife didn't have money for a private grave, and so, you understand . . ."

"But there's nothing to remember him by? Not even a stone?"

"What does that have to do with it—you can always put up a stone. You can do anything, even a statue if you want. Whatever you like. If you have the money you can do anything; am I right or not, ma'am?"

Near the grave a solitary visitor was walking back and forth along the path with short, quick steps, talking to himself.

"That man is a musician," the caretaker exclaimed. "He comes every single day. Don't ask me why, because I don't have the slightest idea."

"What's his name?"

"Antonio Salieri."

Nannerl felt her energy revive. "You can go now. Thank you."

"It's nothing. And let me know about the plaque!"

VI.

"Herr Salieri?" she said, approaching very slowly.

He had an unassuming appearance: slender, typically Italian, in a tight jacket covered with decorations of which he was evidently very proud. Observing her, he arched his eyebrows in a mask of restraint; his lips, in the shadow of an aquiline nose, were almost nonexistent.

"Who are you?" he asked suspiciously.

"Mozart's sister."

He said nothing, evidently much affected, then he stated, "I didn't know he had a sister."

"I'm not surprised," she murmured, putting her hands in the pockets of her coat. "I don't imagine he ever spoke of me."

"Did you have a good relationship with him?"

Were these proper questions? "And you, if I may ask?"

Marvelously, the faint line on the face of the little man opened into a smile of utter kindness. "I would have liked to have a pupil like Mozart. That was the first thing I thought as soon as I met him. He had no need of a maestro by then, but when he was a boy—oh when he was a boy it would have been so exalting to confront such a genius! Do you know anything about music, madam?"

"I would say so."

"And have you had good teachers?"

"In fact I was a piano teacher myself."

"Oh, really? That's very interesting. Have any of your pupils had a successful career?"

"Only one, as far as I know."

"That is already a great deal, don't you think? I will confess to you one thing: for me it would be a greater satisfaction to be remembered as a teacher rather than as a court composer. Glory for oneself is never intoxicating the way a relationship with an evolving talent is. And the applause we may receive personally is not as satisfying as that which is addressed to our students. And I consider myself fortunate, for one of my boys is beginning to give me satisfaction: young Ludwig van Beethoven is undoubtedly the best, yes . . ." And he walked off along the path, mumbling to himself again.

"But where are you going? I need to talk to you!"

He turned, with his eyebrows so arched with surprise that they practically reached his hairline. "About what, may I ask?"

"About my brother, obviously, and also music."

"Regarding your brother, I haven't much to tell."

"But you knew him!"

"Yes, of course, but our personal relations were very limited. Forgive me, madam, I have to go now."

"Then why do you come here?"

Salieri gave her a strange look. A gust of wind lifted his gray hair and the lapel of his jacket.

"Why do you come here, if you hardly knew him?" Nannerl insisted.

The man took a deep breath, and in a low voice said, "Do you believe that terror can be colored by lightness?"

Nannerl didn't know how to respond.

"Madam," he insisted, "try to think of Tamino and Pamina, when they go through the waterfall and the flames: only a moment before, we were trembling with them before the gate of terror; and then those ethereal notes rise from the flute, floating over a little march that is like a fable. The test that has been passed consists of hovering fear, of odorless sweat. You understand what I'm saying, don't you?"

She nodded, even though by now she was convinced that the man was raving.

He continued, with a veiled melancholy: "Here in this place I still hear echoes of *The Magic Flute*—that sublime synthesis of every human passion and every operatic style, filtered by a delightful levity. Nothing redundant, that's certain; rather, a complex, marvelous delicacy, an apparent innocence that leaves the most capable of performers lost, since the least mistake, a single one, even just the shadowy shadow of a mistake, is enough so that the entire passage rolls disastrously over him."

"Forgive me, Herr Salieri. But why are you telling me these things?"

"Didn't you ask me to speak to you of music? And is it possible to speak of Mozart without speaking of his incomparable music?" He had closed his eyes, and was directing an imaginary orchestra. He reopened them and seemed transformed into an ascetic. "The soul of Mozart remains near his body, for it can't detach itself from life, which he so loved. For that reason, in this place, I can still hear his music. Outside, it died with him."

"But it's not true! His music is anything but mortal. It will last for all time."

"Do you know *Don Giovanni*?"

"Yes . . . ," she answered, hesitantly.

"Never have notes so dark and cruel been heard, as if saturated in an odor of putrefaction. The hereafter looms, invades, and leaves no hope. Do you follow me, madam? Death is dissolution, for Mozart. It is the irremediable loss of what is created in life. This is what your brother believed, and what is inexorably verified."

Then he looked at Nannerl with extreme attention and his eyebrows descended, knitting together over his eyes, which lost every trace of good nature. "You do not share my thoughts!"

"To tell you the truth, I have to admit I don't fully understand them. I don't know either *The Magic Flute* or *Don Giovanni* thoroughly."

"Is that possible?"

"For a long time I had lost contact with Wolfgang," she confessed in a small voice. "So I did not have access to his last creations. Or his last thoughts."

Salieri's expression turned uglier. In an instant she forgot his slight build: the man seemed suddenly aggressive, possessed of a twisted, dark, and violent nature.

"Were you envious of him?"

"Never!"

"Are you sure? There would be nothing strange: being related to a genius can't be easy."

"I wasn't envious of Wolfgang. And I won't let you suggest it."

Her protests fell into a void. "Envy is an effective poison, don't you know, madam."

"Envy kills only the heart of the one who feels it."

"You think? I don't believe that: it can also have a harmful effect on its object. And I mean a slow, subtle action that develops through the years."

"I have never been envious of my brother. Is that clear?"

The caretaker, too, shoveling snow again, must have heard this passionate declaration. And in the same instant, Salieri stepped out of the role of ambiguous accuser and became again the gentle, affected little man he had been a moment earlier. He looked at Nannerl with childish candor while he murmured, "Then show it."

"I still don't understand you."

"His manuscripts are in the hands of the widow. And that woman certainly cannot grasp their value. They are in danger of becoming wastepaper. The children will make them into confetti, they will be sold to some traveling dealer or, worse, will sit in a corner to get dusty and rot!"

"What does this have to do with anything?"

"Get them! Steal them from that woman, if necessary. You, as his sister, can assert your rights. Then promote the compositions of Mozart, have all the works published, or his genius will remain unknown. So that at least our descendants may know his miraculous melodies, their formal perfection, their simple complexity. So that the men and women who come will be passionate about music through the music of Mozart. So that your brother's brief life has had meaning—for that, if nothing else!"

Then he came close to her and warily added, "In any case, be on your guard, madam: your brother had many enemies. There is a rumor circulating that he was poisoned."

And he went off along the path with his short steps, no longer muttering to himself.

VII.

She couldn't take her eyes off it, a thing immersed in a bluish liquid, a small thing, barely human, that had nevertheless once lived inside a woman. A grayish being perhaps born dead, or perhaps dead as soon as it was born, with tiny curled-up limbs and eyes so tightly closed that they appeared pasted; but there were four eyes, because the thing had two heads. The corresponding ears were fused, like two candles too close to the fire of the hearth and to each other. There were two noses, two mouths, and two foreheads, and the neck was a sort of forked branch, and so wide in relation to the shoulders that it took up almost their entire breadth. What was the purpose of preserving such a freak of nature?

"The object of the scholar is knowledge, and knowledge of the abnormal improves that of the normal." The man appeared to have heard her internal question and had answered as if reciting from memory. "But these sights are not suitable for a lady. Shall we move to the study? Matthias von Sallaba is expecting you."

Nannerl followed him, passing a table on which stood the trunk of a man without its front wall, so that heart, liver, and lungs were on display; it was a plaster cast, conscientiously painted in shades of purple, pink, and pale blue.

"Sit down, please. Here, I was just looking up for you the working of acqua toffana. Have a look, if you'd like."

And he put a volume down under her nose.

"Excuse me, but what is this acqua toffana?"

"The poison that your brother claimed to have ingested. The rumor was put about by the widow, isn't that so, Thomas?"

"You always speak the truth, Herr Sallaba."

"Thank you. By the way, Thomas, I imagine you know the composition and origin of that potion. Am I right?"

"Certainly: arsenic and lead, with a delayed reaction."

"Congratulations."

"The name comes from a certain Giulia Toffana," Thomas continued, like a good student, "a shrewd peasant from the land of Sicily who invented the formula and, as she was dying, passed it on to her stepdaughter in turn; and she, named Girolama Spara—"

"Is it true?" Nannerl asked nervously.

The interruption seemed to disconcert them both.

"Naturally, madam," Thomas declared. "Without the shadow of a doubt. All documented—it's no legend. As I was explaining, the abovementioned Girolama was a real witch and was hanged in the Campo de' Fiori in Rome—"

"Is it true or not that my brother was poisoned?" Nannerl cried.

For a moment the two seemed bewildered. They looked at her, they looked at each other, then Sallaba said with firm conviction, "No, madam. My knowledge leads me to exclude it."

"I also exclude it!"

"Besides, you yourself, even if you have no medical knowledge, can find proof in that volume, given that you can read: the symptoms do not coincide."

"But then why, may I ask, was he so certain of it?"

"What can I tell you? We'll never know. The only certainty is that a sensitive soul can be convinced of anything."

"Well put. I wasn't closely acquainted with poor Mozart, but I had cared for a dozen artists before him, and each had his oddities, his obscure fixations."

"Morbid excitability is an inevitable component of genius. Of course, for those who are without genius this is something difficult to comprehend: I don't expect you to accept it, unless by faith in our expertise."

Why were these two men struggling to discredit her? Only because she was trying to understand something? "Then, if it wasn't poison, can you explain to me what he died of? And please use terms suitable for my meager intelligence."

"It's very simple," said the chief, with an imperturbable smile. "Acute miliary fever."

"And what is that?"

"Would you like me to describe the effects? Here you go: the body of your relative was burning more fiercely than fire, and both his hands and his feet were swollen. Not to mention the stomach, which in the last days of his existence became enlarged and, even after death, continued to fill with liquids that migrated to the surface, so that his remains resembled a single abnormal bladder."

"That's enough, thank you."

"Then trust and accept the diagnosis: acute miliary fever, certainly not the effects of acqua toffana or any other hypothetical substance." Scratching his beard, he continued: "Let me think, how many cases have I seen since the start of winter? Fifty, I would say. And how many pints of blood have I drawn? Probably a hundred. But I can't guarantee that figure; certainly I did not take the trouble to count them."

"If I may," the other intervened, "I remember precisely how much blood we took from dear Mozart: five pints in the last week of his life alone! And before that, seven. Twelve in all, I'm saying, but it was of no use, alas."

"Medicine has no power over the divine will."

"Well put, as always. And remember the terrible spasms he suffered before he died?"

"Naturally," the chief said gravely. "His limbs appeared to be shaken by an earthquake. Sometimes he sat up suddenly, eyes staring into the void, panting and raving with inarticulate sounds. He managed to utter a few phrases that made sense, otherwise it was only words in other languages or invented words."

The two-headed fetus, the stripped bust, the anatomical instruments, and the flasks and medicinal herbs—all were confused in Nannerl's mind with Wolfgang's body weakened by fever and bloodletting, shaken by uncontrollable spasms. His breath came noisily,

swelling his cheeks, panting, as if he were producing his final music—
and in the meantime, the two pompous quacks blathered on, their
voices mingling in an indistinct swirl. She heard one of the two utter
a definite word, a known word; and then the word was repeated, and
the two went on to another, but that word remained in her mind, and
she held onto that word to recover herself. She took a deep breath
and again was able to distinguish the terrible voices of the doctors, but
now the word was there, in front of her, tangible, she saw it, she could
even touch it: it was "kingdom."

"What—what did you say my brother said?"

"Eh? Oh yes, in his delirium he sometimes repeated that he
wanted to return to his kingdom, and similar nonsense about a queen
lost somewhere or other."

"Yes, poor man. He was no longer present in his mind. These
manifestations are frequent . . ."

She hurried to the door, pressing a handkerchief to her mouth, but
the odor of alcohol and medicines assailed her more intensely than
before, along with the sight of the monstrosities on display, and she
had to stop and lean against a wall. With surprising speed, Sallaba
reached her and took her pulse.

"Madam, do you not feel well? Thomas, get a remedy right away."

"No, no, for pity's sake," she cried, slamming the door behind her.

VIII.

Could this be the place? Nannerl checked the address, then put the
piece of paper back in her purse. The building was low and dilapidated, and on the street, from one end to the other, she didn't
see a soul. Sebastian opened the carriage door, and in silence she
descended.

She made her way into a small, dark, dirty courtyard with a brick
staircase on the far side. Walking on tiptoe and holding up her skirt,

she reached the staircase, and when she had arrived at the fifth floor, she knocked: only twice, lightly. The door opened, and instinctively she searched for a face at her height, but she had to lower her gaze: it was a child who had opened the door, a small child who looked at her as one looks at a stranger, and yet who was identical to Wolfgang.

"Who are you?" he asked cheerfully.

"I am . . . Nannerl."

"Mama, Mama, there's a lady!" he yelled, and ran away.

Furtively she went in and found herself in a poor, untidy room. The piano was open, as if her brother had been there working just a moment before, and bundles of scores were piled on the case. She began to look through them and saw that some were covered with hideous scribbles.

"What do you want?"

Constanze, the widow, was behind her: sensual and disheveled, wrapped in a shabby dressing gown, and hostile toward her.

"How did these scores come to be in such a state?" Nannerl asked quietly.

The woman shrugged her shoulders. "What do I know, it must have been the children. Please go."

"You should keep them somewhere else. You mustn't risk their being ruined."

"I haven't touched them since Wolfgang died. Everything's the same in here."

"But where are the other scores? This can't be everything."

"Some I sold, some his students have."

"What? He was giving lessons?"

"Yes, of course! How do you think we lived?"

"And whom did you sell them to?"

"Dealers, whoever happened along . . . But what do you want from me? Go away, Nannerl!"

But she didn't go. She turned and frantically began looking through the scores and trying to put them in order, assemble a whole piece, at least one; but suddenly there fell into her hands a different piece of paper, not a sheet of music but a parchment, and it took her breath away. She laid it on top of the piano, smoothed it, and saw again the image of herself lying on a bed in the old Mozart house, and of the boy, Wolfgang, who held out that parchment. "Look what I found," he had said, asking her to forgive him, and she had stubbornly refused . . . And then on the meadow, on the castle, on the figures of two children with crowns on their heads fell a warm transparent drop, then another, and the drops spread, mixing with the folds of the paper, erasing those already faded marks.

"Why is the lady crying?" asked the little boy from the doorway.

"Go to the bedroom, Karl," Constanze said. Then she approached. "Listen, Nannerl, I'm really sorry, but if you came here to grieve, you could do it just as well in your own house. These rooms have already seen enough sorrow."

"You're right— I'm sorry," she said. "In reality I came to—to buy the scores. All you have."

"What?" Constanze said, astonished. Then she went to the door and opened it with a peremptory gesture.

"I'm serious, Constanze. I want to buy them."

"I've already told you too many times to get out! And now, for goodness' sake, I would be grateful if you would do it."

"I'll pay you. I'll pay you now, right away. You need money, don't you? That's why you started the rumor of poison: so that people would talk about it, to create a scandal, to move some powerful person to pity. I imagine you have already submitted some plea, some request for money for the poor widowed mother of children whose husband was unworthily murdered—or am I mistaken?"

After an instant Constanze shouted, "It was Wolfgang who spoke of poison! I didn't even know what that acqua toffana was."

"Listen to me, let's not waste time. I'll give you three hundred florins."

Constanze was speechless, although she tried not to show it. Then, with a small smile, she said, "I know that you're disgustingly rich, but do you really go around with all that money? And where do you keep it? I mean, that might be interesting information."

"Four hundred."

The smile died on her lips and she looked at Nannerl suspiciously. "Why do you want to buy them?"

"I want to have them published. Cataloged, from first to last, and published. They cannot end up in the hands of some dealer. It's all that remains of him!"

"Who cares what remains—he's not here anymore, Nannerl. He is dead!"

"You'll also be paid by the publishers. You'll get a good income from it, I guarantee you. It will be useful for bringing up the children."

After an interminable silence, Constanze said, coldly, "Five hundred."

Nannerl seized the parchment. "Only if you give me this, too."

"It's easy for you," Constanze said disdainfully. "It's all your husband's money."

"I want this, too, Constanze."

"Then take it!"

IX.

She sprang lightly out of the carriage, and when Sebastian looked up from the step, she had disappeared.

"Baroness! The bag!"

"Oh, of course, how silly." She turned back and took from his hands a bag full of scores. "Unload the rest, please, and leave it at the foot of the stairs."

The villa shone with a warm orange light. Panting, with the suitcase tight in her arms, Nannerl ran to the door, opened it, and hurried in, crying, "Baptist! Jeanette!"

Her husband met her with an air of bewilderment. "What, you're back already?"

"Aren't you glad?" she asked in amusement, and laying the bag carefully on the table, she drew him affectionately to her.

"Of course, Nannerl. Only I imagined that your journey would last longer. I'm surprised, that's all."

"Oh yes, my love. Everything was done with a speed surprising to me."

"What do you mean, done?"

Suddenly Nannerl freed herself from him and hugged the child. "Jeanette, look what I brought you." And from the pile of baggage she took a large pear-shaped object, laid it on the floor next to the dollhouse, and unlocked it. Inside was a violin. "Do you like it?" she asked with shining eyes. "I can show you the basic idea—assuming I can still remember something—then we'll find a teacher. And for you, my treasure," she said to the boy, who arrived with a sword in his hands, "I brought a flute. Look how beautiful it is, as splendid as the hilt of your sword. If you like the violin more, don't worry, you can exchange them, and then we'll get other instruments, all you want, if you like playing them."

Jeanette grabbed the strange object. First she examined every part of it with scientific attention, then she started a horrendous twanging, while the boy blew in every hole of the flute, producing piercing shrieks, and Nannerl laughed deeply.

X.

"Look, Baptist, this is his handwriting. I've managed to collect so many of his works! I still have to get in touch with some of the students, and then with the orchestra players, and whoever else might have original scores. And then I'll have to put them in order, transcribe them, and find publishers. I want to have all his compositions published in a systematic way, to make sure that every single note, every embellishment, every marking is just what Wolfgang wanted, and that no one is permitted to change anything. It might also be a good idea to promote a biography, as faithful to the truth as possible, and tell everything, starting from his childhood years, of which I alone have precise knowledge. I want everyone to know who Mozart was; I want to immerse myself in this undertaking, so that his name may cross the boundaries of the centuries and be launched into the future!"

All this time Baptist had remained seated at the desk, in silence, playing with the stopper of the inkwell. He screwed it tight, wiped his fingers with a cloth, and stared at his wife. No emotion was visible in his gaze.

"Why do you want to do this, Nannerl?"

"What? Do you mean to oppose it?" she asked, surprised and annoyed.

"Not at all. I only wish to know why you've decided to do this."

"Because otherwise the music will be lost. It's so obvious. Why do you ask?"

"And if it should be lost, what would be so bad about that?"

For a moment she was silent, widening her eyes. "Baptist, what's gotten into you?" she murmured.

"Will you please explain what would happen if that music should be lost?"

"But don't you see? These compositions are astonishing. They open up a whole new path. In recent years, Wolfgang had reached heights never touched before, by him or by others. It's unacceptable that this legacy should disappear."

"It's unacceptable for whom?"

"For me, but not just me. It should be also for you. You should be happy that I'm trying to preserve it."

"So you're doing it to please me? As you tried to please the esteemed Colonel d'Ippold with the warm hands?"

"Why do you bring up Armand now?" she asked in dismay. She went over to him, resolutely. "Please, let's set things straight: that man has nothing to do with my decision. And if you think about it, you, Baptist, don't play a big role, either. It's a matter that has to do with me and my only brother, who, by the way, was a great composer. He has died, and I want his music to survive."

"Now, then, Wolfgang is your only brother? And was he not when you could barely pronounce his name? And was he not in the years when you were forced to give lessons to pay for his studies, and you hated him with all your heart?"

"Now it's different."

"Tell me why!"

"Because now I am choosing to be occupied with him, just as I chose to reject him."

They placed their fists on the desk and confronted each other, breathing hard, their faces tense and close. For a moment they were silent, then Nannerl said quietly, "I want to do it because—because I miss music, Baptist. Because to give concerts, or compose, is no longer so important for me; but to be involved in music is, and always will be. I want to do it because the idea of analyzing those works, of dating them, of going to publishers, of checking the proofs, of authenticating Wolfgang's compositions with respect to the thousand false ones that will surely emerge from all over—because the idea of doing all this, Baptist, is thrilling to me."

She left him and went to the window. Before her eyes unfolded the landscape that she had looked at a thousand times at night, wondering where Vienna was. "The same emotions can be felt in such a different way. It's true, for a long time I cut my brother out of my life—not to mention my father. And perhaps I didn't want to touch an instrument because inevitably, if I had, I would have thought of the two of them. But now I understand that to both I owe something. I understand that both are part of my story, and it doesn't make sense to deny it, because to reject the memory of them would mean to reject myself."

Baptist listened without interrupting. Under his thick mustache was the hint of a smile.

"In these years," Nannerl continued, "I haven't lived in pure silence, but as if within a 'rest.' In music, rests are as significant as a torrent of sound. A rest makes possible what precedes it and what follows, and lacking such a passage, I wouldn't be able, now, to occupy myself with composition in a way so different from the way I always thought and dreamed and imagined—but with the same intensity."

Then she turned to him and confronted him with gentle firmness. "I can't be a wife, a mother, and no more, all my life, Baptist. I need to do other things, too, and it's no longer possible for me not to do them. I don't know if I'll be able to be involved with our family in the same way I've been until now, but I also know, on the other hand, that if I didn't undertake this activity I still wouldn't be able to: because I am not what I was yesterday. Today, Baptist, I am again Maria Anna Walburga Ignatia Mozart."

XI.

"Children, get rid of all the guns, bows, arrows, and even the slingshots, if you have any: I do not want anyone shooting a feathered dart into my rear."

Nannerl, absorbed in checking the manuscript of a fantasia for piano, looked up and saw the monumental grand piano entering, carried by four workmen on the orders of her husband, and meanwhile Vincent and Hermann were lifting up the big table and putting it in a corner, and Jeanette, incredibly, was picking all her dolls up off the floor and putting them in a basket.

"What? You've had it brought here?"

"Yes, as you see, and from what they tell me, time has helped it rather than damaged it. The action is in excellent condition, and before the move I called a tuner. In a couple of months it will need a light touch-up, but just so that it settles. Gently, men, it's a precious object. Nannerl, where do you want it?"

"Oh . . . by the window, I would say."

"Hear that? Do what my wife says. Where's the stool? Ah, here it is. Nannerl, this is new. I allowed myself to choose it, but if for some reason it doesn't go, you can change it even for a chair for a queen. Good, I'd say we're good. Vincent, if you don't mind, see the gentlemen to the door and take care of the last details. Thank you all."

As the room emptied, Nannerl opened the lid and propped it up, then clapped her hands and listened to the resonance of that beat fade in a thousand ripples. Then she stroked the strings in all their length, feeling them scratch her fingertips pleasantly, and suddenly she rushed to sit on the stool beside Baptist.

"I didn't remember that it was so marvelous," she murmured.

"I've always known it, Nannerl."

"What?"

"That sooner or later we'd come to this. And I've always waited for you—and the wait was so long that I had almost forgotten whom I married."

She was silent while he gently slipped a hand under her dress to feel her skin, and yet he looked only at the ivory of the keys.

"I knew I didn't have with me a woman like others, but a Mozart who had decided not to devote herself, for a while, to music. I knew that you would go back to it, and marrying you, I also married that certainty, and knowing you over the years, I understood that the depths I now see in you cannot be reached through joy alone. When I asked you to play this piano, and your only response was to shoot me in the buttocks, I was much more thoughtless and talkative than I am today, and also much more restless. Now, instead, I'm happy, so happy that you will stop punishing yourself, but at the same time I'm frightened: because you are about to set sail, and the truth is I don't know where you'll land. Yet I have to do my part, I have to stay beside you, of course, because to be with you is my greatest pleasure, but without weighing on you."

He took her hand, brought it to his lips, and gallantly said, "*Madame, jouez ce piano pour moi . . . je vous en prie.*"

Carefully she placed the fantasia on the stand. Wolfgang had designed a passage simple to execute but revolutionary. It began with a broad arpeggio in D minor, establishing a melancholy nocturnal atmosphere, which seemed to clearly presage a dramatic outcome. Instead, after an interminable pause, a little melody arose, rich in half tones, light, tortuous, transporting the thoughts of both player and listener into some watery realm, to be suddenly undermined by those heavy, terrible chords, like sudden stabs of pain. Then a frenetic fragment, accelerating, preparing for a conflict—you wait for it, you know you have to reach it, and instead the music returns to that light melody. How could Wolfgang have had such intuition? How many disparate musical cells does this piece contain? How many intangible, superior visions? Suddenly a violent cascade of sound invades the entire space, and the hands speed along the keyboard, from one end to the other, crossing, and then two spaced-out chords, and an unlikely finale, which overturns every premise. It's a game, barefoot children chasing a ball who stick out their tongue at you, or a carillon that enjoys its own insolence and hammers you with those sharp sounds: and you think, before the piece ends, we'll have to go back to the beginning. We'll have to return to sorrow and, so, close the circle. But no, instead that game repeats with childish insolence, and the children end it with a light laugh that is a gay mockery. This piece is the confounding of expectations. Perhaps Wolfgang felt that and wanted to communicate it: each of us lives in expectation of something, but reality is always different from every conjecture and even every aim; in reality, an accident always happens that the most imaginative mind wouldn't have conceived of, and it's pointless to torture oneself about what hasn't happened, which can obscure what actually has. And while she played and thought all this, Nannerl seemed to see her brother beside her, in a gold jacket carefully buttoned, and he was happy that his sister had understood. And behind him she seemed to feel Frau Mozart tightening her corset, and she felt the contact with her soft, welcoming body, and her instinctive and boundless love, and opposite her was Herr Mozart, with his violin, and he—he was playing with her! He touched the strings lightly with the bow, supported only by the sounds his daughter produced, and like those who make music in ensemble, he exchanged with her rapid glances, and that silent contact canceled out every trace of the difficult past and let only affection emerge, and Music. She imagined that Victoria, too, was sitting in a corner, her attentive listener, in a flowered skirt, and on her face the pleasure of one who is gaining personal success; even Armand was present, in a brilliant general's uniform, mute and distant, and then there was Tresel, and Martin, and between one note and the next she seemed to hear Ebony's angry neighing . . .

After she played the last chord, Nannerl rose without even thinking and made a deep bow. There was a burst of applause, she closed her eyes, and tears flowed down her face slowly. Ever since she had rediscovered tears, she gave in to them easily; her eyes were a generous fountain whose waters streamed at the snap of a finger. Could tears, like the piano, be a matter of practice? Nannerl laughed and cried, happy in her tears, and when she opened her eyes she saw only Baptist near her, her only spectator, who observed her in silence with his beautiful eyes, in loving acceptance.

Finale: Scherzo

I.

Tightening the knot of the foulard that the wind was threatening to steal, the old woman approached a man muffled in a cape and tapped his shoulder with one hand. "Hello, sir. I'm here. Tell me what the problem is, please."

"Here," said the engineer. "As you see, we've dug a hole five feet deep exactly, because a part of the pedestal had to be sunk in the ground. The statue, as you know, is very heavy. And the deeper we went, the clearer it became that the soil is very loose and probably full of holes. Would you like to look from close up?"

"I trust you, I trust you. But tell me, what are those workers doing?"

"Surveys, Baroness. If the ground really is unstable, I'm sorry, but . . . the statue of Mozart can't be put up. Too risky."

"Oh, good Lord! And what will I do with it?"

The statue, suspended high up on a pulley, grimaced, but didn't seem offended.

"I imagine you'll have to find another square. But in Salzburg there are many beautiful squares."

"Yes, but imagine! We would have to start the whole process over again. To get the permission has taken me a lifetime. And I don't have much time left. I'm sixty years old, did you know?"

"Actually, I did, but believe me, you look ten years younger. Even fifteen, easily."

"May I remind you," she said, raising an eyebrow, "that I'm not the one paying you for this work."

He laughed. "I know, I know. It was a free compliment!"

"I'm grateful. So, how long will it take to finish the surveys?"

"Not long. If you like, you can stay here and wait. In fact, I would be delighted to offer you a hot drink in that café beyond the square. I looked in this morning, quickly, and they have some very inviting pastries."

"Thank you, but I can't. I have so many things to do. Would you be so kind, instead, as to come and tell me at home? It's not far."

"It will be an honor, Baroness."

"Then I'll wait for you," she said, and went off.

Nannerl's pace was not that of a sixty-year-old. She cleaved the air with the decision of a prow and passed the French soldiers who guarded the streets without bowing her head; in fact, they greeted her with respect. She went as far as the café beyond the square, entered, shook hands, smiled kindly at the citizens for whom Mozart, and his sister, had for years been glory and pride. She had the counterman bring her a bag of the pastries that had tempted the engineer, then, at the flower seller, she bought a bunch of violets and one of daisies, and took the road to the cemetery.

She loved the holy quiet of that place, and the slow steps of the grieving mourners, and it seemed to her that she heard the voices of those who observed human events from a distant land. She reached a graceful tomb, and around the name of the dead man scattered the violets as if on a meadow, then she sat on the bench opposite the stone and spoke in a low voice.

"Today I rose in a strange fit of restlessness, with the fear that what I have done up to now is not yet enough. The more I immerse myself in the endless mass of works that Wolfgang left to this world, the more I pledge to spread his marvelous musical soul, the closer I feel to that soul. And yet, my love, from time to time I find myself fighting with people who want to make it a commodity, who want to get rich off Mozart, something that never occurred to us."

She interrupted herself, realizing that a woman was looking at her curiously. She made a polite gesture indicating that she didn't wish to be disturbed, and the woman immediately went off.

"I know what you would say, Baptist. It's natural that certain people want to take advantage of the name of someone who has been successful; it's inevitable, and the intention itself constitutes the testimony and proof of that success. Therefore, my actions are good and just, and I shouldn't be afraid; and yet sometimes I wonder what Wolfgang would think, if he would approve the direction I've chosen, or if he would consider it mistaken. Because I don't know what he would say to me."

She rose and tenderly caressed the high-sounding name of the baron, her husband. She placed a kiss on her fingers, then touched the cross and slowly left.

The other grave that awaited her care was modest but no longer bare: for Nannerl was not the only one to dedicate floral homages to Leopold Mozart.

"Do you know, Father, that in a published anthology of Wolfgang's compositions for the piano, four spurious pieces were inserted? You would be horrified, certainly, but I find it enormously funny. First of all, let me tell you that I couldn't prevent it, and it isn't my fault: clear? Second, the idea that some innocent doesn't know Mozart's handwriting and takes someone else's mess for it makes me laugh. Who knows how long it will be before the knowledge of the centuries traces a clear line between what is his and what isn't. So, for the moment, dear Father, we have to resign ourselves and wait."

She took a few steps toward the gate, then turned back, chose a daisy, and set it at the top of the cross, murmuring, "I love you, Father." And, at peace, she went home.

II.

Sebastian, having exchanged the duties of a coachman for those of impeccable butler, was waiting for her at the door. "Baroness," he said in a complicitous whisper, "that Italian has come back."

"Oh, no—why did you let him come in?" she asked, scrutinizing a man with a large build lounging on a chair.

"Even I don't know how he managed it. One minute he was on the landing, the next in the middle of the study."

"He hasn't touched the scores?"

"Heavens! I haven't let him out of my sight for a moment."

"Good. Come with me, please," she said, and went through the archway declaring, "Your perseverance is admirable, Signor Bencini."

He wouldn't let her continue. He began to revolve around her like a top, babbling, "My dear, dear Baroness, I see you looking even better than usual today—do you know, blue becomes you? It makes the color of your eyes even more intense and alluring."

"Spare the compliments or I'll begin to fear you're asking for my hand."

He laughed nervously, and his belly quivered. "Think of it! The baroness is witty as well. Oh, oh, oh."

"You wouldn't marry me? I'm a little past my prime, but still presentable, they tell me."

"Well, of course, naturally," he stammered, "you are even today a grand, a beautiful woman, and without a doubt, I—"

"Bencini, why have you come again? I am not selling Mozart's manuscripts. Have you got the idea? I am not selling any manuscripts," she repeated, unruffled yet severe. "Must I tell you in your own language for you to understand?"

"But I—I have come purposely from Florence. It's a long, difficult journey, days and days in a coach, in severe weather—it's not a joke, you know."

"Yes, I know," she answered distractedly, placing the bag of pastries on the piano and picking up a package of proofs.

"Have you ever visited my country, Baroness?"

"I, no, but my brother and my father traveled all over Italy."

"Then if you ever decide to undertake a journey to the land of opera, you must be my guest. And I warn you: I accept no excuses. I will welcome you to my abode in the hills like a true sovereign, or, rather, more like an empress! I will put my maid at your disposal. You will taste the prized Tuscan cuisine, and one beautiful sunny afternoon I will take you through the streets of the city and you will admire the baptistry in its imposing, shining elegance. Oh, I beg you, bestow on me that honor."

"Spare your entreaties, Bencini—at my age, it certainly isn't the thing to start on a journey," she said, sitting down at the desk and preparing paper and ink. "Now, kindly let me work. Sebastian, please, accompany him to the door."

"But I," Bencini said, looking at the servant with a somewhat fearful air, "I promised that I would bring back at least one manuscript. Please, Baroness, put yourself in my shoes."

"I have an idea they would be very big on me."

"Hear me, oh most dear lady!" he cried, near desperation. "Consider my request, which isn't excessive: one score! Only one. Only one tiny little manuscript of dear Mozart's. Ultimately what does it cost you to lose one bit of paper? And, furthermore, I assure you," he added in a conspiratorial tone, "that I can pay well."

"It's not a matter of money," Nannerl said, giving him an icy look. "I won't sell them, and that's it. Go and don't ever come back again."

"No-o-o! I won't go!" he shouted passionately. "I will not go unless you, cruel creature, let me look with my own eyes at the precious papers, at least for a moment!" And he fell on his knees at Nannerl's feet.

"Should I throw him out, Baroness?" Sebastian said. "I fear I can't manage it alone."

She sighed. "All right, Bencini. I will let you look at the manuscripts, as you wish."

"Oh yes! Thank you, adored Baroness!"

"Look and that's all, clear? Get rid of any idea of buying even one. And while you're looking, I don't want to hear a word. And now promise me that as soon as you go out of that door you will disappear from my life forever."

"I swear it," he said, kissing the hem of her dress.

"We are agreed. You can examine this shelf. Handle every piece of paper with religious care. Now let me see your hands."

He showed her his palms, which were fat but clean.

"Perfect. But if you dare to make even just a tiny crease, I warn you, Bencini, I will send you flying out the window."

"I won't, I promise. You will find the scores more beautiful and tidy and clean and smooth than when you handed them to me."

"I hope so," Nannerl said, then whispered to Sebastian, "Make sure he doesn't take anything."

While he was looking, she returned to the desk and began passing the pen from one hand to the other, wondering how to begin the letter.

Most esteemed Herr Krabbe,

With great delight I received your edition, and I much admired the quality of the paper, not to speak of the leather binding, which has been beautifully stamped. What bewildered me was the surprising insertion of those four Minuets, which, alas, do not seem to me to be by Mozart. Their structure is too simple to belong to his last period, and if Wolfgang had composed them in his youth I would know them. You must have inserted them certainly thanks to a zeal for which one can only praise you, my conscientious friend; but I wonder where you found the manuscripts, and if it's not too much trouble, I would be grateful if I could examine them, if only out of curiosity. In any case I would advise you not to insert those pieces in the next printing.

"What in the world is the Kingdom of Back?"

Jumping to her feet she upset the inkwell. Bencini was staring at a score with a skeptical expression.

"No, that no! You weren't supposed to look at the other shelves! That music is not my brother's. Sebastian, weren't you checking on him?"

"It isn't your brother's? Then who wrote it, may I ask? The handwriting seems his."

On the old woman's face appeared perhaps the most foolish expression of her life. Since she said nothing, the Italian tried to guess the author by the style: "So, let me see, it could be Haydn. It's a composition clearly intended for children. Yes, from the development I would say Haydn."

"No. Not Haydn."

For thirty seconds, no sound was heard apart from the ticking of the clock.

"May I play it?" Bencini said, and he was at the piano before she could resist him, and as he gave life to the notes, she felt her own inner strings vibrate.

It was a short, simple piece that she had written in loving homage to Wolfgang and their excursions through the places of the mind and the capitals of Europe, both so far away now. She hadn't composed anything else, for she hadn't felt the need, really, but that sweet musical piece was an expression of affection in brief, whispered notes.

"It's pretty," Bencini commented, playing. "It has echoes of a game, and yet there is a thread of melancholy. At this point it gives a sense of comfort, certainly. However, this title is strange: *Kingdom of Back* . . ." He delivered the last chord and looked at her. "So tell me, Baroness, is it Haydn or Mozart?"

"Well, on the . . . surname I would say there's no doubt, it's . . . Mozart."

"A thousand florins!"

"What?"

"Deal done?"

And without waiting for a response he threw down a pile of banknotes on the piano and went off triumphantly, with the score under his arm.

"Baroness, should I stop him?" said Sebastian, and she remained staring at him openmouthed. Then slowly she walked to the window and looked beyond the glass: down in the street Bencini was pursuing the score, which the wind had torn from his hands. The page floated irregularly, like a butterfly, and as it was about to be seized by the sausagelike fingers of the Italian, it seemed to fly away laughing. The echo of that laugh reached Nannerl's heart and she, too, burst into a noisy laugh, laughing so hard she cried. She leaned on the windowsill, unable to control the contractions of her stomach and the sense of fun that completely possessed her. She opened the window and spread her arms like wings and threw back her head, letting the gusts of wind ruffle her hair; in a moment it had freshened the air of the house and swept to the floor her letter to the publisher.

When she turned, the man in the cape was standing beside the servant. "Oh, engineer, do we have the answer?" she murmured, composing herself in a hurry. "I got some pastries for you. Sebastian, please, prepare some coffee."

"Better not, Baroness," the engineer said, very seriously. "You must come right away."

III.

"It's incredible! Every time one digs in the ground a find is made. But, really, did the Romans have to live right under the statue of my brother?"

"They went as far as England, Baroness."

The square was still crowded with workers and the hole in the center, now deeper, revealed a mosaic with a legend in Latin. The workers were carefully cleaning it.

Nannerl approached. "Excuse me, I know you're doing your job, but could you move aside a little, please. Otherwise I can't see anything."

The workers promptly did as she asked and she tried to decipher the writing, but there wasn't much light at the bottom. The first word she managed to bring into focus was *Nihil,* and she repeated it aloud.

"Do you know Latin, Baroness?" the engineer said with a hint of envy.

"Not very well. I studied it a little, many years ago. My brother taught me, to tell you the truth. Now, if my memory is right, *nihil* means 'nothing.' "

Then laboriously she deciphered the two words beside it, one and then the other, and it seemed to her they were *felicitas . . . intret.*

Her face broke into an incredulous smile. She looked up at the statue of Wolfgang and stopped at his mocking sneer: it's really a joke worthy of him.

"Here forever happy are we, and nothing bad will ever be. Thank you, my king. Thanks to you!" she cried aloud, with the joy of a child.

The engineer thought it might be the first sign of senile dementia and rushed over to her protectively: "Baroness, do you feel all right? Do you want to sit down?"

Just then Bencini arrived, chasing his precious piece of paper. "My score! My score! My original score by Mozart! I paid a fortune!"

The piece of paper ended up on the monument, right on Mozart's face, like a slap. Then a gust of wind seized it and bore it off into the sky.

AUTHOR'S NOTE

Hic Habitat Felicitas,
Nihil Intret Mali.

The Roman mosaic found on the site of the monument to Mozart, which bears this inscription, is preserved in the Caroline Augustus Museum in Salzburg.

Mozart's Sister is a work of fiction, but the events that inspired it actually happened and the main characters really existed. Maria Anna Walburga Ignatia Mozart was a child prodigy and, together with her brother, performed at the courts of Europe as a child musician. The family letters are testimony that in her youth she also composed vocal music, although none of her works have come down to us.

The relationship between Wolfgang and Nannerl, very affectionate in childhood, passed through moments of cold hostility and was then extinguished altogether; in the last years of Wolfgang's life, the two had no contact. After the death of the maestro, however, his sister contributed greatly to the promotion of his memory, collaborating with his biographers, authenticating his compositions, and overseeing their publication.

Mozart's Sister

READER'S GROUP GUIDE

The name Mozart is synonymous with musical genius, calling up the powerful notes of *The Magic Flute*, *Don Giovanni*, and *The Marriage of Figaro*, reminding us that what is now classical was once revolutionary. But most of us don't know that standing in Wolfgang's shadow was another talented musician who played and composed at his side for many years before the two parted ways— his own sister, Nannerl. In *Mozart's Sister* we experience life as the other Mozart child, an equally passionate musician who, though eclipsed by the sun of her brother's greatness, eventually found her way back to the music they both loved. This reader's guide is intended as a starting point for your discussion of her story.

1. In an early letter to Armand, Nannerl claims to have given up on her higher musical ambitions, saying that she is "truly happy" with what she has and asks "nothing more, truly nothing" of music. Is this true? As she is courted by Armand, has she in fact given up on music? And if so, is it a decision she is truly at peace with?

2. Reacting angrily when Armand asks about why she doesn't play anymore, Nannerl relents and tells him her whole story. Why? What do Nannerl and Armand have in common? Why is each attracted to the other?

3. How does her brother's birth change Nannerl's life? Immediately? In the long term? Specifically, how does it change her relationship with her father? Do you think she would have been happier had Wolfgang never been born? How are the two Mozart children alike? How are they different?

4. Sibling rivalry and parental favoritism play a huge role in shaping Nannerl's life. Do you have siblings? What is your relationship with them like? Did you ever feel favored and perhaps unfavored by your parents?

5. On page 18, Wolfgang tells Nannerl that she won't be a successful musician because she will have a "bunch of children." Why does he say this? How does Nannerl react to his taunts? Is he right?

6. What kind of man is Leopold Mozart? Is he a good father or a bad one? Is Anna Maria a good mother? To both of her children?

7. On page 28 Leopold takes the violin away from Nannerl. Why? Is it his own prejudice against girls or simply a sign of the times? Why might the violin have been considered an inappropriate instrument for a girl?

8. Does Nannerl ever really fight for her dreams? Why or why not?

9. What is Mozart's attitude toward his work? Toward Nannerl's work as a composer? Do you think he was supportive of her talent?

10. After her father tells her he is taking Wolfgang to Italy but leaving her behind to earn a living for them as a piano teacher, Nannerl burns her musical compositions. Why? What does this action represent to her? This is the beginning of a dark period in her life. What happens to her and why?

11. How are Nannerl and Victoria alike? How are they different? Why is Nannerl interested in teaching Victoria? What does she see in Victoria's experience?

12. Victoria steals a composition of Nannerl's—the only one that Nannerl hasn't burned—from Tresel. On page 145, when Nannerl discovers Victoria playing the piece she reacts badly. Why? Why wouldn't she want her music played?

13. Why does Armand forbid Victoria to take piano lessons? Are his reasons in her best interest or are they selfish? What eventually makes him change his mind? Do his feelings for Nannerl play a role in this decision?

14. How does life change for Nannerl when Wolfgang and Leopold return from Italy? Why are she and her brother never able to recapture the magic of their youth? Who would you say is responsible for their drifting apart? Nannerl? Wolfgang? Leopold?

15. On page 207 Tresel tells Nannerl that Nannerl only loves Armand because he is unhappy. Do you think this is true? Why would an unhappy man be attractive to Nannerl? Why is Armand attracted to her?

16. On page 211 Leopold tells Nannerl that she, not Mozart, must be the one to write his requiem mass. Why would he choose her?

17. Why does Nannerl start writing music again? To please herself or to please Armand? Discuss the events that take place at the costume ball. What does Nannerl discover about herself, her fiancé, and her student? How do these revelations affect her?

18. Why would Mozart seduce Victoria? Do you think sibling rivalry or spitefulness played a role?

19. In the end, Nannerl and Armand don't get married. Why? What do you think of Armand's reasons for breaking off the engagement?

20. What did Nannerl think of Baptist when she was introduced to him by the Countess and her mother? How does her opinion of him change when she meets him again nine years later in Sankt Gilgen? Who do you think has changed? Him or her? What draws the two together?

21. What does Ebony, the horse, symbolize to Nannerl? When the horse is injured and needs to be put down, why does she want to be the one to do it?

22. When Baptist goes to Herr Mozart to ask for his daughter's hand in marriage, Leopold wants to give her the harpsichord. Why does Baptist refuse it? Do you think Leopold has regrets about his treatment of his daughter?

23. What is Nannerl's biggest regret?

24. Discuss Nannerl's meeting with Salieri.

25. Why does Mozart's death inspire Nannerl to buy her children musical instruments?